BEAT THE DRUMS SLOWLY

BEAT THE DRUMS SLOWLY

Adrian Goldsworthy

Weidenfeld & Nicolson
LONDON

First published in Great Britain in 2011 by Weidenfeld & Nicolson
An imprint of the Orion Publishing Group Ltd
Orion House, 5 Upper St Martin's Lane
London WC2H 9EA

An Hachette UK Company

978 0 297 86038 9 (cased)
978 0 297 86039 6 (export trade paperback)

A CIP catalogue record for this book is
available from the British Library.

Typeset at The Spartan Press Ltd,
Lymington, Hants

Printed in Great Britain by
Clays Ltd, St Ives plc

The Orion Publishing Group's policy is to use papers that are natural,
renewable and recyclable products and made from wood grown in
sustainable forests. The logging and manufacturing processes are expected
to conform to the environmental regulations of the country of origin.

To Bill Massey and Carole Divall, with thanks

As I was a-walking down by the Lock Hospital
*   Dark was the morning and cold was the day*
When who should I spy but one of my comrades,
*   Draped in a blanket and cold as the clay.*

Then beat the drums slowly and play the fifes lowly
Sound the 'Dead March' as you carry me along
*   And fire your muskets right over my coffin,*
For I'm a young soldier cut down in his prime.

Got six of my comrades to carry my coffin,
*   Six of my comrades to carry me high,*
And each of them carry a bunch of white roses,
So no one may smell me as we pass them by.

• • •

Lyrics, c. 1780, to an old tune probably now most
familiar as the 'Streets of Laredo'. There are many
variations on the lyrics.

THE ACTION AT CACABELLOS 3rd January 1809.

Royal Horse Artillery

2nd Position GRENADIER Company

3rd Position GRENADIER Company

CHURCH

BRITISH SKIRMISHERS

FORD

SKIRMISHERS

FRENCH

1st Position GRENADIER Company

VILLAGE of CACABELLOS

RIVER CUA

Reserve Division Paraded to witness PUNISHMENT

Outposts formed by 95th and Hussars
(Forced to Withdraw)

ADVANCING FRENCH CAVALRY

THE RETREAT TO CORUNNA

BRITISH ROUTE
FRENCH ROUTE

Vigo
Santiago de Compostela
CORUNNA
Ferrol
Ourense
Lugo
LIGHT BRIGADES MARCH TO VIGO
Nogales
Villafranca
Cacabellos
Bembibre
Oviedo
Astorga
Benevente
R. Esla
BAIRD
Leon
Zamora
Mansilla
Mayorga
Sahagun
MOORE
NAPOLEON
SOULT
Valladolid

DSV 11

I

The first horseman splashed through the ford with barely a check, cloak drawn tightly around his neck against the night's chill. A glance behind showed that his companion was having difficulty with his borrowed mount.

'Come on, Williams,' the man called back, trying to sound friendly even though it dismayed him that a fellow officer was so lacking in this essential accomplishment of a gentleman. 'Not far now.' His encouraging smile was lost in the shadow of his cocked hat and the gloom of the night. Cloud for the moment masked the bright moon, leaving only a faint glow off the snow-covered fields.

'Doing my best,' replied Ensign Williams, for although he disliked Captain Wickham and resented his condescension, he was obliged to respect his superior rank.

'Go on, Bobbie! Go on, girl,' he added more quietly. The mare flicked her head up, then tugged at the reins and took a couple of paces backwards. She did not like the look of the fast-flowing water, or perhaps it was the rushing noise and the clicks and reflections from the chunks of ice that had come from the mountains not many miles away. Williams prodded his heels against her side once again. Ears twitching, the horse began to turn away.

'Get on with it!' The impatience was obvious in Captain Wickham's tone, his consciously suave demeanour beginning to crack. 'We must not keep Lord Paget waiting.'

They were riding to join Lieutenant General Lord Paget, eldest son and heir of the Earl of Uxbridge and the commander of the cavalry forming the vanguard of the British Army. Wickham obviously relished using the title, and had already done his best to imply a degree of familiarity. Although belonging to the same regiment, the 106th Foot, the captain had been given a staff appointment back in August, secured through the offices of powerful friends. Williams had often wondered whether these knew or cared anything about the actual talents and character of the man whose advancement they fostered. Personally, he had seen enough of Wickham to despise him both as a soldier and as a man.

'Use your whip, damn it!'

Williams had no whip, as indeed he had no spurs, although since he instinctively felt the latter to be cruel this caused no regret. His boots were the same as those issued to the ordinary redcoats of the regiment, as were his gaiters.

An ensign was the most junior of commissioned ranks in the British Army and Williams had been an officer for barely four months. Before that he was a Gentleman Volunteer, a man without friends to secure him a commission or the money to purchase one. A volunteer marched in the ranks, carrying a musket, wearing the uniform and doing the duty of an ordinary soldier. All the while he lived with the officers of the regiment, waiting until battle created a vacancy and he had shown sufficient courage to deserve it. Back in August he had fought the French in Portugal and both of those things had occurred. Not only that, but he had survived to receive the promotion.

Now it was just a few days short of Christmas in the year of Our Lord 1808, and the British Army had marched from Portugal into Spain. They were riding to join the foremost vanguard of that army, although Wickham had still not told him why he had been summoned from his battalion.

Pulling on the reins, Williams tried to guide the mare back towards the ford. Suddenly she went sharply in that direction, turning full circle.

'Damn it, Bobbie,' he muttered. 'It's only water.' A religious man, who often seemed rather sombre when he was not with his few close friends, Williams rarely swore, but had always found that riding encouraged the practice. His friend Pringle had bought the bay mare from among the horses captured from the French at Vimeiro. It was a scrawny beast, for French dragoons took poor care of their mounts, and her left eye had been lost long ago to infection, leaving a gaping, empty socket. Yet she was normally willing, if insanitary in her habits – 'likes pissing on her own hay', was Billy Pringle's verdict. He had christened her Roberta, but quickly shortened it to the less respectable Bobbie or even Bob.

'For God's sake!' hissed Wickham. Waiting on the far bank, he was beginning to feel the deep cold of the night, and tugged his heavy boat cloak even closer around him. Williams wore nothing over his red jacket, with its ensign's epaulettes and shoulder wings marking him out as a member of a flank company. Ensigns in the rest of the battalion wore only a single epaulette on the right shoulder. He possessed no cloak, and although his soldier's greatcoat was warm enough, it was far too awkward to wear on horseback.

Big flakes of snow began to tumble lazily through the air. Even though the savage wind had gone, the night was still bitterly cold. Williams had always thought of Spain as a land where a tyrannical sun baked the earth in endless summer. Portugal had in truth been hotter even than that imagining. Yet the regiment had marched into Spain to face weeks of torrential rain, and now the temperature had fallen and the rain turned to sleet and snow.

Desperate, Williams reached back and slapped the mare's rump. She protested, tossing her head, but still shot forward so sharply that he almost lost his balance. Then they were in the ford, icy water spraying up and drenching his trousers. She almost stumbled on the rutted slope at the far bank, but recovered and then was out.

'There, that wasn't so bad, was it?' said Williams softly, patting the mare's neck.

Wickham set off at a brisk trot as soon as Williams joined him on the other side, for it was better to be moving than standing in the cold. Even so, the chill seeped into the ensign's soaked lower half. Soon Wickham's affability was restored. He did not much care for his fellow officer, thinking him rather a dull clod of a man, somewhat inclined to surliness, and also knowing him to lack any useful connection. Yet it was always simpler to be on easy terms with people, and he avoided unpleasantness whenever possible. Wickham knew himself to be good at being pleasant. He dropped back a pace to be beside the ensign, and grinned.

'Not as warm as Roliça, eh? Or as hot as the drubbing we gave the French that day?'

'That was hot work,' replied Williams flatly. That had been the regiment's first action, a bitter scrambling fight up a warren of rocky gullies. Their colonel had been killed early on, along with several other officers, and more were wounded or captured. In spite of this they had taken the hill and held it, but little thanks to Wickham. The captain had been drunk by the time the advance began, and lay insensible before the battle was finished. Worse still, Williams had seen him murder a French officer who had surrendered. 'A grim day,' he added.

'But glorious.' In truth the captain remembered almost nothing of the battle, and was puzzled at his companion's lack of enthusiasm. He changed the subject.

'How are my grenadiers?' Wickham had for a time commanded the Grenadier Company in which Williams had served as a volunteer and now as an officer. The grenadiers were the biggest soldiers in a battalion, awarded the place of honour on the right of its line. Wickham was a little above average height, and the straightness of his carriage and the skill of his tailor always made him seem taller again. Williams was a big man, more than an inch over six foot and broad shouldered. At the moment he was also very cold, and sore from riding for the first time in months. He merely confirmed that the company flourished, now led by Pringle.

'Good old Billy,' said Wickham, realising that he would have to labour at this conversation. 'I do miss him and the other

4

fellows. By the sound of it you should have Hanley back with you soon.'

That was good news, for along with Pringle, Lieutenant Hanley was Williams' closest remaining friend in the regiment – poor Truscott still being in hospital at Lisbon after losing his arm. Williams nodded, but said nothing, and once again Wickham was forced to continue.

'Hanley is a lucky fellow, doing duty with Colonel Graham.' If Wickham had less esteem for a senior officer who was not a lord then he did not show it. After all, everyone knew that the elderly Graham had been wealthy enough to raise his own regiment. His rank was a courtesy, but his talent for diplomacy and ability to speak half a dozen languages had made him indispensable as the army had driven into Spain. Very few British officers spoke Spanish – or indeed any language apart from their own. Hanley was fluent, having lived for some years in Madrid, trying and failing to establish himself as an artist before poverty and the French invasion forced him to leave. Wickham had remembered this, and recommended him when the army com-mander was searching for Spanish-speakers. It had enhanced his own reputation as a man well suited to providing practical answers to a problem. Now he hoped to repeat the success.

'It is quite remarkable to have two linguists in the same company,' he said. 'It rather belies the opinion of the rest of the army that we grenadiers are conspicuous for the size of our bodies rather than our brains.'

Williams was baffled. 'Two, sir?'

'No need to be modest. Hanley may be more accomplished from living over here, but I remember you embarked on a serious study of Spanish on the voyage from England, and no doubt have improved with experience. So when I discovered that Lord Paget had need of an interpreter, I could not help thinking of you. It will be no bad thing for your career to become known to such a distinguished officer.'

Dread flooded over the ensign. It was true that he had got hold of a Spanish grammar, and sought instruction from Hanley, and endeavoured to practise. So far his efforts had been rewarded with little progress.

'Do you know what his Lordship requires me to do?' It was a struggle to keep his voice level.

'No idea,' said Wickham blithely. 'Don't worry, old fellow. I am sure you will serve most handsomely. Don't Billy and the others call you "Jack the interpreter"?'

Williams' already flimsy confidence collapsed, and he silently cursed his friend's sense of fun. The day after Vimeiro, in the full flush of excitement on gaining his commission, he had offered his services to a baffled official from the commissariat department, the civilian clerks who ran the army's supply system. The man was trying and failing to explain to some local muleteers that he needed them to gather early the next morning with their animals. In his mind, Williams constructed a flawless instruction, perhaps a little more Spanish than Portuguese, but he felt that an appropriate accent would make the difference. According to Pringle – and Williams was convinced that his friend embellished the story on each of the many occasions since then that he had told it – he produced the following confident oration.

'Portuguesios, the commissario – wants the mulos – tomorrowo – presto – la, la!' Pringle accompanied each performance with fervent gestures and forceful expressions. At the time his friend, and the other officers in the group, had laughed so much that Williams doubted the accuracy of their recollection. He did remember the grave disappointment of the commissary, who reasonably enough felt that he could have done as much himself.

'I am not sure my best is very good,' was all that he thought to say now.

Wickham silently damned the man for his gloomy disposition, and decided that efforts at genteel conversation were wasted effort. Anyway, the cavalry brigade should not be far away now, and they could see a faint glow reflecting off the clouds from the chimneys of Sahagun up ahead.

'Let's push on,' he said, and urged his expensive gelding into a canter. Williams kicked in his heels to follow, but Bobbie stubbornly refused to go faster. He tried again with more force, and the mare lurched, seemed to stagger, and then was running in her fast, jerky motion. The big man stood up in his stirrups to prevent the saddle slamming against him with every beat. Bobbie was awkward, but fast, and soon closed on Wickham.

They slackened pace when they saw a long dark shadow in the gloom. The moon emerged from behind clouds and they saw that it was made up of many shapes. They walked across some sort of bridge or causeway, and then, without a word, Wickham again surged forward. Williams used more force than before and when the mare took off in pursuit he lost his right stirrup. Fighting for balance as he was pounded by the saddle, he bounced in his seat and swayed from side to side, as they rode alongside the long column of light dragoons in their fur caps. No doubt the cavalrymen were suitably impressed by his horsemanship, but Williams was too concerned with his frantic efforts to stay on to spare this any thought. Somewhere he lost the other stirrup. His legs began to swing wildly.

Wickham reached the front of the brigade and reported to the general and his staff. A few moments later Williams arrived, sawing desperately on the reins. Bobbie decided to respond abruptly, skidding to a halt in a patch of mud topped by only a thin sliver of ice. Williams lost his balance and tumbled sideways, slumping down into the snow- and mud-filled ditch beside the track. The smell suggested that some of the horses from Lord Paget's staff had added to the mixture.

There were sniggers, and a low comment of 'Who gave you permission to dismount!' – the ancient rebuke of regimental riding masters dealing with raw recruits unable to stay on a horse.

Bobbie stood meekly beside Williams, as he pushed himself up, something he did all the more quickly when she began to urinate noisily.

'May I present Mr Williams, my Lord,' said Wickham, unable to resist exploiting his subordinate's discomfort. The cavalry officers laughed uproariously, until their commander raised a hand. Lord Paget was a handsome man, a horseman since boyhood, and wore the tight overalls and heavily laced, fur-trimmed jacket of the hussars with a perfection that Beau Brummell could not have surpassed. He was also a serious soldier and widely believed to be the ablest leader of cavalry in the King's service.

'To what do we owe this honour?' he asked, the tone a mild rebuke to the effect that Wickham had forgotten his duties and not yet made a formal report.

'General Paget's compliments, my lord, and he understands that you have need of an officer able to speak Spanish.' A younger brother, also a general and as widely respected, commanded the Reserve Division.

'Does he? Well, yesterday you might have been useful, but we have other things to occupy us now. Still, you may as well stay for the dance.'

It took an effort for Williams not to cry out his joy. Even the shame of falling off his horse in front of the cream of the cavalry's officers – and no doubt of London society as well – no longer mattered. He would not to be called upon to exercise his supposed talent as a linguist. He hauled himself back up on to the mare.

Lord Paget was peering at a fob watch, doing his best to read its face in the moonlight. 'It's time.' He looked up at one of his aides. 'Tom, do me the honour of riding over to General Slade, and remind him that he is to begin the attack from the northwest of the town at six thirty, and drive the enemy towards us.' He turned to Wickham. 'Take Mr . . . ?'

'Wickham, my lord.'

'Take Captain Wickham with you. He seems to be well mounted. The other fellow can come with us.'

The two men rode away, cutting across the fields. 'And pray God that bungler doesn't make a hash of it.' Williams was close enough to Lord Paget to catch his whisper, but did not know whom he meant. As the column moved off, he fell in at the rear of the general's family of staff officers. A lieutenant with side whiskers almost as luxuriant as the general's rode beside him and soon proved himself a friendly companion.

'There are French cavalry at Sahagun. Maybe a brigade, but we can't be sure. Probably foraging, or the far outposts of Marshal Soult's army. So we're off to wake them up a bit.'

'We?'

'The Fifteenth Light Dragoons, old boy,' drawled the staff officer, who then turned to the man riding behind them at the head of a squadron. 'Nearly as good a regiment as the Tenth Hussars.' The officer behind them ignored the good-natured provocation.

'The Tenth are my lot. They're out there somewhere with Old "Black Jack" Slade. They drive the French from cover, and then it's view halloo and sabres and glory before breakfast. Have you ever been in a cavalry charge, Williams?'

'I confess not.'

'The main thing is to stay on your horse.' The hussar chuckled, and the mockery was so good natured that Williams happily joined in.

'Quiet back there,' shouted a voice far louder than their conversation. 'We're getting close now.'

The moon had gone, and the pale light of dawn was growing, although there was no sign of the sun. In the fields there were patches of milky-white mist. They rode on, hoofbeats mingling with the snorts and heavy breathing of the horses and the creak and jingle of harness to produce a noise so different from the sound of infantry on the march. If anything, the road was in worse condition than the stretch Williams and Wickham had come down. Patches of ice combined with deep ruts to make the going treacherous. Bobbie stumbled and skidded several times, as did most of the other horses. Several fell, although Williams did not see anyone badly hurt.

Muffled shouts and a single shot came from somewhere in advance of the main column. Minutes later, an hussar galloped up to report that the outposts had run into a French piquet, and killed two and captured half a dozen. Several more had escaped, riding back to give the alarm. Lord Paget led the regiment on, but progress was slow when they had to file across two bridges spanning a drainage ditch. Neither had a parapet, and their surface was slick with ice, but, to Williams' surprise, Bobbie strode across without any hesitation or false step.

He could see the rooftops of Sahagun clearly now, and somewhere a bell was tolling.

Lord Paget took the 15th to the right of the place, following a fork in the road. As Williams looked across the fields to their left, he could see a dark mass formed outside Sahagun, perhaps a quarter of a mile away. There were horsemen there, but in the mist and gloom it was hard to know their strength. The cheerful hussar officer had no doubt about their identity.

'Johnny Crapaud is up early for once.'

Lord Paget turned and gave the order himself. 'Form open column of divisions!' Cavalry drill was something of a mystery to Williams, and he had no idea whether a division was a troop or a squadron, but the intent seemed clear. As in the similar infantry formation, the regiment would march with sections one behind the other, with enough space between them so that each could wheel and form a single line either to the front or facing either flank.

The dark mass began to move as the 15th changed formation, heading eastwards away from Sahagun.

'Walk march – trot!' The general's order was repeated down the extended column. The British cavalry advanced rapidly, moving parallel to the enemy, quickly gaining and then passing them. Small shapes came out of the darker mass as the French sent out flankers, individuals and pairs of riders, whose task was to screen the main force. They came close, and Williams could clearly see the outline of one man's broad-topped shako. He was probably a chasseur, like the men they had seen in Portugal, and the counterparts to the British light dragoons and hussars.

'*Qui vive?*' a voice called out. The challenge was repeated.

'Ignore them,' said Lord Paget.

'Well, we haven't been introduced,' hissed Williams' companion.

'*Qui vive?*' The wind picked up, driving away the mist, and he could clearly see the French chasseur holding his carbine, and yet in spite of their refusal to answer, he did not fire. It began to sleet.

The main body of the French had stopped. It took a moment for the general to see this, and then he halted his own column. There was movement in the French mass as they deployed into line facing towards the British. The sleet turned to snow, then slackened and died away to nothing.

'*Qui vive?*' Still no answer, and Williams began to think the enemy outposts quite stubbornly obtuse. Behind him the 15th wheeled left to form line to confront the enemy. He remained with the general and his staff, ahead of and just to the left of the centre of the new line. A small escort of a dozen men from Lord Paget's own regiment, the 7th Hussars, guarded him.

Williams reached down to loosen his sword in its scabbard, suddenly nervous that the frost would make it stick. It slid comfortably and he let it fall back into place. He had anticipated the order by only a moment.

'Draw swords!' There was a scraping as the hussars' blades grated against the metal tops of their scabbards. The light cavalry-pattern sabre was curved and rather clumsy, but its heaviness lent power to the edge. Williams carried a Russian sword, less curved and lighter, but well balanced, and he was tempted as always to flick it through the air, enjoying its feel. Instead, he shouldered the blade just like the hussars. Williams had never fought with a sword, for in the battles of the summer his weapons had been musket and bayonet. He had shot and killed the sword's owner, and now for the first time wondered whether it was an unlucky weapon. That was superstition, and he tried his best to dismiss the thought.

'*Vive l'Empereur!*' A cheer came from the French cavalry. Williams almost smiled to hear again the familiar shout. Then there were flashes and puffs of smoke as the flankers fired their carbines, the noise of the shots coming almost instantly as they were so close. Williams did not see anyone fall, and the French horsemen were soon spurring their horses back towards their main body.

Unscathed, the 15th gave a cheer of their own.

'The Fifteenth will advance. Walk march!' The line walked forward, the hussars in two ranks; the second waited until the first was a horse's length ahead of them before following.

'Emsdorf and victory!' shouted the lieutenant colonel.

'Emsdorf and victory!' The chant was repeated all along the line, recalling a battle half a century before when the regiment had first made a name for itself.

'Trot!' They accelerated almost immediately, for the French were already less than four hundred yards away. Swords were still on the shoulder.

The French were not moving, and then suddenly their front vanished behind a cloud of smoke as they fired a volley with their short carbines. The range was long. Williams would certainly not have thought to fire at such a distance. He did not hear or feel any of the shots go near him and guessed that they all went high.

'Charge!' They was already closing quickly, and before he used his heels Bobbie began to run, for once without her familiar lurch. She raced ahead, and Williams was riding abreast of Lord Paget, a horse's length ahead of everyone else. The general looked more puzzled than irritated when he glanced to see the infantry officer beside him.

Another volley, and this time a ball snatched the cocked hat from Williams' head. A horse fell in the squadron behind them, the man tumbling to the ground, and somehow the hussar behind him jumped the fallen beast and man without checking. The men had their sabres high now, the point angled forward at the enemy. Williams was bouncing too much in the saddle to hold his own blade steady.

The French were close. In front were three ranks of chasseurs, their shakos protected by light-coloured cloth covers, and their dark green uniforms looking almost black in the dim light. Some were loading, fumbling with paper cartridges and metal ramrods, for even the short-barrelled carbines were awkward to load on horseback. Others clipped the guns back to their slings and reached for their swords.

Bobbie took off, leaping a ditch which Williams had not noticed as he focused on the enemy. The mare landed well, only an instant after Lord Paget's horse, but Williams had not been prepared and almost lost his balance. Behind them the staff and escort, followed closely by the 15th, cleared the ditch and urged their mounts to one more effort, rushing at the enemy.

A few Frenchmen had loaded fast enough to fire again, and an hussar was plucked from the saddle, but there was already movement and jostling among the chasseurs. Their horses were stirring and shifting. Many turned away, instinct making them want to join the herd rushing towards them and run on with them. The riders were nervous, for they had expected a feeble probe by the atrociously mounted Spanish cavalry and not an enemy who charged boldly home. Their volleys had had no impact and now it was far too late to come forward and meet the charge.

Gaps opened in the formation and Williams felt a wild exhilaration as the last few yards thundered past in the blink of an eye. Bobbie shot into a space left by one of the Frenchmen pushing to the rear, barging against the rump of his horse. The man looked back over his shoulder at Williams, his face a rictus of horror. To the right a big horse, aggressively ridden by one of the general's aides, knocked down a chasseur and his mount as they struggled to turn, but were trapped by the press behind. Lord Paget was cutting with his sabre, but as yet Williams could reach no one. Then he was through into the confusion that had been the French second and third ranks. A chasseur levelled his carbine, and the flame was enormous because it was so close and the ball took a chunk out of his right shoulder wing, knocking him back in the saddle for a moment.

Williams' body turned and he flung his weight into a wild slash with his right arm. By chance rather than design the tip of the sword struck just above the chasseur's collar, opening his throat to the bone. Blood sprayed from the blade as Bobbie surged on, finding a gap in the press, and Williams' arm swung round until it was almost straight behind him before he could recover. Another Frenchman came at him from the right, but the man's cross-bodied slash was misdirected, then another horse struck his own mount, and there was just enough time for Williams to duck beneath the blow.

The chasseurs were broken and running, although some still fought, and just behind them was another regiment. These were dragoons, with dark green jackets faced red and brass helmets with black horsehair crests, and they were also in three ranks. Fugitives from the chasseurs pressed into the formation, spreading panic and confusion, and with them came Williams and the first of the hussars, who gave a deep-throated roar that sounded more animal than human as they hacked with their heavy blades. One trooper screamed, and others grunted or sighed as they were caught by precise thrusts from the Frenchmen's straight swords. Williams parried a blow and Bobbie was still going forward as, just like the chasseurs, the second French regiment's horses chose to join the stampede. He was pressed so close to one dragoon that neither man had room to swing and the Frenchmen grinned at the absurdity of their predicament.

The hussars cut mostly at the heads of their enemies. Williams saw a man with his face slashed open from cheek to chin. Another was knocked from his horse by a blow which dented his brass helmet. The hussars' own fur caps were reinforced with nothing stronger than cardboard, and offered little resistance to the enemy's swords. Blade clashed against blade and the noise was like hundreds of coppersmiths all hammering at their work together, and all the while cursing and screaming at each other. More than one hussar was struggling to remain in his seat as their saddlecloths shifted. No one had remembered to halt the regiment and tighten girths before the charge.

Suddenly the press broke up. Both French regiments were running, swerving to the east and scattering into small groups. When the lines met, each side's left wing had overlapped the enemy line. The hussars had wheeled at once to roll up the enemy. On the French left, a still-organised force of dragoons tried to cover the retreat, but they were quickly swept up in the mad rush away from the fight.

Bobbie ran with the flow, and Williams reckoned the mare was enjoying the wild excitement. Everything was happening so quickly and he was reacting by instinct, more than any thought, as the whirling mêlée surged across the snow. He cut at a Frenchman, missed altogether and almost lost his balance, but by that time he was past and approaching another man. Then he saw the man was wearing a round fur hat and realised that he must be one of the 15th so stopped his blow and urged Bobbie to pass to the man's left. Williams nodded to the man as he passed, and was rewarded with an obviously French curse and the gaping muzzle of a pistol pointed in his face. He flinched, eyes snapping closed.

'Look out, sir!' came a cry, and then there was a deafening explosion, but Williams felt no blow, and when he looked the Frenchman in the fur colpak was spurring away, but a British hussar was sprawled almost at his feet, his dead horse crumpled behind him.

'You daft bugger, Jenkins,' said an hussar corporal, who then kicked his mount onwards. He was shaking his head as he passed Williams. 'He shot his own horse with his pistol!'

'Fifteenth to me! To me!' An officer was gathering a group of men, trying his best to organise the pursuit, and Williams followed the corporal as he went to join them. Spotting some twenty French dragoons still moving in order, the hussar captain led his own men in a fresh charge. There were no more than a dozen of them, but the French did not wait to meet them. They split up, scattering in every direction and fleeing in ones and twos. Williams could see that most were getting away. It was so much easier for them to escape than infantrymen.

Even so, as daylight grew, the hussars gathered at least one hundred and fifty prisoners, and almost as many captured horses. Many of the captives had ghastly cuts to their heads and faces. Bobbie was exhausted, her breathing heavy and her sides covered in a foam of sweat. He let her rest for a moment, as he looked for the general and his staff. The captain who had led the little group came past, riding alongside a sergeant.

'Make damned sure you search their valises for anything we can use.'

'Sir!' The sergeant trotted away and was already bellowing orders.

'Especially God-damned nails!' called the captain after him. He shook his head and noticed Williams. 'You would think even those buffoons at Horse Guards would realise that if you send four regiments of cavalry off to war that you might want to make sure they are properly shod.'

'You lack horseshoes?' asked Williams.

'Oh, we've got the shoes, just not enough nails for the farriers to fix 'em on. We must have lost a hundred horses on the march here.'

'Nevertheless, those that remain appear in excellent condition.'

'You think so, do you?' The hussar officer's voice was sharp, but he quickly relented. 'If you had seen them before we embarked! Then they kept us waiting at Corunna and let the infantry land first. We were as well mounted as any cavalry could hope to be. Could be again given time.'

Jenkins passed, carrying his saddle and furniture over his shoulder. He was accompanied by the corporal, delivering a constant stream of abuse.

'Find him something from the French horses,' ordered the officer. 'And make sure you clean up his back. You know how badly the Frogs treat their animals.

'How did we do, Simms?' This was to the corporal, whose moustache was flecked with grey, attesting to long service.

'Biggest balls-up since Yorktown, sir,' was the cheerful reply.

'Splendid!' said the captain, and then looked up as they heard a trumpet call. The 10th Hussars were advancing at a walk, their squadrons deployed in an immaculate line. Williams could see a group of officers in the lead and guessed that Wickham was among them. The exhilaration of the charge, and the sheer relief of still being alive, was wearing off, and now his heart sank at the thought of rejoining a man he held in contempt. Once again, Wickham had kept out of the real fighting, and if that had not been through any choice of his own, Williams was not inclined to be fair at the moment. He realised that he still had his sword drawn, and noticed the red-brown dried blood on the blade, but could remember the fighting only dimly. On the ground by his mare's feet was the corpse of a dragoon. The top of a Frenchman's head had been neatly sheared off, its contents spilled on to the snow and obviously trampled. He hoped Bobbie was not responsible.

'This is a little more than fashionably late,' said the hussar captain, twisting his moustache, and glaring at the 10th.

'Biggest balls-up since Yorktown,' said the corporal under his breath.

2

' "Blood and slaughter – march!" His very words, Williams, and then we advanced. I never saw anything more handsome or soldier-like.' Captain Wickham's enthusiasm for General Slade had carried him along for much of the fifteen-mile ride back to the main army. The captain was eager to press on, keenly anticipating the admiration and envy of the other staff officers for his participation in the cavalry's great victory. Only the weariness of their mounts, and especially Williams' mare, kept them at a gentle pace. The general had halted the 10th Hussars to deliver a grand oration, filled with gruesome details of what they were about to do to the French. Wickham evidently considered this a finer accomplishment than actually having arrived in time to take part in the fighting.

Williams was barely listening, and had shown no more than the barest amount of interest demanded by courtesy, but the captain continued his flow of praise anyway.

'Just think, two regiments of French cavalry utterly overthrown!'

The ensign nodded, sourly thinking that it was all the more praiseworthy since only the 15th had charged and thus been forced to fight on their own a substantially larger enemy force. Williams was tired, cold, and every inch of his lower body screamed at the slightest movement of the mare as she plodded alongside the road, which was taken up by the columns of marching infantry. The whole army under the command of Lieutenant General Sir John Moore was following in the wake of the hussars, pushing ever deeper into northern Spain. They were to camp at Sahagun that night, as many men as possible being billeted in its houses, but Wickham had been unwilling to wait there for them to arrive. Lord Paget and his own staff had already reported to Sir John on the morning's success. Wickham had got Williams to accompany them, but they had been left on the fringe, barely noticed except by the young ADC, who cheerfully clapped Williams on the back. Wickham decided to move on to reach the Reserve Division and give the news to Major General Paget and his officers, who were unlikely to have heard any detail of the action or had a chance to exercise their approbation.

The redcoats trudged along the road wearily. It had been a hard march, begun in a thunderstorm, before the temperature dropped and the sleet and snow began. The tramp of hoofs and feet churned the road to mud which sucked at boots and shoes, straining at the straps on gaiters and making each step an effort. Sodden greatcoats had been removed and tied to the tops of packs, along with the single blanket which was all that had been issued to each man. Williams knew from experience how the wooden frames of the backpacks pressed against the spine, and the straps constricted the chest until each breath was painful.

Thirty-five battalions of infantry had at last been concentrated, along with eleven troops or brigades of artillery and the four regiments of hussars. With more than 35,000 men, it was not simply the biggest army Britain had sent on campaign for generations, as its commander was wont to say, it was *the* British Army, including the majority of its finest corps. Serious losses could not be quickly replaced, and were a catastrophe to occur then it would be many years before Britain could dream of again intervening on the continent of Europe.

The men marched with confidence in spite of their fatigue. Word had spread that the French were near, and there was an aggressive swagger in the redcoats' manner. They were eager to fight, and once the enemy had been routed there would be plenty of time to rest. None of them doubted for a moment that they would win any battle. In that strange way with armies, some news of this morning's charge had clearly spread through the regiments. An orderly from the 3rd King's German Legion Hussars galloped past Wickham and Williams and a great cheer went up from the nearest battalion. The Germans had been nowhere near Sahagun that morning, but the sight of the fur cap and laced pelisse jacket of an hussar was enough for the redcoats.

Ten minutes later they finally reached the staff of General Paget, halted beside the road as the head of the leading battalion of the reserve marched past – Williams recognised the pale yellow facings of the 20th. The German hussar had obviously been carrying a dispatch to the general, for as they rode up, they watched one of his staff sign to acknowledge receipt of the message. The trooper then saluted and rode off.

Wickham was well satisfied by the welcome he received. He began by formally passing on Lord Paget's best wishes to his brother, and then allowed the eager questioning of the general's ADCs to prompt modest but strongly suggestive answers. Williams found it all rather sickening, and would happily have ridden on in search of his own regiment, but was told to stay by the friendly Captain Pierrepoint, the Deputy Assistant Quartermaster General attached to the division. Then the latter was drawn off in conversation by a couple of officers from the 20th, his own corps. Williams was left on the edge of the group, waiting either for the 106th to arrive or for someone to remember his existence.

He dismounted gingerly, the ache in all the muscles of his thighs turning briefly to vivid pain as he swung down. His legs were stiff after so many hours in the saddle, and he almost thought they would buckle underneath him when his boots touched the ground. Williams stamped his feet to bring some life back to them, and could not help hissing in discomfort. He patted the mare on the neck, more through relief to be off her than from current affection.

Wickham was giving another rendition of Black Jack Slade's speech. Williams ignored it and stretched, rubbing his neck. He passed a hand through his fair hair. His hat had been irreparably trampled at Sahagun, so he had left it where it lay, quickly dismissing the thought of searching for a replacement among the enemy dead. Somehow he would have to purchase a new cocked hat from his meagre funds, but he was too sore to worry about that now. He scratched his head. When he had joined the army at the beginning of the year, regulation decreed that hair should be worn long, tied into a queue and then covered in white powder. The rule had been changed in the summer, and it was still a relief to reach up and not feel the thick, flour-like paste. As he felt his hair, he wondered whether it was getting too long once again.

Williams ran up the left stirrup. Instinctively awkward in social gatherings even of such an informal sort, he had long since convinced himself that appearing to be busy, rather than merely standing and looking on, created a better impression should anyone deign to notice. As he walked behind Bobbie, the mare lashed out with a hoof. She missed, just swishing aside the long tails of his officer's coat. He had bought it after Vimeiro, at the auction of the property of a fallen officer of the 50th, and then had the black cuffs and collar replaced with the red of the 106th. The unfortunate man had been as broad shouldered, but considerably larger around the waist. In spite of adjustments the jacket still hung loose around him, suggesting that Williams had suffered from a serious illness, and denying him the trim figure felt ideal for an officer.

He patted Bobbie again to calm her, but suspected this was merely one of her periodic outbursts of malice and not prompted by any particular grievance. There was a sound of more horsemen arriving to join the group of officers clustered around the general. Williams now had his back to them all and did not bother to turn. He slid the other stirrup up, and then reached back to scratch his lower back with both hands, before reaching farther down to the area left tender. A shadow fell over him.

'I trust you are not wounded, Mr Williams?' It was a voice he admired above all others, and for a moment he froze, horrified to be caught in such an ungraceful posture. Then the tall man turned, his face beaming happiness as he looked up at the girl. She overwhelmed him, as she always did whenever they met.

Miss MacAndrews wore a deep blue riding habit, with a snug-fitting jacket over it styled something like the pelisse of the hussars. This was a paler blue, with white lace and ribbons, and a generous fringe of soft brown fur. She had a grey fur hat, only very vaguely resembling the cavalry's headgear, but far more suitable to keep her warm, and her flowing red curls were pinned up beneath it. In a field of snow under a grey sky and amid a tired and mud-stained army, she seemed to shine. Williams fervently believed that her beauty and essential goodness would stand out in any place and any company.

'It seems that I made an appropriate choice of attire for today,' she said. 'Even Father will be pleased at such a victory.' Major Alastair MacAndrews had been a soldier since the American War, where he had been captured when the cavalry had fled and left his battalion surrounded. This had greatly reinforced the instinctively jaundiced attitude of a foot soldier to the more conspicuous and flamboyant mounted arm.

'May I say that your uniform becomes you most magnificently. I am sure that our hussars will crave the chance for ten more such charges, merely to begin to prove worthy of inspiring your costume.' It had taken months for Williams to gain any confidence in her presence, and even now he was thinking hard to devise appropriate compliments.

Jane MacAndrews' blue-grey eyes stared into his, her expression suddenly serious. 'Then I am sure that I must at once go off and alter it. For that would mean more fighting and surely it is inevitable that some men will die. I should hate to be the cause of deaths, most of all merely because of the choice of a garment.'

Williams scrambled desperately for an appropriate response. 'I am sure that in such a cause they would feel honoured . . . That is to say . . .' That was no doubt wrong. 'I did not mean to imply . . .' For all his hard-won confidence, he had been thrown off balance in a minute.

The flicker of amusement began in her eyes, and then she

dazzled him with a smile, and he no longer cared about balance. 'I am cruel,' said Jane, 'to respond so unjustly to generous gallantry.'

'And I am flattered to be felt worthy of such spontaneous ingenuity,' he replied, surprising himself at being able to imply even gentle criticism. He had loved Miss MacAndrews from the very first moment he saw her, an emotion which had grown unflinchingly. Months before he had declared that love, at the same time confessing his inability to ask for anything, lacking any income beyond his pay. Deep down he knew that he had hoped for some affirmation from her – not a promise, for that would be unreasonable to expect, but the slightest acknowledgement that she would consider his proposal, should he ever be in a position to make one. That had not been given. She assured him of friendship, and had certainly lived up to this statement. The disappointment did not reduce his love in the slightest degree.

Jane returned to the attack. 'And do you feel a rapid fluency sufficient to excuse such behaviour? The charge of cruelty remains, and it seems I must be convicted.'

Williams faltered again. 'Never, never,' he pleaded. 'Not unless the sun is cruel because of its brightness, or the stars because of their . . .' He struggled to think of something stars did, for sparkle seemed inadequate.

'Gallantry is no doubt an appropriate defence for a soldier, although perhaps there are circumstances where it is insufficient in itself.' The girl was disappointed that he was unable to continue such a promising exchange for very long. His adoration was so akin to worship that at times it wearied her. She had no wish to be a goddess, exalted, but not given the dignity of directness or exposure to even gentle wit. At nineteen she accepted her attractiveness to men – as far as she could see, almost all men – as a simple fact. This complacency made praise of her perfection unexceptional, and while she found it pleasant enough, it failed to provoke a deep response. So much was anyway habitual, although at least Williams had the virtue of utter sincerity and obviously steadfast conviction.

On its own that was not enough. Jane was genuinely fond of him, but there was no more than a remote prospect that this would one day amount to anything more. Occasionally he showed just a spark of something which might perhaps foster deeper feeling. Yet such matters rarely exercised her thoughts for long. She was young and had no desire to marry until she had seen more of the world. The year before she had been with her mother in America, visiting their family. Since then they had rejoined her father in England, before following him to Portugal and Spain. Life was filled with new and interesting places and people. Marriage and children, even domesticity itself, for the moment had no more than distant appeal.

She decided to lead the conversation in another direction. 'I am aware of your diverse and numerous talents, Mr Williams, but I confess that until now I had not suspected great equestrian prowess.' Miss MacAndrews sat straight backed on her grey, and was a confident – indeed, like her mother, at times somewhat reckless – rider. 'Is it true that you rode in the charge?'

'I was there,' he said. Williams found it difficult to talk about a battle or skirmish. Somehow words struggled to match the confused memories and the stark peaks of anger and fear.

Jane leaned forward a little to whisper mischievously, 'And did you fall off?'

'He did. Right in front of Lord Paget himself.' Neither had noticed Wickham walk his horse over to join them. 'Best to stay with the infantry, old boy.' His smile was broad, the mockery ostensibly generous. Jane laughed, and Williams felt obliged to smile.

'May I say how uncommonly elegant you are, Miss Mac-Andrews. The finest ornament the army could possess.' Wickham had met Jane when the regiment was still in England, but not remarked her to any degree. This morning he was struck by her charms.

'You, of course, have an excellent seat, Captain Wickham.' Williams envied the smile the girl gave him.

Wickham looked directly at her. 'I can ride hard and fast and always last till the end.' He paused. 'There is the whip if I need it.'

Jane blushed, and Williams was not quite sure of the cause, but felt a flash of anger at Wickham.

'And yet I fear your sword was not called upon to do any work.' Williams tried and failed to make the statement sound innocent. Wickham kept his gaze on the girl.

'I do not consider pride in killing appropriate. I'll do my duty, and stand shot' – Williams was sceptical about both claims – 'but if it can be avoided I shall be glad never to shed blood.'

'A strangely gentle philosophy for a soldier,' said Jane in quick response.

'The only fitting one for a gentleman,' was the equally prompt reply. He was still studying her closely, his eyes wandering far beyond her face. Williams struggled with a most ungenteel desire to tip the man off his horse into the grubby snow.

'Good day to you, Captain Wickham, Mr Williams.' Mrs MacAndrews was tall, dark haired and still striking although now comfortably into middle age. She spoke in the formal drawl of the Carolinas – indeed, seemed at this moment to be exaggerating it.

They replied to her greetings. Williams found the formidable wife of his commanding officer as unsettling as her daughter, if in a different way. He also liked her, and was slowly becoming used to her barbed humour.

'I have liniment in my baggage if you are uncomfortable after your journey, Mr Williams,' she offered. 'It rubs on.

'Captain Wickham, it is good to see you. I saw a shawl in Salamanca that I am sure your wife would adore.' Esther Mac-Andrews had obviously noticed the attention the captain had being paying to her daughter. 'Be sure to extend our best wishes to her when next you write. I trust that she is well?'

'When last I heard,' Wickham confirmed.

'I am most pleased to hear it. Come, Jane, the regiment is here and we ought to rejoin them, otherwise your father will make a mess of things when billets are assigned. Will you ride with us, Mr Williams? Or should your prefer to walk?'

He shrugged. 'I fear walking is all that I am capable of at present.'

'Then we will bid you good day. Come, Jane!' Mrs Mac-Andrews set off at a canter. Her daughter smiled down at Williams, then glanced with a lesser, markedly nervous smile at Wickham, before following her mother.

Williams led Bobbie along beside the road. Neither he nor Wickham had felt the need for any acknowledgement as they parted. The ensign stared wistfully at the rapidly diminishing figures of the ladies.

'Bills, you old rogue!' Pringle's animated greeting interrupted his thoughts. 'Glad to see you brought her back in one piece!' The 106th were passing, and the Grenadier Company in their place at the head of the battalion.

The bespectacled Pringle was an inch or so shorter than Williams, but thickset and inclined to plumpness, which the rigours of campaigning had so far not in any way diminished. He came over and nuzzled Bobbie, who responded by snapping at him. 'Ah, your usual friendly self, my darling,' he continued, having just dodged her yellow teeth. 'Hmm, I am sure she had two eyes before I was generous enough to lend her to a friend. How did she do?'

'Fine, but I see what you mean about her gait.'

'Ah well, she is more suited to someone with an elegant figure resembling my own.' Pringle reached back to pat his behind. 'Helps to pad things. I was going to ask you to ride to the rear and check on the stragglers.'

'I'll walk,' said Williams firmly.

'Don't blame you!'

Williams strolled happily past the battalion's column. He knew all the men of the Grenadier Company. Dobson, the old veteran who had taught him so much about soldiering, had nodded as he passed. Williams knew all the officers of the regiment, and there were plenty of men in the other companies whose faces were familiar. Even after less than a day away, it was good to be among the 106th.

At the rear of the battalion a row of ox-carts carried the heavy baggage piled high. Sitting on top of the mounds were many of the wives and children who followed their men to war. Sally Dobson waved when she saw him and prodded her daughter Jenny, who had been looking the other way. There was a cluster of wives from the grenadiers on the leading cart, since apparently they had insisted on their seniority. In a moment all of them were waving or blowing him kisses.

'Where you been, Mr Williams?'

'Gone all night, eh! What's her name?'

'Been off riding with the cavalry,' he replied.

'Bet your arse is sore!' The laughter doubled.

'No, my dear ladies, it is very sore.' There was no malice in their mockery, and its coarseness was unthinking and habitual, and so Williams happily joined in. For a few paces he exaggerated the awkwardness of his walk and the winces each step provoked.

'Here, what have you done to all my hard work?' The heavily pregnant Jenny was looking at his jacket, stained from the fall, smeared in one place with blood from the Frenchman he had killed, and with the right shoulder wing broken and half hanging off. 'You're not safe to be out. Bloody men! Send it to me later and I'll sew it back up for you. Ma will give it a clean.'

Jenny was barely sixteen, but her condition had done nothing to diminish her good looks or her readiness to speak to anyone as an equal, officers included. She was married to the taciturn Private Hanks, whose feet were badly blistered, so that he was riding on a donkey behind the cart. Williams asked him how he was, and received the expected brief but optimistic reply. 'Be all right tomorrow, sir.'

'Good.'

Williams was glad to be home. An argument broke out among the women, all uniting in mutual hostility to Molly Richards. Williams decided it was time to check that the baggage was stored properly on the other carts.

3

That evening the newly returned William Hanley sat with Pringle in the small room allocated to the officers of the Grenadier Company. Williams was out checking that the men and their families were settled, had received and consumed their rations, and were neither being mistreated by nor themselves abusing their hosts. Major MacAndrews insisted that his officers visit the men's quarters twice a day. More often would have given the soldiers no rest. Less would have made it much harder to maintain an acceptable standard of discipline. He knew that other regiments were less strict, but saw that as no reason to change his own regulation. Anyway, standards of internal order appeared to be generally good in the Reserve Division. The grenadiers were in the houses at the far end of the hamlet's single street. No one seemed to know what it was called, but the entire regiment had somehow been crammed into the forty or so buildings, with the officers allotted space in the only big house in the place, a crumbing villa owned by an obscure member of a very minor aristocratic family.

Only a single servant remained in the place, and he left the barest pause after knocking before opening the door and peering in, apparently in the expectation of catching the two officers mistreating his master's property. This would not have been easy. Two low stools and a table with one leg markedly shorter than the other three were the only furnishings left in the badly swept room. The British officers had themselves obtained a meagre supply of straw to spread over the cold flagstones. The candle on the table was also their own.

Much to the man's surprise, Hanley greeted him in Spanish, and listened politely to his praise of Don Carlos, and his confidence that the latter would wish him to extend every hospitality to the English while they visited his home. It was clear from his tone that as far as he was concerned his employer was far too generous for his own good, and that it would have done them all no harm at all if the officers had slept in the snow. Briefly he showed interest when asking whether Hanley was Spanish. Although tall, Hanley's already dark complexion had tanned strongly during his years living in Spain. If the man was disappointed by the confession that Hanley was in fact English, his demeanour suggested that by habit he both expected and embraced disappointment. The man left, crossing himself absent-mindedly.

'Another warm welcome,' said Pringle sourly. 'Sometimes I wonder why I am putting up with such inconveniences to free their country.'

'The Spanish doubt that they need us. They made a French army surrender at Bailen before we won in Portugal. As far as they are concerned we're turning up late to join in as they chase the last remnants over the Pyrenees. Anyway,' he conceded, 'they are none too fond of soldiers, even their own.'

'And me so personable! And with this pretty red cockade.' All of the British troops marching into Spain had been ordered to add a red Spanish cockade to the black one of the House of Hanover which all wore in their hats. Pringle poured some brandy into two pewter cups which formed part of his travelling canteen. 'So what is the news?'

'Oh, I forgot.' Hanley rummaged in his valise and produced a folded and rather battered newspaper which he tossed to his friend. Pringle saw that it was *The Times*. 'It was among the effects of a French staff officer. He rode into a village near Segovia and started ordering people about in an offhand way, so they killed him. Well, as I said, the Spanish aren't too fond of soldiers. It's from the start of November.'

Pringle was impressed. 'I would guess that this is the most

recent English paper anywhere in the army.' He frowned. 'I suspect there is a moral there somewhere.'

'Most of it is about Cintra. By the sound of it your fellow has been exercising himself:

> *Here folly dash'd to earth the victor's plume,*
> *For chiefs like ours in vain may laurels bloom.*

He must have sobered up for long enough to get angry.' They had conflicting opinions of Lord Byron's merits as a poet.

'I don't think Wellesley was to blame,' ventured Pringle, scanning the pages as well as he could in the poor light. Sir Arthur Wellesley had won the Battle of Vimeiro, but before the day was out had been replaced by an older, more senior general, Sir Harry Burrard. The next day an even more exalted commander had arrived in the shape of Sir Hew Dalrymple. Neither had seen much to be gained by farther attacks on the enemy, and had welcomed a French deputation which had arrived under a flag of truce. Negotiation had led to an agreement to end the hostilities. General Junot's French army was to be returned to France in British ships and was awarded all the honours of war, keeping their guns, colours and personal possessions, including a good deal of loot. Wellesley had signed the Convention of Cintra, but it was widely held that he had been ordered to do so by his seniors and did not deserve the blame associated with it.

'All the Spaniards I have met think that it was a good settlement,' said Hanley.

'Well, they weren't the ones who had been robbed and murdered by this particular group of Frenchmen. It got the campaign over quickly, I'll allow, but you know as well as I do that the Portuguese were none too impressed. Maria gave me hell over it.'

'I dare say her mood recovered in time.'

'Oh, indeed yes,' Pringle smiled at the memory. He thought for a moment. 'She really is extremely good at what she does.'

'I know.'

For once Pringle was startled. 'You do? So, it seems I cannot even trust my friends.' There was no trace of any annoyance in his voice. 'At least Bills is too pure of heart. However, she was talking of going to visit Truscott in the hospital. Be rough if after surviving the loss of his arm he succumbed to pleasure!'

'Does he indulge in such pleasures?'

'Don't we all? Well, excepting Bills probably. Truscott is a Cambridge man, though, so you never can tell.' Pringle had attended Oxford. 'You know he says that he must have been there at the same time as Wickham, but does not recall ever meeting him.'

'Have you heard from him?' asked Hanley.

'No, not since you left us. The fellow is probably too busy enjoying himself to write to his friends.' Pringle went back to the paper, skimming quickly through the sheet. 'I cannot see any mention of the Russians.'

Hanley shook his head. A squadron of Russian warships had been sheltering in the Tagus off Lisbon when the British Army arrived. Russia was allied to France, but not actually in a state of war against England until a few weeks later. By that time, they were included in the Convention and allowed to return to their home ports.

'The Navy wasn't about to let the fleet sail away, and Admiral Cotton put up quite a stink.'

'So what happened?' asked Pringle.

'Well, we are English.'

'So I have been told.'

'And so there was a compromise. The ships stay, and the Royal Navy will keep them until six months after Russia ends hostilities. All the sailors have already been sent home.'

'Good riddance,' said Pringle. He had nothing against Russians in general, but at the height of the summer's campaign, Maria had ensnared him and the others in a deadly race against a Russian officer and his soldiers. She wanted to beat them to the hiding place of treasure left by her former lover, an aristocrat who had fled to South America. The Russian count had been ruthless and clever, and they were lucky to win in the end. Williams and Dobson had done most of the killing on their side. The old veteran had taken the Russian's sword and given it to Williams. He had also taken the gold from the man's purse and shared it with the officers. Pringle had bought the horse with his share, and Williams the basic accoutrements of an officer. Hanley was sad to think that he had gambled away most of his own portion. Truscott was probably using his as they spoke, for the army did not make allowance for provisions for convalescing officers.

Pringle laid down the paper. 'So what, apart from the life of London nearly two months ago, is going on in this wide world?'

'Well, I do not really know all that much, and suspect I understand even less,' began Hanley. The last was quite probably true. Born of an indiscretion between a man of business and an actress, Hanley had never known either of his parents, having been raised by his maternal grandmother. His father paid for an education, even allowing him in later years to travel abroad and pursue his artistic dreams. He had also secured him an ensign's commission at the age of ten, before such abuses had been stopped. It gave him an officer's salary without any obligation to earn it. Only when his father had died and his half-brothers cut off his allowance had Hanley been forced to return to England and take up this only opportunity for employment. Half a year later, and he still felt himself very much a civilian. His ignorance of many military matters continued to astound his friends. They trusted his courage, for he had proved that in Portugal, and had schooled him so that there was a better than even chance that his uniform was fit to be seen for longer than the first five minutes after he had dressed. Yet in many ways he remained an astounding griffin.

'Napoleon is here in person,' said Hanley, confirming the rumour that had been circulating throughout the army in recent days. Many had repeated the story, but on questioning their 'certain information' invariably proved to have come from someone else, who in turn had been told by a friend or simply a passer by. The army knew very little of the wider war beyond what they saw day to day as they marched with their regiment.

Major Alastair MacAndrews could not now recall when first he had been told of the emperor's presence in Spain. For some reason he had always believed it. The French army had been beaten, first by the Spanish and then by the British in Portugal, and with the rest of continental Europe now forced to submit to his will, it seemed only reasonable for him to come in person to avenge the defeats in the Iberian peninsula. An overlord made by war could not permit any crack in the illusion of his infallible power. He was bound to come, and it seemed equally reasonable that he would bring with him regiments greater in number and older in war than the young conscripts whom he had sent a year ago to overrun Spain and Portugal.

Such matters had only a general concern for MacAndrews, for he had no say in such great matters and no one was likely to ask him how the campaign should be conducted. Forty-eight was very elderly for a major still to be on active service with a regiment. In the spring, he had been a fractionally less old captain, with no apparent prospect of promotion, for he lacked both money and influence. The 106th was the most junior regiment of the line, lacking any battle honours or the slightest prestige. Lieutenant Colonel Moss had purchased the command of the battalion, and his relentless pressure had finally been rewarded when they were added to an expeditionary force. MacAndrews succeeded to his majority following the sudden death through alcohol and rage of the 106th's senior major.

Moss had died in the first attack at Roliça – privately Mac-Andrews felt he was recklessly dangerous as a battalion commander. Of the two majors, Toye was senior, but he had been wounded and captured at the same time, and that had left MacAndrews in command of the 106th for the remainder of the campaign. They were mentioned in Wellesley's dispatch for Roliça, and more than played their part at Vimeiro. Toye was released from captivity after Cintra, and as the senior man

33

naturally became the new lieutenant colonel. Custom dictated that vacancies created by battlefield casualties were filled in accordance with seniority.

Toye commanded the 106th, but his wound from Roliça proved a bad one, and his recovery, and indeed his life, was placed in jeopardy by a savage bout of fever. After several weeks the doctors no longer despaired of his life, but it was feared that his health was permanently broken. With Toye unable to attempt his duties, MacAndrews continued to lead the battalion, and had taken them north to the border fortress of Almeida. Their task was to ensure that the terms of the Convention were enforced, and the French garrison permitted to leave. In a few places there had been difficulties, when the local Portuguese troops showed an understandable reluctance to let the French escape so easily. The sight of redcoats, as a reminder of their goodwill towards their ally, had sometimes proved necessary. In the event, matters had already been decided peacefully before they arrived, and instead they had begun a quiet spell reinforcing the garrison of the spacious fortress.

'I think we have done well,' said Brotherton, interrupting his commander's thoughts. 'The Reserve Division appears a fine formation, and General Paget and his staff know their business. It would be nice to think that our attachment was a tribute to our conduct in August.' The two men had claimed a room with a table as the battalion office and worked long into the night. They had almost finished and had dismissed the clerks, leaving them a moment to settle any more private matters.

'Aye, perhaps,' said MacAndrews, registering sufficient Caledonian doubt that even a man who knew him far less well than the adjutant would have realised his scepticism. 'Although it does appear to be true that we have been summoned to replace the Sixtieth, on account of their misconduct.' The 5/60th were greenjackets, armed with rifles rather than the inaccurate smooth-bore muskets of the line infantry. Officially the Royal Americans, most of the recruits these days were Germans, and the battalion had enlisted a large number of men who claimed to

34

be German or Swiss from those prisoners taken in August who were reluctant to return to the French army. The same men were equally reluctant to accept British discipline, and on advancing into Spain had plundered and used violence against the inhabitants to such an extent that Sir John Moore had ordered them back to Portugal.

'So we are considered an improvement over a pack of thieves, which I suppose is still a compliment of sorts.' Brotherton was only in his late twenties, but had an older demeanour, reinforced by the baldness that had by this time claimed all of the top of his head as its own. He had a good attention to detail, as well as sufficient knowledge of bribery, bullying and contagious enthusiasm to be very good at turning the battalion commander's wishes into actions. He and MacAndrews worked well together.

'Let us sincerely hope that we can maintain such a good opinion,' said MacAndrews.

'I'll keep an eye on the lads. Doubt there is much to steal here anyway.'

'There is always something.' MacAndrews nodded in satisfaction. 'You are right, though. I believe we are well placed. There was talk of putting us with Bentinck. That would probably be well enough, but on balance we may well be better off here. How do you find the administration of the division?'

'Good. In fact, on the whole, remarkably good, except for the . . .'

'Commissaries.' MacAndrews echoed the expected complaint with a wry smile. The civilian commissariat department had recruited many new officials to oversee the supply of the expedition. Almost none of them had any experience.

'Not very much we can do about that.' The 106th had joined the army just two days ago. Although summoned to replace the 5/60th, they had been tasked with escorting an ammunition convoy, and so spent weeks toiling over atrocious roads with the slow-moving ox-carts. Fortunately a few companies from the Buffs had been sent to take the empty wagons back to Portugal, so that MacAndrews' battalion was left at comfortably over six hundred men. 'I believe that the army is to have a day or two to rest, before we advance again. It is clear that the general expects a major action before very long.'

'Happier now that we are led by a Scotsman?' suggested the adjutant.

'Aye, well enough.' MacAndrews deliberately broadened his soft accent again. 'Sir John has a fine reputation, although I have never had the honour of serving under him.'

'He behaved most handsomely to me earlier, when he rode past with his staff. Stopped and bade me good day, and then asked about the condition of the regiment. Seemed pleased with our turnout after a fatiguing march through foul weather to get here.'

MacAndrews had rarely seen the habitually cynical Brotherton so openly enthusiastic. He guessed that his adjutant had been burning to tell the story, so listened with patience. It was flattering to hear such a high opinion of the 106th, and remarkable how quickly the general had won the utter devotion of one of his officers.

'A long day,' the major said at the end of the story. 'And no doubt longer ones are to come, so I believe we have a duty to rest. We shall parade the battalion at eight thirty tomorrow morning. After the inspection, I think an hour of battalion drill and then the same by company. They can have the afternoon to rest and look more fully to their equipment. Good night, Jack.'

'Good night, sir.'

The room opened on to the corridor, but on the far side was another room which had been allocated as quarters to the major's family. It worried MacAndrews to have his wife and daughter with the army. They had always followed him to garrisons around the world, but he had hoped to prevent their coming to Portugal and then following him to Spain. His wife's determined ingenuity had thwarted that hope, when she managed to find passage and follow the army. He was afraid for them both, and especially that Jane might see things no girl of her age should see, let alone that worse might happen to her. Those last thoughts he tried to force from his mind, without much success.

Yet for all those fears, it was a deep pleasure to have them with him. His hair was white, his career perhaps unlikely to advance, for Brotherton had received a letter from one of the wounded officers left in Madrid which said that he believed Toye would sell out and retire from the army. That meant a new lieutenant colonel would soon buy his way to command of the 106th. Well, that was the future. For the moment MacAndrews led the battalion and had the deep satisfaction of regulating it according to his own theories. He was proud of the result, and confident that they would do well. All of that pleasure was redoubled by the knowledge that he would each day see a daughter of whom he was even more proud, and a wife whose willingness to be with him still caused him the greatest wonder in all the wide world.

It was with a warm sense of joy that he knocked and then entered their room. Smiles greeted him, at least for a short moment.

'You can take off those damned boots or clean 'em, Mac-Andrews! Jane and I have not toiled these long hours to have you spreading filth across the floor!'

Alastair MacAndrews was a very happy man.

4

Lieutenant General Sir John Moore flicked open his handsome
new telescope, but even with its excellent lenses he could
make out very little of the landscape. The hill they were on was
open to pale winter sunlight, but most of the ground beneath
them was smothered in thick mist, which was only slowly rising
and burning off. There was certainly no obvious trace of the
enemy, but Marshal Soult was out there somewhere, his army
corps holding the villages around Saladaña and Carrion to the
north-east.

'Two divisions and a brigade of cavalry. Perhaps fifteen or
sixteen thousand men?' Colonel Graham knew that the general
was running through the calculation one more time and did not
require comment. More than a decade older than his forty-
seven-year-old commander, he understood when to keep silent.
His trust in Moore as a general was absolute, while he still saw
himself as no more than an enthusiastic amateur.

'They have not moved,' the general said very definitely. 'The
prisoners the hussars took confirm that. By the way, did you hear
Georgie Napier say how worried he was when he found a cellar
full of them last night who seemed to have had no treatment for
their wounds? He gave orders for a surgeon along with food to
be sent. An hour later he went back and found them playing the
fiddle and dancing reels!' Sir John permitted himself the luxury of
laughter. The rest of his staff were out of earshot, and although he
was never obsessively serious with them, there was nevertheless a
sense of some freedom having only the older Graham beside him.

'Suggests a good spirit at least,' the colonel commented.

Moore nodded. Soult was out on a limb. The French marshal must by now be aware that the British were close. He would guess that there was force behind the cavalry attack at Sahagun, although he would probably not know how much. Sir John knew the names of Soult's divisional commanders and the numbers of their regiments. He also knew that for the last weeks Napoleon had been assuring the recently arrived marshal that the British were fleeing back to Portugal, and that only a few thin remnants of the Spanish armies were in a position to oppose him. Sir John knew this because he had in his sabretache a dispatch, written by Marshal Berthier, the Emperor's chief of staff, to Marshal Soult – or the Prince of Neufchâtel and the Duke of Dalmatia as they styled themselves, happy recipients of the deluge of titles issuing from the self-proclaimed Emperor. It listed the various French armies in Spain, giving strengths and positions. None was near enough to offer immediate support to Soult, and this was Moore's chance. For a brief moment he would have an all too rare advantage in this campaign.

'We will give the men another day's rest,' he said firmly. 'The infantry have come a long way and have earned it. We'll begin tomorrow evening, march through the night, and be at Marshal Soult on the twenty-fourth.'

Graham waited, but Sir John did genuinely appear not to have marked the date. 'Christmas Eve,' he pointed out.

Moore looked blank for a moment and then smiled, shaking his head. 'Of course. I had quite forgot. Hah, my grandfather would not approve. He was a minister, you know.' Graham nodded. 'However, he was all in favour of smiting the ungodly, so I dare say would forgive us.'

Moore wondered for a moment whether he had been indelicate. Graham had been caught up in the early days of France's atheistic Revolution. Not long married, a Grand Tour of Europe had ended abruptly when his young bride succumbed to illness in the prime of her life and beauty. Returning home through France, he had been powerless to prevent a mob tearing open her coffin and desecrating her corpse in an alleged hunt for illegal weapons. Graham had turned soldier in the ebb tide of his life, waging relentless war against the Revolution and the Empire which followed it. Sir John knew all this, although the two friends had never spoken of it. He hoped that he had not awoken painful memories, and was relieved at the simple response.

'Amen to that. So no plum pudding this year. Ah well, let us hope to see the New Year in well.'

'Pray God we do,' said Sir John, for both men knew how precarious their situation was. They might beat Soult, but the French would concentrate against them in time and they could not resist such great numbers. 'Is Romana ready to move with us?'

Graham nodded in confirmation. 'He assures me that he is.' The Marquis of La Romana commanded the only Spanish army near by. A year earlier Napoleon had sent him with the finest regiments of Spain's army to garrison the coast of Denmark against British depredations. The Emperor already contemplated the conquest of his ally, and found this convenient pretext to reduce the force likely to oppose him. Then ally became occupier, and the old enemy a new friend. La Romana's division – or at least more than half of his men – were taken off by the Royal Navy and carried back to fight the invader of their homeland. That had been months ago, and since then the regulars, their numbers bolstered by enthusiastic but poorly trained recruits, had been badly mauled by Napoleon's veterans. 'However, I doubt that even half his men have muskets,' conceded Graham.

'At least he is willing. The firelocks and cannon we brought for them have not yet arrived, I presume.'

'As usual the transport is lacking. It took weeks for the Galician junta to help Sir David to obtain the animals and vehicles necessary to move his own division from Corunna.'

'Were they willing?' asked the general acidly.

'Yes, I believe they were, but they had already given much of what they had to La Romana.'

In May uprisings had erupted throughout Spain, in sudden

anger at the French occupation, and the imposition of Joseph Bonaparte as king. They had been suppressed – Hanley had witnessed the brutality of the French reprisals in Madrid – but the news provoked a wave of fervent enthusiasm for Spain and the Spanish cause in Britain which had not yet died away. The government sent the expeditionary force to the Peninsula, which eventually ended up in Portugal. The French were defeated there in August, but it was not until October that Sir John's army began to advance into Spain. The aim was to assist the Spanish in evicting the remaining French armies from their country. All of the ministers agreed upon this objective as a most worthy one. London gave its approval, and after considerable thought instructed Sir John to find some way of achieving it. It was generally expected that the means would become apparent to him in due course as opportunities arose.

Everything about it was untidy, unplanned and poorly organised, and from the beginning Moore had viewed the situation with the deep distaste of a man who took his profession seriously. None of his predecessors in command of the forces in Portugal had made any effort to prepare for the move to Spain. No supplies of stores had been gathered along the proposed route, nor even the most basic information sought about the main roads. The Portuguese army seemed equally unsure over whether or not the main road past Almeida was capable of use by artillery and heavy transport at this season, but were mainly inclined to feel that it was not.

So when the advance began the British were divided along two widely separated routes. Most of the infantry went by the direct, northern road, while the cavalry, almost all of the artillery and a few battalions as escort followed a wide loop into Spain, by which they almost came in sight of Madrid before swinging north to join the others at Salamanca. At that peaceful university town, Sir John had concentrated most of his army, although a significant body led by Sir David Baird did not arrive until later. Small detachments and even entire battalions were still on their way to the main force. Fortunately the French had been in no position to exploit this vulnerable dispersal.

'What is the Spanish situation overall?' Sir John asked his friend, already guessing the answer.

'As you would expect. The juntas do too much or too little, and none of it is well co-ordinated.' The French had taken over the Spanish state and its administration, such as it was. Throughout the country, patriots had formed regional juntas, and done their best to organise an administration capable of running the country and, most important of all, directing the war effort. 'I think that on the whole there are now more reasonable men in positions of authority than there were. It has been a while since anyone has talked of invading Portugal! Well, at least as a serious ambition. They still bicker with one another incessantly.'

'And the generals?'

'Are much the same. La Romana is one of the best, and some of the others seem good. Like the juntas they do not always agree. Of course, they lack our own country's dedication to restricting the senior ranks to men of genuine capacity.' Moore smiled at the arch comment. 'Money is by far the biggest problem.'

'That I understand.' Moore had been demanding more funds from almost the moment he assumed command. Everything needed to be in appropriate coin for Portugal and Spain, for the locals were unwilling to trust printed notes in the nervous climate of war. London had proved unable to supply him with Spanish silver dollars in anything like the necessary quantities.

'They have no money,' Graham continued. 'The soldiers are not paid, and the commanders have little money to supply provisions, so all too often they go without food. It is not to be wondered at if they leave. It is enough to make a man consider whether the Royal Navy has been doing Britain quite so good a service as we used to think by preying on Spanish merchant ships. Or indeed that our governments have been so wise in stealing – forgive me, liberating – their colonies.'

'That money would be in Bonaparte's hands now.'

'Probably, but it must be confessed that we contributed a good deal to making Spain such a poor country before the war began, when they were still our enemies.'

Moore had little concern for the past, and knew he must focus on making no errors in the coming days. It had been planned for the British Army to move to Burgos, and support the Spanish armies which formed in a rough line to meet the French on-slaught. The British were still far away, and the line incomplete, when Napoleon, leading with his usual energy, savaged one Spanish army after another, cracking the line open. When news of this reached him, sent by Graham as he travelled tirelessly from one Spanish camp to another, meeting with generals and juntas, Sir John had decided to withdraw. He even began preparations, knowing that his flight without meeting the enemy would appear ignominious and probably ruin his career. In his darkest moments he wondered whether, as a man known for his Whig associations, and never reluctant to criticise those in power for corruption or folly, there were plenty of Tory ministers hoping for this outcome, desiring him as a scapegoat for their own unrealistic plans.

That fear had not changed his mind, nor had the attempts to plead, bully and even subvert his authority made by the gov-ernment's minister in Spain. Moore had stayed, and then advanced, because the soldier in him was so habituated to duty that he was determined to do what he could for his country and its ally. He would strike at Soult and win a victory. It would not win the war, and it might merely delay a French victory that seemed almost inevitable. Yet it should dislocate Napoleon's plans, at least for a while, giving time for the Spanish armies in other parts of Spain to recover a little and improve their resources. The trick was to win this small victory, and still bring the British Army away in one piece. That would not be easy, and it was all down to the decisions he would make.

Graham looked at his friend and knew him well enough to discern the strain he was undergoing. As they rode down the hill he talked lightly of Scotland, of people and places they both knew. When they rejoined his staff there was work to be done, planning routes and orders of march, but he could see that Moore's mood lightened just a little. The ADCs were all bright young men in every sense. Their commander was unusual in insisting on true ability and experience in his staff, and not simply friendship and connections. He had confidence in their diligence and capacities, as well as a strong affection for all of them. This trust was returned with a devotion verging on the idolatrous.

They worked as they rode, escorted by a small detachment of hussars, and passing more cavalry patrols as they went. The general paused to greet each officer. Nearer the camp numbers of messengers went back and forth, going about their business, and more than a few men from the staffs of his subordinate officers were also out and about. Sir John stopped for a while to talk to Captain Scovell, who oversaw the guides – a villainous collection of Swiss, Italians and other foreigners, many of them deserters from Napoleon's army – who carried some dispatches, acted as translators, and showed the route for marches to the rest of the army. Riding on, they were steadily joined by most of the general officers with the army, and others of field rank, until there were some thirty or forty riders in the group. Most conspicuous were the two ladies, both well mounted on greys, and dressed in extremely fetching habits, whose green and blue stood out among the array of red coats.

General Paget introduced Mrs MacAndrews and her daughter to Sir John, who expressed himself honoured to make their acquaintance.

'Your husband commands the 106th, does he not?'

'Yes, we left them at drill.' Esther MacAndrews guessed that the general must be of an age with her husband, but was not inclined to resent the different opportunities granted to some. Born into one of the wealthy families of 'Rice Kings', owners of large slave-worked estates and a grand house in Charleston, she had run away with two British officers escaping from captivity in the last months of the Revolutionary War. One was her lover, whose child she was carrying, but that man had fled and abandoned them when the local militia closed in. The other was MacAndrews, then a lieutenant, youthful and lanky, whose very black hair was already flecked with grey. They had escaped, fallen in love, and married when they arrived in the British lines. She had never regretted any of the events, or the unorthodox, often threadbare life they had lived together. MacAndrews' hair was now wholly white, his frame spare and ungainly, and in every way apart from height he was so different from the classically handsome general.

Colonel Graham flirted prodigiously with mother and daughter alike, at times crowding out the younger ADCs, who were drawn inexorably towards Jane. Moore had already observed that the older man delighted in the company of every woman he met, flattering and praising in a way that was as relentless as it was harmless. One or two lieutenant colonels had also brought their wives with them on the campaign, to his knowledge, and he was sure that other officers had done the same. It surprised him to find such a young miss of respectable family with the army, and he hoped that the father's judgement was not so poor in other matters. He urged his horse on, and let the younger officers swarm around the ladies, for there were too many serious matters requiring his attention to indulge in such pleasures. Yet one thought had struck him, and he could not resist raising it with one of his aides.

'Do you see a likeness, James? In the major's wife?'

Captain the Honourable James Stanhope had failed to follow his leaders' change of subject and looked politely baffled.

'To Lady Hester?' Stanhope's sister was the ardent admirer of the general, and the two of them corresponded, although the brother was unsure whether she was realistic to hope for a closer bond. Sir John's Calvinistic sense of duty had so far denied him the indulgence of wedlock. Yet his enthusiasm now was most marked. 'I do not mean so much as to looks, as spirit.'

For all his praise, Moore was saddened to see any ladies with the column. An even greater cause for concern were the wives and children trailing behind each regiment. It was the normal custom, but he felt it a bad one, especially in winter with the prospect of an arduous and harried flight through the mountains, a fear that was most likely to be realised. Before leading the army from Portugal he had offered passage home for all the soldiers' families. Only a handful had accepted. He had also instructed each battalion to leave their dependants behind. All too many commanders had felt this cruel and had ignored the order. Such lenience was likely to prove misguided, but there was nothing that he could do to remedy it. Other problems and mistakes loomed larger in his mind. For all his appearance of calm, Sir John remained a deeply worried man.

The cavalcade following him was universally more cheerful, encouraged even beyond its usual spirits by the presence of the ladies. Apart from Colonel Graham, few of the staff officers managed to enjoy more than a minute or two beside either of the ladies. Wickham chose his moment carefully, pushing his horse close alongside Jane's grey as the girl was watching her mother being drawn away by the colonel to peer through his telescope at a distant peak.

'You are a most elegant ornament to our hunt, Miss Mac-Andrews,' Wickham said, raising his hat.

Jane turned, surprised by his sudden appearance and the familiarity of his gaze. Yet several voices sounded in hearty assent, and so she felt obliged to acknowledge the compliment with a thin smile.

'Do you speak of war as sport, Captain Wickham?' asked the girl, very aware that he was looking at her intently.

Jane decided it was better to draw others into the conversation. Wickham was a handsome man, with a manner both bold and highly assured. Jane's heart beat faster with mixed excitement and fear from his obviously predatory intent.

'Certainly – perhaps the highest field and challenge of all.' Wickham was closer to her than any of the others, and when he dropped his voice to no more than a murmur only Jane heard him add, 'save one.' His gaze, which had been roving over her promiscuously, now fixed on her eyes.

Jane felt herself blush, and was again annoyed at her weakness. She barely listened as the nearest officers spoke enthusiastically of hunting as admirable preparation for warfare.

'A good officer must naturally be a bold hunter,' said a major, whose long jaw and yellowing teeth gave his own appearance more than a hint of the equine. 'Do you ride to hounds, Mr Wickham?'

'Whenever my duties permit,' lied Wickham, whose lack of funds had prevented his keeping a stable good enough for him to excel. There was little purpose served by cutting a poor figure, and so he hunted only when an acquaintance could be persuaded to loan him a decent mount.

Wickham had turned to look at the major, but Jane knew that his next words were aimed at her. 'I do dearly love the chase,' he said with emphasis. 'Whatever the distance, whatever the going, once I have a view I am not to be denied.' He smiled modestly. 'Although not perhaps on this poor old fellow.' Wickham patted the gelding on the neck, and slowed its walk, letting others close around Miss MacAndrews just as her mother returned to the girl's side.

Pleased with the brief conversation, Wickham happily chatted to some other staff men, and affected indifference to the girl's presence. Without ever catching her eye, he took satisfaction in noticing that Jane glanced in his direction more than any other.

The monks cowered in a way that seemed abject to the French officers, and the leader of the delegation struggled to deliver his petition, making the interpreter's job more difficult. The grossly fat man kept making obeisance and was so flustered that at one point he actually used the nickname of Malaparte. The interpreter made the appropriate change, but it was clear that the Emperor had heard and was amused by the lapse.

The room was not large, even though it formed the whole first floor of the house. Beneath was the kitchen and a few smaller rooms, and above a single stairway led to two bedrooms, occupied for the moment by the Emperor and the Prince of

Neufchâtel. One side of the room was crowded with staff officers, summoned to make reports and receive orders. Two tall men stood near the back, and although neither had met before they were drawn together by the association of their regiments. Each carried a silvered cuirassier's helmet under his right arm, hand grasping the black fur band and letting the horsehair crest hang down. Their left hands supported the hilts of their long, straight swords, held up awkwardly because they were on foot. Surprisingly one of the men, a little less tall than his colleague, but far broader in the body, also wore the cuirass itself, something which most officers abandoned on all occasions apart from parade and battle. If the man felt its weight and discomfort then he refused to show it.

'You would never have credited it,' whispered the taller man to his burly companion. 'Yesterday they were cursing him with every breath as we slogged up that pass. "Shoot him! Go on, Henri, shoot the old bastard!", "Kill him, and then we can get some rest!", "He's close enough, I couldn't miss from here!", "If he doesn't stop and let us rest, I'll do it any minute, I swear I will", on and on as they waded through snow waist deep. The Emperor and Marshal Lannes clustered together with a group of us, heads down and leading them on. Not what you'd expect the master of Europe to be doing.'

'Only if he were a different man.'

'That is true. We made it in the end, although for the last patch they put him and most of us on to a gun carriage and dragged us up. The men got billets in the villages, warm beds, food and drink. Today I saw those same soldiers screaming out "Vive l'Empereur!" at the tops of their voices.'

The noise from the monks subsided, and since his fellow cuirassier seemed disinclined for farther talk, the taller man fell silent. There was still a degree of confusion, but the main plea was for protection for the convent buildings, and security for the relics and treasures kept there. The Emperor confirmed his existing order forbidding all plundering and any mistreatment of the local population as long as they welcomed the French and offered no resistance. He repeated some of his proclamations, reminding them that he wished only the best for the Spanish, that his brother King Joseph brought honest government in the place of corruption and decadence. If they spurned his friendship then they had only themselves to blame for the punishment they received. He even threatened to send his kind brother to another realm and take the crown for himself. The interpreter struggled to convey the menace with which this was delivered, but the suppliants were already sufficiently terrorised, for they had heard so many stories of French atrocities. If some tales had grown in the telling, they were not to know, and in any case the truth was terrible enough.

The monks were ushered out, and the Emperor and Berthier dealt with each of the officers in turn, apart from the two cuirassiers. The Emperor sat on a chair beside a table, on which a map was spread. Far bigger maps, pinned together where they overlapped, covered a good third of the floor. They waited at least five minutes after all had been done before summoning the taller officer and giving him orders to carry. The other man wondered whether he had been forgotten, but simply stood there patiently. There was an even longer pause before the round-faced Prince of Neufchâtel called to him. His uniform was a glorious confection of lace.

'Capitaine Dalmas.'

The thickset man marched stiffly in his knee-high boots and stamped to attention. 'Sire!'

The Emperor's pale eyes looked at him squarely from under that famous lick of hair. As so often he was wearing the dark green undress uniform of the Chasseurs of his Imperial Guard. He pointed. 'I remember you from Eylau.' Dalmas nodded. 'And before that I gave you the cross. That was at Boulogne.' Another nod. 'We have travelled a long way since then.'

The Emperor paused, and his chief of staff asked sharply, 'Where is your squadron?' It surprised Dalmas when the prince appeared to recognise the name of the village. He had never heard it before in his life until they reached it just before dawn this morning. 'It is not on this map,' continued Berthier, 'but should be about here.' He pressed his thumb into the paper.

'Your strength?'

'My own company, of forty-five men, and another from the Legion of the Visula with seventy-three.'

'Horses?'

'As good as any in the army.' Few cuirassiers had been sent to Spain, for the big horses they rode were too valuable to suffer on the bad roads and eat the poor fodder available.

'You think your cuirassiers suitable for detached duties?' the Emperor interrupted. 'You carry no carbines, so cannot fight on foot.'

'The legionnaires have them.' Dalmas' tone was matter of fact.

'Yes, the Poles are good men, why not take more of them?'

'I trust my men. They are the best.'

The Emperor was pleased with such assurance. 'I asked Marshal Ney for a good man, and he has sent me you.' Actually he had asked Ney for his best man, not just the prettiest uniform on his staff. 'I want someone who can fight like a demon and think like a thief. He may well get killed,' he had warned.

Dalmas managed to conceal his surprise. He was a super-numerary ADC on the marshal's staff, recommended by a wounded divisional commander unable to serve, and not one of red-faced Ney's own protégés. Supernumeraries usually got only the difficult jobs, the ones that brought danger with little hope of glory. Silently he wondered whether he was being given a task likely to prove a death warrant.

The Emperor was pleased that his praise had not provoked unnecessary bluster. Ney may have chosen well. 'I have a task for you . . .' He began by explaining the wider situation. With Madrid in French hands, the Spanish armies almost all routed and the British in retreat, the French had been gathering for a new invasion of Portugal and southern Spain. In the last days he had learned that the British were not in retreat, but still moving forward. 'I do not know whether to call it courage or folly, but either way we have a chance to destroy them. All of the forces near Madrid, including my Guards, are now moving north as fast as they can. Marshal Ney is coming to join us and Soult is already there. Some of Junot's men, back from Portugal, are on their way to support the drive.

'This is what will happen.' The three men knelt on the floor – an awkward posture for Dalmas in his high boots – crawling over the maps as the Emperor explained the choices facing Sir John Moore and his own moves to counter them. The British must retreat. The route to Portugal was closed so they must go to the north-west coast and one of the Spanish ports – probably Corunna or Vigo. His own armies were swinging round in a wide arc, rather than rushing headlong at the enemy. The Emperor talked of the ground, of the few roads able to take an army, the mountains they cut through and the rivers and bridges – especially the rivers and bridges.

'I may cut off the English at Benevente. The odds are sixty-five to thirty-five in my favour, but much depends on when General Moore realises that I am coming. If we do catch him there then it is probable that you will not have a chance to do very much.' Dalmas was to take his mixed squadron on an even wider loop to the north-east. He was to avoid any contact with the British, but try to get behind them. Marshal Soult was ordered to give him a company of infantry, a capable engineer and more cavalry squadrons if he wanted them. His force was to get behind the enemy. If possible – and the Emperor believed this to be unlikely, but worth the attempt – get behind their columns and destroy a bridge to slow them down so that they would be caught. More probably, his task would be to find and take a bridge that would allow the French to envelop any position where the English tried to stand. In short, he was to help keep them on the run.

'It is not a duty for which specific instructions are appropriate. I need a man who can use his judgement.'

'Sire.' Again it was pleasing that there were no usual protestations of determination. The captain simply stood up, and nodded.

'Good. I know that I can trust you. I only wish that the English army was three times the size. If one hundred thousand English mothers had to mourn the loss of their sons then we might have peace at last.'

Dalmas barely remembered a world at peace. He had been a soldier now for ten years, far longer than his spell as a school-teacher in St-Omer. A conscript like almost everyone else, he had discovered that he liked the army, and thrived on the excitement of war. He had also discovered a talent for the business, and so he had risen through the ranks and become an officer. His anticipation of farther advancement remained fierce. This was an opportunity to win the favour of the Emperor himself, who never failed to reward a good soldier. Dalmas would do his best to win that favour. The prospect of peace could look after itself.

He stood and stamped to attention. Helmet still under his arm, he bowed rather than saluted. As he left, the Emperor was already dictating a new set of orders for one of the marshals in the south of the country.

5

That evening Williams paid a call on Dobson and his family, as part of his round checking on the company. Dobson and Sally, their children and Hanks, along with Sergeant Rawson and his wife, occupied one of two ground-floor rooms in the little stone house on the edge of the hamlet. The other married grenadiers and their families were in the only other room, which did not have a fireplace, and so the wizened Spanish woman who lived there and her three small children watched the British visitors warily from a corner they maintained as their own.

The veteran sat in some state, bolt upright on a clumsily made wooden chair, smoking his clay pipe. The room was gloomy, and since there was no chimney the air was full of the heavier smoke from the main fire. Only a single candle stub perched in the neck of a bottle gave any addition to the red light.

Williams felt his eyes smarting as soon as he went in. Rawson, always a formal man in spite of his close association with the company officers through his duties, sprang to his feet. His jacket was undone and he began furtive attempts to fasten the buttons. Dobson's son, a drummer, who wore a white jacket with red cuffs and collar as a distinction, also stood up, although less steadily. His father had let him join him in his daily tipple, as a mark that it was soon to be Christmas, and he was approaching his fifteenth birthday. The rum, combined with the heady atmosphere of the room, had left him more than a little light headed.

Dobson himself made no move, since for the night this was his home and he knew that the officer would not expect formality. He nodded.

'Good evening, Mr Williams, sir. Welcome to our humble abode.' When Williams was still a volunteer he had served as Dobson's rear rank man, standing behind him in formation, loading and firing past his shoulder. Front and rear rank men depended on each other and the veteran had made it clear that he expected his to be up to the mark.

'Good evening, Dobson. Good evening, Sergeant Rawson. I trust you are well, Mrs Rawson?' The sergeant's wife was a highly respectable woman, always neat in her attire and God-fearing in her ways. She and Sally Dobson, in spite of so many differences, had become firm friends, and the two families were billeted together now as a matter of course, an arrangement which both found satisfactory. She stood, gave a curtsy, and thanked him for his enquiry. A sharp barking interrupted her, as the little terrier she carried in her basket expressed discontent at being ignored.

The welcome from the others in the room was far less formal, but genuinely warm. Hanks said little, but that was not unusual. Jenny was bright and chatty, and never one to feel bound by deference. He paid her for repairing his jacket.

'Try not to get it shot again,' she said by way of thanks. 'Making work for me.' She shook her head, swaying her thick dark hair consciously. Pregnant, wearing a dress that was patched and worn, Jenny Dobson was still very aware of her looks, even in the ash-filled gloom. 'That's the best me and Ma could do, but you can still see the hole.'

'Thank you for your efforts.' He smiled. 'I shall try to avoid getting shot again!'

Dobson snorted. 'Aye, see that you do! I don't want to be breaking in more new officers at my time of life.' He must have been forty, and had served in one regiment or another for more than half his years. He had been promoted many times and always reduced to the ranks after having one drink too many. In October he had been raised to corporal once again, and it had lasted for almost a month before he went on a colossal drunk and wandered the street, half naked and telling everyone that he was going to shoot Major MacAndrews. By the time he had sobered up even he could not remember why, for he had both respect and affection for his commander.

Dobson's leathery face was lined, but without any trace of weakness. With age, he simply seemed to have grown stronger and harder. Williams had never seen him flag, even on the longest march, and knew the cold efficiency with which he fought and killed.

That thought reminded him of Redman, one of the ensigns in the Grenadier Company when Williams had joined the regiment. Jenny had flirted with him, taking presents and, in time – Williams feared the time may have been brief – taking him as a lover. It seemed more than likely that he was the father of her baby – or if not Redman then his friend Hatch, who had often joined their parties. Williams was sure that Dobson had discovered this, and hurriedly arranged his daughter's marriage to prevent her public humiliation. He was almost certain that Redman had died on the veteran's bayonet in the confusion at Roliça. So much had happened in those few days that his shock had ebbed away, and Dobson had saved Williams' and his friends' lives soon afterwards. Murderer or not, Williams had found that he still trusted the old soldier. Dobson responded with an almost paternal interest in the young officer's success. He was always respectful, and never overfamiliar in public. His daughter did not share these inhibitions.

'You need a new coat,' she announced. 'No matter how much we scrub we can't get the stains from your sleeves.' Traces remained from where the black dye of the original cuffs had run in wet weather. Jenny grinned at him, and gave a sly wink. 'Can't expect to impress her if you look so shabby.'

Williams hoped that the poor light concealed his embarrassment. His close friends knew of his admiration for Miss Mac-Andrews. He hoped that it remained a secret to everyone else, and he feared to make her the subject of gossip. Mrs Rawson was obviously shocked. 'I . . . I do not know what you mean,' he began.

'Suit yourself,' said Jenny saucily. Williams noticed that neither Mrs Rawson, nor Sally Dobson, nor even the Dobsons' youngest girl appeared to dispute Jenny's claim. He feared that his feelings were too obvious. Dobson himself looked mildly amused, but said nothing and continued to puff on his pipe. Williams decided to change the subject.

'And how are you, Mrs Hanks?'

'Fat,' replied Jenny. 'Fat and ugly. I can't wait for the little bugger to pop out!' Mrs Rawson hissed at her language, even though living as a soldier's wife must have hardened her somewhat.

'It'll come in God's good time, Mrs Hanks,' she said, 'and not a moment before. Just hope it goes well and all are healthy.' She and her husband had not been blessed with any children as yet, and she viewed birth with sacred awe.

'Mrs Calloway has promised to help when the time comes.' Sally Dobson had considerably more faith in the wife of one of the sergeants than the battalion's surgeon and his assistants.

'I don't want that old trout mauling me!' Jenny's anger was sudden and sharp, and Williams suspected than an oft-rehearsed argument was about to resume, so changed the subject again.

'Well, you will be reassured to know that the families are to stay here with the baggage when we advance. At least you can make yourselves comfortable and know that there will be a roof over your head.' Williams was pleased to pass on the good news. Then he noticed that the Spanish woman was busy picking lice out of her children's hair. It reminded him of the shock of seeing rows of people sitting one behind the other in Lisbon, each engaged in the same task. On one bridge he had seen the women perched in a row on one parapet and the men on the other, all singing happily as they worked. The sight then as now was enough to make him feel that his own skin was crawling with vermin. He had caught a few lice in his jacket in recent days, but hoped his uniform was not yet badly infested. Bidding them good evening, he left to complete his rounds.

It was not quite so cold as it had been, but even so he wished that he had worn his greatcoat. He nodded to the shadowy figure of another officer, walking along the far side of the street and no doubt going about the same task.

'Good evening to you, Williams.' It was Ensign Hatch, and as usual his voice was more than a little slurred from drink.

Redman had loathed Williams from the very start, and his crony had often joined in the mockery. After Roliça, Hatch had come to make peace, genuinely saddened by his friend's death and with no reason to suspect that anyone apart from the French were responsible. More recently his behaviour had been strange, with an unctuous friendliness accompanied by ostensibly unintended minor insults or provocation. Williams often struggled to understand people, but officers of necessity were often in each other's company and it was better to be affable.

'Good evening, Hatch. Bit warmer, I think,' he said with a smile.

'Then I am sure it must be.'

Williams decided to ignore the tart response and felt obliged to continue a conversation he had begun. 'Still, I'll be glad to be back in the warm, once I have finished checking on the company. How are your fellows settling in?'

'Well enough.' Hatch smiled. 'Squalor suits most of them, and some of the families have already made themselves as comfortable as in their own hovels back home. That grubby brute Peters was already rutting with his sow of a wife under a blanket.' He paused, and frowned as if in deep thought. 'At least, I assume it was his wife. Didn't fancy lifting the blanket up to make sure, eh!' Hatch gave a cheerful wink.

Williams gave a brief and restrained laugh for courtesy's sake. The wit of his brother officers was often a little raw, and at times blatantly crude. Such was the common coin of army life, and if he did not especially care for these things, he knew that most of them were good fellows at heart.

'Well, you'd know, of course,' added Hatch.

'I doubt that.' Williams knew the reply was weak, but was not altogether sure what the other man had meant.

'You are too modest. Everyone knows the Grenadier Company is a well-ordered household. I am sure you know each of your men well.' Williams was suspicious of the compliment, but could not see any barb within it. 'Acquainted with their wives and children as well.'

'Contented men are good soldiers,' said Williams, aware that it sounded prim, and trying to understand what the other man was implying.

'Of course, and good officers keep them so, even if it means stirring out on a cold night to visit their quarters.

'Well, we had better continue with our duties instead of chatting away. Good evening, Mister Williams.' Hatch emphasised the 'Mister', and took a couple of brisk paces away before looking back over his shoulder. 'You know, it is a pity we cannot encourage the lads and their women to bathe more often.'

Williams was dubious. 'Not enough wood to burn to heat the coppers, but certainly an admirable enough ambition.'

'Yes, might also liven up these inspections and let us see some tit now and again.'

Hatch vanished into a doorway before Williams could muster a response. He wondered whether it was only his imagination which made Hatch's conversation a good deal cruder whenever they were alone. It was not something he could easily discuss, even with Pringle or Hanley. Williams shook his head, trying to dismiss both the thought and the encounter while he finished off his rounds.

At least what he saw was encouraging, for it was clear as he went around the billets of the grenadiers that the company was largely content, and he suspected that the mood was general to the battalion. The 106th had enjoyed their day of rest, aside from some inevitable muttering when told that they were still required to parade and then drill for a couple of hours. After that some had carrying and fatigue parties to perform, and sentries were required, although to universal relief they were not called upon to provide piquets today. Many of the officers and all of the clerks toiled to catch up with the company and battalion paperwork. Yet by the middle of the afternoon almost everyone had the chance to enjoy some rest.

Someone from the Light Company had produced a football – battered, patched, but still just recognisably spherical – and a noisy game developed, which at various times involved several hundred players. On the far side of the rows of houses, officers from the brigade played cricket amid the melting snow. With more than forty scouts in such a small area, scoring was difficult. Williams thrashed a few wild runs before a lieutenant from the 91st caught the ball in his feathered bonnet. Pringle enjoyed longer success by aiming his shots between scouts and trusting that the running men would collide with each other as their eyes followed the ball. Hanley, baffled that anyone could enjoy such a patently futile game, had contented himself with sitting near by and sketching the scene. It was rough, and he struggled to capture the sense of slowness and sudden action, so after a while he wandered to the other side of the town and tried his hand at drawing the football. This at least had the virtue of constant flow, although he remained entirely ignorant of any result.

When the cricket match broke up, Williams and Pringle went over to join their friend. There was no sign of the football abating, and Hanley's drawing gave a good impression of the mobs of players whirling around the ball. He handed the pad to them for inspection. Pringle smiled, and Williams nodded enthusiastically as he wished once again to possess such skill himself.

'I have only ever been able to draw trees,' he confessed.

'At least they don't move about,' commented Pringle. He flipped over the pages and cast his eye over a series of landscapes. Then there were the great arches of the aqueduct at Segovia. 'Good to see this in daylight.' Hanley had shown him the drawings the previous night, but the light of their candle had made it impossible to study them properly.

'It is a spectacular work,' said the artist, moderately proud of his sketch, and sharing his friends' enthusiasm for antiquities of every sort.

'Is it still in use?' asked Pringle. 'The preservation certainly looks remarkably good.'

'It crosses the valley and I believe supplies most of the water to the town,' Hanley confirmed. 'There are regular marks and traces of an ornamental inscription at one of the highest points, but I had no opportunity to climb up and see them closely.'

Pringle nodded, but from the small human figures in the sketch he guessed that the height of the aqueduct was considerable indeed and wondered at his friend's enthusiasm at the prospect of taking such risks. Personally, he had no head for heights, but perhaps Hanley was unaffected by such nervousness. 'The marks perhaps indicate bronze letters?'

'I should think so. A priest told me that the inscription declared the work to have been carried out by the Emperor Trajan, but priests are generally inclined to name either him or Hadrian.'

'Local fellows, of course,' murmured Williams of these emperors from Roman Spain, but his mind had drifted away as he caught sight of Miss MacAndrews, returning from another ride. Earlier in the day, he had seen the girl and her mother pass by, both of them straight-backed as they effortlessly controlled their mounts. Too far away to greet them, he found his mood souring when Wickham passed in the other direction and was able to bid them good day. At least the suave officer's face betrayed no particular emotion, but the generosity of the smile with which Jane had greeted Wickham's appearance was a source for concern – and, he had to admit privately, no little jealousy. It was hard to tell at that distance, but Williams felt that her expression became harder when the captain passed with no more than the barest of civilities.

Now the girl was out riding again, but this time without her mother. Beside her, mounted on a saddled mule, rode Mrs Kidwell, the quartermaster's wife, who had joined her husband while they were in Lisbon. She was a plump woman, and her bulk kept the animal to the slowest of walks, which no doubt frustrated the fast-riding Miss MacAndrews. The two ladies paused on the crest of the hill beyond the town. There they were joined by three red-coated officers, and stood for a while to converse, before the group split up. Mrs Kidwell and two of the officers came at a steady pace, while Miss MacAndrews and the remaining man trotted briskly down the road ahead of them. The bearing of the redcoat told Williams that it was Wickham before he could recognise any features.

'I said that one must admire the enterprise of a villain even as you deplore his actions,' repeated Pringle loudly.

Williams was snatched from his thoughts, and looked puzzled.

'We were speaking of whoever it was climbed up so high to steal the bronze letters,' explained Hanley. Williams still appeared to be lost to the world, and so he returned his attention to Pringle. 'The aqueduct at Toledo is almost as large, although these days less well preserved. I have a rough sketch of that somewhere near the back . . .'

Captain Wickham and Miss MacAndrews passed close enough for the girl to raise her long whip in greeting, but neither she nor her escort showed any inclination to stop and talk. Williams could not quite make out the words she spoke to her companion, but the tone, and her manner in general, indicated deep sympathy.

The captain's voice was deeper and carried more clearly. 'I should have been a parson,' he said in a resigned tone, 'in a good living in Derbyshire, encouraging kindness in the world rather than making war. All through the jealousy of a man raised to be as a brother to me. I am almost glad his poor father did not live . . .'

The riders had passed, and perhaps were speaking more quietly, for he could discern nothing more. It did not matter. Like most of the officers of the 106th, Williams had heard this story from Wickham. Knowing the man better, he was inclined to believe that there was more to the tale, but could remember how readily he had sympathised when Wickham had first confided in him such an apparently intimate part of his history. Miss MacAndrews' sweet nature would most likely respond in the same way and this worried him.

'I am forced to question whether that man's intentions are honourable,' he said firmly.

'Oh, I should not think so,' replied Pringle without thinking. He was intent on Hanley's sketchpad, as the latter pointed out features in drawings of other aqueducts and bridges, including one of the great bridge at Salamanca. 'Of whom are we speaking, anyway?'

'Of Wickham.'

Pringle had grave doubts about the integrity and general probity of George Wickham, but when he looked around and realised that Miss MacAndrews was the principal focus of his friend's concern he realised that some delicacy was necessary.

'Miss MacAndrews is a thoroughly sensible young lady,' he ventured.

Hanley stood up. 'She is,' he agreed.

'She is still very young,' replied Williams.

'She also has her parents with her to keep her under observation. I do not think that the major would take kindly to any attempt at his daughter's honour.'

'The mother is even more intimidating,' added Pringle, hoping to lighten the mood. 'You are a fine fellow, Bills, but sometimes just a little too ready to jealousy. You even became suspicious when out of the sweet kindness of her heart Miss MacAndrews was so assiduous in visiting old Truscott in hospital!'

'I grew to suspect that he was enjoying her company and exploiting her sympathy.'

'Well, yes,' said Pringle. 'We only have his word for it that it was the French who shot him! Perhaps it was all arranged as part of some devilish scheme to win Miss MacAndrews' favour?'

Hanley threw his head back in laughter. Williams joined in after a moment.

6

The next day was as restful. The brigades leading the attack were to march at eight in the evening. The 106th were ordered to parade with the rest of the Reserve Division at 9.30, to follow on once the order came. MacAndrews insisted on a spell of drill in the morning, but that still left the greater part of the day to prepare. In the afternoon the commissaries drove half a dozen bullocks into a pen at the end of the street, where they were slaughtered and butchered. The meat was fresh, if rather tough, and to everyone's delight there was an issue of bread that was only just going stale. It made a change from ships' biscuits, which seemed to be either hard enough to crack teeth or soft and teeming with worms. There was time to cook and eat a good meal and everyone was grateful for it.

Mrs MacAndrews kept close to her daughter whenever she was away from their billet. They saw Wickham from a distance, but spoke no words to him. Jane was surprised at being so disappointed, but was struck by the ardent glance he gave her. Then the rain began to fall, and no one was inclined to venture out unless required to by duty.

At 9.30 that night the drums beat for muster.

Rain still fell steadily, washing away the last remnants of the snow and turning the roads into slippery mires. A torrent of water cascaded down from the gutter fringing the roof of the convent and spattered on the stones of the courtyard. Sir John Moore's cocked hat was protected by an oilskin cover, and a heavy cloak kept him reasonably dry. Even so water gathered at each end of his hat and now and then a drip fell in front of his face. Captain Napier had wrapped his pistols carefully to keep the powder within them dry as he handed them up to the general, who pushed each in turn into the holsters on the front of his saddle, and then flipped the tops closed.

There was shouting from outside the gateway, and a moment later Graham brought in a Spaniard, drenched to the skin and covered in mud. The colonel explained that the man was carrying an urgent message from La Romana. Moore sheltered under the roof of the porch as he scanned the letter and translated its contents. The general looked impassive, but all present knew that the contents changed everything. The French were moving north from Madrid. Napoleon was coming.

By the time the 106th had paraded the rain had stopped and a bright moon shone amid the ragged clouds. The men all wore greatcoats, and had their white cross-belts over them. Each man's pouch and pack had sixty rounds of ball ammunition, and between them the pack and haversack carried hard tack biscuit for three days. In spite of the hour, many of the women of the regiment stood silently watching their menfolk, when they marched off the mile or so to join the remainder of the division nearer to Sahagun. A brigade from another division was formed up in column, preparatory to moving off ahead of them.

Then they stood for an hour, awaiting an order that did not come. At the end of that time MacAndrews and the commanders of the other battalions were called to General Paget. After ten minutes they came back, but there was none of the usual rush which accompanied the issuing of important orders. Their horses seemed almost to slouch, and more than one senior officer appeared slumped in his saddle.

MacAndrews nodded to Sergeant Major Fletcher to call the 106th to attention. Before the major had begun to speak a murmur came from one of the other battalions and quickly surged into a roar of dismay. Similar shouts came from other regiments. Williams and Hanley, standing behind the rear rank of the Grenadier Company, both turned as they heard a strange clattering sound. A hundred yards away and facing in the opposite direction a Highland battalion had paraded. First a few and then almost all of its soldiers threw down their muskets in frustration.

'Boys,' began MacAndrews, 'the 106th showed its courage back in Portugal. We also proved to the rest of the army that its youngest regiment not only knew how to fight, but how to keep good discipline. We may not like some orders we are given, but I know that you will always obey them.

'The advance is called off. We will return to our quarters and then the army is to withdraw.'

There was silence. Although many must have guessed what was happening it did not make the shock much less. They were ready to advance and expecting to fight. It seemed shameful to stop when the enemy was near. They knew that they could beat the French, and wanted the chance to prove it once again.

The mood was sullen as the 106th marched back to the hamlet. There was almost no talk, and MacAndrews wondered whether it would not have been better to hear a few murmured complaints.

After the men had been dismissed back to their billets, at close to midnight he crammed the officers into the small church, which was the only place big enough for all thirty men to be in one room. It lacked much of its roof, which was why no men had been quartered there, but with the aid of a lamp it was good enough for his purpose.

'Gentlemen, the enemy is moving against us in great force, led by Bonaparte himself.' That was dramatic news and provoked an excited buzz that for a moment lifted the sombre mood. 'They are perhaps three days' march away, perhaps more, but in numbers at least double our own even before they join up with Marshal Soult. Our Spanish allies are for the moment unable to provide any real support.' There were sneers at this. Hanley, concerted defender of all things Spanish, just looked at the floor. 'If we remain where we are, then we will face enemies on two sides and must be overwhelmed. Therefore, from tomorrow morning, the army will begin to retreat. We of the Reserve

Division, along with the light brigades and the cavalry, will remain a little longer to cover the retreat. I doubt that we will be pressed so early. Marshal Soult does not have the strength on his own, and the other French armies are still too far away. At most we may see some of their cavalry. It is unlikely that we will begin to move until Christmas morning.' He gave a wry smile. 'It will not be much of a celebration, I fear.'

The mood was gloomy throughout the battalion. Williams noticed that some men were more than usually irritable and argued over the slightest disagreements. Others were uncharacteristically silent and apathetic.

Major MacAndrews was far too old a campaigner not to sense the frustration of officers and men alike, and so he determined to keep everyone busy throughout Christmas Eve. Inspections were rigorous, and he urged every officer to look at packs and boots in particular. Most of the latter were in a bad state. They had hoped to draw new ones from store after reaching the main army, only to be told that none was available from the nearest depot.

As far as possible nothing that was not essential was to be carried. Experience had taught him that men burdened themselves with all sorts of useless weight on campaign, most of all trinkets they had scavenged or looted. While he doubted that any inspections would catch and make them discard even a quarter of such rubbish, it would at least be something. Alastair MacAndrews did everything he could to keep the battalion occupied and as ready as possible for the trials of the coming days.

It was not until late in the day that the major was able to snatch a few short moments with his wife, and even then there was much to arrange regarding their personal baggage and little or no opportunity for leisure.

'You're enjoying this, aren't you?' said Esther MacAndrews, only half in jest. 'Tidying up your own little corner in the midst of impending disaster.'

'I trust that things are not so very bad yet.' Yet he had to admit that that the activity and the overall sense of urgency were most invigorating. 'There is danger certainly. A march at this time of year through the mountains and pursued by the enemy is no gentle prospect.'

'You need not sound quite so gleeful,' she mocked him.

He smiled, and then looked serious. 'You do realise that my duties will be heavy, I will not have time . . .'

'You old goat, I should very much doubt there will be time for that!'

'I meant . . .'

Again she interrupted her soft-spoken husband. 'You meant that you shall be far too busy to pay much attention to your wife and daughter. That the journey will be arduous for us, and once again you silently wish that we had not accompanied you.' She reached out and brushed her fingers against his cheek.

'Only my concern makes me think that. In every other regard I am proud to have you with me.' He took her hand with both of his and pressed it gently.

'You are learning charm in your old age.' Esther was only a few inches shorter than her tall husband. 'Do not worry, we shall be careful, and I do believe your daughter and I can take care of ourselves.' Silently she was pleased that this should keep Jane busy. Esther had noticed her daughter's sudden interest in Wickham. Perhaps if they had remained at rest for many more days, she would have been forced to say something to the girl. Memories of her own reluctance to pay heed to the admonishments of her mother had made her cautious, lest a warning have the opposite effect. It was best that the girl work things out for herself, but although sensible and assured in many ways, it was doubtful that she had before confronted as charming a rake as Wickham.

'I will look after Jane,' said Esther firmly. Her husband seemed to detect the edge in her voice, but if he was puzzled he said nothing. Esther wondered whether to speak to him of her concerns. No, she thought, for then he would be bound to do something, and perhaps call the rogue out. Our daughter has sense enough already, or will soon learn it. He has enough to worry about without this additional burden. She smiled fondly at her husband, who was busy trying to cram far too much into one of the valises from his saddle.

'Let me do it, you lump,' she said, taking over.

At that moment, in the little room next to their own, Jane sat on one of the folding beds they carried in their baggage. It had proved an extremely wise purchase, given the dirty and often verminous furniture offered to them in the billets along the line of march. For the tenth time she read the words, the note clutched tightly in her hands.

My dear Miss MacAndrews

My mind can no longer contain anything beyond the thought of you. Instead of sleep come only images of your shining eyes, flawless skin, the radiance of your smile and liveliness of your company. Madam, you haunt me, exalt me, confuse and overwhelm me all at once.

Disappointments in life may be manifold, and yet to see you is to know with every fibre the joy of life and happiness.

It is Christmas tomorrow, a time for gifts. If the whole world were mine for the asking, I would want no more than this. Meet me, if you can. My duties permit me to be on the road north of the village for at least an hour and a half after eight o'clock.

Yours with all my heart – GW

The intended meaning of the second paragraph still eluded her, but the intent of the note was obvious, so bluntly so that it strengthened her resolve to ignore the request. Yet at the same time there was excitement in the secrecy and the boldness of his appeal. No one would ever know that he had slipped her the note when she and her mother had met General Paget's staff on their only ride of the day. Wickham had paid her no particular regard.

Jane had told herself that she would not read the letter again. That vow lasted only for an instant, and she lingered over each word three more times. She was not sure whether or not she liked Wickham, but judged that no particular fondness had developed, although there was a good deal of sympathy. His manner was charming, his appearance most handsome and pleasing to the eye, and his conversation alive with wit – much of it dangerous in its tone. Jane was certain that she did not trust him, or doubt that his interest was less than utterly selfish, and she had to confess to herself that this made the danger all the more delicious. She could not trust Wickham, and part of her wanted to match her wits and her own determination against his challenge. She liked to think that she would not succumb, at least not to any serious extent, but she was not absolutely sure that this was true. For the moment, she tried to hold to her resolve not to go, or in any way answer such an impertinent request.

At least no one else would ever know. With more reluctance than she had expected, Jane dropped the note into the fire and watched the paper blacken and curl.

The retreat began at noon on Christmas Eve. Sir John Moore and Colonel Graham watched the southernmost column set out. Hope's division of ten battalions was to be followed by Fraser's division with another nine. They followed the same route as the advance, trudging along the road to Mayorga, to the bridge over the Esla at Castro Gonzalo and so to Benevente. At the same time Baird took his eight battalions in a separate column to cross the river at Valencia de Don Juan.

Moore stared fixedly at the passing soldiers in their long grey greatcoats, and only a friend as close as Graham would have noticed the marks of concern in his expression.

The men marched without spirit. There was no singing, no laughter, and even the drums of the closest regiment seemed forlorn. The French would face the same grim weather and execrable roads, but they were advancing and everything about them would be eager. The Emperor's presence was likely only to make them drive on faster.

'Two days,' Sir John said softly. 'Give me two marches before the French really know how close we are and the greatest danger should be over.'

'Lord Paget reports no sign yet even of enemy patrols,' Graham confirmed.

'Good. I should prefer not to fight a battle here, but I must if they press me. Baird will be beyond recall. We simply cannot march together at any speed. At this season I will not make the men sleep in the open unless there is no other choice. Look at those fields.' He pointed to the slopes of the hills rising gently beyond the road. 'Not more than a few bits of scrub. There is no wood to make fires or cook, and without those men would start to die. So we must spread the divisions, and let them each take quarters in a different place each night.

'Has General La Romana been reminded that it would be the greatest assistance to us if he keeps his men farther north and avoids our line of march?' Colonel Graham nodded. 'And has he been urged in the strongest fashion to deny the French the bridge at Mansilla for as long as possible, or even to destroy it?'

'He assures us he will. How long he may hold will depend on how fast our friend Soult takes before he strikes. Where shall we concentrate the army again?'

'I am not yet sure that we shall, but if we do it shall not be before Astorga. However, it may prove expedient to employ more than one route. I most strongly doubt that we can maintain ourselves in this part of Spain against the enemy's numbers. So that means embarkation and so in turn depends on where the navy can best come to us.'

'But surely, should enough of the army be together and the chance arrive, you will let us take a rub at the French?' For a moment the elderly colonel implored with all the enthusiasm of an excited child. 'There is not a man in the whole army who will not feel mortified and disappointed at the orders countermanding the advance.'

Moore could not help grinning. 'And I thought we Scots were famed above all for our prudence.' Graham chuckled. 'Perhaps in the days to come. I do not know, and will not waste men's lives without some worthwhile object. If we advanced now, Marshal Soult would be a fool not to withdraw before us. In four days' time we most likely would not have provoked a general action, and by then the corps advancing from Madrid would be upon us.'

Graham understood the necessity, but his enthusiasm was slow to die. 'The men would like a fight.'

'As also would you, and no doubt all the officers in the army! If I were commanding a battalion or a company I am most sure that I would feel the same. I have no doubts about their spirit. It's a fine army.' To himself he added, 'And I'll not be the one to lose it.'

7

On Christmas morning, Sally Dobson and the other wives of the Grenadier Company watched the 106th's quartermaster as he tried to bring some order to the chaos. Mr Kidwell and his assistants ran up and down the line of carts, yelling and pushing to get the baggage wagons, the regiment's equipment and the women and children ready to move. As well as the usual local ox-carts, there were two big wagons, almost as large as the bulky farm-carts used in Britain, although as with the smaller vehicles they were pulled by plodding bullocks instead of dray horses. During the night, the drivers of both wagons had vanished, and now a redcoat stood by each team, bayonet fixed to prod the animals on if necessary. It was just one element to add to the confusion. Children ran in and out of the line of vehicles, shrieking as they chased each other, and ignoring the profane calls of their mothers to come back. The remaining Portuguese and Spanish drivers were clustered in a huddle, yelling at each other in some dispute, which appeared to be on the edge of violence.

'Get those boxes tied securely, you fat-arsed buggers!' bellowed Kidwell.

Major MacAndrews and almost all the men of the battalion were away to the north, forming a piquet line, but his wife and daughter were here, doing their best to help the quartermaster. The mother had a carrying voice and an authoritative manner. Miss MacAndrews was quieter, but had long since made friends with most of the regiment's children and had a good way with them. The girl returned Sally's wave as she passed, walking beside her horse and holding the hand of a sobbing infant, before finding the child's mother. Sally liked and approved of the major's wife and daughter. They were part of the regiment, as important in its daily life as he was.

Mr Kidwell kept swearing viciously as he struggled to bring order to chaos, and then he would notice that Mrs or Miss MacAndrews was near by and would begin a profuse apology, before some new outrage of discipline prompted fresh blasphemies. One of the army's guides passed by, and was halted long enough to persuade the drivers to return to their carts. Most of the children were gathered, and now that all the wagons were full of baggage, the families were allowed to climb on top of the piles, wherever they could find space. The families of the Grenadier Company immediately occupied the first of the big wagons, abandoning their fondness for being at the head of the column. This change to the normal routine prompted angry shouts from some of the other wives, who had already decided that the bigger vehicles were likely to offer the smoothest ride. The quartermaster drew upon an extensive vocabulary, fostered by years of service in the ranks, to resolve the dispute, which essentially granted the case to the occupier, and left the companies somewhat mingled.

'God in his heaven!' wailed the quartermaster. 'Get that damned harness untangled! You!' He grabbed at one of the redcoats standing beside the first of the big wagons. 'You won't go far like that. Unbuckle the bloody thing and fasten it straight and tight.' Frustrated, he watched the man fumble with the wet leather, before quickly pulling him aside. 'Damn it, man! Get out of the way, I'll do it myself. Why in God's name I should be saddled with such a damned useless bunch of . . .' An instinct saved him for the moment, as he glanced round behind him and spotted Mrs MacAndrews close by. 'Oh, sorry, ma'am. I must apologise for my . . .' He stopped in the middle of the sentence, as he spotted the women climbing down from one of the carts and two beginning to fight. 'Oh, the stupid bitches.' He sighed. His apology was half-hearted, as he finished fixing the harness and strode off to deal with this latest outrage. Sally noticed that Mrs MacAndrews was struggling to conceal a grin.

Kidwell wanted to get moving. The 106th, along with the rest of the Reserve Division, was not due to set out until ten o'clock, but he and the other regimental quartermasters intended to hurry the baggage on so that the trudging pace of the bullocks would not hold up the main column when it followed. At dawn, they had begun to marshal the baggage trains, but it was still 8.30 before they were ready. For a short while, it was almost peaceful as they waited for the train ahead of them to move off. Sally Dobson settled comfortably, wrapped in one blanket and sitting on another to soften the hard edge of a wooden box filled with ship's biscuit.

The baggage columns ahead at last began to move, and Kidwell signalled to his own carts to follow them along the road. The rain began at almost the same moment, feeding the mud which already lay inches deep all along the rutted and churned road. The quartermaster breathed a sigh of relief and urged his own mule on, and then cursed once again as he saw that the redcoats were having trouble making the teams of the big wagons move. They yelled, struck at the animals' rumps with the butts of their muskets, and then reversed the weapons to prod with their bayonets. Nothing happened. They jabbed harder, drawing blood, and the beasts finally lurched forward, bellowing in protest.

'Where's Jenny?' Sally Dobson had sudden realised that her daughter was nowhere in the wagon. 'Oh, Mrs Rawson, have you seen my Jenny?'

'Perhaps she is on the front cart?' The fastidious Mrs Rawson put down the dog in its basket to lean out and peer forward.

Sally was becoming agitated. 'Can you see her? Oh, where is Mrs Hanks? Where is my little girl?'

The other wives took up the shout, while the sergeant's wife tried to calm her friend. 'Private Hanks is with her,' she said. One or two of the married men had been permitted to help their wives prepare for the move. All had then returned to duty, but because of his wife's condition, Captain Pringle had told Hanks to stay with the wagons until he was sure that Jenny was secure. 'She cannot come to harm.'

For some reason the carts of the regiment in front of the 106th stopped, and they too were forced to halt.

'Our Sal,' said Sally to her younger daughter, named after her, but always called Sal by the family. 'Get down and go and find your sister.' The ten-year-old, happy to be doing something, scrambled down, putting her feet between the spokes of one of the big wheels and jumping, in spite of Mrs Rawson's call to be careful. The girl splashed happily through the puddles, running past each cart and looking for Jenny.

Sally leaned precariously from the top of the great mound of crates at the front of the wagon and watched the child go. 'Oh, Mrs Rawson, I will not rest until I have Jenny beside us.' She spotted another of the company's wives in the cart ahead. The pretty Mrs Murphy had drawn her shawl tightly around her, cradling her baby in her arms and singing softly to him. Not one of the wives chosen by lot in the summer, Mary Murphy had somehow managed to find passage on board a ship and had got to Portugal, eventually walking all the way to Almeida to find the regiment there.

'Oh, Mrs Murphy!' Sally's voice was strong in spite of a persistent cough which had troubled her for years. 'Have you seen Mrs Hanks?' Mary shook her head, but stood up, and tried to help by looking.

Esther and Jane MacAndrews, drawn by the noise, stopped to talk to Sally, although found more coherent explanation from the sergeant's wife. They split up, the daughter riding to the front of the column to search, while her mother went down the opposite side.

The carts ahead began to move. The Portuguese and Spanish drivers yelled and prodded to get their own vehicles moving again. Sally Dobson was watching her little girl run back towards the team of oxen on the big wagon at the moment when the redcoat had a flash of inspiration. He jabbed with his bayonet, and at the same time shouted out the same command the locals were using at the top of his voice. The oxen almost galloped off.

'Look out, Sal!' screamed Sally Dobson, and then the crates she was resting on shifted with the sudden, jerky movement and she was pitched forward and falling. Her head struck the edge of the iron-rimmed wheel, and her shriek turned into a short grunt as she slid down in front of it. The oxen were still pulling with all their strength, and the big cart rolled inexorably forward, the wheel passing squarely across her chest, crushing down with the huge weight of stores and people, pressing her into the mud. The passengers felt the wagon lift slightly, but only slightly.

Sal Dobson stared in open-mouthed horror. Mrs Murphy screamed, and an instant later the shriek was taken up by all the women and children, as they saw what had happened or word of the horrible accident reached them. The redcoat driving the cart sobbed, and then dragged at the yoke to halt the team, stopping the wagon just before the second wheel reached Sally.

Esther MacAndrews had turned when she heard Sally's shout and had been just yards away – so close that she thought, or perhaps imagined, that she had heard the crack of bones amid the driving rain. She never for a moment doubted that the body lying in the mud was lifeless, but dismounted anyway. Mrs Rawson had already jumped down, catching her skirts for a moment on the side of the wagon, but it did not worry her that her legs were exposed as she rushed to help her friend. Esther herself ran to the little girl, and grabbed Sal, hugging her and turning her away from the grim sight.

Mr Kidwell was there in a moment, shouting to see why they had stopped, until he realised the ghastly cause.

'We must fetch Private Dobson,' he said. 'Poor, poor man.'

Esther did not want her daughter to see and, passing Sal to Mrs Kidwell, she walked towards Jane, who was riding back to find out what was going on. She reached her, patted the grey on the neck, and spoke softly.

'Mrs Dobson is sadly killed. Ride to the grenadiers and tell her husband to come here. I shall try to find the older daughter.'

Jane gasped at the news. Then nodded, and without saying anything – indeed, unable to trust her voice to speak – she flicked her long whip to set the horse off across the fields. Her mother went over to the group around the body to tell the quartermaster what she had done and offer help in any other way. The two redcoats lifted the corpse out of the road, and Esther noticed one of the men shudder as he felt the unnaturally loose body and limbs.

Kidwell had to get the carts moving again, for they could not delay the rest of the baggage. One of his assistants took over guiding the one cart and he walked alongside the other, leaving the two soldiers to start digging a grave with a spade taken from one of the wagons. Mrs Rawson stayed behind, her arms around poor Sal, and the older woman forced herself not to cry so that she would not upset the child. The major's wife got back on her horse and rode along the line of carts, looking in vain for Jenny or her husband. Then she went back to the forlorn group standing in the rain beside the shape wrapped in a blanket.

'Good morning to you, Miss MacAndrews.' The adjutant raised his hat in greeting. He had stopped his horse when he saw Jane approaching. 'Are you looking for your father?'

'No, I am looking for the Grenadier Company. There has been a horrible accident and Mrs Dobson is dead. I have come to tell her husband.' As Jane spoke the words it all seemed unreal.

Brotherton let out his breath. 'How truly terrible. Then I must not detain you, although perhaps the poor man would prefer to remain in ignorance of his loss for as many more minutes as possible.' He pointed behind him. 'You need to bear more to the right. Captain Pringle has established himself in a small barn. He will be able to tell you where to find the unfortunate fellow.'

Jane rode on, gave her horse to the sentry outside the barn and went in. There was a strong smell of damp straw and the feeble fire the redcoats had lit produced more smoke than warmth. It was not Pringle she found with the reserve of the Grenadier

Company, but Hanley, whose warm greeting faded when he saw her expression.

'What on earth is wrong? Are you unwell?'

The girl explained once again. Sergeant Rawson paled at the news.

'Where is Dobson?' Hanley asked him.

'With the piquet the captain has just gone to relieve. May I guide the lady, sir? One of us ought to stay here. I know Dobson well.' Hanley was by now used to the tone employed by sergeants when their request was not a request, but already decided.

'Of course.' Hanley turned to look at Jane. She was wearing her hussar-style riding habit once again, its shade made darker by the rain. 'It is very kind of you to go to this trouble,' he said.

'It really is nothing.'

Rawson walked beside the grey horse. It was not far, and within a few minutes they had topped a low rise and come upon a line of redcoats standing at ease behind a dry-stone wall which offered some small shelter from the wind-driven rain. Pringle was standing beside Bobbie, sharing a steaming mug of tea with a group of men. They had erected a greatcoat on some sticks to give just enough protection to a fire and boil a kettle. Billy Pringle disliked tea, and never drank it for pleasure, but could not refuse their generosity. The men's spirits were still low, and news of the accident made them drop even farther. Dobson said nothing when Sergeant Rawson explained what had happened. His face was wet from the rain, drops of which hung on the peak of his shako, but nothing about his expression seemed to change. The two men walked off, heading back to the road where Sally was being buried. Rawson talked, trying to distract the old veteran. Dobson walked stiffly, as if in a dream.

'Poor devil,' said Pringle. 'I thought he and his wife were tougher than granite and would outlast all of us.' Like Hanley he thanked the girl profusely.

Jane ignored the praise. 'I keep thinking of the poor girl, and her brother only a little older.' She closed her eyes for a moment. 'I would like to gallop, to feel the rush of air and not to have to think for a while.' Pringle nodded in understanding. 'Would such a thing be permissible? Or would it be your duty to arrest me?' Her laugh was thin.

'Probably best if you do not go too far. The outlying piquets are a quarter of a mile ahead of us. Mr Williams is with them. They are just short of the main road. If you get that far then it is best to turn back. It's an open line, but try to stay behind our piquets. We do not believe the French are anywhere near, but a degree of caution would be prudent.' Pringle's glasses were misted with rainwater. Even so he did his best to show the earnestness of his expression. 'Thank you,' he repeated.

Jane nodded to him and rode round to go through the gap in the wall which led down the slope. She went quickly through the field, for the ground was firmer than she expected. With her left heel and the whip on the other flank she pushed the grey faster and faster. Sorrow still gnawed at her, and for the first time since before they went to help the baggage train she thought of Wickham. He was still a challenge, and if the danger no longer seemed so delightful, at least it was distracting.

She crossed another low rise and in the distance saw a score of redcoats, and a little way ahead of them a row of sentries spread widely apart. Williams was there, and the girl noted how he both stiffened to attention and grinned as soon as he spotted her. Today, this enthusiasm seemed lacking in subtlety and more than a little annoying. Beside the tall man was Ensign Hatch, crouching down into the shelter of his dark cloak. The two officers appeared to be waiting in silence as she approached. Jane knew they did not get on well, and if she was inclined to agree with Williams' low opinion of his fellow officer, at the moment this silence added to her distaste for his awkwardness.

'Good morning, Miss MacAndrews,' Williams called in greeting. 'And may I also take this opportunity of bidding you a very merry Christmas!' Having so far failed to obtain a replacement for his cocked hat, he was wearing the woollen forage cap he had worn as a volunteer, red-topped and with the numeral 106 on the front. Soaking wet, it had fallen into a shapeless mass on his head.

Jane was unable to return Williams' greeting with warmth, and a small part of her even took an unjust satisfaction in seeing his reaction as she passed on the terrible news, and he became ashamed of his jollity.

Hatch murmured a vague, 'How tragic,' as he joined them.

'If you will forgive me, I believe it is unwise for you to go any farther,' said Williams. 'The army will be withdrawing soon. If you go straight back, you will pass Mr Pringle and his men, so that you will be sure of the way.'

'Do you have the hour, Mr Williams?' Jane asked in reply, not deigning to respond to the implied criticism of her ability to find her own way.

'I fear I do not.' A watch was another luxury denied to him by his meagre funds.

Hatch produced a fine fob watch, his expression suggesting disdain for any gentleman who lacked something so useful. 'Just short of nine, Miss MacAndrews.'

'Thank you.' Jane smiled with no particular warmth, but it was more attention than she had granted Williams this morning and he noticed this with resentment. 'I shall go back, then. Good day to you both.'

They watched her trot away and vanish into the fold of ground.

'A most elegant young lady.' Hatch knew the comment would irritate the other officer, even though he could not object to it.

'Indeed,' was all that Williams managed.

Hatch looked at him, and wondered again that the face of a murderer could appear so innocent, even rather dull. At Vimeiro he had overheard a dying sergeant tell Dobson that he had not said a word about Mr Williams killing Redman. The sergeant had been wrong, but Hatch did not know that. Instead he was forced every day to see the murderer of his friend living among the officers as if nothing had happened.

'A fine seat,' said Hatch, who was no more than an adequate

horseman himself, but was sure that this nevertheless gave him the advantage over Williams.

The taller man frowned, trying to work out whether there was a deliberate and coarse ambiguity in the comment. 'Indeed,' he said after a while, before adding, 'Miss MacAndrews is certainly a fine horsewoman.'

'It is the natural accomplishment of good birth,' said Hatch firmly, and again Williams wondered whether this was unconscious clumsiness or a deliberate insult based on his own lack of skill and his background.

Hatch's face was impassive and innocent. He was not a bold man, and even if duelling had not been forbidden by the Articles of War, he doubted that he would have had the courage to call out a known killer.

Williams changed the subject. 'A deal warmer, although I wish the rain would stop.'

'You do appear to have a deep interest in the climate, my dear fellow.'

Williams gave a brief snort of amusement, leaving Hatch disappointed at his sarcasm. He felt distaste as Williams unslung the musket from his shoulder and checked that the pan was securely wrapped in rag to keep the powder dry.

'Do you not find that an encumbrance?' Officers in light companies often carried a long arm, but these were usually finely made gentlemen's weapons, and not the heavy Brown Bess carried by ordinary soldiers. Hatch carried a pistol as well as his sword, but felt more armament than this was unbecoming in an officer.

'It was not last summer.' Williams saw no need to conceal his path to a commission, and was indeed proud of his rise from volunteer.

Hatch searched for a more sensitive subject. He could think of no means of exposing Williams as a murderer. For the moment, all he could manage was to pick away at his composure and reputation while avoiding an open quarrel. Thomas Hatch was not an especially subtle man, even on a cold morning when he was – regrettably – fully sober. Yet some marks were easy, he thought, as Miss MacAndrews appeared on a distant rise.

'Some lucky fellow, eh?' Hatch was pleased with the anger obvious in Williams' face, before he added, 'I mean, to think of the man who might one day call such a fine lady his wife.'

There was a drumming of hoofs on the spongy turf. It was not the girl, but Brotherton.

'You are to withdraw shortly. Does either of you have a watch?'

Again Hatch enjoyed a moment of satisfaction.

'Good man!' said Brotherton. 'In that case, in fifteen minutes' time you, Mr Williams, will take half the men back to the main line and then you and the men can rejoin your respective companies. Mr Hatch, you wait a further quarter of an hour, until nine forty-five, and then return with the remainder. I'll come and collect you to make sure that all is well. Good day to you, gentlemen.' He urged his horse on to visit the other outposts.

When Williams reached Pringle, the captain was preparing to rejoin the rest of the company at the barn. Billy walked beside his men, leading Bobbie, who snapped at the ensign when he patted his neck.

'A sad day,' said Pringle.

'Very sad.' Williams searched for better, less conventional words, but could not find them. Not that talking was likely to be of any great help. 'How is Dobson?' he asked.

'Didn't show much when Miss MacAndrews brought the news. Know he must be pretty cut up, though.'

'I do admire Miss MacAndrews' compassion in carrying the word to him – and indeed her composure in doing so.'

Pringle nodded. He knew full well of his friend's adoration of the major's daughter.

'I fear she was sorely saddened by the experience, but hope she looked in a little better spirits when she returned past you,' Williams continued.

'She did not come back this way,' said Pringle. 'Her intention was to go for a ride. It seemed a sensible thing.'

'I suggested that she return rather than get beyond the army.' Pringle privately suspected his friend's advice and tone may not have been welcomed.

'No doubt she came another way.'

Williams stopped. 'May I borrow Roberta?' The tone reminded Pringle of Sergeant Rawson. It had been old Dobson himself who had taught him that an officer never gave an order unless he was confident that it would be obeyed. Pringle doubted his friend would obey an order to remain.

'Miss MacAndrews will be fine. I am sure there is no need to go hunting for her.' Silently he thought that such a spirited girl would also resent being chased around like an errant child.

Williams had his foot in the stirrup and was already swinging himself up. With his forage cap, rolled greatcoat worn over his shoulder, and musket, he looked an unlikely horseman.

Pringle sighed. 'Go if you must. Just don't get yourself lost! I need Bobbie!'

Williams' urgency conveyed itself to the mare, who staggered immediately into her jerking canter. When Pringle got to the barn Hanley asked about their friend. 'Off playing Sir Galahad,' was all the reply he got.

'In this rain. His armour will rust!'

Williams greeted Hatch with no more than a curt nod and the briefest of explanations. The other ensign had already formed his men up to march off and stood some distance away from them. Not long after Williams had disappeared, the watch showed 9.45 and as if on cue Brotherton arrived.

'Anything to report?' he asked.

'Nothing at all,' said Hatch firmly, and ordered the detachment to march away.

The 106th began its retreat on time, forming with the rest of the reserve and then setting off down the road. Rain still fell steadily, and ran down Dobson's face as he piled stones over his wife's grave to keep animals away. Esther MacAndrews stood and watched the pitiful scene. Having buried three of her own children, she knew how to mourn and felt there was some comfort for the bereaved in knowing that other people understood their loss. She also waited for Jane. Pringle had told the major that his ensign had gone looking for the girl. He had been surprised when he realised that neither was yet back with the regiment. Private Hanks was also missing, although Pringle assumed he had caught up with the baggage and was looking after his wife.

As each regiment marched past the forlorn group of figures around the grave the drums went silent and each mounted officer drew his sword and raised it in salute. When Dobson, Sergeant Rawson and the two redcoats marched on, Esther MacAndrews waited until the men of the light brigades passed and only the hussars were left behind.

'No one behind, apart from the French, and there is no sign of them,' she was assured by the fourth hussar officer she stopped. Like the others he could not quite conceal his opinion of anyone who had let a girl ride off on her own in the middle of a war. 'No doubt your daughter has ridden ahead and is already with her father.' There was the clear implication that the rearguard was equally no place for an officer's wife, however handsome. 'I am sure the best thing you could do, dear lady, is to join them.'

'Thank you for your advice.' Esther MacAndrews let her courtesy slip, but could see no purpose to remaining behind. She drove her horse hard along the road, splashing through the deep puddles, and using her whip whenever the animal tried to go round. The rain had stopped, and a red sun sank beneath the horizon as she passed a dozen German hussars singing in their own language. Only when she caught some of the words did she remember that it was Christmas Day.

8

Captain George Wickham had one brief pang of disappointment when he realised that he would not be able to make his assignation with the red-headed girl. General Paget kept all his staff very busy, and more than a few times vented on them his own annoyance at the necessity of retreating.

'No time for that, Mr Wickham,' he had bellowed angrily, at the captain's suggestion that he take a ride around the northern flank of the army. 'You are no longer with Betty Burrard. I expect my aides to work.' In August Wickham had been appointed to the staff of Sir Harry Burrard, who was as indulgent to his staff as he was slow moving.

Wickham followed the commander of the Reserve Division as he rode through the rain, chivvying his battalions on. Later, he had the great pleasure of being sent once again to carry a message to the general's older brother, with instructions to stay with him and observe the withdrawal of the cavalry. It was pleasant to find that Lord Paget welcomed him warmly. Black Jack Slade was even more handsome in his greetings. Their officers were lively and spoke of the latest society gossip.

Viscount S___ had eloped with the wife of Colonel Powlett. Wickham was not sufficiently acquainted with aristocratic society to guess the man's identity, but knew enough to keep silent and appear to understand. In most cases, the answers to such mysteries were either soon revealed or unnecessary to join the conversation. His judgement was swiftly vindicated.

'Can't say I blame Sackville,' said a magnificently dressed hussar captain, laughing, his waxed moustache standing out stiffly on either side of his face. 'You must have seen Mrs Powlett in the Row, Ferrars. You'd certainly remember her. Famous frontal development!'

They soon turned to the topic of Miss Clarke, and here at least Wickham knew enough to follow from the beginning.

'Will it damage the Duke?' he asked. The Duke of York was head of the army, and as good an administrator as he had been poor as a general back in Flanders. His former mistress had recently revealed to the newspapers that she had been using her influence over him to gain commissions for her friends, the friends of her friends, and indeed anyone inclined to be generous to her.

'Oh, Freddie will manage,' said a major from the Blues, and then paused as he took a pinch of snuff from an intricately decorated box. Balancing the pinch on a practised hand, he carefully returned the box to its pocket, before inhaling. 'Might have to retire for a month or two, but no more than that, I should think.' He prepared for a colossal explosion, and then looked puzzled when no sneeze came.

'From what I hear Annie Clark is enjoying all the attention, and now gets invited to many a salon formerly closed to her,' the major continued with great assurance. 'She's still a pretty little thing, although past her prime. I can remember seeing her on the stage when I was just a boy. Grew me up in a hurry, I can tell you!'

'Is that how you joined the army?' asked the hussar with affected innocence.

'As good a way as any.' The major chuckled, and seeing that the joke was acceptable, Wickham joined in.

Somehow, the talk turned to cricket. Wickham recognised the name of Lord Beauclerk from listening to Billy Pringle, who was obsessed with the game, but found that his attention soon wandered as the conversation became more technical. It was a shame not to be able to take a run at Miss MacAndrews. Wickham was not quite sure whether or not she would meet him. Even if she did, it might not be until the next assignation that she would finally succumb. She had spirit, and he suspected was more than a little the coquette, but like most of these young pieces she was also naive and required coaxing, which only made the result all the more gratifying. Perhaps she had gone to the meeting and his failure to arrive would cause her to lose her temper. So much the better, for the step from rage to passion was a small one if well guided. He smiled.

'You look happy,' said a very tall infantryman on Lord Paget's staff.

'Just thinking of a filly who is well on the way to being broke.'

'Four-legged or two?'

'Two. I think I shall soon get a saddle on her.' The nearby officers laughed.

Wickham knew himself to be an intensely physical man, and if his love for his wife had long since faded, hers was undiminished and they took great pleasure in each other. Lydia was now in England. There had been places in Lisbon, and plenty around the cloisters of Salamanca, but it had now been weeks since he had enjoyed a woman. The enforced celibacy oppressed him, and he had even began to notice some of the drabs among the soldiers' families. Then the 106th had arrived with MacAndrews' daughter, and for the last few days he had dreamed of a mass of red curls, a trim figure and smooth skin. The whores in Portugal and Spain had been well enough, but now he craved the complexion and manners of an Englishwoman. Soon, he thought to himself, soon; for the moment it was far more useful to ingratiate himself with influential men.

Jane found no sign of Wickham on the road to the north of town. There was indeed no sign of anyone. She felt her anger flare, and drove her horse into a faster run, splashing through the puddles on a track barely used by the army. After five minutes she turned and cantered back in the opposite direction. Her sense told her to go back. Her rage made her want to see the man long enough to snub him, and make it clear that in future she would not contemplate either his attentions or indeed any degree of familiarity. Part of her wanted to see him smile, and wondered how he would excuse his lateness. Jane walked her horse into a little hollow, where the ruin of a shrine and a steep bank crowned by a holly bush gave shelter from the wind, if only a little from the rain.

Jane was not sure how long she waited. She wondered about dismounting, but her grey was a good fifteen hands and she could not be certain of climbing back on to him without assistance. She was cold and wet and told herself that she was a fool for ever letting herself be drawn on by the dashing captain. Her rage turned entirely against herself, especially since she was no longer quite so sure where she had joined the road and so where the battalion lay. The thought that she had taken this risk only to distract herself from the sadness of Mrs Dobson's death merely made her own behaviour seem selfish as well as foolish.

Miss MacAndrews walked her horse back on to the road, and headed towards where she thought the army lay. The road dipped ahead, then rose to a little hummock. There was move-ment on the edge of the dip. Two thin poles wavered in the air, and a faint glint showed that they were topped with pointed steel heads. Beneath them were riders, wearing strangely shaped hats with square, flat tops, all covered in a buff oilskin. They were going away from her, and Jane wondered how she had not seen them come down the road past her. A track led off away from the road into a patch of trees, and she assumed they had come that way.

Jane was about to call out, feeling that on such a foul day it was better to ignore her pride and ask for directions from the patrol. Then something stopped her. The men did not look anything like the British hussars. She had never heard of British lancers and wondered whether the men were Spanish. She spoke little of the language, and doubted that she would be able to understand any directions. Oh well, she would simply have to rely on her own memory and hope it did not take too long to stumble back on to one of the outposts. If Mr Williams was there, she would pretend to be entirely confident of the path and not need any assistance.

One of the horsemen turned and looked startled. He said something to his companion, and both turned their mounts to face her.

'*Qui vive!*' The challenge was given in a guttural accent, and only after a moment did Jane realise that is was in French. Would the Spanish use the language? she wondered. The two cavalrymen spurred their horses towards her and she realised that they must be enemies. The girl turned her horse and sent him cantering along the path off the road. Fear fought with anger at her own folly. She used the whip mercilessly to drive the grey ever faster.

Her horse was fit, and unburdened with a large rider and heavy equipment, and Jane soon left her pursuers behind. Within ten minutes she had lost them, but in the process had lost herself. Wandering for a while, all sense of direction gone, she found a road and gambled that following it in a direction chosen on a whim was the best chance of finding the army again. Then two more lancers appeared and gave chase. She rode for twenty minutes, but the grey was tiring and she could not shake them off. One was now some way behind the other, but neither showed any sign of giving up.

Williams wandered for a long time across the fields and beyond the road, unsure where Miss MacAndrews was likely to be. Part of him hoped that it was all unnecessary and she had had the good sense to return long before now. He wished he knew when now was, and he felt the lack of a timepiece far more than when Hatch had paraded his own. Williams was fully aware that he ought to turn back. He could not do it, excusing this weakness by telling himself that searching for just a few minutes more could make all the difference. In his heart he knew that he would not abandon her, and also that he could not ride up and down for ever. The army was moving and he had duties to perform. He had a dreadful thought of being left behind by the entire army, a sudden terror that long hours had passed without his realising and that the battalion and everyone else had gone.

Then he heard a woman scream and a great wave of fear and horror swept over him. It came from the left, beyond a straggling row of trees, and he wrenched on the reins to turn Bobbie and then slammed his feet against her side. She protested, but ran.

Williams bounced in the saddle, almost lost his musket as the sling slipped down to his elbow and banged against his side. The scream came again, and then was cut off short. The musket slid again and he just caught it with his right hand and held it down against his leg. The rag covering the lock stayed in place, as did the cork he had put in the muzzle to stop the water getting in.

With only one hand on the reins, he steered clumsily, and Bobbie took him so close to one of the trees that a low branch slashed at his face and drew blood. Then they came into a patch of open ground, with a thicker stretch of woodland beyond it. Some sense drove him to the wood, and he followed a track running through it. There were shouts – men's voices yelling at each other – and he pressed on.

Round a bend in the track, Bobbie swerved hard to avoid a braying and bucking mule. The mare's hoofs narrowly missed Jenny Dobson, sprawled on the ground, her eyes closed and a trickle of blood coming from her lips. Her cap had fallen from her head and her long dark hair was spread around her like a fan. A few yards away a big soldier in a silver-grey helmet with a black horsehair plume and wearing a long blue cloak stood in the centre of the track, long sword drawn and facing Private Hanks. Hanks fired his musket, but the flint sparked on to damp powder. The Frenchman turned to look at Williams, and his hope that it was one of his own comrades died at the sight of a red coat.

Hanks lunged with his bayonet, striking the man's body squarely. The Frenchman reeled, staggering back a step as the other man looked in bafflement at his blade bent almost double. A rapid jab with the sword, and Hanks dropped his musket to claw at the steel sunk deep into his throat.

Williams forced Bobbie between the two men, and before the Frenchman could react, the tall officer jabbed down with the butt of his musket and struck the man on the peak of his helmet.

Bobbie's chest pushed against the Frenchman's sword, still embedded in Hanks' neck, but although it had fallen from his grasp, the wrist strap prevented it from falling. As the mare pushed, the sword was wrenched from Hanks' flesh, which pumped blood like a fountain, and the enemy soldier was falling. Williams hit him again, breaking his nose with the end of the musket, but the blow unbalanced him and he slumped down from Bobbie's back, rolling as he fell.

The Frenchman was on his knees, his cloak open to reveal a metal cuirass, but he was groggy from the blows and slow as he fumbled to get his fingers back around the handle of his sword. Hanks choked and gasped as he died, kneeling down and then toppling forward.

Williams pressed with his hand to get to his feet, and then kicked the Frenchman in the face, tumbling him back. He drew his sword, point reaching out towards the cuirassier, who pushed up and forward so that the tip of the Russian blade went through his left eye. He died with no more than the gentlest of sighs.

Breathing hard, Williams looked around him. Hanks and the Frenchman were both obviously dead, the former in a pool of his own blood. Bobbie stood on the path, idly munching at the long grass, so that the froth around her mouth was turning an unsightly green. He walked over to Jenny and was glad to see that she was stirring. A bruise was blossoming on her cheek and he guessed that the Frenchman had struck her, cutting off her last scream.

'It is all right,' he said, and then realised the folly of that statement when the woman's husband was lying dead a few feet away. 'Are you hurt?' He worried that the child might have come to harm.

'Bastard!' she said. 'God-damned French bastard!' She reached up, licked her fingers, and rubbed away the blood from her face. 'Going for a girl when she's about to have a baby. Bloody French.' She began to get up. 'Come on, give me a hand,' she commanded.

'I am afraid the Frenchman has done for your husband.' Williams tried to make his tone as gentle as possible.

Jenny glanced at the corpse. 'Poor Tom,' she said flatly. 'He weren't much of a man, but he were kind.' Williams was to be disappointed if he expected any greater grief.

He heard a man shouting from back the way he had come. The voice was not speaking English. 'Can you ride?'

'Reckon I can. You'll need to lift.' He helped Jenny climb on to the mule, and was surprised at the ease of lifting her in spite of her current bulk. Then he turned, picked up his musket, and went over to Bobbie. By the time he was in the saddle, two men had appeared around the bend in the path. One was another cuirassier, in a long blue cloak just like the dead man. The other wore a cocked hat, and a very dark blue jacket and breeches. He shouted, and cocked a pistol.

'Go on, Jenny,' yelled Williams. As long as the girl was with him he could not risk fighting, especially as he did not know how many more men were behind the two Frenchmen. The girl hit her mule with a stick and the animal trotted away. The man in the cocked hat levelled his pistol, but the cuirassier stopped him, and instead began to draw his sword.

Williams walked his horse after Jenny, wondering whether the man wanted to avoid the sound of a shot, or perhaps was squeamish enough not to fire when there was a chance of hitting a woman. Jenny's mule was surprisingly fast, and a glance showed that she was leaving him behind, so he trotted on to follow her, still looking warily behind him.

Capitaine Dalmas watched the red-coated officer ride off, and wondered what an Englishman was doing outside the outposts of the army. He strode along the track, saw the dead British soldier, and his own man stretched out in the grass. Guibray had been a good man. Not imaginative or fit for promotion, but a brave, reliable soldier, whose only weakness was the speed with which he was distracted by women. Like a lot of the fellows from those early days of the revolutionary army, he had fallen into bad habits when discipline was so slack. Dalmas guessed that he had seen the girl and that had prompted the attack. Still, perhaps he had simply stumbled across the English. He was supposed to have been watching their horses, inside a sheep pen in a fold of the ground.

'Let's hope the English did not get to the horses,' said the engineer Lieutenant Maizet. Dalmas had noticed a tendency in the man to state the obvious. He had brought him because his eyes were keen and his memory good, and anyway his other officers had things to do. They had come to watch the English army, and make sure of the routes they were taking. Dalmas wanted to look at their patrols and outposts and judge how vigilant they were likely to be. He did not want to fight, still less to be drawn into running skirmishes with the rearguard. They would look and then go north and wait for better opportunities as the retreat continued and the enemy grew tired. It would be better if the British officer could not get back to their lines quickly, in case the commander of the rearguard started to get too aggressive. Dalmas had left the remainder of his cuirassiers some distance back. The Poles were with him, stretched out in a line to observe, and the Englishman was already behind that line. He should not be able to get back to his own people. That was enough. Nothing useful would be gained by devoting too much effort to finding him, and the girl would prove to be a liability as Guibray's useless death had shown.

'Yes. Well, we might as well go and see.' The cuirassier had been silent so long that the engineer officer had almost forgotten his own question. Now he surged through the undergrowth beside the track, and the other man struggled to keep up. A moment later they found the three horses where they had left them. It had been a chance encounter, then, or one brought on by Guibray's lust.

There was little time to talk as Williams and Jenny rode across the rolling fields.

'Have you seen Miss MacAndrews?' he hissed as soon as they had left the two Frenchmen far enough behind.

'Her?' Jenny frowned. 'No.'

He decided not to pass on farther news until they were safe.

It was hard to see far in any direction, and he was unsure how many French were there. After five minutes he turned west, thinking to swing round and get back. Before they had gone more than a few hundred yards, some movement caught his eye. Two lancers whose blue jackets had yellow fronts emerged from a sunken road a quarter of a mile away. They did not seem to have seen him, and he quickly led Jenny back into a dip in the ground, where they followed the line of a gully. For a moment he stopped, got down and then edged his way up to peer over the bank. The two lancers were some way away, but another patrol was nearer, barely three hundred yards from where he lay, letting their horses crop the grass.

Williams tried going east, but all the while they were also going north, farther and farther away from army. The day was getting on, and by now the reserve must have marched. Probably the light regiments and the cavalry of the main rearguard were already drawing back. Yet as he tried to loop east they kept spotting the blue-jacketed horsemen. He thought of doubling back to try again in the west, but the line seemed solid. Then they stumbled on another pair of lancers on the farthest side of a small walled field. It was still raining, and no one bothered to attempt a shot. Williams and Jenny fled as fast as her mule would run. The Poles gave up the chase after a few minutes, but he felt it prudent to keep going at a trot for longer. They came to a stretch of better road, and went for a mile before they slowed to a walk. Williams was surprised when he looked at Jenny and saw the exhaustion in her young face. Her condition had slipped from his mind as they dodged the French patrols.

It was now late afternoon, and the rain slackened a little and then died away as the grey light of a cloudy winter sky began to fade. The land was rising steadily. They came to a valley, and the river that curved through the bottom was fast and swollen with rain from the mountains. Jenny was swaying on the back of her mule, and clearly could go no farther. Williams saw a small stone building clinging to the slope above the river. Telling her to stay, he rode over, dismounted, and walked cautiously up to the heavy wooden door. He knocked, felt foolish for doing so, and then lifted the catch to open it. He guessed it was a shelter used by the shepherds, as there were signs that animals were sometimes kept inside. As his eyes adapted to the gloom he saw sacks and a pile of straw and then neater piles of the chopped straw the locals used for most of their fuel. It would do.

Jenny looked almost ready to faint when he brought her over. He helped her down and then took her inside. She asked for the bags on the mule and he took them off and put them inside before bringing the animal in as well. Hopefully they had left the French behind, but it would be better not to advertise their presence. By the time he came back, the girl had lit the stub of a candle. He was surprised at how practically she began arranging the wide single room.

Williams went to attend to Bobbie. The clouds had split to let the setting sun shine its red light across the drab landscape. Even the wind had dropped, and for the first time in hours he felt a sense of peace, until sudden movement caught his eye.

The grey horse looked bright in the fading light. Miss Mac-Andrews, hat gone, and hair streaming behind her, struck again with her whip to keep the horse going, its sides a foam of sweat.

Williams swung himself up on to the mare, musket held across his body, left hand on the rein and the other slapping her rump as he urged her on. He headed for the gap between Jane and the closest Pole, but they were still a good quarter of a mile away. The man seemed to be gaining on her, and Williams bounced as he raced down the slope, but no longer noticed the discomfort. There was a shout as the second lancer spotted him, and slowed his horse cautiously.

Jane looked up, saw a man in a red coat, and only as she turned towards him recognised who it was. The leading Pole shifted direction to follow her.

Williams was sure the lancer would reach the girl before he could get to them. He stopped, dismounted and wrenched the rag off his musket's lock. Then he reached to yank the cork from its muzzle. The Pole was some two hundred yards away, the girl nearer. He prayed that the musket would spark, and that the charge had not been so shaken around by the long ride and its use as a club that it would not fire the ball with any real power.

He let them come closer, almost fired, but just stopped as Bobbie chose to swing her neck against him. He took a couple of paces forward and kneeled. They were one hundred and fifty yards away, an absurd range for a soldier's musket. Yet if he waited Jane, who was swinging towards him, would soon be between him and the pursuing lancer. He took a deep breath, half let it out, aimed at the horseman's chest and then raised the muzzle to allow for the distance.

It was a miracle when the powder in the pan flared and the main charge went off. It was even more of a miracle that the ball fell true and gouged a deep furrow on the man's left arm just beneath the shoulder. The lancer rocked with the force of the blow, felt his limb go dead, and dropped his lance to steer the horse with the other hand as he turned and retreated. Williams did not know that he had hit, but saw the man turn as the smoke of the discharge began to clear.

It was unfortunate that the grey horse panicked at the noise of the shot or perhaps the sudden flame and smoke, and bolted. Jane bounced in her seat as the animal swerved sharply, and with strength she thought long exhausted galloped towards the river. The girl dragged at the reins, but the animal did not stop. Williams barely noticed the two Poles retreat down the road as he clambered on to Bobbie and set off in pursuit of the girl.

At the high riverbank, Jane just managed to steer the animal away from the water. It reared, and somehow she stayed on the side-saddle, and then the grey horse galloped again, running along the top of the bank. As its weight fell on earth undermined by the recent floods, the ground gave way. The bank crumbled, and Jane for the first time screamed in fear as the grey lurched to the side and toppled into the river. She fell free, and the shock of the icy flow was terrible as she sank under the waves. When she came to the surface again she was being swept along, the horse already some distance ahead.

Williams drove Bobbie on, running at an angle, trying to judge where he could get in front of the girl. A bend in the river hid her from view, and he rode on in dark fear until with massive relief he saw the white of her face emerge from the brown water again. She was close to the near bank, and that gave him a chance, but he could see that she could make little headway in the torrent.

He lost sight of her as he cut across another bend, and then he was at the bank. Jumping down, he scrambled on to a boulder standing proud of the flood. Again there was a surge of relief as the girl came into sight. She was close, and he hoped that he would have a long enough reach as he lay on the stone and stretched his musket out.

Jane dropped beneath the surface again, then came up spluttering and saw Williams just yards away, his musket extended. With all her strength she reached towards him, struggling against the appalling weight of her waterlogged clothes. Her hands stretched up, and as her arms rose her head again went under the water, but she felt the touch of wood and her fingers closed desperately around it. Then her other hand found the musket's butt and clung on.

Williams felt himself shifted violently to the side as the girl grabbed hold and was stopped. For a moment he feared that he would slide off the rock and end up in the river with her, drowning or freezing instead of saving. He pulled slowly, terrified that a sudden move would loosen her grip, but she came towards him and her head emerged again. Jane was close enough for him to take one hand off the musket and grab under her arm. He pulled harder now, for the current still dragged the girl away from him. Gloved hands slipped on the soaked wood and Jane lost her hold on the musket, but Williams let the weapon go and it slid into the water. His other hand was now under her other arm and despite all the wet cloth he held her tight, pulling her to the edge of the stone.

It was still a huge effort to lift her out of the water, and Williams would never have believed that the small woman could possibly be so heavy. He lifted her out and knelt, pressing her against him. Jane's hair looked almost black as it was pasted flat against her head. She was shivering violently, and the skin of her face was icy to the touch.

Williams raised her by the arm, but after a few steps she staggered. He reached down, shifted the weight and lifted her in his arms. Unable to think of a way of getting on to the horse, he managed to loop Bobbie's reins over a couple of fingers and led the mare as he walked up the hill to the stone hut. Jane's grey had vanished downstream. There was also no sign of the Poles and he hoped that they had gone, especially since his musket was lost to the river.

For a while Jane clung to him, her shivers shaking him as he walked. Then she passed out and hung limply down. The shivering had stopped and he worried that this was bad sign. As he carried her into the little building her skin looked almost blue in the candlelight. Jenny had already got a fire going, but the chopped straw produced only a modest heat. The pregnant young woman moved surprisingly easily as she came to look at Jane. Jenny touched her cheek.

'Get her clothes off!' she ordered.

'What?'

'Strip her! She'll die if you don't warm her up. Get them clothes off and then hold her close so that she can feel your warmth. I'll cover you with one of the blankets and that coat of yours.'

'But . . . ?' he began.

'For Gawd's sake get on with it. I'll build up the fire.' She turned away, dismissing him to his task and muttering, 'I never thought I'd have to persuade a bloody man to do that.'

Williams looked at the unconscious Jane and was no longer sure that she was breathing. He began to fumble at the buttons of her pelisse. The material was sodden, his gloves slippery, so he pulled them off with his teeth and began again. It was still difficult, for there were nine buttons on the jacket and each fitted tightly. Her dress fastened with hooks at the back, and only a few ivory buttons, so was a little easier, although he found it difficult to balance the unconscious girl and go about his task at the same time. At one point Jane stirred, made a noise some-where between a sigh and a moan. Her eyes opened and a panicking Williams just managed to stop himself from dropping her as he prepared for an outrage which he no doubt deserved, but she did not seem to focus and quickly passed out again.

In the end it was done, and if in private thoughts he had dreamed of such a moment, his imagination had not made it like this. Fear for her safety drowned out all other emotions.

'Not bad,' said Jenny. She had stretched a blanket on the bare earth floor and Williams gently laid Jane down on it. Another, and Williams' greatcoat would go on top of them. He took off his jacket, itself very wet, and then stopped.

'Might it not be more proper if you . . . ?'

'Me? I'm about to have a baby in case you hadn't noticed.' She shook her head. 'I'd have thought you'd jump at the chance,' she added.

Williams got down and pulled the girl to him. There was a faint motion of breathing, but she felt so very cold that his fears for her grew strong again. Jenny covered them.

'Sleep if you can,' she said. 'I'll keep watch.' She produced a tiny pistol from the pockets of her skirt. 'It's easier for me to sit by the fire than lie down these days.' She settled down carefully, pulling the remaining blanket around her like a shawl.

Williams pressed Miss MacAndrews to him, and thought he saw the blue tint fade from her skin before he dropped into an exhausted sleep.

9

Hanley shook his head. A company of green-jacketed rifle-men were marching down the street, so Pringle did not try to shout a response, and merely shrugged. In the gap before the next company arrived, he dashed through the mud to join his friend.

'Nothing,' he said. 'There is no sign of Miss MacAndrews or Bills anywhere in the town. Nor does anyone appear to have seen them.'

They had marched sixteen miles by the end of Christmas Day. It had been hard going, with the road little more than a mass of mud. Time after time they stopped and waited while a bogged-down cart or gun carriage was shifted by brute force. The rain fell with barely a break and the few Spanish they saw stared at them mutely. There were no cheers of welcome for their allies. Very few of the people of Mayorga had waited for their arrival. Many of the houses had been boarded up, but shutters and locked doors had been forced by the men from the other divisions billeted there the night before. Perhaps that was why the locals had fled.

The 106th was one of ten battalions to cram into the three hundred or so little houses, so the officers responsible for quartering had simply divided the streets into ten sectors and given each one to a particular regiment. There were none of the usual chalk marks on doors allocating the place to a set number of men from a company of a particular regiment. Instead as a unit arrived its men piled into the houses twenty or thirty at a time. The heat from the small fires did little to warm them, but in time the warmth of packed bodies made the single room of most houses almost oppressively hot. There was little talk, and scarcely any singing or liveliness as exhausted men steadily consumed their cold rations. Most of the women looked worse, and even the children were subdued, staring mutely at nothing.

'Dobson and the others have caught up.' Hanley had seen the veteran in a corner of one of the houses, being looked after by Mrs Rawson.

'How is he?'

Hanley was not sure. 'Silent,' was all that he could think to say at first. There had been something disturbing about the emptiness of his expression. Hanley thought that he had looked so very ancient, like a hollowed-out tree ready to fall. Beside him his son and young Sal kept crying in spite of all that Mrs Rawson and the other women did to calm them. The veteran appeared to take no notice, and had spoken only once, to ask about Jenny. 'Private Hanks and his wife are not with us,' Hanley reported. 'No one seems to have seen them.'

'Perhaps her time came?' wondered Pringle.

The thought pleased Hanley. 'A baby at Christmas. Seems appropriate somehow.'

'Probably not to be recommended in the circumstances, for the mother or child,' said Pringle grimly. 'Well, we must hope that they catch us up soon. For the moment, I'll not make any mark on the company roster.' If Hanks remained absent for any length of time, then there would be little choice but to mark him as a deserter, liable to be flogged when he was found. His previously good conduct would count in his favour, but the slightest suspicion of turning his coat and joining the enemy would make the punishment more savage or even place him in front of a firing squad. 'There is still time. Time for all those left behind to appear.' His voice was fervent with hope.

'A hell of a day.' Hanley sighed.

Pringle clapped him on the shoulder, and suddenly felt happy. 'Make the most of it, tomorrow might be worse!' He threw back his head to laugh, and the mood was infectious, because after a moment his friend joined in. Some of the riflemen filing past looked at them strangely, and that only made them roar all the louder.

Mrs MacAndrews did her best to be busy, bringing some organisation to the two-storey house allocated to all the officers of the battalion. She had also been out to many of the other houses, asking after the women of the battalion. It was pleasing to see Mrs Rawson so solicitous for her dead friend's husband and her children. Esther had realised she was not needed and moved on.

Her husband had done all required of a battalion commander, before setting out to visit the cavalry brigades and light infantry regiments as they closed on the town. At each of the brigade headquarters he asked whether they had seen a young lady mounted on a grey. Often the first answer was a facetious wish that they had as it might have brightened a drab day.

'No word,' he told his wife when finally he got back to the billet. 'No one has seen Jane. Some had seen one or two officers riding on their own, but who knows whether they saw Mr Williams or someone else. Some have duties, and by the sound of things there are already a few stragglers.'

'Is that what our daughter is?' Esther almost wanted to make her husband angry, but neither of them was betraying any emotion, still less talking of blame.

'Williams is a capable young man. If he has found her then he will be well able to look after her.'

'Not too capable, I trust?' She tried to lighten the tone.

MacAndrews gave a thin smile, remembering his own flight with Esther so long ago. He doubted they were in any position to judge, until the father in him overruled such weak and indulgent thinking.

'At least there have been no reports of the French so far,' he added. 'If they are lost, then it is to be hoped that they are not at risk from the enemy. They have horses and can go faster than we will march. We may well see them tomorrow.' The conversation was whispered in a corner of a room they shared with the Kidwells, Brotherton and a few other officers, so he could do no more than take his wife's hand and stare into her eyes. 'We will get her back.'

'Yes,' said Esther with new resolution. 'I will not conceive of it otherwise.'

Wickham slept soundly that night. He was tired, but he had increased his acquaintance with many important men during the day and it was to be hoped impressed them with his charm and capacity. He was too fatigued, and the little town too crowded, for him to think of seeking out a meeting with Miss Mac-Andrews. It was probably better to leave time for the girl to vent her anger. As her rage slipped into puzzlement at why her charms had failed to draw him to their meeting, he could apologise and explain that only his duty to the army had kept him away. Wickham was as happy as a man could be, sharing a tiny and poorly lit room with three other officers from General Paget's staff.

His good spirits carried him through the next day, when the road was as bad as ever and the rain just as constant. The Reserve Division marched for twenty miles, and Paget and his staff travelled farther, moving up and down past the marching men to keep the pace steady. Wickham guessed that he had ridden twice as far as the soldiers had walked, but consoled himself with the thought that such hardships were the price of staff work, and that in time he might move to higher rank and lighter responsibilities.

In the 106th, Major MacAndrews insisted that all officers remain with their companies unless specifically ordered elsewhere, and so Pringle and Hanley were with the Grenadier Company at the head of the regiment. The major had always emphasised long marches in training and so they were at least as well prepared as any regiment in the army, but that did not make it any more pleasant.

It was still a hard slog. Pringle noticed that quite a few of the grenadiers had toes sticking from holes in their boots, and even more had soles that flapped with each step. Private Hope and little Jackie Richards had their feet wrapped in rags as some protection. Murphy went cheerily barefoot through the mud. One of eleven children on a tiny plot of land in Kerry, he had rarely worn shoes before he joined the army.

The men grumbled as they trudged along. It was surprising how much this helped, and the mood of the company and the battalion as a whole was more resigned and in many ways happier than the day before. Word had spread that they were heading for Benevente, where there were food and stores and even the prospect of turning round and having a go at the French. It gave them an end to anticipate. After a while, the jokes became more rowdy. Hanley was amazed when someone began an ironic rendering of 'God Rest You Merry Gentlemen!' and for a while all of the grenadiers were bellowing the words out like a challenge to the weather and the world as a whole. Only Dobson stared blankly ahead, his mouth closed. In the end the rain won, and one by one they sank into a silence, but it still seemed a good deal less melancholy than the previous day. Hanley tried to remember the look of the men and wondered whether he could catch it on paper.

Captain Pierrepoint of Paget's staff rode past and stopped for a moment to pass on the news to Pringle as the grenadiers slithered on through the mud.

'The French cavalry have caught up,' he told Pringle. 'Lord Paget set the Tenth Hussars on them just outside Mayorga and sent them rolling back! Better go. No rest for the wicked!'

Pringle waved farewell to Pierrepoint and watched the staff officer ride off. At the same time he listened to the story of the cavalry's success spreading through the ranks. Most of the other company commanders rode their horses, but while a small part of him cursed Williams for depriving him of his own mare, Billy Pringle suspected that it was no bad thing to show the men that he could keep pace. To reinforce the point, he was carrying Williams' pack, refusing to add it to the baggage on his own mule, and wondered again why his friend insisted on carrying so much heavy and no doubt unnecessary equipment. Tied to the side was a huge naval telescope, intended to be mounted on a tripod, which the man's mother had bought for him from a pawn shop when he went for a soldier. It was powerful, but not really practical. He knew, however, that the dutiful Williams would never part with it. Well, Bills could damn well carry the ruddy thing himself as soon as he got back and then, good example or not, Billy Pringle would ride a few miles.

No one in the 106th saw any sign of Williams or Miss Mac-Andrews, or indeed Hanks and his wife, that day. Nor was there word of them.

'They may be past us already,' said Major MacAndrews when he told his wife that the French had closed on the rearguard. 'If not, Williams has the sense to go north and join Sir David Baird's division. This is friendly country, so the locals should help them.'

'Yes.' Esther said no more and did her best to fight down doubts. She rode away to check that the 106th's families were managing well enough with the baggage train. Some were now walking, including Mary Murphy, with her baby in her arms, and Sergeant Rawson's wife, holding young Sal by the hand. The axle on one of the carts had broken so that it had to be abandoned. Pioneers had set light to it and the column of dark smoke was whipped away by the sharp wind. A few of the women squeezed on to the other vehicles, but there was not room for all and so they walked. Mrs Rawson had the basket containing her dog slipped around her other arm.

'Would you like to come up on my horse for a ride?' Esther asked the little girl.

'Isn't that kind, Sal.' Mrs Rawson's enthusiasm failed to prompt more than the slightest of nods from the little girl. Setting down the basket and ignoring the yaps of protest, she lifted the girl up and Mrs MacAndrews took her and set her in front of the saddle.

'If you are very good, I will show you how to use the reins.'

They stopped in a large village that night, and there were more signs of the angry soldiers ahead of them. Doors and shutters had been ripped off and chopped up to make fires. There were few inhabitants, although it was hard to know where they had gone. Even fewer of them offered any hospitality willingly. Sir John Moore was ashamed and angry at the misbehaviour of some of the redcoats, and at the same time frustrated by the lack of support from his allies. Spanish failures had already lost them the campaign. Now that he had made an effort to distract the French and placed himself in a highly dangerous position as a result, the behaviour of the locals beggared belief.

'The people of this part of Spain seem to be less well disposed than those I have hitherto met with.' He was reading aloud to Graham from his letter to La Romana, urging him to publish a proclamation asserting the duty of all the communities, and especially the town mayors, to prepare food and assist the British army in every way. 'When the magistrates are not present, to give regularly, the soldier must take, and this produces a mischievous habit.'

Silently Graham thought that there were always a few soldiers ready to take even at the best of times. 'Yes,' he said. 'I believe that remains within the bounds of courtesy and yet still stresses the imperative for action. However, I am not sure how much the locals will listen.'

'It is their country.'

'Yes, and they know that the French are coming to occupy it, and do not know when we or a Spanish army will return to drive them out. If the French are refused food and quarters, then they begin hanging and shooting people.'

'So the peasants are more afraid of them than fond of us.'

'I fear so. One can hardly blame them.'

That night the report came in of a cavalry raid. The Grenadier and Light Companies of the 106th were among the troops roused from their billets to form up in the streets in case they were needed. After an hour they were dismissed.

'Well, that broke the monotony of sleep,' said Captain Headley of the Light Company.

'At least the rain has stopped,' ventured Pringle. The sky had cleared and was full of bright stars, now that the waning moon had almost set. It was a lot colder.

'Snow soon,' suggested Headley with a wry smile.

'Oh well, it is nice to have things picturesque.'

On the next day they had only five miles to go to Benevente, but it took them most of the daylight hours. The Reserve Division deployed to cover the withdrawal of a large convoy of ammunition – some baggage had been captured by a party of French cavalry during the night, and as the day went on more and more squadrons were spotted by the outposts, probing tentatively at Lord Paget's hussars. The British rearguard was sufficiently ordered to deter any serious attack.

In the afternoon a forlorn group of half-naked and bruised men staggered in loose files past the 106th. The light dragoon escorting them said that they were stragglers who had drunkenly abused the people in a small hamlet a mile off the road. The locals had caught them as they made away with their loot, surprised them, and beaten them badly. His task was to take them into the town for more formal punishment.

In spite of such a discouraging sight, MacAndrews enjoyed the day. It was good to have sense and obvious purpose to their movements rather than merely plodding along a quagmire of a road. Officers and men alike looked better with a task to perform. Yet there was something unreal about it all as thick fog often made them seem alone in the plain beside the river. It was dark by the time they crossed the bridge and proceeded to Benevente itself. The town was noisy and chaotic, the streets full of soldiers, many of them drunk and some prostrate.

That evening the major gathered the officers of the 106th and read to them the Order of the Day:

The Commander of the Forces has observed with concern the extreme bad conduct of the troops at the moment when they are about to come in contact with the enemy, and when the greatest regularity and the best conduct are the most requisite. He is the more concerned at this, as until lately, the behaviour of the part of the army at least which was under his own immediate command was exemplary, and did them much honour.

The misbehaviour of the troops in the column which marched by Valderas to this place exceeds what he could have believed of British soldiers. It is disgraceful to the Officers, as it strongly marks their negligence and inattention . . .'

MacAndrews wondered whether Sir John was striking the right tone. 'I am told that the commander exempts the corps of the Reserve Division from his admonishment,' he said aloud to his officers, for it was clear that many of them were offended. 'Let us ensure that he has no cause to change that opinion.' It seemed improper to add farther commentary to the general's words, but again the manner of the conclusion seemed to him ill judged, even though he believed every word to be both sincere and no doubt true.

It is impossible for the General to explain to his army the motive for the movement he directs. The Commander of the Forces can, however, assure the army that he has made none since he left Salamanca which he did not foresee, and was not prepared for, and as far as he is the judge, they have answered the purposes for which they were intended. When it is proper to fight a battle, he will do it; and he will choose the time and the place he thinks most fit: in the meantime he begs the Officers and Soldiers of the army to attend diligently to discharging their parts, and to leave to him and the General Officers the decision of measures which belong to them alone.

The army may rest assured that there is nothing he has more at heart than their honour – and that of their Country.

'Gentlemen!' MacAndrews spoke loudly to halt the flurry of murmured conversation. He had caught phrases such as 'must have a chance to face the French', and 'is it caution, or something worse?' and did not wish to give them the opportunity to vent their frustration at having to retreat.

MacAndrews banged his hand down on the table he was leaning against. 'Gentlemen. I should not need to emphasise that this is an <u>Order</u> of the Day. It is not the custom in the British Army, and certainly not in this regiment, for junior ranks to subject orders from the commanding general to discussion. I shall not detain you longer. Many of you have duties – not least ensuring that your men are as well provided for as possible – and I would advise the remainder to take every opportunity to rest. There is no doubt in my mind that we will have plenty of fighting as well as many more hard marches.'

IO

Jane woke slowly. She was on her side and something heavy rested on her. The dying fire gave only a faint glow and it took her a moment to realise that it was a man's arm clad in a loose shirt. A bulky, warm presence leaned against her back and she presumed it was the owner of the arm.

Her mind moved slowly and the memories of yesterday were dim and weak. Then she remembered Wickham's note and how she had gone to meet him and fear snapped her into full consciousness. Was this it? Had she lost her honour and perhaps ruined her life, bringing disgrace on her parents? A rebellious part of her felt that it was severe punishment indeed, since she could remember none of the supposed ecstasy of such a moment. Perhaps it was true that only the man gained the pleasure.

No, this was not right. She could remember clearly her anger because Wickham had not appeared. So who did lie beside her, breathing so softly and still sound asleep? Jane lifted the arm as gently as she could so that she could turn on to her back, and then twisted her head to look. A large head lay beside her, and even in the poor light the hair on it was clearly fair and not Wickham's dark brown. Turning a little more she saw that it was Mr Williams, looking even more boyish than usual.

Jane was not sure how much comfort to take from this. She still remembered nothing of how she had got here, and a quick exploration revealed that she was almost completely naked. That did not appear to be true of Mr Williams, but she was unsure how much significance to rest on this. Again she lifted his arm, and began to slide out from underneath, raising her head to look around. A stamp and a snort, followed by movement in the shadows, revealed a horse, and there was just enough light to see an empty eye socket, so that made it Pringle's mare. A mule was behind it. That explained some of the more earthy smells in the room. Clothes – her clothes, she realised – were stretched out around the fire, draped over bags and saddles. Beyond the fire Jenny Dobson sat with her back to the wall, her head down almost on her chest as she slept.

Memories rushed upon her of the French lancers, of her flight and the horse shying and plunging her into the river, and then the icy water and someone – yes, Williams – reaching out to grab her as she swept past. There was no recollection after that at all. Jane slid out and let the man's arm drop so gently that he slept on without the slightest stir. She did not know whether or not she ought to be aware whether anything else had happened, but there would be some small comfort in being clothed.

She felt her shift. It was cold, and still perhaps a little damp, but surprisingly unstained, for the river had looked to be full of mud. Jane pulled it on and felt just a little more confidence.

'Up and about, are we?'

Jane started, even though Jenny spoke in no more than a whisper. She smiled nervously, but for the moment could think of nothing to say that would not sound foolish.

Jenny stirred the fire into life, and added the last of the chopped straw. She lifted a small pistol from her lap, carefully relaxed the hammer and laid it down beside her. 'How do you feel, miss?' she asked with an unusual degree of deference.

'Thank you, I believe I am well.' Jane found herself trying to be overly formal because the situation was so very irregular. 'But I shall be glad to be dressed. Would you help me?' She had put on the small stays she wore over her shift, but needed someone else to tie the laces. In Portugal she and her mother had shared a maid, but her father had forbidden them to bring the girl on campaign – Jane suspected in a doomed attempt to make them stay in the comforts of Almeida – and more recently mother and daughter had performed the service for each other.

'Good for the figure, these.' Both women were still speaking quietly. Jenny fingered the stiff support, which was a delicate pale pink. She liked fine clothes, and longed for the day when she would own many of her own. That would come soon, she told herself. 'Tight enough?'

Jane nodded. 'Thank you, yes.' She drew on her stockings and then reached for her silk drawers. Jenny had never seen such a thing before last night, nor even known they existed. Her admiration was fulsome.

'I got them in Charleston,' said Jane, finding talk of clothes pleasantly distracting. 'The lady in the shop assured us they came from Paris, but then they will say anything.' It all sounded so exotic to the sixteen-year-old Jenny.

'Bet men like 'em,' she said, shocking the other girl, but she continued obliviously. 'Well, leastways taking 'em off.'

'I cannot vouch for that one way or the other,' came the prim reply. Yet the point could no longer be avoided. Jane looked down, still struggling with the words. 'Last night,' she began. 'When I came here . . . did . . . That is to say, did he . . . I mean, Mr Williams . . .'

Jenny's look was unbelieving and included just a hint of scorn. 'He saved your life twice. When he pulled you out of the water you were like a block of ice. You'd be dead now if he hadn't kept you warm.'

'But did he . . . ?'

'Ravish you in your sleep!' Jenny scoffed, only narrowly stopping from using a more blunt term. She could not believe the naive ignorance of a woman several years her senior who always appeared so confident in public. 'Him. 'Course not.' She laughed at the thought. 'Expect some would, but not him.' She looked her straight in the eye. 'You've got a good one there.'

'Perhaps Mr Williams has misinformed you. In no sense is he mine.' Jane was relieved. She was sure that she was relieved. She also felt unnerved by the younger woman's knowledge. 'How is your husband, Mrs Hanks?'

'Dead,' said Jenny brutally. 'A Frenchie got him. Mr Williams there killed the Frenchie, and here we are.'

'I am so very sorry,' said Jane after a moment. She wondered whether it would take time for the sorrow to sink in. Then she remembered the accident of yesterday morning, which somehow seemed an age ago. 'I fear I have some more dreadful news to convey . . .'

'Poor old Ma.' Jenny seemed genuinely moved, but there were no tears or obvious displays of feeling. 'Dad will take it hard. Poor old bastard.' This appeared to close the subject and there was silence for a while as Miss MacAndrews drew on her petticoats – a second shorter one went over the first in deference to the cold – and then her riding boots.

'So old Mr Williams saved you and me both, and here we all are. I told you, you've got a good one there.'

'And as I explained before, Mrs Hanks, in no way is the gentleman mine.'

'Please yourself.' Jenny's smile was broad and she was evidently enjoying the young lady's discomfort. 'But he could be if you wanted. He's handsome enough in his way. Bit dull maybe, but loyal.'

'Then you marry him.' The response was unthinking, and then Jane thought how cruel the words must sound to a new widow.

'Nah, he's got no money.' Jenny's reply scarcely suggested any annoyance. The assurance in her tone surprised the other girl.

'And do you feel wealth essential for happiness?'

'Ask me when I'm rich.' Jenny gestured at the sleeping man. 'Look at him, out like a log. You could always creep off and see the lodger any time you got bored.'

Miss MacAndrews gasped aloud in shock. Jenny guffawed, while silently remarking that the other girl had known what she meant. Williams began to move, and a few very male groans punctuated his stirring to consciousness. He sat up and blinked, unsure where he was. He glanced around blearily, seeing the two women, the animals and the little room. The realisation that one of the ladies was Miss MacAndrews cheered and surprised him. It was closely pursued by the recognition that she was not wearing a dress. Amazement was swiftly chased away by excitement, which engaged in a bitter but indecisive battle with respect for her modesty. His face changed again as the memories returned, recent fear mingling with disbelief and wonder. He blushed, or perhaps it was the red light of the fire, but then Jenny noticed that the young lady's complexion had also changed.

'I hope that you are fully recovered, Miss MacAndrews?' he asked, dropping his gaze at last.

'Thank you, sir, yes, I believe I am unharmed.' He did not notice the emphasis on the last word. 'And also that I owe you my thanks.'

'Pray do not mention it.' Both of them were now looking anywhere but at each other.

'I'm well too,' put in Jenny after a moment, 'although the little beggar is kicking me black and blue.'

Williams insisted on going outside 'while Miss MacAndrews completes her toilette'. They both ignored Jenny's just audible. 'Not as if he hasn't seen it all already', but Williams had to look down in case he was smiling.

Somewhat later they shared a little of the food from Jenny's bags – neither of the others had anything to eat with them, although Williams had a canteen of water. He urged Miss Mac-Andrews to eat, and when Jenny added her encouragement, Jane no longer felt bound by courtesy. The girl was soon greedily spooning up a bowl of the stew which Mrs Hanks had kept simmering. Jane was weak, but the warm food soon began to make her feel stronger.

Afterwards they began to speak of practical things. Williams was also pleased to find a map in one of the holsters in Pringle's saddle, and a pistol with a small powder flask and a dozen or so shot in the other. The map was the work of Hanley, copied from one borrowed from Major MacAndrews. There were few maps in the army, and most of the ones bought in England or Portugal and Spain themselves were woefully inaccurate. Hanley had added to the impression of greater fiction than fact by embellishing the original with drawings. Next to Leon, he had drawn a little Roman soldier. Segovia had a tiny aqueduct, and Astorga, rather obscurely, a statue of a naked woman holding a vase. On a largely empty patch to the north-east, he had written 'Here be dragons' in an ornate script.

At the time, Williams had enjoyed the wit. Now he rather wished for something more true to the landscape, although he doubted that much if anything of value had been lost from the original sheet. It had surprised them all how little many Spaniards knew of villages and towns even fifty miles away from their homes.

It was still early in the morning when they went north. On his own, Williams would most likely have tried to slip through the French lines and rejoin the rearguard. With two mounts between three, and one of the three likely to give birth at any moment, he judged this to be impractical. Instead he hoped to join up with Sir David Baird's column.

Jenny rode her mule. Miss MacAndrews perched herself as best she could on Bobbie, sometimes using the left stirrup, and balancing her right leg on the front of the saddle. She had not ridden astride since she was very small, and suspected that it would be too uncomfortable to do so now for any length of time. Although the thought was more than a little absurd, for the moment she was also determined to cling on to whatever traces of modesty she still possessed. Williams was happy to walk. Given Mrs Hanks' situation, they could not have gone much faster for any length of time.

Williams was glad that he took them across country in as direct a line as he could manage when rain clouds blocked all save the dimmest sense of where the sun was. It meant that they spotted the cavalry on the road before they were themselves seen. They were in the far distance, little more than a dark bluish streak on the road below them. Pringle had left a small glass in a pouch on the saddle, and he extended this and thought that movement above the tiny figures hinted at tall lances. He wished that he had his own telescope to be absolutely sure that these were French and not some of the hussars covering the British retreat. Yet unless the going was atrocious, Baird's column should be a good deal farther ahead by now. The cavalry must be French.

They kept out of sight as best they could, staying away from the tops of hills. They stopped every hour for Jenny to dismount and rest, although she was fiercely and often profanely uncomfortable whatever they did. Early in the afternoon they stopped at a small farm and, piecing together some halting Spanish, they secured some flat loaves, and a bowl each of oily soup. The coin Williams handed over was worth far more, but he and the others were so grateful that none of them cared.

In the late afternoon they halted for well over an hour in a patch of wood as French cavalry passed them in the valley below. They were cuirassiers, their body armour just visible through parted cloaks, and through Pringle's telescope Williams recognised the two men he had encountered yesterday. Both were clearly officers, and the one in the helmet presumably commanded the cuirassiers.

The French officer raised a hand and no doubt shouted a command, which Williams was too far away to hear. The column halted and he worried that they might be planning to search. Yet he could think of no good reason for the enemy to waste their time chasing a few stragglers – it saddened him to apply the word, but from a military standpoint that was all that they now were. You simply do not matter, Williams thought to himself, partly so that the truth sank in, and also in some superstitious hope that the conviction would carry to the cuirassier officer down in the valley.

Perhaps it worked. The French troopers dismounted, and one of the lancers had to be helped down by his comrades, which suggested a wounded man. Williams wondered whether his shot had caused serious injury. A practical, if callous, part of him felt some satisfaction that this would encumber the enemy. The cavalrymen fiddled with their saddles and then began to march on, leading their horses by the reins. Williams assumed they were resting the mounts, and that suggested they planned a long journey. He watched them continue along the track and disappear, and only then felt secure enough to accept that they were not concerned about him and his companions.

Even so, they waited something like an hour after the French had gone before they moved on. Without a watch, it was hard for any of them to be sure. Williams decided that it would be too much of a risk to press on in pursuit of Baird's division, now that the French cavalry were sniffing at his trail. So they would head for the bridge at Mansilla, which he knew the Spanish army were supposed to be guarding.

When it was almost dark, they approached another farm. Only a woman and some children were there, but the mother welcomed the travellers with great kindness, especially when she saw Jenny's condition. There was considerable confusion as the woman tried to work out just which of the two visitors was married to the foreign officer. Eventually she dismissed the matter as some Protestant folly and permitted Williams to sleep in the small barn with the animals, while the two young women each had a straw-filled mattress in the single room of the house, along with her and the children.

There were traces of mist the next morning, but it soon burned off and a winter sun – still markedly stronger than the thin rays at this season in England – gave them warmth as they travelled. They saw no sign of any Frenchmen. Williams insisted on keeping watch when they stopped in the middle of the day for a long rest and to eat. Jane was equally insistent that she take a turn, and so went to the edge of the hollow where they sat in a long-abandoned sheep pen. The woman in the farm had given them slices of ham, apples from a store and a fresh loaf, and angrily refused any payment.

Williams and Jenny ate in silence. Kind though he was, she was left with the distinct impression that she rarely entered his thoughts. He had tried several times to express his sorrow at her mother's death and his concern for her father. Jenny was sure that the sentiments were genuine. She just did not want to talk about it, and still less did she wish to speak of something that clearly troubled the young officer. He had raised the matter once, asking why she and her husband were so far from the battalion when he stumbled across them.

'Thought the baby was coming,' she had said eventually, avoiding his eyes. 'I weren't going to be laid up in some field, or with half the regiment gawping at me. So I told Hanks to take me somewhere quiet and warm. We'd have caught up again once the kid was born and I felt strong enough.' She hoped that she sounded convincing. 'Poor Ma would have loved to be a grandma,' she added, changing the subject and then dropping into silence.

Up on the lip of the hollow Jane stretched out and lay looking down the slope beyond. She scratched her arm, and hoped that the itching she was beginning to feel was no more than the inevitable result of wearing clothes which had also been dunked in a river for the third day in a row. She ran a hand through her hair and wondered what state it was in. Mrs Hanks had given her a scarf to wear against yesterday's rain, but although it was cold today she had done without a covering. She knew her parents would be worried, and that they were still a long way from being safe, yet she had to admit that there was pleasure in such a wild, gypsy-like life. A fresh itch began on her left thigh.

Williams tried not to stare, but knew that his gaze returned again and again to the girl lying in the grass. Since their first meeting Miss MacAndrews occupied a great many of his waking thoughts. There had always been a physical element in those dreams. He was forced to admit that for the moment the carnal was dominating.

'Dirty devil,' said Jenny. He looked confused. 'Don't think I don't know what you're thinking.' She shook her head. 'All alike, all alike.'

That night they came to another lone house, but calls and then banging on the door produced no response. They must be near Mansilla by now, and perhaps the people had gone to take shelter there under the protection of their army. Williams prised open the shutters a little way and then reached in with his clasp knife to raise the catch. He shrugged.

'Your father showed me,' he said to Jenny. He climbed in and opened the door. It was too low to admit the animals, so he tethered them in the lee of the sloping roof. They had had little to eat apart from grass in the last few days, and he thought he noticed a new thinness. He would have to hope they could find better fodder soon.

By the time he went into the house, a fire was burning and filling the room with smoke. They had made good progress during the day and all were tired. After eating more than half of their remaining food, the three of them slept without undressing, each lying to one side of the fire.

Jenny's cries woke them hours later. She looked scared and Williams reached instinctively for the sword that lay beside him.

'The baby's coming!' The girl sounded her age, very young and very frightened. Williams was terrified.

11

'It's him, I am sure of it,' called out Derryck. 'There on the white horse among that group of officers!' The boy's voice cracked with enthusiasm. 'I am sure it is Buonaparte!' The ensign's face was scarred and his nose bent from the wound he had suffered at Roliça. Those injuries, and the short captivity which followed, had done nothing to dampen his spirits, but even so Hanley had never seen the lad so excited.

'Ugly bugger, ain't he?' commented Hatch, who had now fixed his own glass on the distant horsemen. They were standing on a rise behind Benevente, looking back over the plain to the river and the low hills beyond it. The distance was great, and he doubted that either of the ensigns could see much with their little glasses. 'How could any fellow choose to miss out on all this?' Hatch added more softly.

'See what you think,' said Pringle, and passed Williams' bulky telescope to Hanley. Billy wondered whether Hatch was implying something about their absent friend, although that seemed unlikely. Surely no one thought that Williams had deliberately left the column? Better not to say anything, rather than risk starting talk. Whispers in the mess could sometimes carry a long way.

It took a while for Hanley to find the horsemen, and longer still to twist the lens into focus after the short-sighted Pringle had been looking through it. One white horse stood out, but there was nothing else distinctive about the blue-coated rider.

'I do not believe it is,' he said reluctantly. 'That man looks as tall or taller than those around him.' It was hard not to be disappointed. The days were long gone when he was a simple, utterly faithful admirer of both the passion of the Revolution and the order brought by the Empire. There was still a great thrill at the thought of seeing the man who had overturned all of Europe.

Pringle agreed, but the younger gentlemen – there were two more ensigns apart from Derryck and Hatch from the 106th, and a couple from the 28th – were unwilling to concede.

'It must be him. Look! Those cavalry down there are his own guards!' Derryck was looking with the naked eye, and his vision was truly remarkable, for when Hanley turned the glass on the horsemen he saw their red jackets, dark fur hats and green trousers. He had fled in horror as men in these same uniforms – the jackets had been slung rather than worn in the May heat – had cut to pieces a crowd in Madrid. They were the Chasseurs of La Garde Impériale, veterans of many campaigns and Napoleon's favourite regiment.

The previous night the British had blown up the bridge over the Esla. It was not destroyed, for the stone structure had proved notably stubborn, but for the moment it could not be used, and so the French cavalry climbed their horses down the bank and forded the river. Only a few outposts of British hussars were visible in the plain to oppose them. As more squadrons crossed, the French threw out skirmishers of their own, and soon there were puffs of smoke and a distant popping of carbines.

A staff officer arrived behind them. 'Have I missed the fun?' he asked. 'Oh, hello, Hanley. How are you this fine grey day!' It was Major Colborne, Sir John's military secretary. Hanley had made his acquaintance during his time with Colonel Graham and now made the necessary introductions.

'Buonaparte is watching the advance,' Derryck blurted out when he was named to the staff officer.

'Is he indeed,' came another voice. It was Lord Paget himself, his uniform a riot of blue with gold lace and accompanied by an infantry officer attached to his staff. Derryck was most impressed, and wondered how long it would take him to grow such whiskers.

'There is an officer on a white horse,' said Pringle. 'More than that we cannot say.' The ensigns, now cowed by the higher authority of a general and a lord, just managed to restrain their protests.

'Well, whoever the devil is, we shall give him a warm welcome.' Down in the plain a concentrated group from among the piquets charged. The leading Frenchmen gave way and retired some distance. Soon, they reached their supporting squadrons and the heavily outnumbered hussars were in turn chased back the way they had come.

'Good,' said Lord Paget, taking in the scene. 'That will give us some time. Come on, Colborne!' He set off at a gallop to take direct charge.

Colborne had seemed an especially pleasant and capable fellow, but it was a relief that he had left without asking what the infantrymen were doing here. In truth Colborne himself was supposed to be on his way to join Sir John farther up the road, but had been unable to resist the sniff of powder.

The Reserve Division had been allowed to rest for all of the previous day, while other sections of the army continued the retreat. Hanley and Pringle had found the time to visit the castle. The redcoats billeted within its walls had left, but the signs of their presence were everywhere. Remnants of carved legs were all that was left of antique furniture broken up and burned. Some paintings had been added to the flames, while others seemed merely to have been wantonly smashed. Someone had added charcoal beards to a scene of nymphs disporting themselves. Tapestries were left discarded after being used as blankets.

'We're as bad as the French.' Hanley was outraged at the destruction. Pringle had rarely seen his friend so angry.

'Hardly that,' was all he could think to say. 'And remember, it's cold, and they have had a rough time. Nor are they much in love with the Spanish at present.' The defence was out of habit. He liked and admired his own soldiers and the army in general. Yet even he was shocked. Worse came when a false alarm during the night created a panic. A mob streamed through the streets. Many were drunk and more than a few were women. The regiment had been called to arms and had then waited for hours in a cold drizzle until dismissed. In the confusion scores of the carters hired in Portugal had taken their teams and fled, abandoning the vehicles.

The 106th had marched at dawn with the rest of the Reserve Division, past the pyres made from the abandoned wagons and the stores they had carried. Pringle and the Grenadier Company were left behind to hunt out a few dozen men who were missing. A few officers and sergeants from the other companies had been left with the grenadiers to deal with their own men. It was clear that other regiments had done the same.

Most of the missing were soon found, lying in drunken stupor in the alleys around their billets. No one was sure where they had found the liquor. A few took longer to find, and in the end only Dobson remained unaccounted for. Then an agitated young priest appeared from nowhere and began berating Sergeant Rawson. Hanley heard the commotion from the far side of the street and when he joined them caught enough to realise that the man was complaining about the behaviour of a big English soldier.

The priest took Hanley and the sergeant to a little chapel, tucked away in a minor alley. Troops had been billeted there on the previous two nights. Benches had been burned, or pulled into little groups, and even the altar rail had perished. There was rubbish, even excrement, in one corner, and the whole place stank of wood smoke and concentrated humanity.

Dobson sat on one of the remaining benches, stark naked except for his shako, singing in a hoarse voice and every now and again taking a swig from a dark green bottle. The verses he sang lacked any significant religious content. The priest began a fresh tirade, screaming at Hanley that the British were all barbarians and telling him to get this Visigoth out of his church at once. It was hard not to sympathise, and the officer made no attempt to explain the peculiar circumstances. Hanley felt ashamed to be wearing the same uniform as men who had treated a once beautiful church so callously. He was also flooded with sympathy for the old veteran.

'Come on, Dob,' said Rawson in a strong but kindly voice. He stepped forward slowly, and patted the old soldier on the shoulder. 'We need to go, my friend.'

Dobson looked at him without recognition. He plunged into a new song, this time at least prominently featuring a parson, albeit one whose conduct was unlikely to win recommendation from the established Church.

Rawson tried again. 'We have to go, Dob.' The expression in the bloodshot eyes was still vacant. Hanley came closer, and adopted the coaxing voice he normally reserved for children.

'Let's leave, shall we?'

Dobson's face filled with sheer hatred. 'You bloody bastard!' he screamed as he sprang to his feet. His first punch struck Hanley on the side of the chin and sent the officer flying backwards. There was a flash of pain before he lost consciousness.

He woke to the sound of sobbing.

'Oh, my Sally, my poor, poor Sally.'

Rawson's face was bruised as he patted the veteran on the back.

'Sally, girl, I miss you.'

Hanley stood carefully, but there seemed no prospect of renewed violence.

'My Sally, my darling best Sally.'

'That's good, Dob. Let it out.' Rawson's voice was tender, in marked contrast to the harsh bark with which he gave orders.

'She's gone. Just gone.' Dobson noticed Hanley. 'It's you, Mr Williams. Come and pray for her. Please, sir, you know the right words.'

Hanley was sensible enough not to correct him. He had no religion, and the more he saw of an often cruel world the less he was inclined to believe in God. Yet he caught the desperation in the man's voice, and so knelt beside him on the flagstones of the desecrated church. The priest had fled at Dobson's outburst of violence, no doubt to summon more assistance, so he could not be asked to speak the words, but nor was he there to protest.

'Our Father, who art in heaven,' he began. A glance showed him that Dobson was staring upwards, his face imploring, eyes wide in awe. Hanley stumbled over the words, and found that he too was crying. He missed lines and jumbled the order before he ended. 'For ever and ever. Amen.'

'Amen,' echoed Dobson. 'Thank you, Pug, thank you so much.' The veteran had given Williams the nickname when he was a volunteer. Hanley wished more than ever that his friend was with them, and tried desperately to think of anything else he might say and do.

Rawson gave Dobson his greatcoat and hoped to find something more substantial for him before they marched off. The veteran still appeared to have little idea where he was. By the time they were ready to leave, the grenadiers and the stragglers formed up on the slope beneath the group of officers, the sergeant had found him boots, trousers and a shirt. Dobson's pack, haversack and musket were still in the billet, so apart from his jacket he was largely restored to a soldierly condition. He had relapsed into silence again.

Pringle knew they ought to leave, but the spectacle of the cavalry action held them all. A fading hope also made him linger. Pringle suspected that MacAndrews had superstitiously chosen the grenadiers in case the presence of his friends somehow made it more likely that Williams and Miss MacAndrews would appear. He doubted that the major had much hope. Even so, only someone who knew him well would have detected any trace of concern for his missing daughter. Neither she nor Williams had reached Benevente. Of that they could be sure, for Major and Mrs MacAndrews as well as himself, Hanley and some of the other officers had gone all around the place. Perhaps they had joined Baird and his troops. If so, then they might see them at Astorga.

Sergeant Rawson marched up and stamped to attention. 'They are ready to move, sir.' Pringle acknowledged his salute.

'Thank you, Sergeant.' He had felt it best to leave the sergeants to sober the drunks up so that they were capable of marching. He preferred not to know the methods, suspecting that they were scarcely likely to be according to regulation, but also guessing that they would have been far more effective than anything he could devise. 'Any trouble?'

'No, sir. Nothing we couldn't handle.' Rawson looked uncomfortable. His left eye was swelling into a blue-black bruise. 'Mr Hanley, sir, may I ask how your jaw is?'

Hanley rubbed the area ruefully. He smiled. 'I suspect as comfortable as your eye, Sergeant. I would never have believed that a man could hurt so much from slipping down some steps.'

'Yes, sir. Very nasty, sir.' Rawson was relieved.

'We must both be more careful to watch where we tread.' Pringle knew what had happened and was willing to let them lie about it. None of them wanted to see Dobson before a court martial and given anything up to one thousand lashes. Pringle wondered for a moment whether this made him a bad officer, of the sort Sir John had criticised in his recent order. Hanley was not really concerned about such things. Lying in a good cause had never bothered him in the slightest.

'It still beats me where they found the stuff,' he said to Pringle after the sergeant had gone back to the company.

'Ah well, that's hard to say, but one of the fellows from the Twenty-eighth was telling me that they were quartered in part of the convent, and that the priest left in charge kept assuring them that their cellars were empty. Then one of their subs spots a wall that looks newly built, so gets his men to knock a hole in it. It opened up into a deep chamber, and when they lowered him they found a great vat full of splendid stuff. As they were filling their canteens – and I suspect any other bottle they could find – the priest came down and asked if he might have some.

'They weren't too impressed, and one of the boys shouts out that he wasn't willing to share when he had plenty and they had none, so why should they share now. '

'It is a reasonable point of view,' conceded Hanley.

'Oh yes, unfortunately he took action as well, and tipped this vastly fat friar head first into the vat. The sub heard the splash and had them haul him out.' Pringle chuckled. 'Terrible for a man of God to lie so.' Pringle had studied to go into the Church of England, until even his father was willing to concede that he was utterly unsuited to such an occupation.

Excited shouts from the other officers drew their attention back to the plain outside the town. The British hussars had charged more than once, pushing back the leading chasseurs until they drove too far and had to flee for their own lives. Over time the French must have come at least a mile from the river. Their squadrons had started to scatter into little clusters of individuals.

With a shout audible even at this distance a fresh regiment of hussars, joined by the remnants of the outposts, swept in against the French flank. Hanley managed to focus on the charge and distinctly saw Lord Paget, his sabre held high. The ensigns cheered as the French gave way.

'One could hear all kinds of things coming at the same time from this one Athenian army,' quoted Hanley, 'lamentations and cheering, cries of "We are winning", and of "We are losing".'

Several of the youngsters looked at him oddly, but most were too excited to pay any real heed. Hanley was widely considered to be a little odd, although of course a splendid fellow in many ways.

'Thucydides?' Pringle had a broad grin. 'Well, this time I believe it is certain we are winning.' The French were streaming back to the river, chased by the British hussars. 'Regardless of this spectacle, it is certainly time for us to go.' There were protests, voluble ones from Derryck, as they walked down the rise to join the company. Billy wished that his friend had not chosen a passage from the disastrous Athenian expedition to Sicily. He hoped it was not apposite to their own wider situation.

They reached La Baneza after dark. There were milestones on this road, something neither Pringle nor Hanley had ever seen in Portugal and rarely enough in Spain. They counted twenty-four, and yet it was surprising the pace they kept up. It was so much easier marching independently than as part of a great column. Pointed towards the 106th's billets, the men had just settled when orders came to move. The light brigades had arrived and this meant that each regiment now had to squeeze itself into a smaller number of houses. It was late, and both Hanley and Pringle were very tired when they finally flung themselves down on to piles of straw in a room shared with half of the company. Dobson sat in the corner, attended by Mrs Rawson, who did her best for the children. He still said almost nothing, although he had come to apologise to Mr Hanley, and to thank him and the captain.

Wickham had good fortune that night. He arrived carrying orders to Sir John's staff at just the right time to be invited to join them for dinner. The fare was good, and the company included a number of distinguished officers as well as the general's own aides – all very useful acquaintances. The most spectacularly dressed guest was also the most melancholy. General Count Charles Lefebre-Desnouettes wore a heavy blue coat, lavishly embroidered with gold. He had led the charge of the chasseurs, but his horse had failed him by the riverbank as he and his men tried to cut their way out. He was captured, along with a good few of his men. Later in the day, the English general had permitted a message to be sent to the enemy, summoning his extensive baggage and allowing him to appear at this meal in fitting style. His sword had gone, and Sir John had generously unbuckled his own and given it to the count to wear.

Quietly, Moore had also asked Colborne whether or not he should ask the prisoner to give his parole, a signed promise not to attempt escape. The military secretary advised against it, recalling an incident years before in Sicily, where a French officer had been most offended by such a question.

'I am glad you told me this,' came the reply. 'Of course, I will not ask.' The matter was dropped, and every courtesy paid to the distinguished prisoner. The ordinary chasseurs taken in the fight were entertained more modestly, although the hussars guarding them did prevent an angry mob of locals from slitting their throats.

Sir John later asked Colborne whether he would escort the prisoner as the army continued its retreat. He was unsurprised and fully satisfied with his military secretary's refusal on the grounds that he had far too many more urgent duties. Lord Paget's staff proved equally reluctant to leave him. Wickham presented himself as an obvious choice, and General Paget freely expressed a willingness to do without him for a day or two.

All in all it was most satisfactory. The next day Captain Wickham travelled inside the coach with the French general. They travelled at speed, and soon caught up and passed the brigades ahead of them. The count looked scornfully at the signs of disorder, with ragged groups of stragglers, many of them barefoot, staggering along through the mud. Some of the men were drunk, and more walked with expressions of blank hopelessness.

'My chasseurs would cut through this rabble like a hot knife through butter,' he said, shaking his head.

'It is dreadful,' conceded Wickham, seeing no reason to associate himself with the mobs of drunken redcoats. 'Our men usually join the army rather than face the prison cell or the gallows.'

'We are more fortunate in our conscripts, and the Guard picks the finest men from all the regiments. But how will your country take this retreat?'

Wickham shrugged. 'There will be anger, but the sensible will know that some officers at least have done their duty.' The general was growing more amiable, and Wickham was both comfortable and performing an honourable, and not undistinguished, task.

'My Emperor does not forgive failure.' Lefebre-Desnouettes repeated the sentiment several times. 'He sometimes forgets victories you win, but never defeat. Even in a relation.'

Wickham was intrigued. 'Are you from his family?'

'The countess – my wife – is a cousin of the Emperor,' said the general, always happy to tell of the connection. 'A distant cousin,' he added modestly, satisfied with the obviously deep impression this had made on the English officer.

'You should have been born French, my dear Captain Wickham.' The count spread his hands. 'Well, of course, everyone should have been born French. But a bold young officer like yourself could be a colonel by now, perhaps a duke or count, and married into the family of the master of Europe.' Lefebre-Desnouettes had no idea whether or not his escort was either brave or capable, but knew that a little flattery was seldom wasted.

'You are too kind, my dear count.' The reply was enthusiastic, in Wickham's rusty but competent French. 'Although I confess it is true that good men are held back in our Service by the preference given to the friends of the powerful. I know all too well how a man whose friends neglect him is shamefully lost.'

'The Emperor looks for merit. He does not ignore the advice of friends, but with us a man can rise high and rise quickly,' said Lefebre-Desnouettes, who had been a count for barely a year. 'Yet he is sometimes more generous with titles than with funds. Since the Russians surrendered, he has starved we Guard commandants of the money needed by the regiments. Yet he still wants the chasseurs and the others to be as finely equipped as ever. Always it must be the best – the best horses, the finest fur for colpaks and saddlecloths. I agree his Guards must shine in splendour, so that men fear them and ladies swoon as we pass. I just wish that he would pay for it.' In truth Lefebre-Desnouettes' debts came more from the gaming tables, but he was not about to make such a confession to a stranger.

'Now we must pay to dress his regiments or suffer his rebukes.' The count chuckled. 'It is a terrible thing, my friend, when a man's duty means he can no longer afford to pay for his wife's pleasures, or even pamper his mistress!' In truth the general was very concerned about his wife, and only his wife, but style mattered in talk with anyone, save the closest of friends. Better to let the Englishman hear what he expected.

Wickham grinned. 'I know something of such things.'

'You have a wife?'

'I have a wife. I also have many debts.'

Lefebre-Desnouettes winked. 'How about a mistress? Or more than one perhaps?'

Wickham spread his hands deprecatingly. 'I am only a poor captain, not able to match the establishment of a general!'

'Yet surely a man of any vigour and spirit needs diversions from the stern call of duty.'

'Ah, well, I have my eye on a certain young lady.'

'Hah, I knew it, you dog! Even out here in this wilderness I knew it! Is she a blonde? I hear you English like blondes.'

'Sometimes, but this one has red hair.'

'And . . .'

Wickham was happy to boast. 'A face full of spirit, lips softer than any pillow and the curves of a Venus.'

'But does she know how to use them?' asked Lefebre-Desnouettes.

'Not yet, I think, but the task of teaching her will be a great pleasure in itself.'

They laughed, the French general slapping his hand against his leg and letting tears stream down his face. He seemed to be letting go of some of his low spirits.

'I envy you,' he said at last. 'To have such a prospect waiting. I regret that escorting me takes you away from such a worthwhile quest.'

'It is an honour.' Wickham was genuinely enjoying his association with a general and aristocrat, even one who was so recently minted and an enemy.

'But less of a pleasure. I fear I cannot compete with your little red-headed piece, but perhaps we can dine in the best manner permitted by our situation. I trust you will join me.' The general's servant had prepared a basket with a wide selection of bread, cold meats and cheese, as well as a few of those barbaric pies provided by the English. There were also half a dozen bottles of tolerable red. They ate and talked more of horses, and Paris, and women, until full stomachs and the warmth of the wine made the general drowsy.

Wickham watched him doze and wondered when he might next have a chance to renew his pursuit of the MacAndrews girl. He had not been near the 106th for days, although he had seen her mother at a distance and thought that she looked rather haggard. The delay might actually help his cause, bringing the young miss nicely to the boil. With that happy thought Wickham let himself drift into sleep, by now used to the bouncing of the coach on the badly rutted road.

12

Jenny screamed and yelled, employing a vocabulary fostered by growing up in the regiment. Fresh panic consumed Williams with every cry. He had seen a cat produce a litter, and had to assume the principles were the same. This did not seem especially comforting.

'Keep calm, Mrs Hanks. You will be fine,' he said unhelpfully.

Jane MacAndrews tried to distract him with tasks, setting him to boil water in the camp kettle, and then to sharpen the clasp knife he carried, and prepare and clean a short stretch of cord. In a life spent in garrisons throughout the world, her mother had always attended when the time came for one of the officers' wives to give birth. Once old enough, Jane had accompanied her, watching as Esther MacAndrews calmly took charge, made sure that the attending army surgeon was neither too drunk, nor dangerously incompetent. There were a few times when her mother had delivered the baby herself, or with the help of one or two of the more sensible women. Sometimes Jane had watched, although she preferred to be outside, looking after any young children in the house. Seeing something was not the same as having to do it, and now she felt sick at the thought of being responsible, and terrified that there would be complications.

'Keep calm, Jenny,' said Williams once again, his nervousness prompting informality.

'Get about your business, sir,' snapped Jane. 'Now the knife is sharp, plunge the blade into the boiling water.'

Jane was glad that Jenny seemed also to have a good idea of

what to do. Soldiers' families lived their lives in public, and births, deaths and plenty more in between were all carried out in plain view. That also meant she knew what could go wrong. Fear as well as pain fed her yells, and with each cry fresh panic consumed Williams.

He fell back on the language of the battlefield. 'Steady, Jenny, steady.'

Williams fussed and got in the way, then started to talk too much, offering constant advice and encouragement to the mother. Finally he knelt on Jenny's hand, provoking a string of epithets which Jane felt it was probably just as well she did not understand. Miss MacAndrews told him in no uncertain terms to go outside and keep himself busy. They would summon him if his presence was required.

The door of the cottage slammed behind him. The screams were muffled now, and if he tried hard Williams could almost pretend that he could not hear them. He paced up and down, feet crunching in grass stiff with frost. The sky grew red, and he watched the sun rise over the mountains. He looked to the animals, brushing them both down more times than could possibly be beneficial. A loud cry came from the house. Minutes later it was repeated, and he found himself running to the door and yanking it open.

'Get out, Mr Williams!' Miss MacAndrews' voice was surprisingly controlled and of unquestionable authority. Jane was perhaps as frightened and nervous as he was, and was surprising herself at her ability to conceal this. Seemingly assured, she did her very best, hoping desperately that it was right and that nature would do the rest without any hitch.

He closed the door and went back to his pacing. Then he thought that he ought to pray and knelt down. For a while the thoughts came in words, until these faltered and there were just unexpressed emotional pleas. The sun rose higher in a patch of blue sky that looked as if it would soon be swallowed again in dark cloud. He went back to pacing.

The cry was distinctive, unlike any of the noises of the past hours, and wonderfully pure. Williams went to the door cautiously, opening it like a naughty boy expecting to be scolded again, but unable to resist the lure. This time there was no angry shout. Jane was wrapping something small and reddish pink in a piece of clean linen from Jenny's baggage. The mother lay back exhausted, as her son bellowed heartily.

'Noisy little bugger,' she said before sleep took her. Miss MacAndrews looked exhausted, and lost in blissful wonder as she rocked the child gently and calmed him. Williams thought that he had never seen her looking more truly beautiful.

'Take him,' she whispered. 'I have things to do.' He did not resist for this was still a place where authorities other than those of the army prevailed.

The boy was tiny and snub nosed, and far lighter than Williams could have believed possible. At first he was afraid that it was so delicate that it must break under his touch. One hand had come loose of the wrapping, and as he lifted it back beneath the little blanket he could not resist touching each minute finger.

Jane looked up to see the officer walking slowly around the room, gently rocking the child in his arms. Williams' face was split into a grin so broad that it could almost have come from some printed cartoon.

The girl was drawn by instinct to children – indeed, almost any children at any time. She could never resist any baby, even if the last few hours had most certainly not altered her desire to wait some years before having any of her own. Reason told her that Jenny had had an easy time of it. Her senses screamed out that it was still painful and dangerous, and if truth be told part of her was terrified of the risks involved. Yet she was pleased to see Williams so taken by the infant, for it spoke of a natural kindness. He might make a good father, and indeed a good husband, if not necessarily for her. That assumed that he was equally capable of more practical assistance than simply cooing at a baby.

'Mr Williams,' she announced, 'it is clear that we cannot move today. We need food – Mrs Hanks especially needs to regain her strength. We shall also need fuel for the fire. I will not let either

her or the little one go cold. Most of all we need milk for the baby. I understand that it is often some time before the mother provides enough.'

Williams was startled from his reverie. The boy had begun to suck his index finger and that in itself seemed such a truly remarkable and delightful sensation, even though it confirmed Miss MacAndrews' judgement.

'Well?' she said.

'Of course, I shall go at once, but . . .' He lifted the boy slightly; the infant began to cry.

'Let me take him.' Jane sighed happily. 'He can rest beside his mother soon.' She took the little bundle and almost instantly the crying stopped. Williams stood beaming at them both. Miss MacAndrews gave him an arch look.

'Of course, of course, I am going.'

'Do not take too long,' she said, as the child began to search for a source of sustenance on her.

Jenny had been woken by the crying. As Williams left, Jane carried the boy over to his mother.

'How do you feel?' she asked.

'Split in two,' came the blunt response.

'Would you like to hold him for a while?'

'I've been carrying him for months.' Jenny's voice was weary and hard edged. 'Someone else can do it for a bit.'

Jane wondered whether mothers often took a while to develop affection for their infants. In truth she was more than content to clutch the tiny life to her. Going to the fire, she one-handedly collected a bowl of stew she had prepared with almost their last provisions. She took it over. 'Have something to eat.'

They said little while Williams was away, mainly because the mother had small inclination to discuss her offspring, while Miss MacAndrews could think of little else.

'You should marry him.' Jenny had insisted on getting to her feet and walking haltingly up and down the room. It seemed unwise, but she was determined and less inclined to follow orders

than Williams. Jane was still surprised at her sudden pronounce-
ment. She did not reply.

'He's good and kind.'

'Was your husband not those things, Mrs Hanks?' Jane was
stirred to directness of her own.

'Oh, in his way, he was kind enough. There are worse men.
Dad chose him to try and keep me in his world, just like him and
Ma, following the drum and never dreaming.'

'Is that so very bad?'

'Well, look what happened to her.'

'And yet you would have me marry a soldier, who however
good and kind may well get killed one day.'

'You wouldn't be here unless you was going to wed an old
sodjer. Father or not, you'd be off sitting in fine houses and
drinking tea. "Good day to you, squire, will you favour me with
the next dance, and try not to stare at my . . ."'

'Jenny!' The baby burst into tears as Jane shouted to interrupt
the flow. Her pride at not being easily shocked continued to be
eroded by Mrs Hanks' directness. Yet there was something
bizarrely fascinating about her image of polite society. She did
her best to calm the child.

'I do hope Mr Williams returns soon. The boy is very hungry.'

'Typical man, never will wait for anything.'

'Poor boy, never to meet his father.' Jane once again endeavoured to change the subject. Part of her wanted the widowed
mother to show more natural feelings, even at the cost of
upsetting her.

Jenny put her head on one side. 'Well, he may, one day.' She
laughed at the surprise. 'You don't think it was Hanks, do you?
No, this little lad's da is a fine gentleman. Drunk off his head at
the time, but I owed him a favour.'

Somehow the revelation was less shocking than perhaps it
ought to have been. Jane had now spent days in Jenny's company, and they had talked longer and more freely than might ever
have occurred in more normal circumstances. Apart from that,

she had overheard a few conversations among the officers which hinted at such things.

To her relief, Williams came in at the perfect moment to permit them to drop the subject. He had ridden in search of an occupied farm or village. The first one he found was empty, and although there were two skinny cows and a calf in a byre he had decided to keep this as an ultimate reserve, in case he did no better elsewhere. Riding on, he had come to a cluster of five or six houses. There was no sign of any men, but women came to the doors. With some difficulty, he established himself as English, in need of food. With considerably more effort, involving a prolonged mime, which produced only laughter and confusion, followed by pointing at a baby in the arms of one of the women, which provoked a fear of kidnap, he was finally able to explain that there was also a child to be fed. The people were poor. They were also extremely generous. He suspected that had they been less distant he would have been followed back by half a dozen womenfolk trailing their own offspring in their eagerness to fuss over another.

Apart from bread, vegetables, some smoked ham and a few eggs, all in a basket, he brought a jug of goat's milk, which he had carried gingerly as he rode on Bobbie's back. There were also some old but carefully cleaned clothes for the child. One of Jane's gloves, placed in steaming water for some time and then pierced at the end of the finger, formed a makeshift teat. It worked surprisingly well, and the boy was soon sucking away with every sign of satisfaction.

'Have you decided upon a name, Mrs Hanks?' Jane felt this was a better topic for conversation, as well as an important step for the mother to take. 'Perhaps after his father,' she added automatically, before realising how inappropriate this was.

'Well, I did wonder about Billy,' said Jenny mischievously.

Williams, who knew from the roster that Hanks' name was Thomas, was puzzled. He also knew that neither Redman nor Hatch was called William.

'Then I thought that Mr Williams here has been so good to us, perhaps I would ask if he would mind me naming the lad after him.'

'That is most generous,' agreed Jane.

'But I can't call him mister, can I?' They both looked at Williams, who refused to catch their eyes.

'I confess that I do not know your Christian name, Mr Williams,' said Miss MacAndrews. 'Pray tell us what it is?'

The moment could no longer be avoided, try as he might.

'Hamish,' he said softly.

There was silence, and then Jenny roared with laughter. 'You poor sod,' she said.

Williams stared apologetically at Miss MacAndrews. 'In every other respect my parents demonstrated the fullest affection towards me.' His smile was thin. 'My mother is very proud of being a Campbell.'

'Now Campbell could be a good name,' Jenny mused.

Sensitive over such issues, Williams decided to protect the child's interests before any damage was done. 'Perhaps it would be fitting to name him after your father?'

'He would like that.' Jenny decided. 'Fine, Jake it is.' It seemed to end her interest in the boy, at least for the moment. Oddly, hearing it aloud made Williams realise that he had never once heard anyone call Dobson either Jacob or indeed Jake.

'Jacob Hanks,' he said aloud.

'If you like,' replied the boy's mother.

Williams was unconcerned enough not to insist on standing guard. He had seen no sign of the French when he rode out earlier in the day. They ate well, and after a few serious spells of crying, the baby became calmer and slept at last. It was early, but they were all exhausted in their way. Jane was twice woken when little Jacob stirred, and heard the child's mother hushing him back to peace before she dropped off to sleep again. Williams slept heavily, oblivious to even these small noises.

Jane woke first, and when she had waited and was sure, she stole over to Williams and looked for a long while at the baby resting beside him. Gently at first but, when this seemed to achieve nothing, somewhat more forcibly, she shook the man's arm to wake him.

'Mrs Hanks has gone,' she whispered as soon as she saw sense come into his eyes. Little Jake began to cry.

13

It was a strange procession. The man led, walking ahead of a scrawny, one-eyed horse on which the woman with a baby was perched. The man wore a red coat, although it did not fit him very well, and it had brass shoulder wings, one of which was badly mangled. This suggested that he was an officer, and if the strange misshapen hat appeared to contradict this, then he certainly wore a sword like an officer. The red jacket suggested an Englishman. It also seemed unlikely that the leading French patrols would have a mother and child in tow.

'I keep looking around for the kings,' joked the Spanish captain to his lieutenant.

'We're a few days early,' responded the junior officer automatically. 'And I reckon we'll see an emperor first.'

'Yes. And not bringing any gifts we'd care for.' They were the rearguard of the Army of Galicia, and General La Romana had left this brigade to hold the bridge at Mansilla. The captain knew a hopeless task when he saw one. He commanded the remnants of a regiment which now numbered scarcely two hundred men combined into a single battalion. Barely half wore the white coats with green front and facings, still less the cocked hats and red plumes in which the full regiment had paraded at the start of the year. The uniforms were threadbare and patched, but at least recognisable. The remainder of his men still wore the remnants of their civilian clothes, with just a red rag tied around their left arm to mark them as soldiers. All of his men had muskets, and that was something in this army these days, but the flints were poor and none of them had more than twenty rounds in their pouches. This was the second day when they had had no food apart from the little they could dig up. They had had no hot food for a week.

Both officers had been among the men rescued by the Royal Navy from Denmark. The captain had also lost a brother at Trafalgar, but preferred to remember the more recent friendliness of the English, and his far deeper loathing for the French. He and his men waited, and did their duty. The old soldiers among them must have known as he did that they could not withstand any serious French attack.

The sentry challenged them, prompting the redcoat to call out 'Amigos!' in such an atrocious accent that it farther convinced the captain that this strange couple must be English. He waved at the soldier to bring them over. A few words of English learned on the voyage from Denmark, combined with even fewer words of Spanish from the new arrivals, were enough to confirm that this was an English officer cut off from his own army and seeking to rejoin them. The captain assumed the young woman was the man's wife and could not help envying him. To see such a gloriously beautiful girl on so grey and hopeless a day was an unlooked-for and precious joy. His own wife was in Saragossa, and he did not know whether she had survived the siege of the city earlier in the year. Yet when he watched his lieutenant lead the couple away towards the bridge he envied the man even more the freedom to leave.

Williams was pleased to have reached Mansilla before the French, and even happier with the sense that they were now with allies. It was the same day that Jenny had absconded, and somehow her disappearance made them both feel more vulnerable. As they came closer to the town, the landscape seemed less empty and more hostile. They saw no enemy soldiers, but one stretch of mud road was pitted with many prints from shod horses, and Williams suspected that they were French, and heading towards Mansilla. He said nothing to Miss MacAndrews, but he feared that the French already held the bridge, and for a moment he had despaired because he could see no other way of them ever reaching the British Army again. They waited for a while, and the pace slowed as he tried to avoid open ground and stay under cover.

The Spanish lieutenant was friendly, in obvious awe and adoration of Miss MacAndrews, but communication proved difficult and they said little as he took them through the Spanish lines. A few shallow ditches and earthworks had been constructed. Williams was scornful when he saw most of the allied soldiers sitting and watching while only a few dug, and then he realised that there were no spades or tools for others to use. Apart from that, the soldiers looked weak and emaciated. Some shivered as they sat or crouched, staring hollow eyed at nothing.

'Typhus fever,' said the lieutenant as he noticed the British officer's gaze. Williams resolved to get Miss MacAndrews and young Jacob away from this place as soon as possible, and not stop to rest and search for something to eat as he had planned. The hope of finding another mount now seemed hopeless. He had not seen a single horse as they went through the Spanish lines and camp. If he had been able to find the words to ask the lieutenant, he would have been told that the Army of Galicia had no cavalry, or at least none with horses to ride.

Capitaine Dalmas was not at all surprised at the absence of any Spanish cavalry screen, and happily profited from it. Taking just two lancers with him, he scouted the approach to the town, while the rest of the mixed squadron waited a few miles short of the enemy outposts. At one point he caught a glimpse of the English officer and a woman riding a mule. Dalmas and his two men were in the shelter of a treeline, looking down a ridge at the little figures. He did not need to learn the way from them, since he already knew where Mansilla lay, but it had amused him to see how they stuck to the least visible path. Most of the same route was suitable for his own men. Sending one lancer back, he summoned the squadron to follow him. As he watched the English officer and his woman reach the Spanish outposts, he knew that his men were arriving in a narrow valley just behind him. There they were invisible to the Spanish. Foot patrols were unlikely, and the enemy had no horsemen, so his men should be safe from discovery.

Dalmas knew that Marshal Soult's army was near, and that an attack was planned for today. He was well placed, almost behind the far right flank of the enemy position, ready to join the fighting if an opportunity presented itself. It was a curious chance that these same English had crossed his path again, but he dismissed that thought as he dismissed them. Instead he thought of possibilities, balancing what he might achieve with the cost to his command and its influence on his ability to fulfil his orders. It was the sort of problem Jean-Baptiste Dalmas loved.

After half an hour Williams and Miss MacAndrews were crossing the stone bridge at Mansilla, having waved goodbye to their guide. The British officer could not see any sign that the bridge was ready to be demolished and had small confidence in this rearguard's ability to hold it for long. It was yet another reason to press on. At the end of an hour they were climbing up the slope to the ridge.

'Why not take the road?' asked Miss MacAndrews. They had spoken little all day, and he knew that she felt he should have gone hunting for Mrs Hanks, instead of pressing on as if nothing had happened.

'Our army is over there.' He pointed with a confidence he did not feel to the north-west. 'The road takes us a long way out of our way. It's also clogged up with the Spanish baggage and stragglers.' He did not add that he wished to be as far away as possible from the disease-ridden soldiers, or that he feared the road would soon be full of French cavalry, chopping mercilessly down with their sabres.

'I do not believe that I could have found Jenny quickly,' he said, beginning the explanation he had rehearsed in his head. 'She had a head start, and that mule is surprisingly fast.'

'Could she really travel far or fast so soon after her

confinement?' The reply came quickly, suggesting that Miss MacAndrews had also been thinking of what she would say.

'I confess to know little of such things.' To himself he added that he rather doubted whether she did either. Part of him resented the unkind fate which seemed to make Miss Mac-Andrews freshly angry with him just when he felt that their friendship was deepening. Who was that Greek fellow in the myths who had to keep on rolling a boulder up a hill? Tantalus? No, he was the one unable to drink or eat. It annoyed him that he could not remember.

Williams did his very best to sound reasonable, and, he hoped, persuasive. 'She could have gone in any direction. To search would have meant taking Bobbie away and leaving you and the baby on your own – perhaps for many hours.'

Jane said nothing, and Williams was unsure whether she approved of his concern or resented his judgement of her inability to fend for herself and protect the child.

'The French were nearer than we thought, so the risk was even greater,' he added.

'It remains a puzzle to me why she left. How could anyone abandon such a dear little child?' On cue the baby began to scream hungrily. Miss MacAndrews held out the glove for Williams to fill from the bottle of milk he carried. The officer pulled the cork from the mouth of the green bottle and began to pour. He had washed the bottle as thoroughly as possible, but there was still the faint scent of ardent spirits.

He grimaced. 'I begin to fear that we may be raising a drunkard,' he said, and was pleased to be rewarded with a smile. He handed back the glove, but the task of balancing on the awkward saddle and feeding the boy while still steering Bobbie defeated the girl. Williams took the reins, in spite of her protests, and led the mare on up the slope. Once again he was depressed by the thought of angering Miss MacAndrews.

'Perhaps she was temporarily deranged?' Jane said as the baby sucked contentedly on the finger of the glove. One fear had been nagging at her all morning since they had left. 'What if Mrs

Hanks comes to her senses and returns? How could she ever find us and her son?'

Williams paused, wondering how to explain, for in the last months he felt that he had come to know Jenny well. 'I do not believe that she intends to return.'

His certainty was obvious, but Jane was unconvinced. She could not imagine abandoning any child, still less a helpless infant. 'It would be most unnatural for a mother not to feel the deepest bond with her child. Perhaps not immediately, but I cannot believe that it would not swiftly grow in Mrs Hanks. For all her ways, she struck me as kind.'

'There was no reason for Hanks and his wife to be so far away from the army's outposts when I stumbled across them. I think they were planning to run.' He doubted Hanks had played much part in the decision, but did not question his wife's power of persuasion. 'Jenny does not care much for the life of a soldier's wife.'

Miss MacAndrews considered this for a while, thinking back to the many times Jenny had spoken eagerly of wealth and splendour. 'It seems unlikely that a deserter would give her anything better.'

'He could help her get away more easily than she could on her own, and offer some protection as they travelled.'

'There still appears no great reason for her to give up her child. Would not her husband be reluctant to aid such a deed? Or was he a vicious man?'

'Not at all. Gentle, slow, and very quiet.'

'Then surely . . .'

'I suspect that she would have left him and the baby as she left us.' Williams spoke forcefully, interrupting the girl. 'I cannot be certain, but I doubt that Jenny ever planned to raise the child herself, or return to her parents and the army. Where she is going I do not know. Perhaps to find a rich Spaniard or even a French-man? Perhaps she hopes to get to England? She often speaks of London.'

Jane frowned. 'Nevertheless, I cannot believe her so callous as to abandon her baby to a fate even more precarious than her own.'

'She did not, did she?' Williams smiled ironically. 'She knows us both well enough to be certain that we would do everything for the babe, giving our lives if necessary.' Suddenly it all seemed so comic to him. 'I fear this is the price of having a good reputation!'

Jane was amused, but still wondering whether the officer was right when the distant popping of musketry interrupted them. They turned to stare back across the river as the Spanish soldiers ran to arms. Three squadrons of French cavalry had appeared and were walking their horses inexorably towards the bridge and the town beyond. Behind them were another three squadrons, and more cavalry were appearing at every moment.

The Spanish captain did his best with his battalion to anchor the flank. He formed them behind one of the ditches, so that it would be hard for the enemy to sweep over them, and for a while he kept his men from wasting their shots, even though the rest of the brigade was firing at absurdly long range. When the closest French squadron approached them, he waited until they were less than two hundred paces away and gave the order. They emptied a handful of saddles, and the French halted to reply with their own carbines. Elsewhere the Spanish brigade was collapsing. They fled before the French horsemen could reach them, but men on foot struggle to outrun horsemen and soon the chasseurs and dragoons were among them, stabbing and slicing as they passed.

Perhaps the captain could have kept his men together and reached the bridge in some order. The soldiers were nervous, but they trusted him, and enough were experienced and knew that flight was far more dangerous than keeping together. The line split into two wings. One retreated a hundred paces and then halted, ready to fire to cover the rest of the battalion as it pulled back past them. The squadron ahead watched them warily. Those elsewhere were distracted by other, far easier targets.

Then there was drumming of hoofs behind them, and a new force of French cavalry appeared as if from nowhere.

'*Colloseros!*' yelled the lieutenant, using the Spaniards' nickname for the big cuirassiers. Dalmas' men had rolled their cloaks and strapped them to the valise on the back of each saddle. Their swords were drawn and their armour and helmets gleamed in the pale sun. To their left the Poles had untied the red and white pennants on their slim lances, and the little flags whipped in the breeze as they lowered them to the charge position.

The line collapsed. It probably did not matter, for there was no time to form a square, and anyway the captain doubted that his men were capable of performing the drill. As his soldiers fled, he drew his pistol and pulled back the hammer. He aimed carefully, lining up the barrel to point at the fast-approaching leader of the enemy lancers. The man had an immense blond moustache and the Spanish officer decided that this was as good a reason as any to end his life.

He waited, ignoring his lieutenant's cries to come on. At twenty yards he squeezed the trigger, willing the shot to strike squarely in the middle of the Polish officer's yellow-fronted coat. The hammer slammed down and the flint sparked, but the low-grade powder in the pan merely fizzled and failed to set off the charge. It seemed fitting for such a day. The Polish officer's sabre cut down across his face, destroying his left eye in a moment of searing pain. One of the lancers in the rank behind impaled him neatly near the heart, and then swung his arm round so that as he rushed past the lance was yanked from the Spaniard's falling body. The Pole rode on.

From the hill beyond the river, Williams and Miss MacAndrews could not see the fate of individuals. The French squadrons simply washed over the few thin lines and clusters of Spanish infantry.

'Poor devils,' said Williams quietly. 'We need to move quickly.'

14

'We must attack.' Graham translated the Spanish general's words. 'He believes that Bonaparte is overextended, his army straggling back through the mountain passes. If we together march to the south-west, we can strike at his flank.'

Sir John Moore struggled to control his anger. La Romana was no doubt a brave man, but command of an army required a good deal more than courage. This new proposal to attack was just the latest in a succession of wildly unrealistic plans put forward by the Spanish general, ideas all the more fantastic in view of Romana's frequent expressions of despair at the state of his own army.

'Tell him we do not have food or transport,' Sir John said to Graham. 'We cannot fight, and so we must continue to withdraw. Tell him he must let me have this road and find another for his own men. He must. If we both retreat by the same route we will go slowly and the French will catch up with us when we are in no condition to fight.' Moore waited for his friend to repeat what he had said, and was pleased to hear a definite emphasis in the later sections.

The British and Spanish armies had come together at the town of Astorga. That should not have happened, since Sir John had specifically asked his ally to follow a different route and avoid the town, and had believed the matter to be settled. Instead there were five thousand or more half-naked and emaciated men in the place before he added five times as many of his own soldiers. By the sound of things, most of the Spanish had not eaten for three or four days, and it was obvious that many were desperately sick.

He dreaded to think how many had already died, or been left behind on the road.

'He repeats his complaint at the misbehaviour of our soldiers,' said Graham wearily.

Sir John forced himself to wait a moment, lest his rage become apparent. He also noted that the Spanish general had changed the subject and suspected that this was meant as a distraction from the main issue.

'Tell him that as commanders we must each look to the discipline and welfare of our own men. That soldiers without food are inclined to take whatever they need.'

The Spanish soldiers were desperate. They broke into houses searching for food and drink. Others rifled the stores carefully prepared here to support both armies. The British quartermasters and commissaries were already struggling to prepare some of their supplies for immediate issue, others for transport and the rest for destruction, when the system was thrown into chaos by mobs of starving Spanish troops. His own soldiers – Moore had never before in his life believed that he could be ashamed that they were his – were quick to follow suit. They hunted for food and most of all for wine. Spanish and British soldiers threatened the townspeople if they did not get what they wanted. They were equally ready to turn on each other. There was fighting, and he would be surprised if no deaths had occurred.

'His officers must take back control of their men, as my own will do with our soldiers,' said Sir John. Privately he doubted that order would be restored until the troops left the town. At present it was simply too easy for individuals to vanish into the streets, and avoid the gaze of the regimental officers and sergeants who would recognise them and be able to inflict punishment.

Astorga was a grim sight, and the acrid smell of smoke was everywhere, filling Sir John's nostrils. Fires burned on open patches of ground as stocks of stores were destroyed to deny them to the enemy. Dead horses and bullocks lay in all of the yards and even in the streets, killed because they were no longer able to go on. More animals were still waiting dumbly for execution. There had been sufficient order to issue a musket to every Spanish soldier who lacked one. Moore's own men got less attention. Blankets, uniforms and boots so desperately needed were all too often burned instead of being given out.

La Romana sighed heavily, and then plunged again into another enthusiastic oration. Sir John waited for the translation.

'He says that Bonaparte himself has left the army,' explained Graham. They had already heard the rumour, but did not know whether it was true. 'Surely this is a time to strike, when the French are without their leader.'

Sir John restated the impossibility of attacking, and the risk they would run remaining where they were. There were only two passes into Astorga, and in other circumstances he would have been happy to hold them. At present there was simply no useful object to be served. In the end, Romana gave up his wild plans with a most generous grace.

'The Spanish artillery cannot use the road to the west,' Graham summarised the general's explanation. 'So they must continue north to Lugo. The rest of the Army of Galicia will march to Orense, away from us.'

'Express my thanks.' That was good enough. Sir John had already decided to send some of his own brigades by the western roads, which in time would take them to the port of Vigo. It spread the burden when it came to quarters and supplies, and it would also give him a chance to hold the port open, should he have to shift the rest of the army in that direction.

One problem was dealt with, although he still had to decide how much of his army to send by the western route. Explaining his actions to London was unlikely to be so simple. He returned to a small room in the house chosen as his headquarters, trying to compose the letter he would write. If only the ministers could see the wretched state of the Spanish soldiers, starving and riddled with fever, or know what it meant to deal with such unpredictable and disorganised allies. How could he fight on his own, when the Spanish were so woefully unprepared? He was sceptical that the government, at such a safe distance, still in a comfortable haze of optimism and false reports, would understand the true position. Even if they did privately, politicians were unlikely to make public acknowledgement of the truth if it was personally inexpedient. Sir John's own time as an MP had taught him that lesson most thoroughly.

Out in the streets of Astorga, Major MacAndrews almost screamed aloud as he saw boxes full of shoes perishing in the flames. He and Esther went to the headquarters of each brigade, asking in case anyone had news of his daughter. His wife was shrewd enough to know as he did that there was little hope. If Jane, or for that matter Williams, had made their way here, they would have sought out and found the regiment. They looked anyway. He knew that Pringle and Hanley were out and about on the same errand. Indeed, it had taken something close to a direct order delivered to the other officers via Brotherton to stop almost everyone else joining them.

There was no news, only the signs of looting and destruction. Most of the Spanish and other British troops had begun to move out earlier in the day, and so the streets themselves were less crowded. Despondently he returned to their billet, and found that he was ordered to attend General Paget.

Hanley and Pringle gave up at about the same time. The Grenadier Company was divided between two big houses, and once again the officers had no separate accommodation. When they had arrived, the town was too full to allow any more generous allowance. Pringle had felt it better for each of them to reside with half of the company, rather than together. Hanley would have preferred to stay with his friend. He felt like an intruder among the men and their families, unable to understand them. Some of the smaller children stared at him in a way that made him feel deeply uncomfortable. He felt a reserve among the adults, and was at a loss how to talk with them. It seemed so much easier for Williams, no doubt from his time as a volunteer serving alongside the men. Yet even Pringle was more at ease with the company than Hanley felt he would ever find possible.

The redcoats seemed separate from him in every way, stronger than he was, while being as wild and unpredictable as infants.

The house allocated to his half of the company was quieter by the time Hanley returned, and had lost just a little of its Hogarthian quality. Most of the children were now asleep, or at least quiet, and the little wine the company possessed had already been drunk. His earnest hope that none had been able to drink to excess appeared to be doomed as he watched a burly fellow named Eyles strutting at the end of the room, next to one of the three locked doors where the owners slept and kept their valuables.

'Br-br-bruck-buck-buckbuck.' The impression was remarkably good, if rather startling in its unexpectedness. He tried again, leaning down to the bottom of the door. Moving on, he began to make more chicken noises at the next door.

'What the devil . . . ?' Hanley began.

'Sam'll have 'em soon,' Sergeant Probert replied. 'He grew up on a farm.' It seemed an inadequate explanation, but none of the expectant soldiers was inclined to add any more. At the third door, Eyles tried again. He stopped to listen and then clucked even more loudly. The answer was faint. He repeated the call and again came the reply.

'Right, lads, that's the one.' Probert sprang towards the door as one of the men tried to use his bayonet to get into the crack and spring the lock. 'Out the way, let Salty have a go.' The sergeant was one of very few genuine Welshmen in the 106th, in spite of their official designation as 'The Glamorganshire Regiment'. At his bidding Jim Salt, a man whose military career began at the suggestion of a magistrate, crouched down over the lock, a curiously shaped piece of metal in his hand.

Hanley was too fascinated to remember that as an officer he should probably be preventing this. They had the door open in less than a minute, and as Eyles repeated his call, a cockerel and half a dozen hens processed into the main room. The speed and savagery with which each was seized and its neck wrung dismayed him, after which it seemed too late for any protest. This was not the opinion of the owner of the house, who must have been drawn by the strange noise. His complaints were shrill, although he did not risk coming fully into the room packed with the frightening foreign soldiers.

At that moment Corporal Atkinson from the battalion headquarters appeared, informing Hanley that officers were summoned by the major. He was glad to go, feeling there was nothing to be said. If the redcoats didn't take the owner's poultry then the French surely would. Hanley wondered about giving him some money as payment, and then realised he was too tired to care.

'We are now the rearguard,' MacAndrews told his assembled officers. 'The light brigades are marching to Vigo. The hussars are staying with us for the moment, but the burden of the work is likely to fall on the Reserve Division. It is the usual form. The rest of the army will be between one and two days' march in advance of us. Our task is to keep an eye on the French, and stop them from getting too forward.'

Hanley was yawning when he got back to the house. A boiled chicken leg was presented to him almost immediately. Eating it reminded him of just how hungry he was. He was also so very tired that even the bare stone floor in a crowded room seemed the height of luxury as he lay down, covered himself in a blanket and was quickly asleep.

The next morning the battalion went only five miles along the grand road, built not long before by the Spanish to connect Madrid to the north coast. A convoy of carts blocked the road ahead of them for a long while. Each wagon was full of sick and wounded Spanish soldiers, whose numbers had swamped the few surgeons in their army. Hanley had never before seen so many faces of people so obviously waiting for death.

The division was to stop for the night and for once the 106th were comfortable. The village did not look much, but the remaining inhabitants were welcoming, and their houses showed every sign of being well maintained in spite of their poverty. There was ample chopped straw to keep the fires going, and more that provided the most luxurious bedding they had enjoyed for a long time. If there was less food than they would have liked, then that was merely a proof that life was not perfect. The officers at least were content to discover very little wine in the place. On the whole the battalion was happy. Hanley was not surprised when he heard the grenadiers singing.

The drums beat to muster ten minutes later. Hussars were falling back past the houses as the Reserve Division mustered in the fields outside. The French were coming and there would be no easy night. As the redcoats stood in formation, big flakes of snow began to drift down, settling for a moment on the tops of shakos before they melted. Soon the march resumed, but it was good to be on a road that had a firm rocky bed, leaving behind the sucking mud of so many miles. Steadily, the route wound upwards, into hills already covered with inches of snow. There was no wind and Hanley soon found that he did not notice the cold. He marched at the rear of the Grenadier Company, and the steady tread of their boots on the hard road became the only sound in the world. No one sang, and no one talked. They were marching at ease, and yet habit and convenience kept them all in step.

Hanley woke with a start as he fell against Murphy's wooden-framed backpack. The battalion ahead had stopped for some reason, and so the 106th had also halted.

'Are you all right, your Honour?' Private Murphy had wrapped his shoeless feet in rags for warmth, and he must have been as tired as everyone else, as well as worried about his wife and child, walking with the baggage. He still looked as if he were merely out for a gentle stroll on a summer's afternoon.

'I am so sorry,' stammered Hanley, still dull witted. He could not believe that he had fallen asleep while marching.

'It takes you that way, sometimes,' said Dobson. The veteran had been much less withdrawn since recovering from his drunk. 'Trick is to make the most of it.'

'Ten-minute rest.' Pringle passed on the order. Most of the

men took off their packs and sat on them. Pipes were lit. One or two men slept.

By the time they moved again, Hanley was starting to feel the cold. The road continued to climb, and as it did, the temperature dropped. The gradient was designed to allow carts to pass, but even so he found his legs were aching with the steady climb. He was hot when they were moving, and had to pull his heavy cloak tightly around him whenever they halted. Pringle came to chat for a while, and then returned to his place beside the front rank. Hanley did his best to keep his mind occupied. He thought of paintings he liked, and tried to remember any where the landscapes were covered in snow. None had ever looked as bleak as these hills. Then for some reason lines of the *Iliad* came to him, and so he tried to recite softly all that he could remember of the poem, with all its vigour, horror, jealousy and friendship. It seemed more immediate to him than ever before. A cynical part of him wondered whether Achilles and Ajax were as scruffy and tired as the men around him. It would have been dust rather than mud and snow, but no doubt the plains of Ilium were uncomfortable enough in their own way. He thought of men in bronze helmets and armour with brazen shields, fighting and dying while infested with lice and weak from dysentery.

They marched all night and into the next day. Major MacAndrews had known a few uncomfortable New Year's Eves in the past. He had been not quite sixteen when they were called out in the dying days of '76 to chase George Washington. He told himself that that cold had been worse and that he was getting soft now. Most of the time he walked rather than rode, using his horse only if he needed to go quickly to the rear of the battalion or was summoned by one of the generals.

The major saw his wife only briefly. Esther rode with the baggage ahead of the battalion, helping and encouraging the wives. Most of the time she kept little Sal perched in front of her. The child said little. At one point Mrs MacAndrews trotted back to speak to her husband as he led the 106th. There was no privacy, and so their greeting was reserved and their conversation light and about little things. Sal said nothing at all, and flinched when the major reached out to pat her hand. The girl's eyes were empty, but lit up with mingled excitement and fear when Esther MacAndrews set off again at a canter.

Esther returned twice more, and took the time to assure the married soldiers that their families were coping. On the final visit, she stopped again beside her husband. This time they said no words, and simply looked. Major MacAndrews reached up a hand and pressed her arm gently. For a while the cold did not seem so bad.

It was a long day, for the battalion covered twenty-two miles and stopped half a dozen times to form up with the rest of the Reserve Division and face the French whenever the latter pressed on the hussars. There was no fighting, but it all took time. They were still on the road long after it was dark, and one day and one year stretched into the next. Opinion was divided over when midnight fell, as none of the officers' watches appeared to agree. At some point it became the first day of the New Year. Fatigue overcame any real enthusiasm.

At dawn the 106th saw a town ahead of them, the road running down through a steep ravine.

15

Williams slipped on a patch more ice than snow and only just broke his fall with his arms. Little Jacob began to cry, jerked from sleep by the sharp motion. Williams pushed himself upwards, almost sliding back again, before his worn boots found some grip. The baby's cries were muffled by the thick greatcoat. The going had been treacherous for the last few hours, and Miss MacAndrews was unable to control the mare, maintain a secure seat and keep the infant warm and safe at the same time. In spite of this, she was most reluctant to give him charge of the boy. Jane had insisted on dismounting, leading the horse and clutching Jacob tightly to her, singing softly to him whenever he grew restless.

Miss MacAndrews was an active young woman, and under normal circumstances Williams would have admired her determination and pluck. Yet as they had climbed higher the snow had grown deeper. Her smooth-soled riding boots gave her poor footing. A shrivelled thorn bush, hidden in the snow, snagged the hem of her dress and tore it. Many brisk walks in more or less clement weather were no real preparation for days of travelling harder and faster than she had ever done before. The girl flagged, although it was some time before Williams could persuade her to admit any fatigue, and convince her that she must ride, at least for a while.

He took over the task of carrying the child, making his long crimson sash into a sling and wearing his greatcoat over the top. After a brief protest, Jacob accepted this new accommodation and dozed off. Now he was awake again, and as Williams opened his coat he saw the little face screwed up as the boy screamed.

'May I have the milk?' he called over the noise of the howling wind. Earlier in the day he had seen footprints like those of dog, only larger. He knew wolves were common in these hills, and hoped that the howling and other eerie sighs they heard were just flukes of the wind among the rocks. They saw seen no sign of human enemies, and that was a relief.

'Really, Mr Williams,' Jane shouted down to him, 'a baby does not always cry because he is hungry.'

A raw scent grew prodigiously until Williams felt it was overwhelming him. He had to concede the wisdom of Miss Mac-Andrews' statement.

'I believe I may need a new sash after this.' He cupped his hand to call to her. Jane smiled weakly. Snow began to fall, whipping around them in the gusts of wind. 'We need some shelter.' The girl nodded.

The baby was still crying. 'Try singing to him,' Miss Mac-Andrews suggested.

They trudged up the slope, Bobbie's head down, but her stride sure footed, and Williams' rendition of 'The Minstrel Boy' drifting on the wind. The top of the rise revealed a distressingly empty valley, but there was a line of human footprints running along the slope beneath them, and it seemed as good a plan as any to follow them. Fortunately the snow stopped and left the trail clear. After a mile they saw a stone cottage clinging to the slope most sheltered from the wind. Knocking on the door eventually prompted it to be drawn back wide enough for suspicious eyes to peer out at them. They belonged to a thick-bearded man wearing a faded red headscarf. His manner was brusque, but seeing in them no danger, he ushered them into his home with considerable dignity. As usual there was just one big room, filled with smoke from the central fire. Three goats occupied one corner, and the man, his wife and their four children – none of them older than seven – lived in the remainder. The visitors were given a patch of the floor beside the fire. The family's meal, a greasy stew, heavy in oil and reeking of garlic, was shared.

It was a sign of his hunger that Williams bolted down the mixture quickly, his obvious enjoyment very pleasing to the wife, whose long, thin hair was grey, her skin heavily wrinkled even though she was barely in her middle twenties. She provided milk for young Jacob, and also heated water, and helped Jane as she bathed the child. It was clearly a process rarely undergone by her own offspring, and all sat and watched in silence, as if this was great entertainment. The husband talked cheerfully to Williams all the while, oblivious to the fact that his guest seldom replied, and indeed understood barely a tenth of the strongly accented words.

For a while Williams and Jane sat side by side, with their backs to the wall and their feet near the fire. Their host continued to speak at length of life in the hills. Jane cradled the baby in her arms. Williams could not quite remember when and how he placed his arm around the girl's shoulders. Miss MacAndrews did not shy away, and indeed was soon leaning to him. He wondered whether he had ever before been so happy. They slept well that night, lying on straw with the baby between them. Jane had Williams' blanket, while he used his greatcoat as covering.

The next day was better in every respect. The snow had stopped and as they continued along the valley, they were sheltered from all save occasional gusts of wind. At times the sun broke through the clouds, and although the glint off the snow was harsh, Williams as always was cheered by the brightness. Miss MacAndrews was reassured to once again have charge of the baby, for the going was good, and the one-eyed mare docile and happy to be moving after a night spent in the cold.

At times it seemed as if they had the world to themselves. Williams tried singing again when Jacob cried and would not be placated, and for a while his deep voice echoed along the valley. Surprise, fear or genuine pleasure quieted the child, who soon afterwards was feeding with every sign of contentment.

Much of the time they talked. Unusually, Miss MacAndrews

spoke of her own life at some length. She told stories of growing up in garrisons in the West Indies and Canada, of the eccentricities of her parents, and the opulent life of her mother's family in America.

'The heat in Charleston is oppressive,' she said. 'One drinks iced water and tries to do as little as possible.'

'It must be dreadful.' Williams clapped his gloved hands together to bring some life back to his fingers.

'And the winters in Nova Scotia would make this seem like a mild spring day.' Her tone was flat.

'Then perhaps we must consider ourselves fortunate.' Williams tried to match her mock seriousness, as he watched the sparkle growing in her eyes.

'Of course, in Canada you spend a lot of time next to a roaring fire, and venture out only when swathed in furs.'

'I knew there would be catch,' he said, and then they both burst out laughing, not stopping until Jacob began to cry. They talked no more until he was calm, and then, somewhat to her own surprise, Jane began to tell him of her dim memories of the brother and sister who had died when she was young, and the sorrow she knew dogged her parents over this loss, and that of an older brother who had succumbed to fever long before she was born.

'Every year, at the beginning of May, Mama would be sad. She spoke less than usual, often remaining in the house for days on end, instead of busying herself with the life of the garrison.' Williams found it hard to imagine the formidable Mrs Mac-Andrews being so subdued. 'Father would be on edge, not quite understanding how she felt, but knowing that she was suffering, and knowing why, and doing everything he could to comfort her.

'They did not snap at me, even though when I was very small I did not understand, and tried as a child to be more lively to make them happy. I was inclined to sing and dance,' she said archly.

'No doubt a delightful performance.' Williams' smile faded almost immediately. 'You were little. It is hard for a child to understand. I can only dimly remember my father. He was big, but his voice was soft and his ways gentle. He always smelt of oil and his clothes were stained with grease.' He smiled. 'My mother complained all the time about the disreputable state of his hand-kerchiefs, saying that they were not fit for washing, but deserved to be burned.' The smile faded. 'I know I felt sadness when he died, but I doubt a child really understands.'

'Or rather understands as a child?' Jane nodded. 'Sometimes I saw Mama weeping. Once I came into the room and she and father were embracing, each of them sobbing as they clung so tightly to each other that it was a wonder they could breathe.

'I never saw anything so sad, or so frightening,' she said.

Williams felt bold enough to hold the girl's hand. 'I never knew my mother to cry,' he said.

Williams listened more than he spoke, but later Jane coaxed him to tell of his own family, of how the young widow raised four children. Jane asked him about his sisters, and he expressed a devout wish that one day she would be gracious enough to let him introduce them to her.

'I shall look forward to making their acquaintance. If they resemble their brother, then I am sure that we shall be friends.' On that more formal note, they lapsed into silence.

In the middle of the day they found shelter in a cluster of a dozen or so buildings around a tiny chapel. The people were wary, until the production of a few coins, and the encourage-ment of a priest who seemed to be the only well-fed person in the place, produced bread, cheese, a little wine, and milk for the baby. They sat at a table in the main room of the only substantial house in the place. Almost the entire population came to stare at them.

Williams tried conversing with the priest in his own fragile Latin and failed to get any response, apart from apparent agree-ment through nods and smiles to everything he said. Later, Jane was able to pick out enough words to hear the man explaining to his flock that England was a desperately cold country, next to Denmark, where God punished the Protestants who lived there with a vile climate and a people inclined to criminality. Several crossed themselves.

In the afternoon, their conversation was lighter. When they spoke of schooling, Miss MacAndrews joked about Thwackum and Square, and was pleasantly surprised when Williams recognised the allusion.

' "His natural parts were not of the first rate, but he had greatly improved them by a learned education," ' quoted Williams. 'Though clearly not to any great profit, as the contradictory views attributed to him make clear.'

For some time they discussed Fielding's hero, the officer insisting on a degree of stern disapproval at the roughness of his virtue, while Miss MacAndrews defended Jones on the basis of his essentially good heart.

'And at least from the beginning he shows finer feelings,' she said. 'How does it go? ". . . for though he did not always act rightly, yet he never did otherwise without feeling and suffering for it". He may do wrong with Molly, but at least tries to set things right – and that to a woman who has deceived him, and been as much the cause of his ruin as her own.'

The situation of the poacher's daughter was too close for his comfort to Jenny's indiscretions with Redman and Hatch and perhaps other officers. It was a sad thought, and quickly followed by fear that the girl had walked away to her own death somewhere in the grim mountains.

Then Williams looked at Miss MacAndrews and saw her far more animated than for days. Talk of books was an escape from their own plight, and it was clearly doing her good. Frowning, he tried to think of a good answer.

'Yet is it enough to make a hero fairly virtuous, winning our sympathies because those around him are worse? Should not the hero – or indeed the heroine – not have high qualities in his or her own right?'

'That sets a high standard,' came Jane's swift response. 'The hero must triumph over adversity, but surely it is no less a triumph if the obstacles come from his own weaknesses. Indeed, perfect virtue is less than inspiring. Or would you have every hero an Aeneas, who only comes to brief life when behaving in a blackguardly manner to poor Dido?'

The sudden shift to the classics chimed well with Williams' taste and knowledge, and soon their discussion blossomed to consider more of the Ancients. Jane remained surprised at how familiar he was even with the poets, for his distaste for Ovid was based on a fair degree of acquaintance. She defended his poems for the richness and beauty of the language, as much for the sake of argument as from any firm commitment. Like their controversies, this was keenly fought, but always with goodwill, and indeed with much laughter.

They went higher just once, to cross over a saddle and enter a valley that pointed in a better direction. As darkness began to fall they could see it led down to a distinct track. It was too late to follow it, and the discovery close by of a shepherd's stone hut with a turf roof provided them with a decent prospect for warmth and shelter overnight. There was no sign of recent occupation, but the stocks of chopped straw had been disturbed and scattered by the visit of some small animal. They were still ample, and there was space to bring the horse inside. Soon a fire was burning, and the place had a warm comfort about it in spite of the smell of horse and harness, and the remarkably powerful odour produced just after they arrived by young Jacob.

While Miss MacAndrews cared for the child and assembled a meal for them from the provisions they had obtained earlier in the day, Williams attended to Bobbie, realising that he had been inclined to neglect her in recent days. Afterwards they ate, and took turns to hold the baby and sing softly to him until the lad at last was claimed by sleep. Jane smiled with considerable fondness as she placed him gently down in a nest of straw covered with a blanket. The smile broadened when she noticed Williams looking dismayed as he held up his sash. The officer laid it down with some distaste and then began to clean the pistol he had found in Pringle's saddle holster. His sword lay beside him awaiting the same treatment. Jane looked at her jacket sadly, and wished for a needle and thread to restore some of its buttons. Still more she wished that she had some means of repairing the tear in her skirt, which she was convinced had grown longer. That only prompted more unavailing wishes, and she ran her hands through her long hair and thought gloomily that it must be in a dreadful state.

They busied themselves about their separate tasks for a while, sometimes sitting, sometimes weaving around each other as they needed. Miss MacAndrews was carrying her jacket to drape it over the piled saddle when she realised that she had trodden on the hem of her dress. Putting her weight on the other foot, she reached down to pluck away the material and hold it out of harm's way. She lost balance and stumbled, falling against Williams just as he turned towards her. His arms closed around her by instinct. Each was surprised, and for just an instant there was a flicker of fear in Jane's eyes, their pale blue-grey looking dark in the poor light.

Neither spoke and neither moved. The fire crackled, and Bobbie stamped his front hoof and snorted to himself.

With a boldness he had never dreamed he possessed, Williams leaned down and kissed Jane on the lips. He felt her tremble faintly – or was that him? Did she push him away for a moment, or was that also his imagination? It did not matter because then she was kissing back. The jacket fell and her arms clasped him, just as his own pulled her tightly to him.

They kissed hungrily, mouths beginning to part, and Williams lifted her in his arms until her booted feet were in the air and her face level with his. For a moment their lips separated and Jane sighed her affection as he kissed her cheek and neck devouringly, until she turned her head and forced their mouths back together.

He set her down, and one hand ran through her curls. Jane's hair was long and thick. In the last week it had been drenched by river and storm, had rested as she slept on dirt floors in smoke-filled rooms. Williams had never felt anything so soft, unless it was her skin.

'Jane, I love you, Jane,' he whispered in a brief pause between kisses.

His chin felt rough to her, rubbing against her own face. His fine hair had begun to create a thin stubble after days without shaving. She did not care, and her hands grabbed either side of his head, as if she could somehow pull them even closer together. She moaned softly.

Williams' other hand ran down the small of her back, feeling the rigid stays, until it was lower, touching soft flesh beneath the layers of fabric. It all seemed so easy, so very natural. Memory led him to the ivory buttons on the shoulder of her dress, and this time they slid from their places so very easily.

Jane hesitated, pulling away from his kiss, but not the embrace.

'I think I love . . .' she whispered, and neither was sure who moved so that their lips were together again.

He unfastened the first of the hooks at the rear of the dress. At the second it noticeably slackened its grip around her. When the third was open he slid his hand beneath, feeling the laces of her stays. His other hand began to gather a bunch of her skirt, clasping her leg through it and lifting.

Jacob woke and screamed, bawling out his protest at a world where he was not granted instant food and attention.

Williams felt the change. The girl no longer met his kisses, and a slight shift made their embrace no longer so natural.

Little Jacob cried. Miss MacAndrews pushed gently. Williams leaned forward to kiss her closed lips, desperate to preserve the moment. Miss MacAndrews became more forceful. He let go of her leg, and then his other hand came away. He could not bring himself to step back.

She looked at him, head leaning slightly to one side, then moved away, and her loosened dress began to fall from her shoulders until she grabbed it and held it in place. Trying to do up the hooks at the back, the girl went over to the baby. She picked the boy up, cradling him and crooning softly.

'Get some milk.'

Williams obeyed, although all of his movements felt sluggish.

166

They said nothing else for the rest of the evening. Miss Mac-Andrews' expression made it very clear that the earlier incident was not to be repeated. After a while, with Jacob at peace again, they lay down with the baby between them. Williams slept little. His mind was still exhilarated and reeling from the ecstasy of holding the girl, of feeling her lips on his, her warmth, her softness. He did not know how far ardent passion would have carried them. The honourable, God-fearing and decent gentleman he hoped himself to be knew he should feel guilt for his own loss of control, and assured him that it was as well the interruption had come. He had been given a taste of the true bliss he could expect if ever he proved so fortunate as to make Miss MacAndrews his wife, and that in itself was a wonderful thing, and more than sufficient. Another, regrettably persistent voice cursed the infant for choosing such an untimely moment to wake. All of him, noble and ignoble alike, tried to preserve every memory and every sensation of those few brief minutes.

Miss MacAndrews seemed especially distant the next morning, and Williams also struggled to converse easily. The pair avoided each other's gaze. They spoke only when the situation required, usually about the baby. Jane was worried that he had developed a temperature. Williams did not think the child's forehead felt any different, but the concern began to nag at him as they followed the track.

'I wonder what has become of Mrs Hanks?' Miss MacAndrews asked after a particularly long spell of silence. In spite of her coarseness and outright vulgarity, Jane had rather liked the other girl. It troubled her to think that she had really abandoned her child.

'I hope she has better fortune than her foolishness deserves,' came the reply, and she could not decide whether his mixture of stern judgement and sympathy was admirable or a mark of coldness.

Not long afterwards, they heard the shouting. Then shots rang out, echoing up from a bend in the valley.

16

Bodies lay everywhere. In this alley it was hard to walk and not tread on human flesh. Major MacAndrews wished that his wife had not insisted on coming with him. He could see that she was at least as tired as he was, and a natural protectiveness convinced him that she was less able to bear it. It was also a shame that she should have to see this. There was no reason to expect that they would find any sign of their daughter, or indeed his missing officer. Nevertheless, they both tramped through the streets, as they did at each new town on the road. Behind them came the grenadiers and Number One Company. The rest of the battalion was allocated to clear up different parts of the town.

There were hundreds stretched in the mud of Bembibre – perhaps even thousands. Most were men, but there were a good number of women and even a few children.

'Good God alive,' said MacAndrews as he looked down at a child of no more than ten, bare legged and sprawled beside her mother. He could no longer remember a worse New Year.

'Animals.' It took a good deal to shock his wife. 'Just animals, or perhaps worse because beasts cannot know right from wrong.'

Nearly all the men wore filthy and stained red coats. Here and there was the dark blue of an artilleryman or hussar, and just occasionally the green of a rifleman. A few moved, stirring slightly or moaning. The rest lay completely still, snow beginning to gather on them. Everywhere were dark red pools. From many an open mouth a thin stream of thick red liquid trickled.

'Is the whole damned army drunk?' Esther asked her husband. It was not a joke. In her voice was a doubt he had rarely heard before in all their long years of marriage. Amid such appalling scenes of collapse and disaster, her worst fears no longer seemed impossible. She shook her head, and some of the familiar spirit returned. 'No wonder you lost America.'

MacAndrews took her hand, then had to let it go as they stepped around a circle of half a dozen redcoats and a couple of their women, all passed out where they had been licking the same pool of spilled wine. Behind them, the men of the 106th prodded, kicked and yelled at the prostrate figures. A few were already dead from the cold.

The Grenadier Company worked its way down a section of one of the side streets. Hanley stayed outside, supervising the men as they woke the sleepers in the street and dragged the dead clear of the track, while Pringle led parties of men into the buildings. In one house his grenadiers found a cellar flooded with wine where a row of barrels had been sprung open. Three redcoats floated where they had drowned when they grew insensibly drunk. The air was heavy with the smell of strong wine. Billy Pringle struggled to breathe as he leaned against the wall.

'Waste of good wine,' he managed to croak, and then with a gesture set the men to work clearing up. There was neither sign nor scent of any corruption, and he wondered whether that was because of the cold or the alcohol. Concentrating on such an unimportant point kept him from facing the full squalor of the scene.

Hanley watched almost dispassionately as grenadiers came out of the house carrying the sodden corpses and piled them up outside next to the wall. As he had often found since joining the army, the sights of war had an unreality about them. The still, silent stack of bodies added to the impression of some overly romantic painting of a massacre, although in all those he could remember the corpses were far more decorous. None of the men looked that different from his own soldiers, and he found himself staring at the grenadiers, trying to guess whether they were stirred by disgust or envy at the sights. Then his thoughts were interrupted when Sergeant Rawson growled at two of their men who had lifted the skirts of some drunken women and were comparing observations.

There was not enough water to waste by pouring it over the prostrate forms. Some could be shaken or struck awake. Murphy and Eyles began lifting men, so that Dobson could slap them with great vigour across the face. It worked in most cases. They even started wondering in jest how many blows from the veteran would be needed. One Highlander took no fewer than six, and as the man staggered off, the bruises were clear on his face. Hanley wondered whether there was a danger of making the victims even more insensible. The 106th were tired, and had hoped for rest once they arrived rather than this arduous duty. He was sure they were beginning to relish the violence, taking out their anger on the men who made this task necessary. Even so, a good third of the drunkards could not be roused, and many more were doubtless concealed in the houses.

The two companies reached one of the main roads, just as Sir John and his staff passed. Hanley watched as the general nodded to Major MacAndrews, and raised his hat courteously to the major's wife, but the general's gaze remained high, almost as if he could not bring himself to look at the chaos. Bembibre was in wine country – the 106th had marched past a long succession of well-tended vineyards as they came down into the town. As the leading divisions arrived at the town, soldiers had dispersed in search of the cellars. Some of their officers were too tired to stop them, many more lagging behind exhausted and reaching the town long after the damage had been done. The few that tried succeeded only in preventing some of the redcoats from joining their fellows. When casks were smashed to destroy the contents before harm could be done, soldiers and their women lapped like dogs at the liquid and the mud it had fallen into. The other divisions had marched this morning for Villafranca, leaving behind this debris.

'Infamous, quite infamous.' Hanley just caught the words as Moore passed.

Once the general and his staff were gone, the grenadiers hustled the recovered men into the road, and jeered them as they began to stagger off towards the gate and on to the road to follow their regiments. Among the drunks were a few men with bandaged feet, whose exhaustion had made them fall behind. There was some sympathy for their plight, although not as much as Hanley would have liked to see.

On the whole, the discipline of the 106th held. The entire battalion was quartered in a cavernous church that night. Mac-Andrews had the Colours stacked on the altar and sentries placed to honour them, and also to prevent the rail and everything else being torn up for firewood. The commissaries had brought them meat from slaughtered oxen. It was tough, but could eventually be boiled so that it was good enough to eat. There was little apart from the meat to add to the stew, until a crate of stale biscuit was discovered and distributed to be added to the liquids boiling in the camp kettles. The grenadiers acquired a couple of sheep, and Hanley guessed that Eyles was capable of other impersonations apart from making chicken noises. There was some wine passed around, but nothing excessive, at least under the gaze of the officers. Dobson had also given loud expression to his enjoyment in hitting drunks, and the big man had made it clear that he stood ready to dole out similar treatment to anyone there.

Hanley sketched for the first time since the retreat. The light in the church was not good, and he tried to capture the weird shadows, and the ungainly, in some cases almost grotesque, figures of the ragged soldiers and their women. He and Pringle chatted with each other and with some of the other fellows until weariness caught up with them. They slept well, and to everyone's surprise went undisturbed by any fresh alarms.

Parade the next morning revealed twenty-eight men absent from the battalion. It was fewer than MacAndrews had feared, although still a shameful enough total. As far as he could tell, the other regiments in the reserve had suffered similar losses. Pringle and Hanley were both relieved to see Dobson in his place beside Rawson on the flank of the company formation. None of the grenadiers was missing, and both officers suspected that this was due in no small measure to the veteran. They hoped that his new-found abstinence would last, as would his determination to impose the same restraint on others. Pringle was sure that one or two of the men had vanished during the night, and had no doubt been out scavenging, breaking into houses, and stealing wine and valuables. The mutton shared with the officers last night was surely only a tiny part of what was taken. Fear of Dobson, more than fear of the sergeants, let alone concern for his and Hanley's vigilance, had meant that all were back by dawn, and at least fairly sober.

The battalion soon resumed the task of routing out the drunks and stragglers. It was colder this morning, and the 106th's enthusiasm for the task had worn thin. It was no longer a game, and the general feeling was that such fools should be left to their fate. A few of their own missing men were found, some emerging sheepishly with bulging packs from houses. MacAndrews had Sergeant Major Fletcher search each one and throw away any likely plunder.

Few of the drunks could be roused. Those most inclined to recover and press on had mainly been found the day before. Time seemed to have permitted few to sober up. Some may well have done so during the hours of darkness, only to drink themselves into a deeper stupor.

The Grenadier Company swept along one of the longer streets, doing what they could to get the stragglers moving. Pringle and Hanley walked side by side, but at first neither had anything to say and they strolled along in silence. Before long parties of hussars began moving back through the town.

'Reckon the French are snapping at our heels,' said Pringle.

Hanley was stamping his feet to keep warm. Even with his cloak over his jacket he felt chilled to the bones. 'About time. I have grown tired of this place.' For all his fatigue, he was looking forward to the march and the warmth it would bring.

'Yes, the French are welcome to it.'

'I am beginning to feel that way about all of Spain.' Hanley was obviously in low spirits. As they watched two of the grenadiers lifted one of the prostrate drunks and shook the man. He protested, but slumped to the ground as soon as they let go. They kicked at him and swore at him, smashing the bottle he clutched in his hand. The soldier – his jacket had yellow facings – refused to get up, and so with a final curse they left him.

Two hussars trotted past. 'Did I tell you that I had a chat with some of the fellows from the Twenty-eighth yesterday,' began Billy Pringle. He loved telling a good story and was always eager for the latest gossip in the army. 'One of their captains has been pretty sick so was travelling stretched out in a cart, rolled up snug and warm and sipping champagne no doubt.'

'Lazy devils, captains,' muttered Hanley.

'Well, there he is, going on his merry way, when he hears some noise and notices an hussar riding past. "Hey there, dragoon!" our gallant captain calls out. "What news?" Much to his surprise the hussar looked angry. "News, sir? The only news I can give you is that unless you step along like soldiers and don't wait to pick your steps like bucks in Bond Street of a Sunday with shoes and silk stockings, damn it, you'll all be prisoners!"'

Pringle was already beginning to laugh at what he knew was coming. As usual it was infectious, and his friend could not help grinning in anticipation. '"Who the devil are you?" says our hero from his chariot. "I am Lord Paget, sir, and pray who the devil are you?" So the poor unfortunate captain goes white as a sheet and stammers out his name. Then the general makes him get out of his cart and march with the men!' Billy had gone bright red, his face creased in the deepest amusement. Hanley found this as entertaining as the story itself.

Ensign Hatch appeared from an alley, leading a file of redcoats from his company.

'Seen anybody we know?' he asked cheerfully.

Pringle had not yet recovered himself, so it was Hanley who shook his head, assuming that Hatch was asking after stragglers from the battalion.

'Well, easy enough to understand a fellow deciding that

captivity might be a good deal more comfortable than struggling on with the rest of us.' The ensign was still smiling, but Hanley was not quite sure whether there was an edge to his voice.

At that moment Brotherton rode past, calling out that the regiment was to muster on the far side of the town. The French were coming and it was time to go. They left the remaining drunks. In spite of all the efforts there still seemed to be hundreds lying unconscious in the streets and houses.

The 106th had not brought its full band on campaign, but MacAndrews had insisted that a dozen fifers bring their instruments. He formed these up with as many drummers beside the battalion and had them play during the muster. When the division moved off, they marched at the head of the battalion. Hanley had never particularly liked the thin music of these instruments, but had to admit that now he found himself standing tall, and marching with an enthusiasm for more than simply getting warm. The music appeared to call out to the stragglers, and a few dozen swayed to their feet at its call, and trickled out of the town to follow the column as it began to climb the long slope beyond the town.

Major MacAndrews was on horseback for the moment, and the added height allowed him to see the untidy little procession of the division's baggage, a mile or so ahead at the crest. He could not single out his wife, but there was reassurance in knowing she was there. Halfway up the slope their brigade was ordered to halt and form up facing back towards Bembibre, covering the last outposts of the cavalry as they pulled back. The French cavalry were already entering the town, prompting the whole place to stir into life like a disturbed anthill. The 106th watched as men and women who had lain like corpses were seized by an instinctive terror of the enemy and sprang to their feet. Hundreds were running.

It was too late. The French cavalry were not inclined to burden themselves with too many prisoners. Perhaps they were also angry at their repulse by the British days before, or contemptuous of such a rabble. The 106th were too far away to hear the screams. They saw the glitter of swords being drawn, watched as the horsemen broke up and rode among the mob of fugitives, hacking down efficiently and without mercy. They killed men, women and children alike. Pringle had passed Williams' telescope to Hanley, and so he saw more detail as one green-jacketed chasseur chopped down to fell a plump woman in a drab and tattered dress, then urged his horse on, passing a fleeing soldier and decapitating him with a single cut. He snapped the glass shut, and wished he had never looked. He could not see Hatch, who must have been back with his own company, otherwise he would have asked the ensign whether French captivity still appeared so comfortable.

'Bastards.' Hanley heard Dobson's angry comment beside him, interrupting his thoughts. For once, that particular insult did not seem so distasteful to him. The grenadiers were gripping their muskets tightly in silent rage. None of the fugitives reached the safety of the reserve. The French came out of the town, but formed up warily when they saw the British rearguard. There was no attempt to molest the withdrawal, and the enemy simply watched, shadowing them from a distance. Battalions retired alternately until they reached the crest, so that several were always formed in case the enemy pushed on. They did not, and soon the whole division was marching together, leaving the hussars and some outposts of the 95th to cover the rear. Twice more in the day all or part of the division stopped, when it seemed that the enemy cavalry was coming closer. Nothing happened before they again resumed the retreat.

In the early afternoon the 106th were left behind. The road curved around a spur, and this, combined with a straggling patch of woodland, allowed them to form line so that they would become visible only when the leading Frenchmen turned the corner. The battalion eagerly anticipated the volley they would pour into them when they did. The rest of the division marched on, moving as noisily and visibly as they could, and only a few patrols of hussars remained behind, for the valley was too narrow for the cavalry to operate effectively in any numbers. It was no doubt this that made the French cautious. After half an hour the hussars came to report that the enemy had halted. Reluctantly, MacAndrews took his men back to rejoin the rest of the reserve.

No one paid much attention any more to the dead horses, oxen and mules which lay by the roadside. There were human corpses as well, some of them women, and a few the tiny forms of children. It was a long time since anyone had thought of stopping to bury them. Nor was much attention paid to the stragglers from the divisions ahead of them, some sitting mutely, staring into nothing, others stumbling on with feet wrapped in bloodstained rags.

'Better hurry, boys, or the French will get you!' called Murphy to some they passed. The sergeants more formally yelled at them to press on and rejoin their regiments. The lucky ones were given lifts behind one of the hussars, but they were few.

Hanley counted nineteen milestones before they stopped, outside the village of Cacabellos with its bridge. They formed up again in columns at quarter-distance facing towards the enemy, but the French failed to appear. The men were allowed to stand at ease, and he heard more talk than had been usual in the last few days. They knew the rest of the army was in Villafranca, just five or so miles farther on, and there were hopes expressed that it contained plentiful food, good billets and a rest. Best of all were rumours that the general would at long last let them loose on the enemy.

'He's been biding his time,' said Murphy. 'Luring them on before we hit 'em hard.'

'We'll show 'em ,' said a private named King, whom Murphy disliked intensely. Today his overall goodwill permitted him to accept the man's support.

'Sure we will! Just like Portugal. Mark my words, our Johnny-boy will give them a drubbing they'll long remember.'

'Bastards need a lesson,' was Dobson's only comment, but Hanley thought his tone was dubious.

Johnny-boy himself arrived not long afterwards. His horse was lathered in sweat, and his normally impassive face alight with cold rage. Sir John had just come from Villafranca, where all the worst indiscipline of Bembibre was being repeated. The redcoats broke into homes, stealing and threatening the inhabitants. They broke into army stores, scattering, destroying or spoiling as much as they took. Doors were ripped off hinges, anything wooden prised away and burnt. Nothing and no one appeared to be safe in this drunken rampage. Hearing that even the Reserve Division was shedding stragglers and had left men behind at the start of the day, Sir John was determined to shame at least these back into order. He reined in his light bay with some savagery, making the animal rear in front of the battalion columns.

'All my life I have been proud to be a soldier of Britain. This red coat,' he stretched his arm out wide, 'is as much a badge of honour as my sword.

'Now I am ashamed. Ashamed to wear the same uniform as men who so forget both honour and duty as to misbehave so very disgracefully in the very face of the enemy.' Graham did not believe that he had ever seen Moore so publicly angry. 'Men lie drunk instead of attending to their duty. They steal and destroy instead of listening to their officers. Some of those officers neglect their men and permit them to perpetrate such abuses.' MacAndrews was unsure it was quite proper to criticise officers in front of their men. Such damning verdicts, even if justified, were hardly likely to encourage obedience to those very men. Yet he understood the fury and shame of the general. The 106th behaved better than most, and that consoled him, but he confessed that even in the battalion there were more abuses than he would have liked.

'So many men were left behind at Bembibre. I have never wanted one of the men under my command to die or fall into enemy hands without great need or useful purpose. Yet now I cannot envy the French. What sort of victory have they won over hundreds of British cowards – for none but unprincipled cowards would get drunk in the presence, nay, the very sight, of the enemies of their country. What a rare prize for Bonaparte!

'Such conduct is infamous, utterly infamous. I am ashamed to be the commander of such a parcel of cowardly rogues. Sooner than survive the disgrace of such infamous misconduct, I hope that the first cannonball fired by the enemy may take me in the head!' MacAndrews was not unusually superstitious, but the phrase struck him as unlucky.

Graham followed the general as he galloped off, back along the road to Villafranca. The battalions of the reserve remained in column.

'Poor old fellow,' Dobson muttered, even though he and the general were of an age.

'Don't think we're to blame,' whispered Sergeant Rawson in reply. 'Sergeants not doing their jobs in other regiments.'

'And officers,' chipped in Murphy.

'Hush, man! It's the sergeants that matter. Now quiet yourself, here comes our own ray of sunshine.' Rawson had noticed General Paget walk his horse forward. Now that Sir John had disappeared, their own commander, a man to whom temper came naturally, would take over and let his men know that they had crimes enough of their own.

'I have nothing to say about the other divisions of this army. You are the Reserve Division, the corps chosen to occupy the place of honour. When a single one of you gets drunk, it brings shame on your regiment and shame on your country. The French are over there!' He pointed down the road along which they had come. 'If any one of you gets drunk, his dishonour threatens disaster to the entire army. We cover the retreat, and you cannot damned well do that if you are lying stretched out in your own puke.

'I don't care what you rogues think you have done in the past. Every moment now you must consider yourselves in the place of greatest honour on the field of battle. There can be no excuses, no pardons. As a reminder, the division will camp here, outside the village. You have all damned well lost the right to sleep under roofs and can bloody well make do with the bare earth and the sky for covering. This is your punishment. I shall share it with you, but the worse punishment is to lead men such as you. You shall not disappoint me again!'

As they were dismissed, Murphy let out a long breath. 'Do you think we have upset him?' Privately he worried about his wife and baby having to sleep in the cold.

Orders arrived that no soldier would be permitted among the houses unless at all times commanded by an officer or NCO. Work parties went in for food and fuel. The commissaries were able to organise a reasonable amount of both. Food was again mainly meat from slaughtered bullocks.

It stayed dry, but the temperatures dropped and Pringle distinctly saw the frost gathering on Williams' backpack as it lay beside him. Each company managed to make one decent fire, and in turn the kettles from individual messes were supported over the flames to cook.

Pringle was visiting the sentries when they heard an unearthly sound of mingled moans and slithering. The nervous grenadier crossed himself and then aimed his firelock as they saw a dark shape crawling towards them on the ground. His companion reached a more optimistic conclusion.

'Wild hog,' he said, and licked his lips.

Billy Pringle told them to lower their weapons and ran to the shape, for he was sure now that it was a man. Later, as four men carried him in a blanket up to one of the fires, he was no longer so certain, and wondered whether he was looking at a corpse who simply had not actually stopped breathing. Hanley almost vomited at the sight. The man had dragged his shirt up over his head, whether for warmth or against the pain, and when they peeled it back it stuck several times on dried blood. His nose was split by a sabre cut, one of his ears gone altogether and the other a twisted remnant. Both cheeks were slashed open, and even his lips were hanging by slim threads of flesh. There were cuts to his arms and legs, and his jacket was slashed and stained in more places than they could easily count. They put him by the fire, and he thrust his fingers into the embers before he could feel any warmth.

'Frostbite,' Pringle whispered to Hanley.

In an uncanny voice which had more of a wounded animal than a human being about it, the man told them that he had been left behind in Bembibre. When he tried to eat, the fragment of meat fell out from his mutilated cheeks. Some wine went down, although as much or more spilt in every direction. They carried him to the village, getting him to one of the carts soon to head for Villafranca.

'Quite a day,' said Pringle, sighing as they watched the man carried off.

'Then make the most of it, tomorrow could be worse,' replied Hanley.

'What do you think, Dob?' asked Pringle, noticing that the old soldier stood near by.

'Biggest balls-up since Flanders, sir,' came the reply. It was easier to laugh than to think.

17

Another shot rang out as Williams made his way cautiously up the last stretch of the slope. He held his sword high. It was his only weapon. He had left the loaded pistol with Miss Mac-Andrews, and told her to flee at the first sign of danger. Whether or not she would follow the order was another matter. There were boulders on the slope, each slippery with ice, and patches where he sank down into several feet of snow.

It took a good five minutes to reach the top. Williams took off his forage cap and laid it down. Gently, he raised his head to peer over a large rock perched on the thin crest, and found himself looking straight into a man's face.

Williams flinched by sheer instinct, gasping out a startled yelp and ducking back down. At the same instant, he heard a flurry of robust, and definitely Anglo-Saxon oaths. Williams looked up again. The man wore the distinctive Tarleton helmet, with its high crest running from back to front. As far as he knew, only the British used the headgear, and then only for the light dragoons and some gunners. The man's dark blue jacket had red facings and three rows of brass buttons trimmed with gold lace. His overall trousers were grey, with a red stripe and more brass buttons. They were also undone, and the man's purpose in coming to this quiet patch sheltered by a cluster of rocks was immediately obvious. He noticed Williams' red coat, and looked relieved.

'Bloody hell, you gave me a turn, you daft sod.' His accent had the burr of the West Country – perhaps even Bristol itself, where Williams' family had lived for some years. His face was round, the cheeks ruddy, and the little hair visible beneath his helmet was close to the colour of straw. The impression of a slow-paced yokel was shattered, however, by the quick wit evident in his eyes and expression. He noticed the officer's epaulettes. 'Oh, sorry, sir. Didn't expect to see an officer.' The man stiffened to attention automatically. His hands were too busy to permit a salute. Steam rose into the air with the sound of a cascade impossible to stop.

'That's quite all right.' Williams smiled and kept his gaze high. 'You are something of a surprise to me, Driver . . . ?'

'Parker, sir.' The uniform was that of the Corps of Royal Artillery Drivers, formed just two years earlier. Such men were attached to each brigade of foot artillery, in charge of the horses, limbers and wagons that towed and supplied the guns. In the old days these tasks had fallen to civilians contracted for each campaign, who had frequently proved unreliable. The corps was under the control of the Board of Ordnance, which also oversaw the artillery, although it remained distinct in uniform. In its brief existence it had also acquired a reputation for indiscipline.

'Well, Parker, once you have finished, you can take me down to see whoever is in charge.' Williams turned and waved to Miss MacAndrews, indicating that things were safe and that she should ride round the valley floor to join him. For one short moment he had dared to hope that they had stumbled on the main army, although it seemed unlikely that they should be so far east. A longer glance at the little column was enough to crush that thought. They were not yet safe.

It took them a good five minutes to walk down the steep slope. Looking around, Williams realised that the valley they had been following led into a much wider one. Here the track was well defined and wide. A trail of hoof-prints and ruts led down as far as the halted column of artillery. There were two guns, each of them quite big by the look of things, with their limbers pulled by six horses. Four horses drew a long, four-wheeled wagon. A smaller cart was pushed to the side of the road and its team unharnessed. Two of the horses lay dead alongside it, and

Williams guessed that the shots had dispatched the animals. About a dozen men stood around the vehicles.

The man in charge wore the four yellow stripes of a quarter-master sergeant on his sleeves. 'Groombridge, sir.' He was short, very broad in the chest and must have been pushing fifty. He wore the uniform of the Royal Artillery itself, with its infantry-styled jacket in blue, and a shako.

'Pleased to see you, Mr Groombridge. My name is Williams, of the 106th. Although I must say surprised as well.'

'No more than us to see you.' Groombridge was precise in his speech, and his face gave nothing away, all the time exuding absolute confidence. He was not about to be impressed by some raw ensign. 'Didn't think any of us were out this far.'

'May I ask where you are going?'

'Mansilla, sir. We're taking these guns and equipment to give to the Dons. Beg pardon, sir, I mean the Spanish army.'

'Mansilla fell to the French days ago. We saw it happen.'

'We, sir?' Groombridge's voice betrayed the faintest trace of relief at this indication that the officer was not alone. At that moment, Jane walked Bobbie around the curve of the valley just over a hundred yards away.

'I am escorting Miss MacAndrews, the daughter of my commander,' explained Williams. 'We became cut off when the army began to retreat.' The drivers noticed that the rider was a woman. As she came closer it became evident that she was young and attractive.

Groombridge concealed his disappointment well, and if he was surprised at an officer traipsing around the countryside with a young woman then this was equally well hidden in manner of all good NCOs. 'Yes, sir. Very good , sir.' His eyes were pale grey, and still conveyed the innocence of childhood – at least until Mr Groombridge was roused. Then the rest of what Williams had said sank in. 'Retreating, sir?'

'How long have you been away from the army?'

'Three weeks now. We landed at Corunna and then waited there for these nags to arrive. It meant we left in dribs and drabs.

Lieutenant Simmons was in charge, but he fell ill ten days back, and told me to push on.'

Williams tried to explain what had happened in the campaign, realising that much could have happened since they were cut off. He doubted the British Army had halted yet, and the massacre at Mansilla made it even more unlikely that Romana's forces were in any fit state to resist the enemy.

'I think it would be best if you came along with me, Mr Groombridge,' said Williams, doing his best to adopt a tone that suggested no real alternative.

'Yes, sir.' The sergeant rather suspected that the lone officer would be coming along with him. 'We can't push too hard, though, because of the horses. There never was much strength to them, and we have been short of fodder.

'It breaks my heart, but we have to abandon the forge here.' He gestured at the two-wheeled cart whose team had been removed, and the two dead horses beside it. 'Poor things were lame.' Williams noted that the sergeant's tone made it absolutely clear that he was not about to abandon the guns or wagon to travel more quickly. In fact, he had dismissed that thought himself, at least for the moment, but it would be worth remembering that Groombridge's respect for rank extended only so far, at least for the moment.

'It's a pity.' The sergeant's accent had a trace of Kent. 'Because it's the only decent bit of work among the whole lot. Those carriages are twenty years old if they are a day.' He was pointing at the guns. Something had seemed odd about them from the beginning, and Williams at last realised what it was. They had twin trails, rather than the single, solid block trail now in use. 'Reckon we've been giving the Dons all the stuff we don't have a use for ourselves. And of course nobody much uses twelve-pounders any more, so the limbers and the ammunition cases are full of rusty old shot and charges of grape from the navy. God knows what they expect the dagoes to do with that. On a brass gun of all things. Won't half knacker the barrels.'

'Any other weapons?' asked the ensign.

Groombridge, who had joined the Royal Artillery as a boy, struggled for a moment with the idea that anyone who had two twelve-pounder cannons might require additional armament.

'Oh, I see. Four muskets, sir. The Wee Gees don't normally carry them, but as we were off on our own I reckoned it were worth having a few. There's two hundred cartridges.' Williams guessed the odd nickname must refer to the drivers.

'Provisions?'

'Biscuit and salt beef for another week. Rum for a fortnight. That's for myself, the two artificers and the ten drivers. Two sacks of oats left. We had some rye from a village a few days back, but I won't use that unless we get desperate.' Seeing the puzzled expression, the sergeant explained. 'It makes them crap. Sorry, sir, I mean it purges the horses something powerful.'

'Well, hopefully we can find some better fodder before long. Thank you, Mr Groombridge, that all sounds excellent.'

'Sir.' Groombridge saluted, and silently wondered just what the young officer felt he had added to the strength of their little band. Then he noticed that the pretty young woman on the horse was feeding a baby. Well, isn't that bloody marvellous, he thought to himself.

They pressed on. Miss MacAndrews took the baby and rode in the wagon. The driver was a cheerful Irishman, and one of the two artificers who also sat among the baggage and stores showed a great fondness for little Jacob. 'Raised four of my own,' he explained, and assured the young miss that the lad was not at all fevered and seemed in the bloom of health.

Groombridge rode a mule. He was still uncertain of what to make of the ensign, but had to admit that the arrival of a baby and a good-looking young woman had taken the men's minds off their sense of isolation.

Williams led Bobbie for a while, as the pace of the draught horses was slow. Later he rode for the first time in days. There was something reassuring about being among British faces and hearing English voices once again. Part of him regretted the inevitable loss of intimacy with Miss MacAndrews. There seemed now little chance that the all too brief and swiftly interrupted moment of lovemaking would be repeated. Nothing in the girl's demeanour had given him cause to hope for this. That had not prevented him dreaming of it, even when he told himself that he should not.

Meeting up with the little convoy also brought him new responsibilities, all of which needed to be handled delicately. Groombridge seemed a proud man, and was obviously highly experienced. Williams did not wish to offend him. That evening they halted in a tiny village. The inhabitants were relieved that no food was demanded, offered a little straw for the animals, and cheerfully made a fuss of the girl and the baby. Jane was given a tiny room to herself. The men were put in a barn with the horses. It was a big building, once used by the royal postal service until this shifted to the new road. By candlelight Williams and Groombridge studied the map. Nowhere as insignificant as this village was marked, nor was the little road they followed, but Williams had a fair idea where they were, and it was close enough to the sergeant's own guess for them both to be confident.

The main road was shown, and Williams had heard enough while he was still with the army to know that it was planned to follow it as far as Benevente, and probably Astorga.

'Napoleon himself has come against us with the greater part of his army. We must be outnumbered two or three to one, and the Spanish cannot help.'

'They don't seem to want to keep their own bloody country,' observed Groombridge.

Williams felt it better to ignore the comment. 'I do not believe that the general will be able to stop and fight. So he'll keep on going. Now, if we are here,' he pointed at the map, 'roughly, anyway, I would guess we are ten or fifteen miles north-west of Astorga. If you look the road will get closer if we keep going straight – and I reckon that's the way this track leads. We can't cut across to join them. We don't know where the French are, and cannot hope to sneak through with guns and a wagon.'

Groombridge nodded. 'The horses wouldn't stand for it anyway. I wouldn't trust them to last ten minutes off the track. If the snow gets deep or we reach a big slope we shall have to double up the teams anyway.'

'Yes, so our best hope is to keep going and try to reach the main road and the army higher up. Maybe Nogales or Lugo?' Groombridge nodded again. 'Say two or three days' time?'

'Depends on the road,' said the quartermaster doubtfully. 'And the nags.'

'I know.' Williams paused. 'Tomorrow I think that I will ride across the hills and see if I can pick up any word of the army as I get nearer to the grand road. Might help to guide us as to where to find them.' A difficult exchange with the villagers, incorporating as many gestures as words, had shown him a path leading off to the left which would take him towards Bembibre.

'Sir.' Groombridge's tone was neutral. Williams wondered what he thought of an officer who turned up one minute and then swanned off on his own the next. He thought for a moment of asking the sergeant to pay particular attention to the care of Miss MacAndrews and the child, and then decided that any hint of doubt over this or anything else was inappropriate. 'Do not wait for me, but push on at the best speed you can make. I'll find you.'

'Yes, sir.'

The next morning Williams had only a brief chance to speak to Miss MacAndrews as she and the baby were helped into the wagon. He explained what he was doing, loudly enough for the closest men to hear.

'It is a good day for a ride,' said Jane.

'It is,' he said.

'Try not to fall off,' she said, reviving the old joke. Her smile was something to treasure, even if part of him rather wished for some sign of concern at his departure. 'Young Jacob will miss you.'

'I shall not be gone long.'

Williams turned to Groombridge, but again spoke loudly. 'I expect to catch up with you in the afternoon at the very latest.'

'Sir.'

As darkness approached at the end of the day, Groombridge settled the men in an empty farmhouse. There were pens – uncovered, but better than nothing – for the horses and vehicles. There was little forage to be had, apart from some chopped straw, so that meant using a good deal of their own supply.

There was no sign of Williams. That was a little disappointing, for he had begun to form a reasonably favourable judgement of the young officer. His plan certainly seemed a sensible one.

Jane found herself worried. The building had only a single room, and although the men had rigged up some ropes and draped blankets over them to cordon off a little corner for her, she was very aware that she was now with a dozen or more soldiers she did not know. It was not that she felt concerned over their behaviour, for they had been universally kind. Instead she began to realise how reassuring the presence of Williams had been. Whatever his fears – and she guessed they had been considerable – he had never once suggested to her that they would not find their way back to the battalion and her family. She missed him, more even than friendship would command, and that threw into even greater confusion the turmoil of feelings from the last week. The thought that he would abandon them never once crossed the girl's mind. Trying to be cynical, she was convinced that he would not have the imagination for such a betrayal, but knew that was not the reason for her conviction. The fear grew that he had run into enemies or an accident.

A muffled shout stirred the room into life. Jane stood to see over the hanging blankets. Groombridge had one of the muskets and was pulling back the flint to cock it.

'Who's there?' he called.

'English,' came a call from outside.

'It's Williams,' a different, familiar voice shouted.

Groombridge relaxed the flint, and motioned to one of the

drivers to unbolt the door. A corporal in a red coat with the white facings of the 32nd came in. More men followed. There were two men in jackets with the buff facings of the 52nd, four with the light green of the 5th or the 36th, a pair in the yellow of the 26th, and another man with yellow facings and the kilt of the 92nd. The Highlander and one of the men from the 52nd had heavily bandaged feet and were using their firelocks as crutches.

All were bone weary. Williams had stumbled across them in ones and twos earlier in the day. They were stragglers, who had moved away from the main route to avoid the French. All of these men still carried muskets, which was a good sign. The stories they told were not.

Once they had been given a place by the fire and fed, Williams had Groombridge place a sentry, and took the quartermaster sergeant out into the cold, walking some way before they began talking.

'It's bad,' Williams began.

18

The drums beat the Dead March as the prisoners were led towards the big tree. Dobson's young son kept his face as rigid as possible, but there were tears in the boy's eyes as he brought his sticks down in the slow rhythm. Half the drummers were from the 106th, and the remainder from the other regiment with a soldier condemned to hang.

The battalions of the Reserve Division formed a hollow square facing inwards, and had been paraded all morning to witness the drumhead court martial and punishment of men arrested during the last few days. They stood in a field of snow on a low ridge to the east of Cacabellos. The village, with its narrow stone bridge, lay behind them. The 15th Hussars provided piquets, supported by the 95th, who were excused from the punishment parade by this duty. In any case, only a small number of their soldiers were under arrest – the result either of good conduct or greater skill in avoiding detection.

General Sir Edward Paget presided, and was confirming his reputation as a keen advocate of the lash. Already some two dozen men had been tied to triangles formed from sergeant's half-pikes and flogged. Young Dobson was glad that he had not been chosen as one of the drummers to inflict the punishment itself, even if this other duty was grim enough. Most of the sentences were small by the standards of an army that could inflict a thousand or more lashes, even if it was rare for more than a few hundred to be delivered at one time. Hanley had seen a flogging soon after he joined the battalion, but had been glad that there was none since then. MacAndrews was a reluctant flogger, preferring other punishments unless the crime was serious. Today, most of the charges related to theft or drunkenness, and the major was willing to accept that some object lessons were necessary.

That had not prevented him from pleading for the life of Reade, the man now sentenced to be hanged. Formerly a sergeant, he had been broken to the ranks about an alleged failure, which was widely believed not to have been his fault. The man's spirit had been shattered by the experience and the insult to his pride, and he had taken to drink. Yet in this case, MacAndrews was sure his excursion into Cacabellos had been a hunt for something to wear on his feet now that his boots had given out. It was simply unfortunate that he had run into a patrol of provosts, and when he tried to escape had fled around a corner and knocked down an officer. The major had no doubt that this was an accident. For the general this was of little importance. The man had been in a place forbidden to the soldiers, and was there with the intention of theft, whatever his motives.

Sir Edward had given his verdict, and then dismissed the court so that they could prepare for the execution. He took the opportunity to inhale some of his diminishing supply of snuff, and wondered whether there was any chance of getting more. The general noticed that Captain Wickham had returned and so nodded to the man, only half listening to his explanation that the French prisoner was now in the charge of an officer rendered an invalid by fatigue. Paget had barely noticed Wickham's absence, and doubted that it had in any way reduced the efficiency of his staff.

Another hussar galloped up, reining in violently so that his horse skidded to a halt, flinging up mud and ice from the ground. The rider saluted.

'Colonel Grant's compliments, sir, and strong forces of French cavalry are pressing our outposts. He estimates there to be some five hundred, with more squadrons advancing to join them.'

'Have they risked a charge?'

'No, sir. Still skirmishing, but the fire is growing heavier.' Sir

Edward had heard the occasional shot, so that the report confirmed his impression of what was happening.

'Very well,' he said to the man. 'That was a clear and soldier-like report. You may return to your squadron.'

The hussar saluted and sped back the way he had come. General Paget made no obvious move to act on the information, but returned to the business of the punishment parade.

MacAndrews found himself close to Wickham, and so bade him a good day, civility winning out over his dislike.

'One of yours?' asked Wickham as Reade was led away and stripped of his jacket.

MacAndrews disliked the 'yours' from a man still on the roll of the 106th. 'Aye, one of ours. Do you not recollect Reade from Three Company?' Wickham had been a lieutenant in the same company, and had failed to deliver the order which had led to the man's disgrace. MacAndrews tried to drive the point home. 'He was a good sergeant.'

'No, I cannot place him,' said Wickham, and his face appeared genuinely unstirred by any memory, or indeed significant interest. 'May I convey my best wishes to Mrs MacAndrews and Miss MacAndrews? I trust they are both well, in spite of the rigours of the campaign.'

'Mrs MacAndrews is as well as can be expected,' said her husband flatly. 'Miss MacAndrews foolishly went riding too far on Christmas Day. She has not been seen since.'

'Oh . . . I did not realise . . .' For once Wickham's calm was shattered. 'I am so very sorry to hear that.' The sentiment was genuine, although it did begin with annoyance that he would be unable to seek diversion with her. Fear quickly followed. Mac-Andrews spoke of her riding out. Did he know why? 'Such a truly terrible thing. However, perhaps she has merely been unable to return to our lines?'

'That is our hope.' MacAndrews kept his voice level. 'Thank you for your concern.' He turned and strode back to the battalion. Wickham misread distaste in the voice for menace, and feared being called out. A major could not challenge a captain, but since he hoped for promotion before long that offered little assurance of safety. All over a daft slut who'd got herself lost in the middle of a war. The unfairness pained him. If the man could not look after his daughter properly, then it scarcely seemed reasonable to blame anyone else.

Wickham sat on horseback among the general's staff not far from the tree as the execution party reached it.

'Proceed,' said Sir Edward to the provost officer. Two ropes had already been flung over suitable branches. They were made into nooses and these were placed around the condemned men's necks and fastened. The pair were then lifted up so that their feet rested on the shoulders of some crouching provosts. These stood up carefully, and the ropes were made fast to the branch. One last roll, and the drums stopped. When the signal was given the provosts would step away and let the men drop and swing. If required, they could return to pull the men's legs and speed their deaths rather than allowing a slow strangulation.

Sir Edward waited to give the order. He was thirty-three, although he looked older. For all his temper, it was not so much passion which moved him now, but a desire to do his duty.

Another hussar appeared, this time riding right across the centre of the square. He was especially gaudily dressed, and Wickham recognised General Slade. Command of the cavalry had fallen to him since Lord Paget had been rendered almost blind by an attack of opthalmia.

'The French are upon us!' he called out, reining in his horse directly in front of Sir Edward and his staff. 'They have twenty squadrons to our three, and so we have begun to retire.'

'I am sorry to hear that,' replied Sir Edward as calmly as he was able. 'It seems, however, somewhat odd for you to bring this information yourself rather than sending an orderly dragoon. I must not detain you, since you must be eager to return to your piquets.'

'No, no, Sir John must be informed immediately.' Wickham had a momentary hope that he might be given the task, until

Slade set spurs to his horse's sides and set off at a great pace down the slope towards the village and bridge.

'Good God,' murmured one of the ADCs, unable to restrain his surprise.

Sir Edward permitted himself another pinch of snuff from the holder suspended on a chain next to his watch. He inhaled, and a moment later sneezed explosively. He walked his horse forward until he was in the centre of the square. Shots were now coming more frequently and appeared to be getting closer with every passing moment. Pringle, standing at the right of his grenadiers, thought that the general's face was racked with thought. If it was an act, then it was a good one.

'My God!' he bellowed out at last. 'Is it not lamentable to think that instead of preparing you to receive the enemies of our country, I am planning to hang two robbers? Nevertheless, I shall always do my duty.' He turned and pointed at the corner of the division's formation closest to the road down which the French were advancing. 'But even though that angle of the square should be attacked, I shall hang these villains in that angle.' He pointed now at the tree.

They waited. More than one of the drummers around young Dobson was sobbing. Reade looked vacant, as if life no longer had any great savour for him and this last disgrace was a release. Paget broke his silence, turning his horse in a circle as he scanned the faces of the paraded men. 'If I spare the lives of these men, will you promise to reform?'

No one reacted. There seemed to be no sound beyond the gentle sigh of the wind. For the moment there was no more sound of gunfire.

'Will you promise?'

'Yes,' hissed Pringle in a whisper. He guessed that other officers were doing the same.

'Yes,' boomed out Dobson's voice. Rawson echoed the call immediately. Then all the grenadiers and the rest of the regiment took up the cry. 'Yes!'

'So be it.' Sir Edward signalled to the commander of the

provosts. The two men were quickly lowered and released. Other provosts dismantled the triangles to signal that there would be no more floggings. The officers called for three cheers for the general, which were most heartily given. MacAndrews wondered whether a last-minute reprieve had been planned from the start. He had known more than a few commanders fond of such theatrics, believing that enough fear was created, and, better still, gratitude won, so that future offences were less likely. Old Billy Howe had been a great one for such things in America.

Little clusters of greenjackets from the 95th started spilling over the crest above them. There was more popping as they turned to fire at the as yet invisible enemy. The hussars were also falling back.

As the square broke up, each of the battalions of the reserve formed column at quarter-distance and began to file in turn down the hill towards the bridge. The 106th was in the rear. It took time for the others to make their way through the narrow streets and over the bridge and MacAndrews had to halt his battalion. He turned them about in case the French arrived more quickly than expected. A troop of horse artillery with six guns each pulled by half a dozen horses caused farther delay.

When the logjam cleared, he sent Pringle with the grenadiers to form in a patch of open ground to the right of the road, before sending the next four companies of the battalion over the bridge. Together, this was half of the 106th, and since they stood on the right of the formation they were known as the right wing. The 52nd had extended along the riverbank and he had his own companies deploy on their flank. The 20th were on the other side of the road. Then the left wing crossed and formed line closer to the high towered church which stood on a rise beside the road.

Pringle waited for the order to bring his own company across the bridge. He had them in line, two deep, with the front rank kneeling, all at an angle to the road. The men were loaded and ready. The right flank was only a few yards from the bridge, but the ground dipped between the last few houses and the crossing point, making it hard for Pringle to see what was happening on the far bank.

Feet pounded as a company of the 95th came jogging down the road. Another followed close behind, and Pringle stepped back to allow the greenjackets to cross. Other riflemen were going into the houses. One of the men looked quite drunk and wandered aimlessly in the street until a comrade dragged him through the door.

Sir Edward Paget remained on the far side of the village, using his telescope to scan the high ground and the road. The 15th continued to pull back, and Wickham began to wonder when the general would himself retire. They could already see French squadrons on the road, and others were just cresting the high ground so recently occupied by the division. There were chasseurs in green, and a regiment of hussars in grey, wearing shakos rather than the fur hats of the British light dragoons.

'Time?' asked Sir Edward.

'A quarter past one, sir,' replied one his officers, checking his fob watch. A clatter of hoofs announced the arrival of Sir John himself, along with Graham, Colborne and some of his other officers.

The generals exchanged greetings, and Moore explained that he had met Slade on his ride here and hurried his pace accordingly. 'It appears that he now considers himself ADC to Colonel Grant of the Fifteenth,' joked Sir John, before listening to Paget explain the situation.

Wickham saw the French horsemen get closer. Using his own glass brought them even nearer. The French hussars had red facings and white lace on the fur pelisses which they wore over their jackets. Shifting his gaze, he saw glittering from the brass helmets of a squadron of dragoons. They were at some distance, but it suggested that enemy reinforcements were approaching fast. The music of a band drifted through the air, playing a jaunty tune. A mounted band seemed unlikely, so that suggested the approach of infantry. Surely it was time to leave.

As if in answer to a cue in the theatre, one of the leading

French squadrons gave a cheer and charged. Others came behind it in support. Most of the 15th were some way back, filing through the main street of the village, and the heavily outnumbered piquet had no choice but to flee in front of the attack.

'We had best be off as well,' said Sir John. They took a side alley, but soon found themselves in the main street, trying to push through an almost solid mass of hussars and riflemen. There was shouting from behind them, and the sound of blade clashing against blade as the French charge met a troop of British hussars formed to meet them.

Somehow the mass shifted. Hussar horses so tired and lame they had barely been capable of a trot half an hour ago now found a burst of energy. Everyone, hussars, riflemen and senior officers, pelted along the road. Those in the lead were already crossing the humpbacked bridge. The mêlée broke up and there were grey-uniformed Frenchmen riding in among the rest. Rifles fired from windows, the sharp cracks of the discharges echoing along the street. A muzzle appeared from a second-floor window just in front of Wickham. He ducked beneath it as he passed, but the explosion was deafening and he was sure the flame touched him.

Horses and men were screaming. Wickham yelped as a Frenchman rode abreast of him, and then he yelled out in horror because the man's head was almost severed from his neck, and simply hung down by a thread of skin, bumping against his chest with the motion of the horse. Another grey-coated Frenchman, this time very much alive, appeared from behind the other. He cut down to slice through the skull of a rifleman running alongside. Then a shot from another window hit the man in the face, pitching him from the saddle to be trampled in the scrimmage.

Wickham felt his horse break through the crowd, his shoes sliding for a moment on the stones of the bridge, and then he was across. He cantered along the road, not sure whether the French were coming after him and afraid to look back. MacAndrews saw him pass, his head pulled down and not looking either right or left.

The grenadiers could not fire into the French without killing their own hussars and riflemen. Pringle stood back from the bridge, knowing that he could not take his own men across until the crowd had gone. He would fire if he had to, but at the moment there were few French to be seen and most were some way back.

'Steady, lads,' he said calmly but firmly over the chaos. He looked along the faces of the rear rank – the men in front were too low to see – and was amazed at how confident they looked. 'Fix bayonets!' Men clipped the rings of the blades around the muzzles of their muskets.

The crowd started to thin. Most of the 15th were across, and the generals and their staffs long since safe. Pringle had smiled to see Wickham pass, looking like a startled rabbit, but then doubted he would have looked too happy in a similar situation. There were dead in the street, but fewer than he expected. At the far end he could see numbers of riflemen being herded away as captives. He could discern no means of rescuing them, and since the greenjackets in the houses were nearer and made no move to help he doubted that it was possible. Perhaps a dozen French hussars were walking their horses down the street towards him.

'Present!' Both ranks raised muskets to their shoulders. 'Front rank only. Wait for the command.'

The French stopped. They had already done a lot of damage. A formed squadron would probably have hurled itself at the single company, but these men were tired from the confused fight and had the sense not to take a risk against an opponent who was clearly ready. They turned their horses and trotted back the way they had come.

Pringle watched them. He wanted to keep his volley if possible. Once the men fired, it would take time to reload and in that time more horsemen might be upon them. Loaded muskets and good order were great enough threats to deter the enemy, at least for the moment.

The riflemen were pulling out of the houses and running back over the bridge. He let them pass, and when there seemed to be no more he sent Hanley with half the company back. There was still no sign of enemy horsemen organising to attack down the street, so he sent his own men back. Walking backwards a few paces, he finally decided that they still had time, and so turned and scampered after his men.

The main line was withdrawing. The 20th and 52nd were on their way up the slope to the ridge behind the church. The 91st Highlanders were already there. Sir John himself rode up to MacAndrews and ordered him to conform to the new position. The 106th remained in two wings. The left wing was to form on the ridge to the north of the road, extending the line of the other regiments. The right wing was farther forward, standing across the road itself. Moore and Paget both trotted along the road to meet the Grenadier Company as they marched back, passing the walled churchyard. Riflemen were already extending in pairs among the rows of trees and vines on either side of the road.

'Good day to you, Captain . . . ?'

'Pringle, sir.'

'Now Mr Pringle, I need your fellows for a special task.' Sir John's voice was calm, reasonable, and conveyed absolute authority. 'Halt here, and form line across the road.' The church beside them was on a hummock, making its high walls and tower loom even taller. 'You must stay here and protect the artillery. The French cannot see them at the moment, but the guns are hidden behind the churchyard. When the time comes they will wheel them out and engage over your heads.' Just behind the company, the road climbed steeply to reach the same level as the church.

'The French are lively today, so I do not think it will be long before they come to visit. Well, they shall have a greater welcome than they expect.' For all his professional coolness, the general appeared to be enjoying himself. Paget and their respective staffs seemed equally jolly. Wickham had not yet rejoined them. Raising his voice, Moore called as they left, 'I know I can rely on my grenadiers to see the French off!'

Sergeant Rawson dressed the line with care. Once again the front rank knelt. They would fire their volley and then ram the butts of their muskets against the ground, pointing them upwards so the bayonets formed a solid line of sharp points to deter any horse from charging home. That, at least, was the theory. Pringle had never done it in practice. Hanley thought to himself that their little band of sixty-seven men was hopelessly out on a limb. Yet his friend seemed untroubled, and the sergeants their usual confident selves. If anything the men were eager to be at the enemy, and he sensed they enjoyed being closer to them than the rest of the regiment.

'We'll teach the bastards for killing women,' said Murphy.

Dobson just nodded, and then saw Hanley and nodded amiably to him.

'Aye, we'll show 'em,' he said firmly.

'Not long now, lads,' said Pringle, pacing along the front of the formation. 'They're only cavalry, so aren't likely to do much thinking.' They grinned at that. 'Wait for the orders, and we'll tumble the rogues in the mud. Now our gunners are going to nip out and be firing over our heads, so don't worry about the noise.'

'You sure they can shoot straight?' called out Murphy cheerfully.

'Oh yes, of course yes. I am sure our gallant artillery can see as well as me.' Pringle took off his glasses and squinted blindly at them. The grenadiers roared with laughter. Hanley envied his friend's familiarity with the men. So often the faces seemed closed to him. He felt useless, with little to do and even less idea of what needed to be done for them to survive the next half-hour.

'Mr Hanley.' Pringle's voice was formal. 'If you would be so good as to watch the left flank, I shall take care of the right.' That was the danger. If the French came at them up the road, and if the men held their fire and then poured it on at the right moment, the enemy horsemen should be stopped cold. Pringle was confident of this. The risk was if the cavalry managed to sweep round the flanks of the company. It would not be easy for them. The road was constricted by walls and the trees and the grenadiers filled most of the open ground.

'Sir!' There was just a hint of nervousness in Sergeant Probert's voice as he called a warning to the captain, breaking in on Pringle's thoughts. The officer turned.

'Thank you, Sergeant, I see them. Well . . .' Pringle struggled to think of something fittingly casual to say, and failed to think of anything original. 'It looks like the ball is about to open.'

19

'Plucky fellows!' said Sir John Moore, focusing his telescope on the two Frenchmen riding over the hump of the bridge. The movement was slow, almost nonchalant. The first man was dressed in the heavily braided blue coat of a French general and a thick white plume crowned his cocked hat. His horse was a grey, so light as to look wholly white even against the snow of the fields. A few paces behind him came an ADC, dressed in a spectacular hussar-style uniform of red and green. All around them, balls flicked up puffs of dust and chips from the stonework as the sharpshooters of the 95th were drawn to such an irresistible target.

'Damned lucky fellows at least!' conceded Sir Edward. He could see the French general raising his glass to study them, just as they were in turn watching the Frenchmen.

Sir John moved his telescope to scan the far bank of the river. 'They must be forming in the depression behind the bridge. I do not believe it will be long now. Any sign of their infantry?'

Colborne answered his question. 'Not yet, sir.'

'Guns?'

'No sign of them.'

'Excellent.'

Wickham was happy enough that the enemy had only cavalry up so far, although to him it seemed just a matter of time before they were reinforced. There seemed little point in waiting here to fight them. Better to pull away, and turn only now and again to fend off the cavalry. There should be no great danger if the rearguard kept moving and prevented the enemy from bringing up their other troops. Considerably more vexing was the generals' insistence on watching the affair from among the skirmishers of the 95th. Surely the ridge to the rear offered not only a better platform for observation, but also greater security, which would permit the calm exercise of control over the fighting. Wickham had been waiting up there, after his escape from the chaos in the village. Then that damned vulgar Scotsman MacAndrews appeared and 'helpfully' pointed General Paget out to him. He worried again that the major held him responsible for the loss of his fool of a daughter. Wickham silently cursed him, and cursed again the unkind fate that had driven him from the comfort of Lefebre-Desnouettes and his carriage. He wondered whether there was any prospect of cashing the Frenchman's promissory note for thirty dollars won in their card games.

There was noise from the others and Wickham returned his focus to the bridge. The French general raised his sabre high, and seemed to be calling to the men behind him. He and his aide still remained untouched by the fire of the riflemen.

Paget admired the courage of the French leader, although he also doubted his wisdom. No doubt he had seen the drunks and stragglers in the last few days, and judged the British to be all such men. The Frenchman was brave, and that was to be admired. He was also an enemy, making his courage dangerous.

Sir Edward reached into his jacket and pulled out a small purse, shaking it so that the coins inside jingled. 'This goes to the man who spins that saucy fellow on the white horse,' he called out. The closest of the 95th grinned, and a moment later one of them dashed out into the road, running along towards the bridge.

'Tom's off,' said a sergeant. 'Lot of brandy in that purse!'

The lone rifleman pelted down the road. Then he stopped and lay down on his back in the churned snow. He cocked his right leg over his left and rested his rifle's muzzle down just next to his ankle.

Trumpets blared, and grey-uniformed hussars, their tall plumes nodding, came trotting in column of fours across the bridge.

Their officer and a trumpeter led them, and the general and his ADC were at least three horse lengths farther in advance.

The rifleman waited. Another trumpet signal and the horsemen urged their mounts into a canter. They were moving quickly now, sabres pointing forward at the charge, and hoofs flinging up lumps of snow and ice.

The rifleman waited. The French general was already within range, but he was a fast-moving target. None of the other greenjackets was firing, wanting the enemy to move on into the trap and also silently urging on the lone man on the road.

With a sharp crack the rifleman fired, the recoil driving the butt back into his armpit as he lay. A thick cloud of smoke covered the target, but all his instincts told him that his aim was true. The general was flung back in the saddle by the blow, and blood was already spreading across his chest. His aide drove spurs into the flanks of his horse, sending the animal into a full gallop in his rage to get at the assassin. He pounded along the road, and at the same time a roar of anger came from the hussars behind.

The rifleman loaded. It was an awkward task to perform while lying down, and would have been impossible with the longer musket, but long hours of training paid off. The ADC was barely ten yards away when the rifle cracked again. The ball hit the officer's forehead, just beneath the peak of his gaudy shako, and had enough force to take a chunk out of the back of his skull. The dead man fell, but his right boot caught in the stirrup and he was dragged along by the panicking horse, his mangled head bouncing against the ground.

The lone greenjacket fled for the shelter of the trees and his comrades. The hussars were close behind, and were gaining on him, but then more and more of the 95th opened up. Men and horses started to fall. The neat ranks of the hussars dissolved. Some men were still pressing on, the officer and his trumpeter at the head of them. Others had fallen, or were trying without success to turn off the road and reach the skirmishers. Another squadron of hussars came across the bridge and the energy of the new advance set everyone going forward again. A third squadron came up behind, and in the rear of them were chasseurs in green.

Hanley turned when he heard the noise. Gunners in their blue jackets and tall tarleton helmets were rolling their guns out from behind the church wall. These were horse artillery, with lighter-weight carriages than the heavier pieces of the foot batteries. All the gunners were fit and most of them were big men. Even so, and in spite of the cold, their faces were red and sweating as they pushed the grey-painted gun carriages into position and then went through the movements of loading. As they worked they shouted and repeated orders.

He turned back to look past the grenadiers. The French hussars were very close.

'Wait for the guns!' said Pringle firmly. 'Wait!' Hanley wanted to give the order, to let the men fire and hide the enemy in smoke. He became sure his friend had left it too late. He could see the Frenchmen's mouths open wide, noticed that all had moustaches and odd pigtails on either side of their foreheads. The horses were straining at their bits, lips back and yellow teeth bared. He remembered the sabres falling, and the dull smacks as the steel sank into flesh when he had fled from the massacre at Madrid. 'Please God,' he thought. 'Fire! Damn it, fire!'

The guns went off first. There were six of them in place. Each was a light six-pounder, but instead of a solid six-pound shot they were loaded with canister. The metal tins contained seventy-two musket balls, each of which weighed one and a quarter ounces. The canisters burst as they left the muzzle, spraying the balls in a focused cone that jabbed towards the enemy.

Hanley flinched at the noise, so much so that he did not notice that most of the grenadiers did the same. An appalling force punched at the air above them, as a cloud of smoke covered the sky over their heads. Pieces of smouldering wadding scattered over them. One dropped on to Hanley's hat and stuck there.

The grenadiers were still below the smoke when the canister balls struck the hussars. Little fountains of red blood blossomed on men and horses, often several at the same moment. Riders and mounts screamed and tumbled. A dozen horses were down, some of them dead or wounded and others tripped by the fallen. Hoofs thrashed in wild agony, and the head of one fallen but otherwise unscathed rider was crushed by a blow. Hanley was appalled at the carnage, closer than anything he had seen in the battles of the summer.

The charge was stopped. Dead horses and men blocked the road, and just thirty paces behind them the Grenadier Company waited with its second rank at the present and ready to fire. The hussars behind turned and went back the way they came. Rifle shots continued to empty saddles, but Pringle kept his volley. His job was to protect the guns, and it was better to let them do the execution. They fired a second time, and even at the longer range the canisters brought down four or five men and horses.

'Well, I think we spoiled their day,' said Pringle. His men grinned back. The French cavalry were already fleeing back across the bridge.

'Mr Hanley, sir?' The officer saw Dobson's lips move, but his ears were still throbbing from the explosion of the cannons and he could not make out the words until the old soldier repeated them. 'Mr Hanley?'

'Yes, Dobson.'

'Your hat's on fire.' Hanley jumped with surprise, and then snatched the smoking cocked hat from his head. He tossed it into the snow, stamping on it. The grenadiers roared with laughter.

The riflemen were in equally good spirits as they watched General Paget give the promised purse to the man who had brought down the French leader. Moore approved, for it had been an intrepid piece of work. It was truly amazing to see the gallantry which the soldiers were exhibiting now that they were squaring up against the French, and so hard to believe that the same soldiers were so recently drunken and disobedient. While General Paget had been flogging a succession of offenders, Sir John had presided over the execution of a man by firing squad back with the main body of the army at Villafranca. The man had looted, and that was common enough, but he had also struck an officer, and that could not be excused. There was no reprieve and the regiments were ordered to march past the open grave before it was filled.

It was an object lesson, and he earnestly hoped the men would profit from it, even though the recent days had done much to shatter his old faith in the British soldier. The behaviour at Villafranca had been as shameful as that at Bembibre or Astorga. Yet there was a desperately feral quality about many of the soldiers. Men without boots or greatcoat looked hungrily at those who still had them, as if willing them to die so that they could take these treasures for themselves. It was good to be fighting, for that showed the men at their very best and gave him simpler problems with which to grapple. The French required a suitable object lesson of their own to make them keep their distance. He feared what would happen if the rest of the army was called upon to fight in its current state.

Sir John extended his glass again and scanned the area around the bridge. He could see nothing, and a second cavalry charge seemed unlikely. Infantry might be another matter, if the French had any. Something drew his attention among the trees and scrub farther along the far bank. Figures in green jackets were moving there. 'What do you make of it, Colborne?'

'Dragoons,' came the answer after a few moments. 'Yes, I can see the helmets.' A century earlier dragoons had been infantrymen who rode to battle, but then fought on foot. These days such a tactic was rare, and he could not think of an occasion when British dragoons had dismounted to fight, but it seemed that the French were willing to try it. He knew they carried muskets almost as long as those of the infantry, rather than the short carbines of his own hussars, so that they were prepared for the job. He focused the glass on a pair of the enemy. They ran clumsily in their high boots, but the spacing between pairs was good and whoever was leading them had some idea of how skirmishers should fight.

'Sir Edward, would you be kind enough to send a company of the Ninety-fifth to the bank on either side of the road. I shall support them with half of the Fifty-second. I wonder whether the enemy believes there to be a ford?'

'I shall have the men extend and keep a close eye on them. The water will be damned cold if there is a way across.'

Throughout the afternoon firing was constant across the river. Skirmishers took cover behind walls, trees and boulders, or crouched in dips in the land. Much powder was expended for little loss on either side. The French dragoons were reinforced by infantrymen and this encouraged them to press across shallow parts of the river. Sir John sent the rest of the 52nd down to reinforce the skirmish line. Soon afterwards Colborne rode to the 106th and ordered MacAndrews to commit first the Light Company and then the grenadiers to aid the riflemen north of the bridge.

Pringle led the company across the fields beyond the church. The snow was deep in places, and several men fell as they doubled over the uneven ground. Captain Headley and the light bobs were to the left of the 95th, so Pringle moved in beside the Light Company. Half of the grenadiers remained formed in line, while he led the rest forward and extended them as a chain of skirmishers.

Hanley remained with the reserve, and tried his best to remember the drills MacAndrews had taught them back in England. It occurred to him that he had never before been required to give an order in battle. At Roliça he had begun the day carrying one of the regiment's two Colours, and managing the heavy flag as he marched in the centre of the line had kept him too occupied to think much of anyone else. At Vimeiro he had taken station at the rear of the Grenadier Company. Pringle had given the orders, and he had simply obeyed like any other redcoat. Throughout this retreat he had simply followed everyone else, doing what he was told, and in truth too consumed by his own discomfort to think much about anyone else's.

This was different. Pringle was some way away, and the company not formed up alongside the rest of the battalion and moving in accordance with the mind and instructions of someone in higher authority. His detachment looked impassive, and yet he felt them all watching him, waiting for him to give orders which could mean life or death to any or all of them.

It would have been amusing if it was not so terrifying. They were looking to him to make decisions – to him, William Hanley, unwanted bastard child and failed artist, who had never been responsible for anyone in his life. He was only in the army at all because he had no money and no other opportunity left to him.

'God help them,' he said softly to himself as the absurdity of it all grew.

'Sir?' asked Sergeant Rawson.

'Nothing, Sergeant,' he said, and turned away to stare to the left, so that no one would see the grin he could not suppress. In that direction there was a low hillock, somewhat beyond the farthest pair of grenadiers. Its slopes and top were covered in grey boulders only half hidden by snow. Hanley was looking at the little rise, and then saw a head wearing a shako appear. A musket flamed and then the head was hidden by dirty smoke. Two more shots followed almost immediately, and then a third.

No one was hit, but the pair of grenadiers nearest the hillock were crouching, trying without much success to find cover. One of them fired back. Pringle was at the far end of the line, a high wall, and the uneven ground prevented him from seeing what was happening. Other shots came from across the river, and now one of the grenadiers was down, clutching his shoulder.

A quick hope that someone else would see the threat and respond flickered to life and then died away. There was no one else. Sergeant Rawson's silence had somehow gained a stronger air of expectation.

Hanley had counted four shots. If the French fought by pairs then that meant eight men. It was important to keep some reserve.

'Sergeant Rawson.'

'Sir.'

'Take sixteen men. A few French have sneaked up on to the rise there. Go on and clear them off.'

'Sir.' Rawson raised his powerful voice to give the commands. 'Eight files on the left will follow me! Fix bayonets.' Amid the scraping, Hanley noticed Dobson beside him.

'Mr Hanley, sir, the words "go on" do not become an officer,' whispered the veteran.

Rawson took his men in line towards the hill. The French noticed the advance, and four muskets flamed. The shots went high, although one clipped the top off the plume on a man's shako. Hanley watched them, wondering whether even now he should listen to Dobson's advice and lead the charge himself. It was not fear which had made him send the sergeant, but the thought that he ought to stay and be ready to commit the rest of the reserve if they were needed to shore up another part of the line. He was doing his best to think before he made decisions.

Rawson halted his men.

'Present!' The muskets were levelled. 'Fire!' The shots came close together, like a brief roll of thunder. 'Come on, boys!' and the redcoats surged up the slope. Shots rang out from among the boulders. Hanley saw Rawson stumble, dropping the half-pike he carried as a badge of rank, but it seemed to be just a patch of ice, because the man was up again, not bothering to retrieve his weapon. Then he fell again, and did not get up.

The grenadiers swarmed up around the boulders. A whistle blew, and Hanley realised that Pringle was waving his arm to beckon him forward, and there was no longer any time to think.

'Follow me!' he called, and jogged forward the hundred yards to the skirmishing line. Pringle gestured at the men to line a wall. A group of several dozen Frenchmen in dark blue jackets and trousers were splashing across the river.

'Let 'em have it, lads!' The grenadiers fired into the enemy, forced to cluster because the ford was narrow. Several were hit, collapsing into icy water. It still surprised Hanley to see a man so animate, running, well balanced and so alive one minute, and then an instant later falling, loose limbed, just like a sack of potatoes.

The light was going, and this seemed to be the signal for the French to give up their efforts at crossing. They had heard the cannon fire again, which suggested an attempt at the bridge, but the lack of any more salvoes suggested that the attack had not come to anything. The British still fired across the river at the least sign of movement.

Sir John Moore and his senior officers and staff rode behind the firing line.

'They're like mastiffs,' Sir Edward Paget said to Moore. 'Can't wait to slip the leash and get at 'em.'

The general nodded, but still found it hard to trust the constancy of such enthusiasm. It would anyway be of little avail without discipline to set courage to a proper purpose. He gave orders for the reserve to begin to withdraw, and take the road to Villafranca. The rest of the army should already have marched much earlier in the day. The retreat would continue, and he suspected that the French would dog them all the way. Paget's mastiffs would have plenty of chance to fight.

As they marched back to rejoin the battalion, the grenadiers were in high spirits. Only one man had been wounded, and even he appeared to have every chance of recovery. Rawson had died on the hill.

'Shot through the lungs,' Dobson told Hanley and Pringle. 'Weren't your fault, sir.' The big man looked the lieutenant squarely in the eyes. 'Just bad luck. Will we catch up with the baggage tonight, sir?' The question was to Pringle.

'Of course, his wife. Well, widow, I suppose.' Pringle did not know the very proper Mrs Rawson well. 'I am not sure. Perhaps tonight, perhaps tomorrow.'

'It'll hit her hard.' Dobson spoke from recent experience. 'Still, she's a good lass.'

The 106th marched the remaining miles to Villafranca under a cold starlight. Several fires burned in the town, and when they went through the main street everything was bathed in a red glow. A big house was burning, and there were more fires where broken wagons and piles of debris had been set on fire. The dead mules and horses were simply left where they had been slaughtered. Slumped forms of men lay in the alleys. No orders were given to rouse them and the regiments did not trouble to discover whether they were drunk or more permanently at rest. The 106th did not leave behind a single straggler that night, and MacAndrews was reliably informed that the other regiments in the reserve preserved an equal record.

Five miles took them to Villafranca, and then another sixteen beyond that to a cluster of ramshackle houses where they stopped and got a few hours of poor rest. There was salt beef in some quantity, hard and tinged with yellow, but the little biscuit available was worm-infested and sour. Fires were lit to boil water and soften both. Many men were too tired to wait. They ate what little they could and then huddled down to sleep. Mrs Rawson cried softly and let Dobson put his arm around her as she cradled Sal's head in her lap.

20

'Pong!' Private Mazey was almost screaming in frustration at the Spaniard's inability to comprehend his own language. 'Pong!' The soldier was barely five foot two, and he stood up on the balls of his feet in an effort to look down on the baffled farmer. The elderly man shook his head. Impatience seethed within the Englishman, causing him to lapse back into his own tongue. 'We want bread, you damned rogue!' Another thought struck him. 'And hogwar.'

Miss MacAndrews pushed her way past the watching soldiers and smiled warmly at the farmer. She had Jacob cradled in her arms. The man's expression softened. The young woman was pretty, and as the father of six and the grandfather of a dozen or so, he was well disposed to children.

If Jane could not frame an elegant sentence in Spanish, then at least she could pronounce simple words and expressions more clearly than the agitated redcoat. 'Bread and water,' she explained. Enlightenment spread quickly across the man's face, dark from long years of hard toil in the hills. Then he shrugged, doubting that he had enough to satisfy the foreign soldiers, but hoping to avoid trouble.

The stragglers had almost doubled their numbers and so halved the time it would take for the convoy to devour its own food. On the second day, Williams rode out again and returned with another twenty men left behind by the main army and wandering off into the hills to avoid the French. There were also two women, one of whom was struggling to carry a one-year-old daughter, while a boy only a few years older clung to her filthy skirts. Both women were barefoot and had lost their woollen stockings. Williams had placed each in turn on the horse as they went back to join the others, giving them a little rest. One of the men was virtually blind, another had hands so swollen that he could hold nothing. The blind man still carried his musket, but three of the others had no weapon at all.

Food for so many became a more urgent problem – greater even than keeping the baby supplied with milk. One village was generous, giving them yellow loaves of Indian corn, cheeses and wine. The senior man in another claimed that they had nothing, and simply let them break the ice on the well and draw water. Williams was away, but Groombridge refused to let the men take what was not offered. The straggle of houses looked too poor anyway to offer them much.

On the third day Williams stayed with the convoy. A German from the King's German Legion Hussars was among the fugitives he had found the previous day. On foot he was short and bow legged, and much darker of hair and skin than he expected a German to be. Johann Brandt spoke English with a thick accent, but seemed to have a good understanding of the language and he struck Williams as a serious soldier. Sitting on Bobbie's back, the man looked at ease, anticipating the mare's moods and controlling her with signs that were barely visible. Williams told him to ride towards the grand road and bring back any stragglers. The hussar showed his tobacco-stained teeth as he smiled, saluted and then sent the mare straight into a canter up the gentle slope of the valley.

Groombridge looked doubtful. 'Do you think he'll be back, sir?'

'Did you believe that I would come back that first day?' asked Williams.

'You're an officer, Mr Williams.' The reply was not necessarily an answer.

They pressed on, with the women in the wagon along with any of the soldiers too weary to walk. One of the draught horses went so badly lame that it was pulled from the traces and had to be shot. The private from the 32nd had been a butcher before he enlisted, although the mess he made of cutting up the carcass suggested to Groombridge that he had not been any great loss to his profession. It still provided them with meat, tough and unappealing, but food none the less. One of the team pulling the wagon suddenly shuddered, and then folded down on its knees, eyes rolled up to show the whites. They unharnessed it and dragged the dead animal free. There were still enough to keep the teams even, but all of the animals were struggling to maintain the pace.

In the early afternoon fifteen redcoats appeared at the crest and marched down to join them. The one at the rear held the reins to a pack mule and they were led by an immense corporal, who topped Williams by several inches. He stamped to attention when he saw the officer, back ramrod straight, and then snapped a salute straight from the manual.

'Mulligan, sir!' The report was made in a bellow. 'First Guards.' His jacket had the shoulder wings of the Grenadier Company.

'Oh Gawd,' came a faint voice from one of the soldiers behind Williams. The officer ignored it. Corporal Mulligan reported that he had been ordered to catch a runaway mule carrying the company records. By the time he had found her, the regiment had gone and even the rearguard was out of sight. Then the French appeared, and he had to shift for himself. He had been cut off for the last three days, but had come across these other men and organised them. Earlier today, they ran into Brandt, who told them about the convoy. The German had ridden on to look for more men.

'Glad to have you with us, Corporal.'

The men were a mixture. There were two Highlanders from the 71st in ragged tartan trews, a man from the 79th in a kilt, and a smattering of men from other line regiments. One pair at the rear of the little column wore the red facings of the 106th. Williams knew the faces, but it was not until the bigger of the two men spoke that he could place them.

'Good to see you, Mr Williams, sir.'

'I am glad to have you, Scammell.' The reply was not fully sincere, but an instinctive courtesy. Scammell and his usual companion Jenkins were among the incorrigibles of the 106th. Every regiment had such men, whose enlistment was usually an alternative to prison or the gallows. They stole or worse at every opportunity. Scammell had been flogged back in the summer, without in any way altering his character. It struck Williams that many of the men he was collecting may have chosen to leave the army, or fallen out through indiscipline rather than accident.

Mulligan confirmed the suspicion, when Williams and Groombridge spoke to him privately a little later. 'There has been a lot of drunkenness. A lot.' The corporal scarcely looked like an abstainer. He was perhaps twenty, certainly no older, but had the assurance and authority of a far more mature man. 'There has been much crime and indiscipline.' His voice carried a hint of painful disappointment. 'Not in the Brigade.' The tone now suggested the impossibility of such a thing. 'Or in general with the artillery and some other corps, but most of the line . . .' Williams felt that he ought to be insulted by the distaste with which the man said the word. All too sadly it confirmed everything they had heard.

The news was generally depressing, although Mulligan had one more optimistic rumour to recount. 'I heard some of the gentlemen saying that the general plans to stop and fight at Lugo.'

If the army halted, even for a few days, it gave them more chance of catching up. Williams guessed that they were already farther north than the main army, although still some way to the east. Their progress was slowing. The horses were wearing out and more than a few of the men needed to take a turn on the wagon if they were to keep up.

'Pity we haven't got newer guns,' said Groombridge, as they watched an exhausted man being lifted into the wagon. 'Those limbers have seats on them and we could carry the lame that way.'

The teams were struggling. The left lead on the wagon was

limping badly, as was one of the animals on the second gun. They shot both and carved them up. Without salt, it was hard to preserve anything, and the meat would be the main meal for that evening. Its taste was unlikely to please. They took the odd horse off the gun and added it to the three left with the wagon.

Before nightfall, Brandt returned, leading Bobbie by the reins and trailing another score of stragglers. Williams nodded to him in greeting, and the German saluted and then grinned broadly.

'Well done, Brandt.' There was no need to say that it was relief to see the hussar return when he could easily have ridden away on his own. 'Now get some rest. I'll have to send you out again tomorrow. It is the price of being the only cavalryman among us.'

The men the hussar had brought were a mixed bag. There were two more riflemen, a sergeant from the 'dirty half hundred', a lance bombardier from the Royal Horse Artillery, and all the rest redcoats, along with one man's wife. They managed to cram everyone into a walled farm, which had a barn big enough for the animals. Taking axes from the wagon, they brought down a tree and built a big fire in the centre of the yard, boiling a mixture of horse meat, rye and the last of the biscuits into a mixture which required stubborn endurance from anyone attempting to eat it. The sole merit was that there was ample for everyone, and some left over to be warmed for breakfast.

The sergeant's name was Jowers. He seemed capable enough, if a little sullen. The lance bombardier appeared to have been given the stripe because of his powerful muscles rather than any sign of wit or ability. Williams gathered the men around the fire after they had eaten. He did not want to make a great speech, and also felt that he did not have the right words.

'Most of you have met me by now. For those who have not, my name is Williams. We are away from our regiments, but we are still soldiers. We are going back to the army and then we'll give the French a thrashing!' He was a little disappointed that this produced no more than a few grins. His right thigh felt as if it was quivering, and he could remember few occasions on which he had been so nervous. 'I know that I do not have to remind you of your duty. It's not going to be easy, and we'll all be a bit thinner, but we will get home.' There was no reaction, and he rather regretted saying anything. When he left to make sure that the women were settled and that the farmer and his family were not being harassed in any way, the NCOs rounded off the occasion.

'If you don't do your duty, I'll have the hide off your back!' said the quartermaster sergeant in the harsh vowels of Kent.

'If you get drunk, I'll shoot you myself,' added Jowers.

Mulligan smiled contentedly. 'God save the King, and all sergeants!'

The German hussar went off again the next day, but the hills lying between them and the main road were turning into mountains. It was harder to move through the deep snow. Six men staggered in to join them in the first half of the day. Brandt returned with another five later in the afternoon. It seemed unlikely that there would be any more.

Another horse dropped dead before they had been gone an hour. Then one more went lame and had to be killed. It left them with three teams of four. On the flat they could still keep both guns and the wagon rolling along at a gentle pace, but there was little flat on the road. When they came to a slight rise, the men helped to push. Bigger slopes – and there were plenty of these – meant unhitching one team to add it in turn to the others before coming back and repeating the process. They climbed steadily. In some ways Groombridge was more worried about getting the heavy guns safely down an ice-covered slope than up it. They had no rope, and only a single small pulley, and he doubted that they would manage the task.

The longest, steepest hill needed all twelve horses for each of the guns. The wagon managed with just eight, but all of the passengers walked. Williams trudged through the snow carrying the little boy on his back. Miss MacAndrews went beside him, Jake wrapped up and held tightly to her.

'You seem to have acquired your own army!' Her eyes

sparkled. They were scarcely alone, but it was the closest they had come to intimacy for days and the thrill coursed through him.

'I am expecting promotion to general at any moment!'

'Or a knighthood!' Jane calmed Jacob as he gave a brief wail.

'Well, perhaps as a start. Although I suppose that I must be patient. And few generals must rely on a cavalry of one!'

'Yes, and with only three eyes between horse and rider!' The girl chuckled.

'What was it you said about the hero needing to overcome adversity of all kinds?'

'Ah, now you make use of too accurate a memory to throw unwise words back in my face.' There was much of her old challenge in her sharp expression, mingling with the amusement. 'You are a general indeed, employing every weapon to win your objective.'

'Well, it is so rare an experience for me to gain even the slightest advantage in one of our conversations that you should not blame me for exploiting it. No doubt even this small success will soon be overwhelmed by your response. I suspect I make a poor showing as a general, and still worse as a hero.'

'Confessing to a virtue less than perfect?' Jane was looking straight up into his eyes.

'There, the attack comes at once, unbalancing me in a trice.'

'Perhaps. Yet, if your memory was truly good, you would recall that I recommended some such imperfection in a true hero.'

Miss MacAndrews' hair was dishevelled, the scarf with which she covered it had worn thin. Her skin seemed pale and strained, her jacket and dress were dirty, with half a dozen little tears and buttons missing. He knew she must be tired. They had travelled a long way in the depths of winter, and she had been nursing an infant for most of it. The weariness was there in the eyes, as was the worry. Perhaps she was less perfectly beautiful than at other times, although his loyalty was inclined to dispute so outrageous a claim. It did not matter. Williams admired her more than ever before. If her beauty was truly remarkable, the character she had shown in these last days demanded respect and adoration that was far, far greater.

'I do not feel myself to be any sort of hero, Miss MacAndrews.' He spoke the words softly, not wanting the closer soldiers to hear.

'You are doing well enough,' said Jane, and then gasped because her smooth-soled boot slid just slightly beneath her. There was an instant before the girl recovered her balance. It was long enough for Williams to grab her elbow as a support. Excitement coursed through his veins. It was the first time they had touched since that night. Memory of her feel, her warmth, of the taste of her lips and the heady thrill of holding her, overwhelmed him in vivid recollection.

'Thank you.' Jane's wide mouth parted to reveal her neat teeth, and her voice dropped to a whisper. 'Thank you, Hamish.'

It was perhaps the first time that he had felt the slightest affection for his Christian name – not for what it was, but simply because she had used it. He had not released her arm.

A curse and the sound of a body falling interrupted his thoughts. The old soldier from the 92nd had stumbled. Williams went immediately to help him up. As they continued on, the man leaned against him. The little boy on Williams' back put his own arm round the Scotsman's head in an effort to help.

'Thank you, sir. My bones are getting old.' The man's breathing was noisy, broken now and then by a grating cough. 'You are a fine man, sir. Almost good enough to be a Scot!'

'My mother is a Campbell.'

Private Donald MacDonald considered this for a while. 'Aye, well, you cannae chose your ain folk.'

They kept going in spite of the snow that began to fall. At one point Williams hinted that perhaps it was time to consider abandoning one of the guns and splitting the team between the other vehicles. Groombridge's expression showed the pain and disappointment as his tolerably approving opinion of the subaltern was sadly dashed.

'The guns are our Colours, sir,' Groombridge said, by way of reluctant explanation for his determination to keep moving the field pieces on. 'And a damned sight more useful than your flags, if you will forgive the liberty. Even old wrecks like these.'

Williams had heard of the near-sacred awe the artillery reserved for its guns, but had not until now appreciated its depth. He dropped the subject immediately. The quartermaster sergeant's nod was much like a pat on the head.

Late in the day they reached a village. The people were at first suspicious, and seemed to be more numerous than in any of the places they had passed through. Williams made all the men in greatcoats remove them to show their red jackets. Once they had been accepted as English, the mood warmed. It was a large place, and winter stores were opened to feed the newcomers. There was ample wine, and before Williams thought of it Groombridge and Mulligan had placed sentries outside the two main stores.

Slow and painful conversation – supplemented by some basic exchanges in Latin with the priest – explained the swollen population and brought new fears. The French were in a place some ten miles or so down in a lower valley to the east. Williams was not quite sure of the distance as the locals talked of leagues and he knew that these were a different length in Spain to Britain.

'*Equites cataphracti et lanciarii.*' The young priest, rarely called upon for such exotic vocabulary, furrowed his brow as he struggled with the words. Williams nodded in enthusiastic assurance of understanding.

'*Sí, sí,* Colloseros,' a visitor from the other village offered his support. The combination of armoured horsemen and lancers sounded depressingly familiar. Williams wondered what fate kept bringing this same French officer across his path. There seemed no particular reason for a small detachment to be here. Then the locals began to speak about a bridge across the River Mimho. It was on the old road they were following, just a couple of leagues ahead, and only a few north of Lugo. Was there a good road leading down to Lugo itself?

'*Sí.*' There was no such detail on his map. He wondered whether General Moore had better charts, but Williams feared that he was beginning to understand.

Dalmas' big horse sped along the road, its large feet drumming on the packed snow. The two lancers were slighter men on sleeker horses, and yet they still struggled to keep up. His mind was alive with the opportunity. He had found what the Emperor wanted; the way to trap the enemy before they reached the sea. It had taken a week of fruitless searches and long rides, but the chance was now there.

The Emperor had gone, called back to Paris by urgent business of state. Marshal Soult was in charge of catching the English. Dalmas had never served under him, but the Duke had a reputation as a shrewd man. He should see the possibilities, give Dalmas the men he needed and then exploit the success in suitable force. It had all been foreseen in the Emperor's orders. Give him a company of voltiguers, mount the light infantrymen behind some light cavalry – no matter whether hussars or chasseurs – and Dalmas would have the bridge secure before the British could do anything about it. He had left eight lancers there for the moment. More than that would struggle to find cover in the little stone cabin that was the only shelter they found anywhere near by.

The rest of the squadron were back in a village where the men and horses could stay in reasonable condition and be fed. Dalmas reckoned that there should not be any enemy in the area strong enough to deal with his men at the bridge. If there were, then he doubted that they would be able to stand up to his full force. It was a risk, but seemed a reasonable one for him to take. Reinforced, he could leave the infantry to guard the bridge and take the cavalry to find the best route to the British. If Soult sent more horsemen and backed them with a brigade or more of infantry then General Moore would be in serious trouble. His whole army might be caught. At the very least they would snap up everything at the rear of his army.

Jean-Baptiste Dalmas knew that he was so very close to fulfilling the task the Emperor had given to him alone. Almost everything was in place. It was a shame that the small man with the piercing eyes would not be here to praise him in person, to pinch his cheek and promote him. Still, the rewards would come, and he could be patient. Once again the confusion of war was fixing itself into a pattern he could control. Dalmas galloped on to see Marshal Soult and make it all happen.

In the village where he had left his men, an old woman with long and filthy white hair screamed abuse at a lieutenant of cuirassiers. Three small urchins added their wails to the noise. She struck at his breastplate, yelling that her daughter had the fever and that no one should come into the little room with its pitiful fire. The tall soldier ignored the blow, and looked past her to see a hunched shape in a bed piled high with blankets. There was a smell of sweat and excrement. He stepped back, hands held up palm outwards to placate the old witch. He left, and told the men to steer clear of the little one-roomed house at the end of the alley.

The woman bolted the door and hoped none of the French would return. She walked to the bed and looked down at the face of the girl lying there. Her forehead was still hot, her skin waxy, and the long dark hair which might normally have been most becoming hung lankly around her.

It was not her daughter, but a stranger found by her grandchildren out in the fields. She had fallen from her mule and been barely conscious. When they took her to their house and laid her out on the bed, the old lady quickly spotted the traces of recent childbirth – presumably ending in tragedy since there was no sign of a child. That had been days ago, and the fever had soon come upon the stranger. The Spanish woman looked after her without thinking why, just as she looked after everyone else who came her way. No one in the village recognised the girl. In her dreams she spoke words in a language no one knew so it seemed that she was foreign – English most likely. That was one reason for hiding her from the French. Another was that they were invaders, who forced their way into people's homes and stole their food or worse.

Soaking a piece of rag, she pressed it over the girl's forehead. The fever would break in the next day or the girl would die. The woman said a prayer, and had asked the priest to do the same. There was nothing else to be done apart from watching over her.

Jenny murmured again without waking.

21

Williams inched his way through the snow. His arms were cold and stiff, and protested as he forced them to keep pulling him onwards. Somewhere behind him were Mulligan and three men, all with muskets and fixed bayonets. Farther back, on the boulders that stood at the bend in the road, were Jowers and another five. He wished he knew all of them better, and had to admit that he was not even sure of the names of some of the privates. Scammell was with Mulligan's party. At least he could be relied upon for stealth if not for honesty of character. None of the muskets was loaded. He had insisted on that, fearing an accident which would betray their presence.

He was close now, and could see the silhouette of the man pacing beside the wall of the bridge. His hat was square topped, so presumably he was one of the lancers, although on this night he cradled a carbine with fixed bayonet.

Williams had a knife, and only that. To take a loaded pistol when he denied his men loaded firelocks would have been unfair, as well as unwise, since there was the same risk of it going off by chance. His sword was too awkward to take when he knew that he must crawl the last hundred yards. The knife had come from the village. It was long and narrow, of the sort the Spanish favoured, and the old man who had given it to him seemed genuinely excited by the prospect that it would be employed against the French.

The sentry turned and came back across the bridge towards him. Williams froze. He had cut a hole in a sheet and wore the thing over his head so that as he lay his jacket and part of his trousers were sheathed in white. Cloud covered the moon's glow, and so the light was poor. He doubted that there was much chance of being seen, as long as he did not move too suddenly.

The lancer stopped. Williams heard a faint humming. It sounded like one of the fandangos the Spanish loved, so no doubt the man had heard it since coming to Spain. Williams knew something about the boredom of long spells on guard. He watched now as the Pole stamped his feet, and then turned to walk diagonally across the bridge.

Williams crawled forward. As his arms brushed against the snow the noise sounded deafening to him, but the sentry did not react and just continued his quiet singing. He turned again and Williams went still, trying even to temper his breathing in case this should give him away. He wished that he had Dobson with him, and then thought of poor Sally, and of Jenny, run off to goodness knew what fate. At least the baby was well. Williams tried to force his mind back to the task in hand.

It seemed to take an age, stopping and waiting each time the man's pacing meant that he was facing in his direction. Williams was getting close. The dim light shone on the sentry's bayonet when he turned, and his sabre clinked as it hung awkwardly. That sound must have been there all the time, and Williams wondered why he had not noticed it. He was almost at the end of the wall on the closest side of the bridge. The noise of flowing water was soft, but seemed to be coming from some way away. He hoped it would help to cover the noise he was making.

The sentry walked towards Williams and he could not believe that the Pole failed to spot him. The serious soldier in him was apt to despise a man who paid so little attention. Useless cavalry, he thought, and then struggled to stop himself from giggling because he sounded like some crusty old infantryman such as MacAndrews or Dobson. The Pole turned away.

Williams pushed himself up with one hand and drew the knife with the other. He stepped forward as quietly as he could. The Pole was still singing and then heard boots crunching on the ice.

Williams dashed at him as the sentry began to turn, but the man's movements seemed sluggish. The ensign's left hand pushed aside the muzzle of the lancer's carbine and grabbed him by the epaulette. The man gasped and then the slim blade slid underneath his chin, pointing upwards. It was less neat than he had intended, but he used all his strength to pull the man farther on to the blade. The Pole gasped, spitting blood over him, and more blood pumped from the wound in his neck. He let go of the carbine, and as it fell the bayonet stuck in the sheet. Desperately the man tried to grab Williams' arms, but his strength was already going. He went limp, became dead weight, and the officer gently lowered the corpse to the ground.

The knife was embedded so firmly that he could not pull it free. As they had marched to the bridge during the night, Williams had tried to think of a way to deal with any sentries without killing them. He had not been able to come up with any plan that seemed likely to succeed. There was no time for regrets. He put the man's hat on, and lifted his carbine, so that if anyone should approach they would assume the sentry was still in place – ideally until it was too late.

Mulligan was with him almost immediately, along with Scammell and one of the men from the 52nd. The other man had gone back to fetch Jowers and his men.

'Neat work, sir,' hissed the guardsman. Williams passed the hat and carbine to the man from the 52nd and took his musket and bayonet. The man was reluctant to give them up, which was an encouraging sign.

Earlier they had seen light from a low building on the far bank. When all of them were on the bridge, Williams left their own sentry in place and led the rest towards it. Up close, they could see only a single door. The back of the building butted against the slope. There was a heavily shuttered window in the wall facing the bridge. Williams put a man either side of it. He gestured for everyone to load and found himself automatically going through the familiar routine. He had only a single cartridge, but if things worked there should be no need to reload.

The door looked less solid than the shutters. He tapped Mulligan on the shoulder and the big man took a step back. Before he could launch himself at the door, it opened, and the dim light of a single candle dazzled men who had spent the last hours in darkness. The man at the door grunted in surprise.

A musket flamed, so close that the yellow tongue touched the Pole's chest as Scammell shot him through the body. Mulligan barged the dying man out of the way, tripped on the threshold and his bayonet impaled a man who was rising from beside the door. The lancer screamed in agony. Another of the cavalryman was pulling a pistol and Williams stepped through the door and fired, the shot appallingly loud in the small room. Mulligan forced himself up, wrenching the bayonet from the wounded man, who shrieked again with pain. Williams had the musket levelled, ready to stab at the slightest hint of resistance. The Poles raised their hands quickly, but their faces looked vacant, still stunned by the rapid onslaught.

Williams wanted to rest, and felt that he could easily lie down on the dirty floor and sleep for days, but there was so much to do. He gave orders to Jowers and Mulligan to deal with the bodies, treat the wounded man, and ensure that the prisoners were kept under guard. Then he took one of the Poles' horses and rode back to fetch Groombridge and the rest of the little column. It took hours for the guns and wagons to negotiate the trackway as it twisted and turned through a series of ravines on the road down to the bridge. The horses were giving out altogether, and the ensign blamed himself for not having thought of this and brought the other horses taken from the Poles to add to the weary teams. The sun was rising when they finally arrived, and the task of organising began afresh.

In full daylight Williams looked at the little stone bridge and wondered whether it was worth it – and indeed would be worth what he felt might happen here. There was a patch of deep red among the ice where he had killed the sentry. That man, and the other two Poles who had died in the attack, were wrapped in their cloaks and laid out by the stone house. Now that the wagon and tools were here he must get the prisoners to bury their own dead. The man Mulligan had bayoneted in the stomach was still alive, although his chances seemed poor.

'Eighty-seven men, four women, including Miss Mac-Andrews, begging your pardon, one child and two babies.' Lance Bombardier Cooke gave the list in a monotone, without any trace of interest or insight. 'Nine of the men sick and have trouble walking. Sixty-eight muskets, about eight hundred cartridges, as well as the ones in the wagon, and three rifles with forty cartridges, and they say powder and ball for another fifty or so.'

'You can add eight carbines and one hundred and sixty cartridges to the list,' said Williams. He and the four NCOs stood on the bridge. 'How much ammunition for the guns, Mr Groombridge?'

'Some,' he said thoughtfully. 'Each has a chest with fifteen rounds of grape and twenty shot and charges ready for use. There is another two dozen of grape in the wagon, and the three barrels of powder. There was a big convoy carrying proper reserves of ammunition to the Dons. God knows what's happened to it.'

'Well, we shall have to make do.' Williams was trying his best to appear supremely confident.

'So you are planning on staying put, sir?' Mr Groombridge's tone contained no hint that such an order could possibly be disobeyed, but was scarcely a ringing endorsement of its wisdom.

'General Moore is taking the army to Lugo. He is probably already there. The talk is that he may turn and fight. That may be true or it may not. He'll be on good ground and it depends on whether the French have the pluck to attack him. From everything we have heard the army needs time to rest and pull itself together.' Williams used a stick to mark out a rough map in a patch of snow.

'We are upriver from him. This is the closest route for the French to cross and we know their cavalry are in the area and know about it. They wouldn't have left anyone here unless they were coming back. The villagers told us about a squadron or two. They are bound to be fetching more men. If they get cavalry across here in any force then they can come round the general's flank. They can do that quickly. It will not be too long after that that there'll be infantry as well. If they are quick they can hit our lads in the flank before they know what's going on. Whatever happens, it will mean the general will have to pull out as best he can and fight off the French from two directions.'

They were listening. Cooke showed no sign of comprehension, but the others looked intent, and that was something.

'The only place to stop them is here. With our handful we cannot hope to delay them in the open. Here they'll be packed together as they cross. They won't be expecting to meet real infantry here, only local peasants. They certainly won't be expecting cannon.'

'We have guns, Mr Williams, but no crews.' Groombridge was raising a difficult question, but it was encouraging that he did not see it as conclusively damning the plan. 'There is only myself and Cooke here. The Wee Gees know how to drive horses, but they have never fired a gun in their lives.'

'Then you will have to show them. You teach and lead one crew, and the lance bombardier will take the other.'

'Yes, sir. Very good, sir,' said Groombridge. Cooke's expression remained unaltered. 'How long do you reckon we have to achieve this?' asked the quartermaster sergeant.

'Hopefully most of today. Perhaps all?'

'Well, that's all right, then.' Groombridge seemed more amused than despondent. 'May I ask on what you base that guess, sir?'

'No, you may not.'

'Ah, I thought so.' He considered for a while. 'Sounds about right, though. We'll have to use them close up. Can't teach men to aim well in that time. Doubt we'll be fast either. So, while I'm performing this miracle, what will everyone else be doing? I assume you have already thought about the other possibility, sir. If there is no bridge then the French can't cross it.'

'Yes, but could we blow it up?' asked Williams. 'I am no engineer, but it looks pretty solid to me.'

'Typical bloody Spanish; do a really good job when you don't want them to,' answered Groombridge. 'To be honest, sir, I do not know. We don't have that much powder.'

'Well, get the artificers to have a look and see if they can prepare things. I do not believe we can rely on that, so we must prepare for the defence. We have to be able to hold them today and probably most of tomorrow. By that time the general will either have sent us help or told us to abandon the attempt.'

There was another obvious alternative, but none of them chose to speak it aloud. 'Right, apart from the gun crews, we'll split everyone else into three groups. The riflemen with half a dozen others will give us some skirmishers. Everyone else is split into two platoons. You will lead one, Sergeant Jowers, and Corporal Mulligan will take the other. Split them up any way you like. From now on keep them together. You'll work as a group and fight as a group.'

Williams gave each of them their tasks before sitting down with paper and pencil borrowed from Groombridge to write a message. He thought for a while about how to address the commander of the army, and for a moment the impudence of what he was doing seemed appalling. He kept things simple and soon it was done.

Brandt carried the message, riding on Bobbie and leading one of the lancer's mounts. As Williams watched him go, Jane looked up into his face and tried to read the officer's thoughts.

'You understand, I trust, why I had to remain,' she said. 'That hussar will be a better messenger.'

'I had hoped to send him back down the road to look for the French.' Williams told himself that his desire to send the girl back to the army was for a practical reason, and not simply because he wanted her safe. After a while, he added, 'Yes, I do understand.' He did not look at her, but watched the diminishing figure of the hussar. Behind them, they heard Groombridge's voice bellowing out instructions.

'The number seven stands to the right of the muzzle. His job is to ram the charge and sponge out the barrel. The number eight stands to the left . . .'

'I could not hope to take the baby with me.' Jane continued her explanation quietly, but firmly. 'At least, not if I was to ride quickly.' Williams had suggested that she pass the child to one of the women.

'Yes,' he said. He still looked away, afraid that if he saw her then he would not be able to stop himself from taking her in his arms.

'And surely the dispatch will be treated more seriously if delivered by a dragoon.'

'Probably.'

'I do understand your concern, and know that your suggestion was a mark of trust, and also intended to remove me from danger.'

'A lone ride through mountains in the midst of a war may not be entirely without peril.'

Jane was pleased to see the faint smile. 'But I simply could not leave when others had to stay.'

'They are soldiers.'

'And the women, and the children?'

'They're followers.'

'And I am the daughter of an officer, raised to understand duty. What would your men think if they saw me ride away to safety? They would think that you had no hope.'

Groombridge sounded frustrated. 'The number nine stands between the right wheel and the muzzle. Before the gun is fired he steps back outside the line of the wheel. And if you don't we'll be scraping you off it!'

'Most of them must realise already that there is little hope.' He tried to shake off the doubt. 'If we are lucky, and they do not come too soon or in too great force, then perhaps . . .'

'So I will stay to show that I am confident of success. More than that, it shows that you believe in it.'

His smile became broader. She understood as well as he could possibly have hoped. 'We had better win, then. I should be broken hearted to disappoint them.' At last he turned to her, and Jane felt she saw more genuine respect mingled with his admiration than she had ever seen there before.

'I should emphasise that my assistance does not extend to digging your ditches or learning to fire your cannons.'

'Shame. I was rather relying upon you.'

She slipped her hand into his.

Corporal Mulligan stamped to attention and saluted. 'Mr Williams, sir. Would you mind showing us where you want these stakes?' He had sent a party away from the river, looking for timber. They found a farm, just under a mile away, but hidden behind the hills. The women and children, along with the sick incapable of fighting, were to go there and shelter. Most of the roof was still on the house. The barn was a ruin, and the men had pulled down as many of the timbers as they could and chopped them into six-foot lengths.

'Certainly.' The girl's fingers uncurled from around his without any other visible sign. 'I will come with you now.'

Williams tried to imagine how the French would come. The road bent sharply as it came down a deep cutting towards the bridge. The low rocky mound stood to the left, and gave them more cover to form up. It was the obvious place to occupy with sharpshooters who would fire at any defenders on or behind the bridge. To the right of the road was an open field leading up to the sheer cliffs which dropped down to the river. Anything forming there was in plain sight and had little cover. So if the French had only cavalry then they would form up behind the mound and back on the road and then charge straight across.

The bridge was narrow, and at most three horsemen could cross at a time. Once they were over, the road wound sharply left again, looping round the slope to which the little stone shack clung. There was another round hill on this side, larger and higher. The riflemen could go there, and with luck dominate any enemy skirmishers on the far bank. Behind the hill, beside the road and out of sight, would be one of the cannon under Cooke. Twenty yards back on the other side of the road the ground dipped a good five feet or so and Mulligan and his platoon would wait there. Jowers and the rest of the men would be on the road next to the gun, as would Williams himself. Groombridge and the other twelve-pounder would be in the lee of the shack. There was not quite enough room to hide the big gun, so they would try covering it with blankets, including the white sheet Williams had worn the previous night. The French would see something odd, but if they were not expecting to meet artillery they might not know what it was. Perhaps.

Williams had toyed with the idea of blocking the bridge with the wagon, but that would have given the enemy cover right on the crossing itself. Instead he wanted to lure them on, bring them across and then savage the head of the charge. To do that he needed to make sure that they could not spread quickly to either side of the road and swamp them with numbers. Hence the stakes.

'I want a line either side of the road. Put them about a yard out, leaning towards the road, and then sharpen the tops.' He thought for a moment. 'How wide is a horse?'

Mulligan pondered for a moment. 'Couple of feet, I suppose.'

'I want it so that a cavalryman can't squeeze through between them.'

'How about we put them a yard apart and then have another line a couple of feet back and in the gaps.'

'Excellent. The ground's hard so it won't be easy.'

'We'll manage, sir.' The corporal was holding a bulky sledge-hammer.

'I got the idea from Agincourt,' said Williams.

Mulligan shook his head. 'Don't know the gentleman, sir.' The officer was not quite sure whether the man was serious.

Williams walked on to the bridge. The two artificers had prised up one of the stones. Underneath was hard-packed gravel.

'Going to be hard to shift,' said the older of the two men.

A shot split the peaceful air. 'Cavalry!' shouted the sentry up on the rocky hill. Williams looked and spotted a lance pennant just above the point where the road dipped into the ravine to come down to the bridge. Far too far even for a rifle shot. 'Two of them, sir!'

So much for surprise, he thought wearily. It was only a patrol, but they would have seen red coats and blue and would know that there were soldiers – British soldiers – around the bridge. Maybe there was one more surprise. Williams turned back to the artificers.

'Make a trail of powder leading back from this hole. Do it so that they can see you.'

'What's the point, sir? We haven't even made space for a charge, let alone put one in place.'

'Yes, but they won't know that, will they.'

And perhaps, Williams thought to himself, just perhaps, it will make them rush.

22

It was raining again, and the drops spattered on to the churned soil as Murphy piled up a little cairn over the grave. His wife's tears flowed as quickly as the rain could wash them away. It was a terrible thing, and maybe worse for a woman, although he knew that he would miss the little chuckles of the boy. He had been growing, and it seemed every day he was more aware of them, and alert to what went on around him. Mary tried to sing, and the words choked so he sang for her as he had heard others lament at funerals. He knew she would have liked a priest, but he had not been able to find one. They had arrived in the dark and left the straggling village before dawn. The child had died some time during their short hours of sleep. Mary had been so weary that it was only when she woke that she realised what had happened. The other women had gathered, and some had tried to rub life back into the little body while others comforted the mother.

In not much more than a day the reserve had marched forty miles, through sleet and later the driving rain. There was little food and no shelter, and no wagons left with room to carry the women and children. Esther MacAndrews was walking as often as she rode, letting one of the exhausted wives sit uncomfortably astride her horse to give them some rest. The major's wife was starting to look old and drawn, but she still fussed over the children and encouraged the women along. She had wept when she saw the little corpse, and pushed her way through the others to embrace poor Mrs Murphy. Esther remembered the black despair of burying her own children.

There were corpses all along the road. The horses were heaped on either side, some cut by hungry men looking for meat and others gnawed by vermin. Dead men were getting more common, almost as frequent as those lying incapably drunk. The cold had killed a lot. At one cluster of bodies, the grenadiers had been sent to rout up any they could. The men had become more brutal, kicking at the prone figures or even prodding them with bayonets. Hanley had walked over to a cluster of red shapes around a shattered cask. They lay in a circle – three men, a woman and a boy of no more than ten. Some of the rum from the barrel had stained wide patches of ice a darker shade. All five of the people were dead, and he struggled to understand the thoughts of such desperate, hopeless folk as they lapped at the drink until they fell asleep where they lay and never woke up. Later they passed corpses fallen in the road and trampled into the mire by men too weary to step around them.

The Spanish guns and transport that had taken this road had nearly all given out in this last stretch. Some of the collapsed animals lay in their traces, tongues lolling out and eyes rolling madly. General Paget ordered parties of men to put them out of their misery. The men of the Royal Horse Artillery were busy painting or chalking 'SPANISH' on each of the abandoned carriages, for they did not want Bonaparte claiming to have taken their guns. The stuff was washing off in the rain almost as soon as they applied it. Pringle had not had the energy to wander over to the officer in charge and ask him whether he really thought it would stop the French Emperor claiming whatever he wanted.

Among the debris of the Army of Galicia's train were carts piled high with uniform jackets and trousers, greatcoats and blankets, and the even greater prize of boots. Quartermasters rode among the mass of soldiers from the reserve calling out for them to leave the stores for their allies. The Spanish were not there, nor likely to be before the French, and the men were in need now. MacAndrews listened to the complaints of one captain from the Quartermaster General's department with every mark of respect and sympathy. He assured him that the 106th would take nothing, and enthusiastically damned the rogues from other regiments who so readily resorted to plunder. At the same time he let his officers turn a blind eye, and it was only when the order came to press on quickly that they drew the men away. There was a rumour that a French column was pushing round the flank to cut them off and so the march continued through the night.

Dobson kept his old worn-out boots and put them in his pack when other men tossed theirs away with a curse. He also took some for Murphy, who had been barefoot for days. Three hours of marching destroyed almost every pair of the new shoes. Uppers came away from soles owing to bad stitching. Worse were the shoes, where two wafer-thin layers of leather sole were padded out by nothing more than clay.

Hanley's disgust vented itself as he stood with Pringle and watched the engineers completing their preparations to blow up the stone bridge outside Nogales. 'Is it not shameful?' he said bitterly as he saw Murphy once again with his feet merely wrapped in rags. 'To supply such trash to our ally.'

'The stuff we get is not always much better.' Pringle was equally gloomy, but had little appetite or energy for anger. 'I dare say some noble man of commerce decided that there was even less likely to be a complaint if the goods were being shipped off to another country.'

'It is a betrayal.'

'It is business – and the man behind it will probably die rich and fat. He will never know the joy of sleeping in a snowdrift and being chased by the French!' Pringle could see his friend still seethed with rage, so decided to be practical. 'There are plenty of cordwainers and cobblers on the books. Perhaps we can get them to repair the wretched things?'

There was a shout from the engineers, gesturing at everyone to stand back and be careful. The last riflemen had run back across to this bank and were reforming on their regiment. An engineer captain lit the powder trail, dashed back to the shelter of a ditch and crouched down. When it came, the explosion was flat, and sounded as damp as the rain.

'How very unimpressive,' said Pringle.

'And useless too.' Wind quickly drove the smoke away and they could see that the blast had done no more than take a chunk out of the side of the bridge. 'Oh, our friends are back,' added Hanley. On the hills in the distance they could see the drab shapes of French dragoons, with their long green cloaks over their uniforms.

The march resumed and the pace stayed quick. Halfway through the day they came to another bridge, with four elegant arches which Hanley was positive were Roman. 'It seems criminal to harm it.'

'They must have heard you,' commented Pringle, after another disappointing explosion had done little more than chip some of the stonework.

'They built well, the Romans,' said Hanley admiringly.

The next stream proved to be readily fordable for a hundred yards on either side, prompting General Paget to tell the engineers to save their efforts for more fruitful projects. All of the hussars had pulled back behind the reserve, their horses quite used up, and so the rearguard was formed solely by the infantry and the Horse Artillery Troop. In the afternoon, the general attempted a ruse, ordering the gunners to unlimber their six-pounders and then leave them in plain view as if abandoned. The captain Pringle had seen supervising the painting of abandoned Spanish equipment was today visibly enjoying the risk to his own cannon. The 28th waited, concealed on the far side of the hill behind the guns, while the grenadiers and Light Company of the 106th watched from a patch of woodland on the other side of the road. A few French dragoons forded the stream when the rest of the reserve moved off. They were reluctant to push any farther, and after half an hour, the general gave up and had the guns hitched back to the limbers and taken away. In the horse artillery all of the gunners had their own horses or sat on the limbers, so they moved off quickly, as the infantry trudged more sedately behind. In the next valley, parties of the 95th were waiting to resume their role as rearmost outposts.

Several times the Reserve Division halted again and formed up, facing the enemy. The riflemen fired a few times with little result, and the French replied with their carbines to even less effect. General Paget was everywhere, cursing the enemy, snapping at his own men and then urging them on or giving orders directly to captains and even subalterns. His staff, including Captain Wickham, trailed behind him, or dashed off on errands whenever the general had a mind to send them.

Wickham was cold and wet and found the day increasingly tedious. Neither side appeared to be achieving anything. Once the general sent him running to the top of a high hill to report on what he could see, and that made him wetter still because there was no shelter from the driving wind up there. Nor was there much more to see. The French were there, a few patrols half a mile or so beyond the 95th and the rest farther back.

When Wickham had half run, half stumbled down the hill, he found the general leaning against a wall as the 91st went past on the road. The Highlanders' gaiters and bare legs were thickly covered in mud. None of them paid any attention when a very tall and extremely thin officer rode past them and reined in next to the general.

'Pray, sir, where is General Paget?' he asked in a strangely deep and very precise voice. He was clearly a man accustomed to neatness and efficiency. Even in the rain his skin looked dry, and he kept licking his thin lips. Wickham had to admit that at this moment Paget scarcely looked like a general. His drab cloak was stained and frayed around the edges, and his hat was both bare of any plume and considerably misshapen from exposure to the weather. It also lay on the top of the wall beside him. His hair was plastered flat against his head and his chin boasted at least two days of bristly growth. His patience was even more threadbare. Neither he nor any of his staff bothered to reply, or indeed acknowledge the man in any way.

'Come, come. Where is General Paget?'

The general donned his hat. 'I am General Paget, sir. Pray tell me, what are your orders?' One of his eyes was half closed, and Wickham knew from experience that this was not a good sign.

'Oh, I beg pardon, sir.' The tone implied that the fault was not his own. 'I am the Paymaster General . . .'

'Alight, sir,' Sir Edward interrupted. His right eye flickered.

The paymaster general hesitated, then drew his feet from the stirrups and swung himself down slowly, as if humouring a child. 'I am the Paymaster General. The treasure of the army is only a short way ahead, but the bullocks are jaded and quite done in – absolutely done in. They cannot proceed farther, and so I must have fresh animals to draw the treasure forward.'

Sir Edward looked around him. When he spoke his voice was low. 'Pray, sir, do you take me for a bullock driver or muleteer?' Already the words were growing louder, as his face became redder.

'Or, knowing who I am, are you coolly telling me that through your own neglect or total ignorance of your duty you are about to lose the treasure committed to your charge, which, according to your account, must shortly fall into the hands of the enemy? Those, sir, are French cavalry.' The general was almost shouting as he pointed at a line of horsemen on the far ridgeline. 'It is possible that you have never seen them before so do not recognise them. Had you, sir, the slightest conception of your duty, you would have known that you ought to be a day's march ahead of the whole army, instead of hanging back with your foundered bullocks and carts upon the rearmost company of the rearguard, and making your report at the very moment when that company is absolutely engaged with an advancing enemy. What, sir!'

The paymaster general was crouching as if he could somehow shelter from Sir Edward's fury, which continued unabated. 'To come to me and impede my march with your carts, and ask me to look for bullocks when I should be free from all encumbrances and my mind occupied by no other care than that of disposing my troops to best advantage in resisting the approaching enemy!

It is doubtful, sir, whether your conduct can be attributed to ignorance and neglect alone!'

'But, sir . . .' All confidence had fled from the paymaster's voice and yet his sense of formalities was still well enough entrenched for this weak protest.

'But, sir! You God-damned rogue! How dare you, sir! You ought to be hanged, and if I could find a high enough tree I shall damned well do it myself!' There was more, but Sir Edward managed to keep most of it under his breath. 'Sir, attend to the duties you have so woefully neglected. Take what you can, but neither your money nor your carts will delay me for even a moment. If your bullocks block the road, we shall shoot them, and if you waste any more of my time I will bloody well shoot you as well. Now go, sir!'

Wickham told Pringle the story as the grenadiers pushed several of the carts over a low cliff not far from the road. The men were enjoying the destruction. As the wagons fell, some of the barrels split open, scattering shiny silver dollars into the snow.

'Nineteen barrels, five thousand in each,' said the subaltern in charge of the escort. He seemed overwhelmingly relieved to be rid of the responsibility. 'God knows how many steps in promotion!'

Wickham watched the falling money with a desperate hunger. He had been pleased to be sent on this errand and had hoped to profit. There had been no chance, and so he watched the atrocious waste. The French would have the silver and many of them would become rich. Down that slope lay the path to comfort, security and respectable society, and it was so tantalisingly close that he almost wept. He looked around, trying to remember the spot, although he could not see any prospect of this being of real value.

The rearguard pressed on, passing over yet another bridge. The 106th were not at the very rear, so for a while heard only the sporadic shots of the riflemen, and the duller booms of the six-pounders as the French pursuers were made to keep their distance. They formed in a valley behind, but the short defence proved enough to slow the enemy, and when the horse artillery and 95th withdrew, the rest of the Reserve Division was able to march unmolested. They pressed on throughout the night, thankful that the rain slackened and then stopped. It was still dry when the sun rose and broke through the clouds.

The 106th reached Lugo around ten in the morning. All ranks were pleased to hear that for a while the reserve would not be called upon to provide outposts, and even the news that this meant continuing the march for another five miles before they could rest did not dampen spirits. They marched through the bivouac of the Guards' Brigade. It seemed a different world. The men were in their shirtsleeves and trousers, sitting at ease around campfires and with jackets and belts newly cleaned and draped over bushes to dry. Cordial insults were exchanged on both sides as the dirty, mostly barefoot 106th marched past. Hanley was at the rear of the company and noticed that the men stiffened to march more formally, Sergeant Probert calling out the step. Half of them wore odd coloured bits of looted Spanish uniform.

'Who are you, bloody harlequins?'

'No, we're soldiers. Who are you?'

The French arrived in the afternoon. Sir John Moore watched their advance guard take up positions facing his own army. The French were in considerable numbers, and he guessed that Marshal Soult had slowed his advance so that he could concentrate a bigger force.

Sir John scanned the enemy with his glass, comparing notes with his staff officers.

'Two brigades of cavalry, a division of infantry already in position and one – perhaps two – more on the way. Assuming that there are two, what would you make that in total, Colborne?'

The ever-efficient staff officer already had the answer. 'Twenty thousand, or perhaps a little more.'

The general nodded. 'Yes, that is my guess.' He had some nineteen thousand or so men. One fresh brigade, standing out in their neat uniforms, joined the army at Lugo. The rest were all very tired, and some virtually exhausted after an order had not been passed on and several brigades had been sent on an unnecessary diversion. Sir David Baird had given it to a dragoon to carry, and the man had got himself drunk. So the men had marched for more than a day over atrocious roads in appalling conditions before the mistake was corrected, and then had to come back the way they had gone.

Sir John knew that his soldiers were very weary. Their spirit was harder to judge. There had been more abuses in the last days, more theft and drunkenness. In anger he had declared that he would rather be a shoeblack than the general of such an army.

'Many officers will be offended at such a harsh verdict on the discipline of their regiments,' one of his brigade commanders had said.

'Well, let them damned well be offended,' Sir John replied coldly. 'As long as they are shamed into doing their duty!' Yet for all his rage, Moore could tell that something of the army's mood had changed. He could see it as they rode through the encampment. It was not just the rest which was welcome. The entire army was keen to fight – even the men whose behaviour seemed the worst. They had all seemed to revive.

The position was not a bad one, and Sir John was sorely tempted to fight, at least if Soult was fool enough to attack. The elderly but ever-enthusiastic Colonel Graham did his best to foster this enthusiasm in his friend.

'Well, Sir John, after we have beaten them, you will take us on in pursuit of them for a few days, won't you?'

'No.' The general's voice was firm. 'I have had enough of Galicia.'

'Oh! But just a few days after them,' Graham pleaded. 'You must take us.'

The colonel got no answer.

The next morning the commander and his staff again rode out to observe the enemy. Colonel Graham's aggressive impulses remained strong, but he was preoccupied by instinctive flirtation with the two ladies who accompanied them. One was the wife of

Colonel MacKenzie of the newly arrived 5th Foot, and the other was Esther MacAndrews. Graham was especially delighted that both were Scots, at least by marriage.

Major Colborne was the first to see the puffs of smoke from the far ridge. The French gunners judged remarkably well and two of the shot bounced so close that they frightened the horses as they skidded past. Both ladies calmed their beasts most handsomely. As the staff withdrew a little way, one of General Hill's aides arrived leading a light dragoon from the German Legion. The man was swaying in the saddle and Sir John at first wondered whether another courier had got himself drunk on duty. Then he noticed that the man's right arm hung limp and useless.

Brandt struggled to stay conscious. The pain in his broken arm burned him with every movement, but he was determined to take the news directly to the general and unwilling to trust anyone else's assurances. It had been a hard ride, and the mare had shied at nothing more than a startled bird whirring out of a thicket, and when she bucked, she had come on to a soft drift and had fallen, taking him with her. The horse he was leading ran off. He was not sure how long he had been unconscious, but Bobbie had remained beside him. Getting into the saddle was hard with one arm, and riding harder through the night. When he reached the outposts of the army he had met with only suspicion and delay. Yet the army was the army, and his stubborn insistence had always ended up with him being passed on to ever-higher authority. At last he had done it.

'I have an urgent message for General Moore.'

Esther MacAndrews noticed something very familiar about the horse. Then the mare turned and showed her empty eye socket and recognition came. A desperate hope grew within her.

23

The first attack came almost exactly as Williams expected. It was late afternoon, and the setting sun had already sunk past the peaks of the hills to the west. The sentry waved his shako on the tip of his musket and then sped down the low hill towards the bridge.

'Make ready!' Sergeant Jowers gave the order to the thirty men formed across the road. Williams was ahead of them, so that he could see the far bank better. Driver Parker stood holding the lighted portfire beside the left wheel of the gun, next to the motley line of redcoats. Groombridge had readily agreed to the suggestion that the bright West Country man should be attached to the gun commanded by the stolid Cooke.

Mulligan's men were kneeling on the slope of the depression, ready to spring to their feet and into view at his order.

'Don't shoot unless they put men on the rocks!' Williams called up to the rifleman he had placed on the high ground. The man, a villainous-looking rogue from Yorkshire, gave him a thumbs-up signal. Looking up, Williams saw that Groombridge had not yet uncovered his gun and was keeping his men out of sight behind the stone shack. He heard the sound of horses. The sentry was puffing as he ran up.

'Fifty or sixty lancers. Might be dragoons behind!' The man was from the 52nd, a regiment Sir John Moore himself had trained to the peak of efficiency. 'No infantry that I can see, sir.'

Williams smiled, and nodded for the man to join on the end of Jowers' line. He glanced back to see the first Poles come trotting down the road. An officer whose drooping blond moustache flapped in the breeze led them, his sabre raised high. The bugler beside him rode a grey horse and wore a yellow jacket. The two men were barely on the flat ground and passing behind the shelter of the rocks when the trumpet sounded. Lances dropped to the charge position, their red and white pennants whipping in the wind. The Poles spurred their horses into a canter, their column driving straight down the road and on to the bridge.

As Williams dashed back to join Jowers, the Polish officer was already on the bridge. A moment later, as he turned, the cavalry-man was riding between the stakes, a bunch of horsemen behind him.

'Fire!' Williams yelled at Parker.

'Fire!' Cooke repeated the order, but the driver had already lowered the smoking match on to the touch-hole just behind the royal crest on the bronze gun. The powder sparked and the flame set off the main charge, making the heavy carriage leap back with a dull boom. All save Cooke flinched, for it was the first time they had been so close to the raw power of a cannon.

The canvas bag split as it was hurled from the muzzle and the nine heavy balls, each an inch and a half in diameter, split away from the iron base and bar to which they were fixed and flew off in a spreading cone. The bridge was no more than thirty yards away and the discharge was still concentrated when it struck the leading Poles. The officer's lower jaw was shattered in an instant, but he was already dead from a second heavy ball which ripped through his ribs and burst out of his back creating a hole a foot wide. The trumpeter's horse went down with the iron bar driven deep into its brain. His own wrist was smashed, the hand still clutching the trumpet flung away. Another man and two horses were flicked aside by the blast.

Williams did not catch Mulligan giving the command in the noise and chaos, but his platoon was standing, visible above the waist where they stood on the rear slope.

'Fire!' He caught the order, bellowed in a voice that augured well for the man's future career in his regiment.

Smoke enveloped the line. The Poles were still pushing

onwards, until the volley plucked five more men from their saddles, and dropped another horse.

Williams nodded to Jowers.

'Forward march!' he called, and the line stepped out. They covered the cannon, but Williams doubted there would be time for the crew to reload. On the bridge the Poles had stopped, their horses milling, and trying to avoid the dead and wounded men and animals. For the first time he heard the screams.

'Halt!' They were less than twenty yards away, exposed now to the far bank, but there had been no shots from his riflemen and he guessed the French had no one waiting on the rocky mound to snipe at his line. He wanted to be sure of doing as much execution as possible and so gave the men a moment to steady their breathing.

'Fire!' Williams gave the order himself and wished there had been a musket spare for him to use and add to the volley. Smoke blossomed, and if the shots were ragged by the standards of a well-drilled battalion, the aim was good. One Pole fell from his horse and plummeted screaming off the bridge into the ravine below. Two more men were dead, one horse slumped to the ground and another rearing, throwing its rider and thrashing its hoofs against the air in agony.

He looked over to the far bank and saw the French reserve, some thirty or forty cuirassiers. Their cloaks were tied to the backs of their saddles and the men's steel armour and helmets caught the red light of sunset. If they came, then they might just be able to barge through the chaos of the bridge and get to them before anyone had reloaded. Then he saw the Frenchmen wheeling away. To his left Mulligan's men were levelling their muskets once again, and he marvelled that they had loaded so quickly. The surviving Poles saw it as well, and began turning to go back. The rear of the company had never crossed at all, and these quickly sped away. Mulligan fired anyway. More men were hit by the lead musket balls. One dropped his lance and spread his arms wide, arching his back, before he fell to the side. Another horse folded, and the rearing animal jumped the wall and tumbled down into the ravine. The Polish officer's horse, wild eyed but somehow unscathed, trotted past Williams.

'Gun ready, sir!' called Cooke, but there was no longer any need. The attack was over.

'Well done, lads,' said Williams. They had lost no one, for the French had never come close enough to use lance or blade.

Jowers drew them back alongside the gun so that they were all in shelter. Williams walked over to congratulate Mulligan and his men. They were grinning, excited, and not a little awed by the carnage they had inflicted. Two men were lifting one of the wounded Poles, propping him up against the wall of the bridge. Another pair went to the trumpeter, who was staring dumbly at the stump on the end of his arm. His face was already pale from loss of blood. Beside him a lance was still quivering from where it had been rammed into the hard ground. Once the men had loaded again, they began shooting the injured animals.

'Visitors, sir!' said the guardsman.

The cuirassier officer was riding towards them. Beside him was the man in cocked hat and dark blue, and behind came a trooper with a somewhat grubby, but recognisably white, handkerchief tied to the tip of his sword.

Williams paced forward on to the bridge to meet them.

It was the man in the cocked hat who spoke. 'This is Capitaine Dalmas, who does not speak English,' he explained. 'I am Lieutenant Maizet of the engineers.' The man's gaze wandered past Williams' shoulders to look at the carnage on the bridge. 'My God,' he said softly, and then realised that this was probably not the best way to conduct negotiations. The cuirassier officer growled at him. 'The Capitaine asks me to translate his words exactly.' It sounded much like an apology. 'But he asks . . . he asks who the hell are you?' Williams wondered whether the French had been considerably stronger.

'Ensign Williams, 106th Foot. I command the advance guard. The rest of the battalion will be here soon.'

Dalmas laughed when he heard the translation. 'He says that

will be more prisoners for his brigade to take. You can surrender now to save everyone's time.'

Williams shook his head. Dalmas was neither surprised at the answer, nor particularly bothered. Rushing the bridge had been a chance worth taking, and in such a gamble speed was everything, so there had been no point preparing the attack and so giving the enemy warning. He said something to Maizet.

'We would like to recover our wounded, and so suggest a truce for the rest of the day.'

That seemed remarkably generous, and Williams could see no advantage in turning it down. 'We will carry them this far. Two men can then come up and take each in turn.'

Dalmas spoke. 'He says you seem very frightened of us.'

'And yet you are the ones coming across under a flag of truce?' Williams turned back and called to Mulligan to begin moving the men. Then he noticed that Maizet was looking at the stone lifted by the artificers. They had made no great impression on the gravel beneath. An engineer would know immediately that there was no charge prepared. Well, that was one less secret. He tried not to show any concern when Dalmas looked intently at the stone building. Had he noticed the gun, and realised what it was? If so, the Frenchman's face betrayed nothing.

Night fell, but with the cloud for the moment gone the stars lit up a landscape still white in spite of the recent rain. Sentries could see well, although the mind could play tricks and the weird shadows invent threats or conceal real ones. Williams allowed half the men to rest at the start of the evening. They piled up all the timber too short to be made into stakes and built a fire, some way back along the road behind the gun. Men rested there, and ate another meal of boiled horsemeat and the last bread given to them at the village. There was a half-mug of wine for each man.

Mr Groombridge was the very proud owner of a timepiece, and it made it easier to regulate the watches. Men did an hour on guard, and an hour resting as best they could in their allotted position. Williams had wondered about changing his dispositions now that the enemy knew them, but could not come up with more advantageous positions. They were in the right place. Every two hours, the other half of each detachment would go to its position and take on the watch. Williams insisted that Mulligan, Jowers and Cooke got some sleep at the beginning of the night. He sent one of the men back to the house to send his compliments to Miss MacAndrews, and check that she, the other ladies and the sick had everything they needed.

Jane sent back her thanks. The women and children were well, but she feared the man with the swollen and frostbitten hands looked near to death. His limbs stank of corruption, and when she came close the girl nearly gagged. The feet of another of the men had the same foul odour. MacDonald the Highlander was coughing, and barely able to stand, but seemed remarkably cheerful. He crawled to each of the men in turn and talked to them whether they could understand or not. He had added his own message.

'Tell yon Campbell that we are all fine. The luckiest fellows in the world to be warm and dry and cared for by fair lassies.' The other women were plump and hard faced, and the old man had looked at Jane as he spoke. He sat back against the wall, breathing hard, his chest wheezing from exhaustion.

'Still, if it weren't for a bonnie lass, I wouldn't be here.'

'Someone you loved?' Jane's curiosity was pricked, and as she tried to change the bandage on a man's foot and fought to control her nausea it was better to be distracted.

'No, not really. She was a great lady, a duchess no less, and I was just a laddie of sixteen with not a penny to my name, but she was famous for her beauty. Fairest woman in the Highlands and spirited with it too. She had a son a few years older than me and he decided to form a regiment. They went around all the fairs that summer. Do you know they give you a shilling when you join?'

Jane nodded.

'Of course you do, you being an officer's lass. Well, the duchess put the coin between her lips.' He puckered his mouth into a kiss. 'And if a boy chose to join he stepped up and took the shilling with his own lips. Seven years or more for one kiss. I'm still here after twice that.'

'Was it worth it?' Jane managed to get the bandage tied. They were running out of cloth that was even vaguely clean.

'Oh, aye.' MacDonald laughed until he coughed, but when he had controlled the outburst he was still laughing. 'But I were a cocky lad in those days. After I had my kiss, I took the shilling and threw it high into the crowd to show that that wasn't the prize I wanted. They all cheered me and so I danced a jig. The bluidy sergeants soon knocked all that out of me when we reached the camp, but it were worth it.

'You know, lass, you could raise ten regiments of your own!' Several of the other men cheered this, and even the blind soldier declared that he would re-enlist.

Jane smiled, and was amazed that they could be so cheerful. The redcoat sent by Williams had told them of the fight. It was obvious that another was expected soon, and she tried not to think about what might happen. Better to keep busy. The girl went to feed Jacob, taking him from the arms of one of the soldiers' wives, a kind enough, if startlingly plain, woman named Rose.

Dalmas found the chasseur captain's ferocious lack of intelligence rather depressing.

'So of course, I shot three of them in reprisal. The usual form.' A chasseur had been stabbed in one of the houses of a village. The wound was no more than a nick on the arm, and the scratches on his face from a woman's nails looked more painful. The captain did not seem to feel it mattered at all what the chasseur had been doing. He toyed with the waxed tip of his luxuriously upturned moustache. The man clearly felt himself to be a dashing figure.

'I see,' replied Dalmas. It was too late to do anything about it. Jean-Baptiste Dalmas waged war ruthlessly, but always intelligently. It worried him that in Spain the French armies were resorting to brutality so automatically. Not especially concerned by their morality, he strongly doubted the utility of such tactics. 'The usual form?'

'Yes. You know – firing parties of three, each musket loaded with two balls. Quick and simple. I got the Légère to do it.' The captain implied that the task was somewhat beneath his men and best left to the infantry. A company of voltigeurs – the trained skirmishers of a battalion – had come with the chasseurs, each light infantryman riding uncomfortably behind a horseman.

The mixed force ought to have been at the bridge before dark, instead of arriving halfway through the night, had this primped-up fool not stopped to demand food from the peasants and then start shooting them. If he had had the company of infantry, Dalmas would not have made the crude attempt to rush the bridge and lost fourteen lancers.

Sourly, he wondered who was responsible for picking Capitaine Lancel of the chasseurs to aid him. Some colonel getting rid of their least reliable man, probably, or perhaps himself so stupid that he mistook bluster for ability. Dalmas could smell the sour stink of the sores on the horses' backs. That spoke of bad practice in the squadron, of conscripts too lazy to care for their horses before themselves. The animals were slow, and with the added weight of the voltigeurs, they might not have arrived in time anyway. Dalmas decided to keep the remaining Poles back, and take them across the river once the bridge had fallen. The marshal had been too cautious to commit a cavalry brigade to his support until it was taken. So Dalmas needed the bridge quickly, and then the fastest of the Poles would carry his dispatch and start the cavalry brigade moving. If their horses were in as poor a state as these, then that move would probably be slow. The Emperor would have understood how much time mattered and hurried. Soult was too cautious, but it could still work.

He would attack at dawn. The infantry commander seemed a sensible enough man, and it would be better for him to see the ground. Dalmas told him to select a dozen men and send them to fire at the British sentries. That ought to disturb their sleep. His own men could rest and be ready for the morning.

The first shots came half an hour later, the flashes vivid in the dark. Williams had only just been forced to take some rest and was dragged out of his sleep by the uproar. Voices ordered everyone to stand to arms. He ran down the road past the gun and Jowers' men as they formed up. Mulligan's group had fired a couple of shots before the corporal screamed at them to wait until they had a proper target. There was no sign of an attack.

Williams peered into the darkness and blinked when another Frenchman fired. The shot flew just a few feet over his head and he ducked back. The riflemen on the hill started shooting.

'Cease fire!' he called. 'Don't waste powder!'

'Waste powder be buggered,' said the Yorkshireman under his breath. He could see the Frenchman quite clearly, a darker shape crawling in the snow. His rifle erupted in flame and smoke. There was a bitter cry of pain from the far bank, followed by agitated shouts. 'Stop firing, lads,' he said to the others.

24

Williams tried to keep his walk slow. Perhaps he should have started out running. No one would have blamed him, but it would not look right if he accelerated now. Another musket ball struck the ground a few feet from him. The range was not long, even for a smooth-bore firelock, and the stupidity of what he was doing only made him more determined to saunter as gently as he could up the slope. The nearest French skirmishers were eighty yards away on the mound. The ones on the far side of the road with less cover were farther, perhaps a hundred yards. A good man stood a decent chance of hitting his mark at that range, and even a conscript might get lucky. He felt the wind of a ball whizzing past his cheek. They were getting far too close, but still he walked. The sound of the rifles was sharper as his men on the hill tried to pick off the French. Muskets gave a duller boom, but some of those shots were from the men with the riflemen and not all were French. At least that would throw the enemy off their aim.

'Try not to get yourself killed, sir,' said Groombridge. The quartermaster sergeant had walked out across the slope to meet him, matching the officer's coolness and copying his stupidity. It was close to dawn and the clouds to the east were a glory of reds and pinks.

'I think they will come soon,' said Williams. 'My guess would be infantry first to clear the way for the horsemen.'

'No sense in staying hidden, then.'

'No, Mr Groombridge. As soon as they get to our side of the

bridge fire and then just keep on firing as fast as you can.' The quartermaster sergeant gave a brief nod. 'Your lads all ready?'

'Yes, Mr Williams. All present.' He emphasised the last words. No one from any of the groups had slipped away in the night. Williams had feared that some would have run, unwilling to fight under a leader they did not know. 'They're up for a good mill,' said Groombridge. 'Tired too, but for many this is the first real chance to get at the Crapauds.'

A musket ball flicked between them as they spoke. They heard a drum beating on the far side of the river and they saw French infantry jogging out to form on the flat beside the road. Williams counted about eighty, with blue jackets and trousers and short black gaiters. That made them light infantry. They had green epaulettes and tall yellow plumes with a green top, and that made them an elite company. Each soldier had rolled his greatcoat and wore it across one shoulder. They had no packs, and had probably piled them so that they could fight unencumbered. He guessed it was one company with thirty or so men detached as a skirmish line on the rocky mound and along the bank.

One of the French skirmishers fired and Williams' forage cap was flicked from his head. He leaned to pick it up, and bowed ironically. A flurry of shots did not come so near, and then a rifle shot was rewarded when one of the Frenchmen sprang up on his knees, clutching at his shoulder.

'In the Royal Artillery, it is the custom to march when going away from a gun, but always to run towards it, hurrying to get at the enemy.' Groombridge emphasised the words, and Williams caught the amusement in his voice.

'An excellent tradition. May I wish you luck, Mr Groombridge.' Williams held out his hand. After a firm but brief shake, the two men turned and jogged back to their positions. As he went, Williams saw cavalry forming behind the infantry. These were chasseurs in green, so more new arrivals. He could not see the Poles or the cuirassiers, but spotted Dalmas and the engineer Maizet behind the infantry.

Mulligan grinned happily as the officer passed. His men lay or crouched in the depression, still hidden from the French, although the previous day's fight had warned the enemy of their presence.

Across the river a whistle blew. The dozen Frenchmen among the rocks all fired at once, balls flattening against the boulders crowning the higher hill and Williams' little group of sharp-shooters. They ducked instinctively, and half of the eighteen voltigeurs on the other side of the road dashed towards the bridge. The Yorkshireman was up again, lying between two rocks, and he fired, followed by the other two riflemen. A voltigeur corporal leading the group was thrown back like a rag doll and fell over the parapet. The men in green passed the rifles back for the redcoats with them to reload and took their muskets instead. Three more shots, and another Frenchman was down, hissing in pain because his kneecap was shattered.

The drums began the rhythm of the charge and the French light infantry started to advance. The column was narrow, just four men wide to fit across the confined bridge.

'Old trowsers!' said Williams, hearing the sound, and some of the men who had been at Vimeiro in the summer grinned.

Three dead horses were piled where they had left them the previous night, forming a low barricade and blocking the bridge, at least to other horses. The leading voltigeurs were already over this barrier and dragging at the dead animals, pulling them to either side so that the column and then the cavalry could pass. On the hill, the three men from the 95th were given back their loaded rifles and slid them forward to aim. The Yorkshireman was happier with the feel of his familiar weapon and lined up the fore and rear sights to point at a Frenchman's back as he leaned over a dead horse. He squeezed the trigger and the butt slammed back against his shoulder. Beside him the other two men fired and the target was lost in the smoke. He saw the flick of stone chipped from the boulder and then the musket ball fired by one of the Frenchmen on the rocky mound ricocheted up. The now jagged ball whipped a furrow through his face, smashing the bridge of his nose and destroying both eyeballs to send him for ever into darkness. He slid down, turning on to his back, and his hands tried to wipe away the blood that must be covering his eyes, but he could not. One of the others swore, and then pulled the man to lie in safety before taking his rifle and beginning to load.

One Frenchman lay slumped on top of a dead horse. Another was crouched down, a trail of blood dripping from his mouth, but other men were kicking the stakes down.

The front of the column was at the bridge. A lieutenant led them, because the company's captain was sick of fever and lying in some hospital hundreds of miles away. He was a small man, his face scarred by sabre and a shot that had smashed through several of his teeth. He had seen the Prussians run at Jena, and had fought the Russians in far worse cold than this at Eylau. A few ragtag English were not about to give his men much trouble. The skirmishers in front were kneeling now. Those on the left fired up the road at a target he could not see, while the men ahead of him levelled their weapons to cover the ground where the cuirassier captain had told them the enemy were hidden.

'*Vive l'empereur!*' he bellowed out with his men as the drummer paused between rolls. Their boots were on the stonework of the bridge, trampling the grubby snow stained so heavily with the blood from the previous day's fight. A line of redcoats appeared just where Dalmas had said. The muskets of his skirmishers banged almost immediately, and one of the British was flung back, a neat hole in his forehead.

'Present!' Mulligan's voice was loud. The French lieutenant saw the men bring muskets up to their shoulders, making them look as if they had turned a little to the right. The line was two deep, the second rank even shorter than the first where the men stood lower down the slope, their muskets pointing through the gaps between the men in front.

'Present!' Jowers' men raised their firelocks. They could see the front of the column now, could hear the French shouts and the beat of the drum. Beside them the gunners waited. Parker involuntarily whipped his hand back when a ball from one of the voltigeurs pinged off the barrel of the twelve-pounder.

From the far side of the river, Dalmas spotted Groombridge and his men yanking the blankets off the gun and rolling it forward. He had wondered whether the British had another cannon. It did not matter.

'Get ready,' he said to the chasseur captain. 'Go as soon as they have cleared room for you to pass.' The man twisted his moustache and grinned like the fool he was, but at least he could be relied upon to be a brave fool. He drew his sabre, and without waiting for his order his chasseurs did the same. Dalmas looked back to see his cuirassiers waiting on the road. That was his reserve, the force with which he intended to shatter any resistance that survived.

'Fire!' called Corporal Mulligan. The volley was better this time, the shots coming almost as one until he pulled the trigger on his own firelock a moment later, having waited for his aim not to be thrown off by the shout.

The French lieutenant collapsed, choking on his own blood from the ball in his throat. The drummer was already dead, his tunic dark as liquid pulsed from his heart. One of the skirmishers lay moaning and two men from the column had dropped.

'Fire!' Cooke gave the order before Williams had opened his mouth and the twelve-pounder leapt back on the twin trails, flame and smoke vomiting from its muzzle. His eyes had barely recovered from the shock when the other cannon fired and this discharge seemed even louder, and that did not make sense. Groombridge had loaded a twelve-pound ball as well as a bag of grape and had increased the charge of powder to give it force. It was a bad habit, and one that in time ruined the barrel, but he was not inclined to worry too much about the future.

One-and-a-half-inch balls ripped through the smoke. One of the skirmishers fell, the left side of his skull ripped off. Another man's musket was shattered and the jagged end of one half followed the grapeshot to drive deep into his belly. Men died at the front of the column, and the range was so short that the balls punched through flesh and bone and passed through to hit the man behind. The bar from one of the rounds of grape buried itself in the dead drummer's forehead.

With the men crowded as they were on the bridge, the cannonball from Groombridge's gun created even worse carnage. The slope meant that it simply snatched the plume from the man in the front rank, but the ball was dipping and the head of the man behind disintegrated in a red spray of bone, flesh and brains. The third man's chest exploded in ruin before the twelve-pound shot struck the man behind him at the waist and cut him in half. In the fourth rank the man was lucky. He was slightly to the side and the ball just missed, tearing off much of the cloth of his trouser leg and leaving the thigh swelling into a bruise, but the skin unbroken. All three men behind him lost legs as the shot smashed through bones, and then it bounced and rose to slice another four voltigeurs in two before it was past the column and humming into the chasseurs, taking the head of one of the horses.

The bridge was awash in blood. The column staggered. Now was the time to press on, but the lieutenant was dying and it was a young sergeant who screamed at the men to charge through the smoke and take the line ahead of them. There was no drum to beat the charge, but enough of the stunned survivors cheered and staggered forward.

Williams heard a dull explosion behind him followed by a sound like a heavy slap, and something knocked him down. One of the gun crew, the number seven, had hit Williams' left side as he was flung backwards, the long rammer embedded deep in the man's own right arm. It was an easy mistake. When he had reversed the ram so that the end with the sponge went into the barrel, the number seven had driven it hard into the muzzle to clean out anything left from the fired charge. The number nine on the right of the muzzle was supposed to press his leather-encased thumb over the touch-hole to prevent any air getting in. Otherwise the sponge risked driving burning embers on to any remaining powder and gases, and the air would ignite it again.

The number seven's own enthusiasm to reload had let him thrust the sponge in before the other man was ready.

Williams was wet from the man's blood, and part of his jacket was scorched by the man's smouldering uniform. The officer pushed himself up.

'Fire, damn it!' he yelled at Jowers, who was as stunned as everyone else by the horrific accident.

'Right, lads, present!' The sergeant recovered and was determined that his men would not fire wildly, so took a moment to calm them. The French voltigeurs were close to Mulligan's men when he shouted out, 'Fire!'

The blue-uniformed men stopped, barely five yards from the fold in the ground. Three more fell in the snow, and one was the sergeant, who was hit in both legs and cursed because his men had been so close. Another voltigeur dropped his musket and clutched at his bloodstained sleeve, but his comrades were raising their weapons and fired a ragged volley. A Highlander in the buff facings of the 71st was hit in the chest and fell back down the slope. More French ran up, but they stopped among the firing men to thicken the line. As they fired, Mulligan's men managed a second volley of their own, and to Williams it seemed as if the flames of the muskets met because they were so close. Men dropped on each side.

'Go on, man!' Dalmas yelled at Capitaine Lancel, and the chasseur at last walked his horse forward towards the bridge.

'Sorry, chum,' said Cooke as he yanked the rammer from the horribly wounded man. It seemed to start the pain, for he screamed and would not stop. Williams looked aghast, but the horse artilleryman ignored him. 'Right, lads, do your jobs. You, Kendrick, put the charge in.' Cooke himself rammed it down, using the sponge because the other end of the ram was a mangled mess.

'Load, you bastards!' yelled Jowers as some of his men turned to stare at the screaming man. 'You!' He pointed at a man in green facings. 'Get him away.'

The redcoat was not used to the rifle. He was from the 52nd, who did practise live firing at targets, and felt himself a good shot, so when he lined up on the French cavalry officer he aimed ahead of him to allow for the movement. Ignoring the smoke and chaos, and the occasional shot from the French skirmishers hitting the rocks around him, he waited, and then smoothly pulled the trigger.

Capitaine Lancel knew that he was lucky, so that it did not surprise him when a ball smacked into his left thigh but did not seem to do much damage. There was little pain and he laughed aloud as he gave the order to trot. His green overall trousers were already growing dark and his saddle was quickly wet as his lifeblood drained from the severed artery. The officer felt light headed as he threaded past the dead and dying light infantrymen.

Over the bridge, Lancel turned left through the kicked-down stakes and his men followed him. The officer saw the thin line of British infantry and the cannon beside them, and then his eyes flickered and it was hard to see or think anything. Lancel slumped sideways off his horse to lie in the snow. His men knew what to do. The enemy was there, and what French light cavalryman needed to know more than that? They spurred towards the English, a ragged stream of a dozen or so men.

The rest of the squadron was still filing over the bridge, and Groombridge was glad that he had chosen to reload with shot rather than grape because it was a beautiful target. He lowered the portfire himself.

The twelve-pounder's roar was less deep throated than the first time, although the recoil seemed no less savage, and Groombridge had to yank one of his men back by the shoulder to stop him from being flattened by the wheel. They had run the gun back after the first shot, following the ruts in the snow as well as they could, but it was never possible to get back into the exact position. The muzzle had turned slightly, and although the alignment was good the shot flew at more of an angle, slicing diagonally across the bridge at shoulder height. It took the leg off a chasseur and broke the spine of his bay horse, crippled the two horses next in line and smashed the shoulder of a fourth before disembowelling the rider.

Two horses folded instantly, and another crumpled down on its front legs. They formed a barrier which the riders behind were going too slowly to cross. The chasseurs stopped, and one fell when his horse reared up in terror.

In the house, Jane heard the cannon fire again and thought that that must be a good sign. The musket shots were fainter, but she told herself that as long as the guns were firing then the fight continued and had not been lost.

'Gun ready, sir!' Cooke called just as Jowers' men brought their muskets up to their shoulders. The chasseurs were bearing down on them, a trumpeter in a pink jacket riding with the leaders, his trumpet swinging on its cords and his sabre raised high.

'Fire!' The cannon added its deep call to the ripple of musketry.

'Fix bayonets!' Williams could not see how much damage they had done, but the only horse to burst through the smoke had no rider and he had to believe that the volley and the grapeshot had halted the cavalry. There was no time to reload, only enough to take one final wild gamble. His own sword was already in his right hand, a pistol taken from one of the dead Poles in his left.

'Charge!' and he turned the order into a long, guttural yell of defiance. The men were shouting too. Another horse barged him as he ran through the thinning cloud of smoke, but there was only blood on the saddle and no sign of a rider. Beside him, the kilted Highlander from the 79th drove his bayonet into the chest of the trumpeter as he knelt on the ground. Other chasseurs lay dead or moaning, and Williams trod on a man's hand because he did not see it and nearly tripped, but then fell against the chest of another horse. He was on the chasseur's left side, and the man struggled to control his frightened mount and cut down. Without thinking Williams rammed the pistol into the rider's stomach and pulled the trigger. A fountain of blood jetted from the man's lower back and sprayed across the rolled blanket behind his saddle.

Williams ran on. There were a dozen chasseurs still mounted, but the charge had been broken and the men milled, so that the redcoats ran in between them, stabbing with their bayonets. Jowers died when a French cavalryman cut down, beating aside his musket and carving a long sliver from the wood, before the man whipped the tip of his blade up to lunge into the sergeant's throat. The Frenchman fell when Cooke slammed the sponge against him, and when the man landed on the ground the big artilleryman reversed the broken pole and drove the jagged end through the chasseur's body. Williams had not realised that the gunners had come with them, and it was too late to do anything about that.

He sliced at the head of a horse, missing it, but making the animal swerve to the side so that the rider's blade missed and only clipped his shoulder wing. He threw the empty pistol at the man's face, and the distracted Frenchman was run through the body by the slim bayonet of a man in the yellow cuffs of the 26th. The Frenchman gasped as the wind was knocked from him.

Williams ran on. The Highlander was ahead of him and he watched the man slam the butt of his musket into the forehead of a voltigeur. He shouted a warning as another Frenchman slid past his guard, but the bayonet jabbed into the Scotsman's stomach. Williams slashed with his sword, cutting open the voltigeur's face before the man could withdraw his blade. The light infantryman reeled back, hands pressed to his long wound, so Williams lunged at his companion as the man staggered to recover from the Highlander's blow. Mulligan appeared from nowhere, the bayonet on his musket bent and bloodied, and the big man knocked the wounded Frenchman down with one hand.

The enemy were going back. The few chasseurs still mounted were already flowing back across the bridge, with the voltigeurs mingled among them. Men slipped on fresh blood or tripped on corpses as they fled, and some were not fast enough and fell to the hungry bayonets of the redcoats, but they were going back.

'Form on me!' Williams needed the men in some sort of order, needed them formed, and had to stop any fool from chasing the enemy to their side of the river.

'Rally!' Mulligan's voice boomed across the valley and more men responded. Between them, they shook the survivors into a rough line halfway between the bridge and the fold in the ground.

A redcoat grunted as a ball fired by one of the skirmishers smashed through his ribs. He sighed as he slid to the ground. Williams' line was very exposed. The remaining riflemen and redcoats on the hill were firing, but more of the voltigeurs were recovering and going to reinforce the skirmish line.

Dalmas saw the moment and raised his sword high. He led, more than two horse lengths ahead of his company of cuirassiers, and they were all big men on tall and heavy horses. He drove the horse on, heading straight for the heap of dead and dying animals, and as he came close he felt that incredible surge of power as his big horse clenched and then extended its muscles, soaring over the barrier. Its hoofs landed, skidded just a little in the slick blood and recovered, and now that he had shown his men how to do it Dalmas was sure they would follow.

'Front rank kneel!' Williams gestured at the men to go down and form a hedge of bayonet points when he saw the cuirassier ride straight at the bridge. No one was loaded, and his hope that the bridge would be impassable was quickly dashed.

The company followed, as they had followed Dalmas in many a bloody charge. They went fast, and the men in the front rank were already rising in their stirrups when Groombridge lowered the portfire and set off the quill in the touch-hole of the old twelve-pounder. It was loaded with grape this time, and the heavy balls struck the front rank of the enemy just as they jumped. Inch-and-a-half balls drove through armour, creating a jagged hole, and then spun through and split the back of the cuirass open like the petals of some ghastly flower. Two of the three riders in the front rank died instantly. All three horses were killed at the same moment as the heavy projectiles smashed into them. They tumbled forward, flopping and sliding instead of landing. The third rider did not get even a scratch, but was thrown from his dead mount, and his helmet struck hard against the base of the parapet, snapping his head back and breaking his neck. Behind them, the other cuirassiers stopped, horses unwilling to go over the chaos on the narrow bridge.

'God bless the artillery,' said Mulligan.

Dalmas reined in short of the line. There was no one behind him and he could see the rear rank of the British infantry reloading.

'*Merde*,' he said, and turned his horse, urging it into a trot. Williams went to follow, but stopped when a volley of some half a dozen shots came from the far bank. His hat was plucked from his head again, and this time there was a fierce sting as the ball grazed the side of his skull just above the ear. Mulligan was thrown backwards by another shot.

'Back to cover!' yelled Williams, gesturing to the men, even though his head throbbed with pain. The dead horses covered the bridge, except at one place on the left where only one animal was jammed against the parapet. Dalmas saw it and sent his horse at that point. He knew his aim had to be precise, for too far one way and the horse would refuse or fall among the still-thrashing legs of the dying horses. Too far the other way and it would smash into or over the wall of the bridge. The horse was only trotting, but the power was there and his line was true as it surged high and over, landing firmly on the roadway. The satisfaction was brief, for he knew that the attack had failed and that his time had run out.

Corporal Mulligan was dead, the hole above the bridge of his nose seeming too tiny to have hurt such an enormous man. Jowers was dead along with three more and at least a dozen wounded. Williams put the remaining man from the 71st in charge of his ad hoc platoon, simply because the man looked experienced. The light infantryman from the 52nd replaced Jowers.

'Get back and reload the gun,' he told the unemotional

Cooke. 'They may come again.' If they did, Williams did not know how he would stop them. More than half of the ammunition for their muskets was gone. He lay for a moment on the snow and breathed heavily, looking up at the sky. He would have to ask Mr Groombridge what time it was.

25

'Good gracious, it's Miss MacAndrews, is it not?' Colonel Graham's tone suggested a happy coincidence on the street of some market town. 'I am most delighted to see you. Your mother expressed considerable concern about your welfare.' He was beaming with genuine pleasure.

Jane looked up, still pressing a pad of cloth down over the wounded man's stomach. He kept bleeding, and there was nothing she could do to stop it. They had no bandages, so were cutting and tearing up the cleanest of the clothes taken from the dead. The room was crowded with moaning men, the wounded from this morning's fight added to the sick. There were fewer of those now. The frostbitten soldier had died, as had MacDonald. The grey-haired Highlander's coughing had grown worse during the night, and then he began to cough up blood and had simply died. The bodies were outside, laid out in a row beside the wall. She and the women did their best to care for those still alive, as well as looking after the children. The less badly wounded or sick men tried to help the worse off, and she was amazed at the patience of them all.

For all the ghastly sights and smells of the makeshift hospital, Miss MacAndrews' manners formed a reply before any conscious thought. 'Good day to you, Colonel Graham.' Her memory for names was excellent, even though the meeting with the elderly officer seemed an age or more in the past. 'I trust that you are well?'

'I am in robust health, I am pleased to say, but all the happier to come into the presence of such beauty.' Jane's dress was heavily stained with blood, and there were dabs of red on her face where she had unconsciously brushed it with bloodstained hands. Graham thought that she looked exhausted, and yet the smile that greeted him was so wide and warm that it genuinely lifted his already buoyant spirits. 'But I am forgetting my manners. Good day to you other ladies.' The colonel went so far as to raise his cocked hat to the soldiers' wives. He was standing in the doorway, and now he turned to call to someone behind him. 'Send for Mr Murray!'

Jane's thoughts came slowly. For hours they had worked, doing what they could and somehow hoping that this little would be enough. 'Has rescue come?' The words were awkward, but they were the best she could frame. Jacob began to cry and the girl tried to tie the bandage in place on the wounded man so that she could tend to the infant.

'Reckon he's hungry,' said Rose. 'Greedy little beggar,' she added.

Graham raised his voice a little to be heard. 'Well, I am not sure that rescue is quite the right word. I am positive that your young Mr Williams will deny that he was in any such need. But, yes, we are here as reinforcement.' He moved to let the surgeon come through the door. Murray blinked as he came into the gloomy room, and then gasped as his eyes adapted.

'Work to do,' he said to his two assistants.

Major Colborne of Sir John Moore's staff stared at Williams and did his best to stifle a smile. In his pocket he had the ensign's message to the general, carried by the German hussar. The words of the conclusion stuck in his mind.

It appears to me that it would be of utility to the army if we were to deny this crossing to the French. The bridge is narrow and offers us some chance of repulsing attacks even by a moderately stronger enemy force. At this moment, we have only heard reports of cavalry – a scouting force of one or two squadrons. No doubt should they secure the bridge, the enemy would be able to summon more troops to exploit the success. I have the equivalent of a company, although composed of men from many distinct corps, and two cannon.

Therefore, I am resolved to stay here and hold for as long as possible, trusting that this decision by a junior officer will not be considered too presumptuous.

I am, Sir, you most humble and obedient servant

H. Williams, Ensign, 106th Regiment

For an ensign to take such a decision was indeed presumptuous, however much he might make claims of humility. It also made perfect military sense.

Sir John immediately recognised the danger. If the French were able to outflank his position at Lugo in any strength, then not only would fighting a battle be impossible, but even retreat would be made more difficult. It meant that there was no longer much point delaying the withdrawal, but first he needed to ensure that this threat was blocked. The message had been written twenty-four hours ago, and there was no assurance that this ensign and his little force had not already been brushed aside.

His thoughts turned naturally to the brigade just arrived from Corunna, whose men were far fresher than the rest of the army.

'Who are your best marchers, General Leith?' he had asked its commander.

'The Fifty-first, Sir John.' The reply did not surprise Moore. They were a good corps and there was talk of training them as light infantry according to the system he had helped to develop at Shorncliffe Camp. Colborne was immediately given command of one wing of the battalion, and told to march at best speed to the bridge. With him went engineers and powder to destroy it if feasible. Now that he had arrived after marching through the night, that looked unlikely. The French had not attacked again, but the voltigeurs were still extended as skirmishers and fired at even the most fleeting target. The cavalry waited farther back, but were unlikely to watch passively if Colborne sent a company or two across the river.

★

Colborne listened to Williams' formal report, as the ensign stood to attention in his ill-fitting jacket and thoroughly disreputable cap. A lot of men would have blustered and boasted. This young officer looked tired, and seemed almost embarrassed by what he had done. He kept praising his men, and particularly Mr Groombridge, and the dead sergeant and corporal. Colborne suspected that he might get a clearer account from the quartermaster sergeant at a later point. Williams appeared to doubt each of the decisions he had made, suggesting that a different plan might have cost fewer lives.

Both men turned as one of the guns boomed.

'Mr Groombridge fires every five or ten minutes just to keep them honest,' explained Williams, far more animated when he spoke of someone else's action. 'He is a good man, sir.'

'Excellent, by the sound of it,' agreed Colborne. He finally abandoned any thought of destroying the bridge. They would retreat. There was no sign that the enemy had enough strength to trouble five companies of steady infantry.

'Cheer up, Mr Williams – you won!' he said suddenly, clapping the ensign on the shoulder. 'And it was a first-rate piece of soldiering.' Williams looked at his feet, and muttered something incomprehensible.

'When were you commissioned?' asked the staff officer.

'In August. I served as a volunteer from the start of the year.'

That helped to explain some of his reticence. The man clearly lacked the funds or connections to begin his career as an officer. That could leave a fellow with a sense of inadequacy, as if he did not quite deserve his rank. The date was also significant. Colborne had not landed until after the battles in Portugal, but the 106th had played a full part in both, and no doubt Williams had earned his commission through courage. His conduct in the last few days also suggested a considerable talent beyond mere bravery.

'You have done well, sir, truly well, and I am sure that the general will feel the same.' Graham was even more effusive in his praise as they marched back to the army. Williams marched with his remaining men, alongside their wagon, which was stripped of everything else so that it could carry the wounded and the women. Three of the injured were in no state to move, and they were left behind in the house in the confident expectation that the French would give whatever aid they possessed. The guns were abandoned, in spite of a brief protest from Groombridge.

'The Spanish army has already left forty or more cannon beside the road, and I do not believe them capable of employing these usefully,' said Colborne. Groombridge drove a spike into each touch-hole, and took the time to cut off the head so that it would be more difficult to pull it out. The old artilleryman then mounted his mule with the rearguard of the 51st and Colborne took the opportunity to quiz him about the recent action.

When it was clear that the French were not going to press the pursuit, Graham rode back to the wagon, but found Miss Mac-Andrews asleep, and so instead rode alongside Williams. The ensign had been offered the use of a horse, but stubbornly insisted on marching with the men. He was carrying the musket of one of the redcoats, who was struggling to keep up. Cooke, the big artilleryman, had no fewer than three firelocks strung over his shoulders as well as another man's pack, and was strolling along as if they weighed nothing at all.

'Splendid, Mr Williams, absolutely splendid.' Colonel Graham's delight appeared wholly sincere, and in spite of his age, he dismounted to walk beside the young officer. His appreciation was not restricted to the ensign. 'You have all given the damned French a taste of British pluck! I do so wish I had been there. Sir John will be most pleased with your conduct.'

After half a mile the colonel grew restless. Colborne had caught up to check that they were coping with the rigours of the march. 'Eh, John, what say you we ride up to that ridge and take a look. See if the Frogs are following close?' Colborne nodded. 'Don't wait for an old man like me,' said the colonel. 'I'll catch up as best I can.' In less than a minute he was streaming ahead of the younger man, riding with all the abandoned enthusiasm of the hunting field.

It was dark by the time the column reached camp. At first, no one appeared to notice Williams and his men as they trudged the last few hundred yards. The camp was bustling, as the army's baggage train began to move out.

Jane woke from her deep sleep just as they arrived. For the moment, she felt refreshed, and for a reason she could not fully explain did not want to ride in the wagon. She eased herself carefully over the tail of the cart, not worrying when she landed in a puddle and splashed yet more mud on to the hem of her stained dress. Then she insisted that Rose hand her down Jacob. The baby stirred for a moment, and it was somehow pleasant for the girl to hush him back to comfortable silence.

She waited for Williams to reach her, as he marched at the rear of his men. He returned her smile.

'Thank you, for doing so much,' he said softly.

Williams' men crossed a bigger track, but he and Jane had to wait as three ox-drawn carts piled high with powder barrels passed. Their ungreased axles squealed in protest. Near by a mule started braying and set off a dozen more. Williams found the sheer noise overwhelming after the comparative peace of their march back from the bridge.

The last of the carts passed, its driver mercilessly prodding the team with his goad, and there were Major MacAndrews and his wife standing and looking at them.

Jane could see that there were tears in her mother's eyes, and knew that her own were glassy. Esther MacAndrews ran to her daughter and kissed her. Neither of them could find words to say.

Her father waited for what seemed a long time. He was not a man who readily betrayed his emotions in public.

Suddenly he whooped, as she had only ever known him to do after drinking plenty of whisky and deciding to dance a reel.

Jane could not help laughing, even when her mother kissed her again.

Major MacAndrews, no longer caring whether or not his behaviour was appropriate for a battalion commander, threw his

hat into the air, caught it, and whooped again. Then he ran to
Jane and took hold of her, spinning her around. He made to lift
her high into the air, and only her protests and a wail from the
baby prevented him.

'You silly old fool,' said Mrs MacAndrews with the fondness
of many years.

At last they noticed Williams.

'It is good to see you, Mr Williams,' said Jane's mother. The
major simply nodded and shook his hand firmly.

A staff officer was already with his men, sending each back to
his own corps. Williams thanked them again. Jane and her
parents waited for him, and together they all walked back to the
battalion's lines. Williams felt that he was swaying as he walked,
the urge to lie down and sleep for ever closing around him.
Sounds became muted, neither readily comprehensible nor in
any way important, and although his eyes saw clearly, it took
time for the images to register in his mind. His feet felt heavy,
each step a conscious effort.

No one had the energy to speak, and the story would have to
wait for a more fitting occasion. There even seemed to be a fear
that if they spoke too much this would all turn out to be a dream.
Major MacAndrews could feel nothing but joy at seeing his little
girl safe and well. His mind had no room for anything else.
Concerns and fears over what may have happened to his only
daughter while she was traipsing around in the middle of a war
were left to simmer as he went back to the battalion.

The Grenadier Company was forming up as they arrived.
Pringle chuckled when he noticed the babe in Miss Mac-
Andrews' arms as she walked beside Williams. He nudged
Hanley.

'That's damned quick work,' he said.

Their amusement was drowned when the grenadiers began
to cheer. It was soon taken up by the rest of the 106th, as men
quickly guessed that it meant the prodigals had returned. Officers
and men alike felt happier because of this good news, and it did

something to lift spirits lowered by the order to continue the retreat instead of fighting Marshal Soult.

Dobson was briefly introduced to his grandson, before Miss MacAndrews carried the baby away. She had grown used to looking after him, and for the moment would continue to do so as she accompanied her mother and tried to keep the regiment's families and baggage together. Mrs MacAndrews was almost as enthusiastic to care for the little boy. From somewhere she had found a side-saddle and had it fitted to Bobbie.

'Oh well, I suppose I am used to walking by now.' Billy Pringle did his best to sound morose and failed dismally, as a wide grin kept returning to his face. Then he cupped his hands to lift Jane into the saddle. Once she was settled, Mrs MacAndrews passed up little Jacob. Jane was weary, but cradling the baby in the crook of her arm immediately gave her energy and a sense of the need to care for someone else. She looked down at his peaceful face and smiled as she urged the mare into a walk.

Williams had little time to talk to anyone. He wanted to sleep and could never remember such exhaustion. People said things and he nodded and sometimes even said words in response, but none of it meant anything. An aide came, leading a horse, and telling him to attend on the general.

Sir John was every bit as warm in his appreciation as Colborne and Graham had predicted. The former had given him a full report, much fleshed out by his conversation with Groombridge and his own observation of the debris of battle.

'Well done, sir.' The general stood beside his horse, watching regiments pass on the road. For all his weariness, his enthusiasm revived Williams. The ensign could not really believe that he was meeting the commander of the army, let alone being praised by him. Then Sir John removed his glove and offered a hand. The handshake was firm and decisive.

'Thank you, sir. You are most kind, but most of the praise more deservedly goes to the men.'

'They shall not be forgotten. Do we have a list?'

'Yes, sir,' said Colborne, waving a piece of paper. He had

written it quickly, resting on his sabretache, the broad bag suspended alongside his sword's scabbard, as Williams dictated.

'Would it be possible for their respective corps to be informed of their good conduct?' Williams' admiration for the men overcame his timidity in the presence of so many senior officers. 'Sergeant Jowers and Corporal Mulligan played an especially gallant role in the defence, and this should be known by their regiments, and those of the other dead men.'

'See to it, George,' Sir John said to another of his aides. 'Now, sir, are you mounted?'

Williams struggled to understand the question. 'I . . . er . . .'

The general understood his confusion. 'Do you have a horse?'

'No, sir.'

'A pity. If you were mounted then I should have attached you to my staff for the remainder of the campaign.'

Williams was stunned, but the compliment was clear. 'That is a great honour.' It was indeed, for no officer as junior as an ensign was likely to be found in any commander's staff.

'Well, I would make you work, so the honour might wear as thin as the seat of your breeches,' said Sir John with a remarkably impish grin. 'But you cannot perform these duties on foot.'

'Again, I must thank you, although if you would forgive me, I feel that I still have much to learn with my regiment.'

The answer greatly pleased the general. 'Such a sentiment does you credit. I do believe that you are a serious soldier.' The trace of Edinburgh, always there in the general's speech, had grown stronger. 'I am glad to see it, for we have too many fellows who consider war to be a game. It is a serious trade, sir, and there is much to learn, and not all can be learned in regimental duty. One day I may call upon you to serve away from your corps. It will be work, sir, hard work, and some of it dull in the extreme, but you will learn what it takes for an army to operate in the field.

'We shall have need of trained men, and serious soldiers, if we are ever to return.'

'Then are we leaving, sir?' The question came before he had

time to consider its brazenness, or he would never have dared to utter the words.

Sir John took no offence, sensing no malice or reproof in the question. 'There is not food to support us for any time, and no useful purpose to be gained by remaining in northern Spain. So, yes, we shall leave. But first we need to give Marshal Soult the slip. You have already helped to make that easier. Thank you again, Mr Williams, you may return to your regiment.'

The Reserve Division set out at 9.30 that night, but halted again within an hour and formed up facing the enemy. Williams was aware of very little, nor did he have the energy to care. It was dark, and heavy rain soon turned into sleet, which made it hard to see any distance. The rest of the army was supposed to have preceded them, but regiments and brigades got lost. When the darker shadows of formed bodies appeared in the night, it was impossible to know whether they were friend or foe until they had come very close.

The reserve would march a short way, and then stop again. Each time the 'enemy' proved to be British. Many corps fragmented in the darkness and confusion. Men were tired, and the enthusiasm at the prospect of a battle had sunk again into despair, which made that fatigue hang especially heavily on hearts and bodies. Williams kept walking, and stopped when everyone else stopped, but he was aware of little. The curiosity of his friends was buried by the sleet and his brief, largely incoherent responses.

The retreat continued throughout the night and the next day. Stragglers were everywhere. Sir John's staff passed one battalion, composed of a lone captain, two sergeants carrying the Colours, and thirty or so men. Yet returning to their familiar task as rear-guard, General Paget insisted that not a single officer or man from the Reserve Division leave his place in the formation. In the light of dawn he halted the men, and they took up position to face any advancing enemy, but were allowed to stand, or even sit at ease in the ranks. There was no food other than some hard biscuit. Rumour said that four thousand loaves baked by the commissaries had been left in Lugo to welcome the French.

There were stragglers everywhere, and orders came for the 106th to flush any redcoats out of a cluster of ramshackle houses beside the road. A wine store had been broken open, and barns found with plentiful stocks of straw. One or both temptations proved too strong for a good few men. The grenadiers dragged men from their peaceful beds, kicking or prodding those who refused to stir.

Williams sat on a bale of straw, sheltered from the wind and sleet just inside the door of a barn. He had been yawning all morning, eyes shutting as his mouth opened wide. This seemed to be the first rest he had had for as long as he could remember. He lay back, revelling in the softness of the straw. Sleep came almost instantly.

'Are we allowed to kick him?' said Murphy, and it was the first joke he had made for days.

'You are not,' Major MacAndrews had appeared from nowhere, 'although I suspect that I am.' Instead he gently shook Williams by the shoulder.

'Takes more than that with our Mr Williams,' said Dobson, and so the major renewed his efforts with far greater vigour.

Williams stirred, and whispered 'Jane?' so faintly that the girl's father could not be perfectly sure that he had heard correctly.

'Get up, man.' MacAndrews tried to be jovial. There seemed no obvious way of asking this young man whether he had con-ducted himself with the utmost respect and decency while stranded alone with his daughter. Even if he could think of suitable words, this was scarcely the moment or the place. 'Get up, we will be marching again soon.'

Williams stood. He had slept for no more than five minutes, but felt surprisingly refreshed.

Hanley thought him almost indecently bright when he joined them outside. His own mood darkened farther when an elderly Spaniard appeared from one the houses and shook his fist at them.

'*Los franceses son mejores que los ingleses, los ingleses son ladrones!*'
Hanley shrugged, but could not think of a reply.

'That did not sound very complimentary,' commented Pringle.

'The French are better than the English – the English are bandits!' guessed Williams.

'Well done, Bills. You really are surprising us all these days.' Hanley's beard was wild and wiry. They had been ordered to clean uniforms in the halt at Lugo, but there had been no opportunity for a shave. 'It is good to have you back.'

'It's even better not to be carrying that damned pack of yours!' added Pringle.

They pressed on. Some men had been stirred into life. Others were left behind, still insensible or too well concealed to be readily found. The sleet held off, and as the sun shone they caught reflections off the helmets of the French cavalry. Later they halted on a ridge, looking back. The advancing French patrols again injected life into men who seemed past caring. Perhaps they remembered the massacre at Bembibre, or perhaps they were simply less drunk this time. A few score of the isolated redcoats banded together. Then there were hundreds and eventually over a thousand. A sergeant commanded them, and they retired in two ordered bodies, halting to fire volleys whenever the enemy cavalry came too close.

'Let us go down there!' Pringle suspected that the voice was Murphy's, but was relieved that General Paget only heard the words and did not remark the speaker.

'Never, sir, never,' he called out angrily. 'I would not risk the life of one good man for a hundred drunkards who have so forgotten their duty as to abandon the Colours.'

Williams felt the judgement a little harsh, but soon it was obvious that the stragglers needed no aid. They went down only when the French were driven off, because the general had noticed that some of the men were inclined to wander again, once the danger had gone. They were herded along the road, marched in groups to their respective corps. Before they went, Sir Edward had every man searched and his pack emptied.

Anything that appeared to be loot was taken from them and piled up. Soldiers from the reserve were free to take whatever they wanted.

Hanley's curiosity took him over to one of the piles. There were candlesticks, bits of plate and some coin, although rarely anything of real value. A bundle of at least seventy cheap spoons was the oddest thing he saw, but he watched as the eyes of a man from the 20th lit up at the sight of this treasure. The redcoat quickly bundled it into his own pack.

They were soon moving again, and marched for the rest of the day.

26

'What, sir? Another damned abortion! Pray, sir, and how do you account for this failure.' Sir Edward Paget's quick temper had flared into new fury. They were at yet another bridge, and the engineers had laid three charges dug into the roadway.

'I fear the first explosion disturbed the powder trail and the other charges did not ignite,' said the engineer, with the confidence of a man whose corps required officers to have studied and learnt the secrets of their craft.

'Then why, sir, did you lay them in such a damned fool way! Remedy the matter at once.' The general looked at the bridge. A great chunk had been taken out of one arch, leaving a path little more than a yard wide in that section. 'How long will it take?'

'Twenty minutes, I should think.'

'Then make sure it requires no more than that.' Sir Edward Paget looked around him. The Grenadier and Light Companies of the 106th were deployed on the bank, and the former were nearest. 'Take your fellows across,' he ordered Pringle. 'I'll wave when you are to come back.'

On the far bank the road forked. The main route went over the bridge, while another turned to go through the arched gateway of a large walled village. They filed towards the narrow strip of bridge. Williams was feeling sluggish again, and Pringle had to prod him to get him moving. As they crossed, Billy looked down with distaste at the fast-flowing brown river.

'If I had wanted to have so much to do with water then I would have joined the navy,' he muttered.

'Seasick again,' Williams responded. In truth his own illness on the voyage to Portugal had been only marginally less severe than Pringle's affliction, but then he did not come from a naval family.

They formed on the far bank, waited until the general waved, and then began to walk back. The company had passed the narrow neck of the broken bridge when Hanley heard the sound of hoofs and turned to see French dragoons rushing towards them. He was at the rear of the company, and the words of command came to his mind as a memory from long and tedious sessions of drill.

'Right about turn, forward!' he called, and sprang ahead, dashing to get across the narrow part and have room for the company to form where the bridge was unbroken. The grenadiers were surprised by the order, but responded quickly and with only a little confusion. Men bumped into each other as they turned. Pringle and Williams were shouting orders and encouragement, as was Sergeant Probert, and the company was hustled back and began to form from one parapet to the other, the men in the front rank kneeling.

'Fix bayonets!' Hanley heard Pringle bellow the order and wondered why his voice sounded distant. He looked over his shoulder and realised that his urgency had taken him too far, for the company was now seven or eight yards behind him. Hoof beats pounded towards him and there was a French dragoon officer bearing down, the man's long green cloak streaming behind as his horse flew along the road. Hanley drew his own sword, knowing he did not have the time to run. He swung wildly at the animal's head, but the dragoon pulled the reins hard and the horse stopped and reared, its big feet thrashing only inches from his face as he sprang back. The gelding spat a great spray of yellow foam on to his face, and then the rider edged it forward and cut down. Hanley just managed to raise his own blade to block the attack, but felt his arm jar with the shock. The dragoon cut again and this time the strength of the blow knocked the Englishman down to his knees and his slim sword slipped from his hand. His eyes closed, anticipating the final attack, when there was a shot which was so close that the noise stunned him.

'Mr Hanley, we've spun him!' yelled Dobson, who had run forward to stand behind the officer.

'Get down, both of you!' shouted Williams as Pringle gave the order to present. Dobson grabbed the confused lieutenant and pulled him down on to the roadway. The company began to fire volleys over them. Hanley was sure that he could hear the balls whipping through the air. The French dragoon lay stretched on the road, and on an impulse Hanley crawled over and unfastened the dead man's cloak. The Frenchman was staring up at the sky, his eyes empty, and Hanley wondered why such sights no longer seemed to prompt much reaction from him.

They continued firing for some time. The French cavalry were kept back, but they dismounted and began sniping from the houses, and soon infantry columns could be seen approaching, so that Paget recalled the company. The engineers were unable to complete their preparations, and the Reserve Division withdrew, leaving the strip of bridge still in place.

They marched on, climbing a winding road up one side of a ridge and down into the next valley. Two hours later they were beside another river, crossed by yet another bridge, and Williams was uncomfortable.

'Are we not very close?' he asked Pringle and Hanley as they watched the engineers once again preparing charges.

'Oh, I shouldn't think so,' said Hanley, luxuriating in the warmth of the dragoon's lined cloak. The temperature was rising and the sky was clear, but there was still a chill in the air, especially when they stopped.

'Yes, Bills, you have missed the efforts of our gallant soldiers of science. They haven't knocked a bridge down yet. It's all been very sad.' Pringle thought for a moment. 'And talking of objects exciting pity, you really do need to replace that hat.' Williams' forage cap had been shot through and wantonly trampled. 'It obviously hasn't been a popular success.'

The engineers shouted a warning and lit the fuse.

'Are you sure we are safe here?' Williams remained unconvinced. The grenadiers were formed only forty or so yards back from the four-arched bridge. A company of greenjackets stood alongside them. Behind was a village and beyond the houses the rest of the division was formed up and waiting.

'They assure us that we are in no danger whatsoever and no doubt that is based upon precise calculation. Now let us wait for the pop!' Pringle was cheerful. They were just a few miles outside Corunna. The fleet was supposed to be waiting in the port and soon they would rest. Even the prospect of a sea voyage did not dismay him. He was tired and simply longed to sleep.

Red flame erupted from the charges on the bridge and then was immediately blanketed in dark smoke and dust. It was louder than any explosion they had ever heard and the shock wave knocked all three officers on to their backs. More grenadiers were flung down and the rest were running in blind panic. The smoke and dust rolled over them. Pringle was coughing and then he was laughing at the absurdity of it all.

'Bloody engineers,' said a voice which sounded much like Dobson. There were thumps as pieces of debris landed. Pringle's amusement vanished when he pushed himself up and saw that Private King was dead and several others injured by the falling pieces of masonry. The Rifles had also suffered casualties.

Both the grenadiers and the company of 95th were ordered to occupy the village and Pringle and their captain split the responsibility and each took the houses on one side of the main road. It offered the greatest comfort they had known for some time, even when the French advance guard arrived and began popping off their muskets from the far bank of the river.

The grenadier officers took the ground floor of the house closest to the bridge, with a dozen of the men on the upper storey. The villagers had left, and the redcoats soon began investigating their food stores. The greatest treasure was three large sacks of potatoes. No one had seen such a wondrous thing as a potato since the days at Almeida. Eyles also led off a group which discovered a well-concealed hen coop and three small sheep. All in all, they had the makings of a grand feast and the officers decided to extend an invitation to the rifle captain to join them. It was issued by shouting across the road, as musket balls flicked the dirt track too often for comfort. Acceptance was signified by more shouting, and the arrangements made. Anticipation was eager, and spirits scarcely dampened when the rumour came that the navy was not there, and that the port was empty of ships.

'Oh, they'll turn up,' said Pringle. 'The Royal Navy always does.'

Jane MacAndrews was similarly disinclined to worry, as she revelled in the luxury of a hot bath, the water brought to the room by the maids from the hotel. The water was cooling quickly, and the bath was small, but it was still the most sensuous pleasure she could ever remember. The past faded, and seemed already unreal, and there was only the warmth, the relaxation and a wonderful sense of being clean. Fresh clothes from their baggage awaited her, and a bed which, if not perfectly wholesome, was at least free from vermin. She and her mother shared the room, for the town was bursting at the seams and its hotels overwhelmed.

Corunna seemed like a different world. The fields outside were green and untouched by snow or ice, and there was fruit on the trees as if summer still lingered. Corunna itself was bustling. People of all ages helped to carry material to strengthen the fortifications. The British were welcomed and fed, even though everyone knew that they were waiting to leave and that the French would soon be here. A battalion stationed here throughout the campaign stood guard with gleaming badges and buttons and their belts a dazzling white, which spoke of hours of effort and considerable amounts of pipe clay. The restaurants were open and so were the theatres. Jane laughed out loud at the memory of seeing scruffy redcoats rolling in the grass like children as they marched down from the bleak mountains towards the town.

Her mother looked at her curiously for a moment, and then returned to fussing over Jacob. The baby was both quiet and thriving, having the chance to remain in one place for longer than ever before in his short life. Jane suspected that her mother had fallen for the little child, and she was already hinting that they might offer to raise him, since his father was dead and his mother vanished. Perhaps they would, and she most certainly would not object, for watching the little ways of the child had been one of the few unalloyed pleasures of her adventures. Williams was another. Her feelings for him had grown. Jane suspected she was in love, although she was not inclined to think about that now or where it might lead. For the moment the glory of this bath and the sheer joy of feeling smooth and free from dirt were wonders greater than anything else in the whole wide world.

The officers' delight in their meal was nearly as intense. When preparations were complete, Hanley called out to Captain Cameron of the 95th, and then Pringle put his cocked hat on the end of a stick and raised it from the window. A shot followed almost immediately, and then two more. In the last hour they had noticed that the enemy fire came in groups of three.

'Come on!' he called across the road. Cameron burst out of the door and sprinted, the long tails of his greatcoat flapping. A fourth shot snapped through the coat and just missed his leg as he leapt into their house. Hanley grabbed him before he could run in.

'Sorry,' said Pringle from the corner. 'It's always been three shots up to now.' He propped the stick and hat against the wall. 'From this point on, I fear that we are obliged to adopt a less dignified posture. William will show you.'

Hanley got down on his knees and crawled across the bare wooden floor. In the far corner, Williams stood by a table, laid out with a somewhat motley but extensive collection of plates and cutlery.

'Why?' asked Cameron, a slim, eager-looking fellow, well known for his pluck and high spirits, as well as the toughness with which he ruled his company. A musket ball came through one of the shutterless windows on the wall facing the river and buried itself in the plaster on the other side of the room. 'Ah, I see,' he said, and happily got down on all fours. Pringle followed him.

The food was brought in the same way, Pringle's soldier servant and two other grenadiers bearing each plate one-handed as they wormed their way below the height of the windows. For all the inconvenience, the redcoats were as cheerful as the officers in taking part in such an unorthodox meal. They also had the complacent happiness from the knowledge that as great or greater portions were left for their own enjoyment. One corner of the table was kept clear.

'We reckon the French can see just that bit,' explained Hanley.

There was mutton and roast potatoes, supported by generous amounts of bread and wine. The last was in some fine glasses discovered in a cabinet. The potatoes were soft, more than a little greasy, and rich with the taste of mutton fat. Williams loved them, adding butter since he had no great taste for the thin gravy.

'You look positively decadent, Bills,' commented Pringle, seeing the exuberant relish with which his friend devoured the meal and then all too transparently began eyeing the remaining potatoes. His personal taste ran to crisper, dryer food, and opulent pies, but after the poor fare and rigours of the retreat he too was revelling in the richness of it all.

'A Highlander is raised to be content with little food in his belly, but we all do love a fine meal,' said Captain Cameron.

'It is strange to be at ease, is it not?' said Pringle. 'I keep waiting for the drums to beat and the order to stand to arms – well, bugles in your case. In the last weeks every moment of comfort was swiftly interrupted.'

'Aye,' said Cameron, 'the French have kept us busy, although I dare say they have regretted provoking the Reserve Division. Still, I hear that Mr Williams has been off adventuring on his own. You have done well, sir, from all I hear.'

'I had able assistance from the non-commissioned officers, and the strength of a formidable position,' conceded Williams. 'The men did their duty.' Together they tried to cajole more of the story out of him, without much success. He preferred to hear about the exploits of the main army, and as the stories alternated they passed the meal with great pleasure. It was also evident that Cameron enjoyed talking about his own men and had a fierce pride in his corps.

'I miss having a piper,' said the greenjacketed officer.

'I was not aware that the Ninety-fifth employed the bagpipes.' Williams' mother had raised him to be enthusiastic for anything Scottish.

'No more they do, but we are the Highland Company of the First Battalion, and more than half of the men marched down with me from Lochaber back when the regiment was forming. So we have a piper on parades, whenever I can find one. My last got himself shot through the lungs at Vimeiro.' The captain's tone implied that the man had been shamefully careless.

Talk turned to the summer's campaign and shared battles in Portugal. As always, Hanley noticed that they spoke most of the ridiculous moments.

'Bald as a coot, bald as a coot, with the sun shining off his pate!' Pringle collapsed into laughter at his own story and barely managed to finish it off. 'Galloping around, yelling out, "A guinea for the man who finds my wig!" and all the while a battle going on about him.' The story of the officer who had lost both his hat and hairpiece at Vimeiro was one of Pringle's favourites. Face bright scarlet and creased, he was incapable of any more talk for some time.

Cameron replied with a tale of a rifleman who fired off all his cartridges at the French. 'Still in a rage, he pours in loose powder from his horn, digs into his pack for his razor blade, and shoots that at the voltigeurs!'

Pringle had barely recovered his composure, and promptly fell into fresh hysterics. They felt the need for a more gentle atmosphere, and for a while fell silent. Cameron had brought cigars, and all save Williams savoured such a rare indulgence. Their comfort was so great that the rifle officer forgot the warning, and laid down his glass at the edge of the table. The crystal shattered into a thousand pieces, spraying the remnants of the wine everywhere.

'You would think they had better things to do!' Cameron said wearily.

'No respect, the French,' agreed Pringle.

It was dark by the time they had finished, which made his dash back to his own company a good deal less dangerous. Soon afterwards orders arrived for yet another retreat. They were to wait until midnight and then walk away from their positions. There were to be no shouted orders, no drums or bugles, and not even formation. Every corps from the Reserve Division was simply to get up and leave, going back to rally on a ridge, lower than this one, but closer to the city. Instinctive protests were roundly damned, and each officer told to obey orders. They did, but to Williams and the others it felt as if they were slinking away.

At dawn the next morning they heard the French artillery commence a bombardment on the houses they had left, and the wisdom of General Paget's instructions became obvious. It was a reassuring sign of the efficiency of the high command. Even more encouraging was the sight of a forest of sails and masts in the bay and harbour.

The Royal Navy had arrived.

27

Hanley sketched, and wondered whether anyone had ever before seen a sight like this. The noise had been appalling, even here more than a mile away from the powder store. Men had been knocked down by the shock, which felt like a rushing wind, although he was reluctant to employ the expression in case Williams grew all biblical when he came back from his errand in the city.

They had been warned that the engineers were about to destroy a store of more than a thousand barrels of powder, which had been meant for the Spanish. Regrettably, no one had informed the engineers that an even larger cache was stored in a warehouse next to the powder store. The first explosion set off a second as some four thousand barrels blew up. Hanley shaded the two quite distinct plumes of thick black smoke. They had climbed quickly at first, looming over the city, but now they were slowing and the bigger plume was spreading at the top, blossoming outwards into a curious, mushroom-like shape. It was beautiful and somehow terrible, as if man could now control the weather, conjuring up great clouds as he plunged the world into destruction.

In Corunna the shock had rocked the houses and shattered most of the windows. A flying shard of glass had cut open the back of Esther MacAndrews' hand and another jagged piece had narrowly missed young Jacob. The baby woke and howled and it was a long time before he would be comforted. One of the little blankets they had got him had been drying in front of the fire. The guard had fallen over and the wool was burning before Jane could rescue it. Her mother complained insincerely that they would now have to go out and buy more things for the baby. A maid was summoned to care for the child, and the two of them set out into the streets. Jane sensed that her mother was enjoying every moment, and seemed especially determined to find what she wanted in a town almost beset by the enemy and preparing for evacuation. Yet life continued and the shops were still open. Jane found herself drawn to a window with a rich display of lace, and remained to inspect it properly while her mother went to the next shop in search of soft cotton.

'Good morning, my dear Miss MacAndrews, it is such a delight to see you unscathed, and indeed looking so gloriously beautiful.' Captain Wickham was immaculately turned out. His boots, buttons and epaulettes gleamed, his jacket had been brushed down carefully, and his trousers were neatly pressed. Sent to help arrange for the embarkation of the Reserve Division, he was now happily ensconced in a comfortable room shared with only one other staff officer. He was well fed, washed and shaved, and had even managed several successful hands of cards the evening before. Now he glimpsed the prospect of completing his pleasure.

'Good day to you, sir,' Jane managed to stammer out. She had almost forgotten the suave officer. The face was familiar, and yet now she saw in it a hard indifference to the needs of others. Surprise and anger mingled. Her complexion reddened, and Wickham saw this as a good sign.

'We were all so very worried,' he said, giving his most earnest stare. 'I was so very worried,' he added more quietly, and before Jane knew it he was pressing her hand.

In the first heat of her rage at him she had taken pleasure in devising cutting remarks, intended to wound and shame him at their next encounter. Then so much had taken place that she had forgotten him. The hatred did not return now, and instead Jane felt a wave of disgust at Wickham, and at herself for ever dallying with the man, or being so much of a child as to see it as excitingly dangerous.

'I missed you, Jane,' he whispered, and his hand slid up her arm.

'Then perhaps you should have the courtesy to attend meetings you have arranged. Although I must inform you that never in the future will they be arranged with me.' Jane would have liked her voice to sound calmer, but Wickham was obviously shocked, so much so that she was able to free herself from his grip and step away. 'I bid you good day, Mr Wickham.'

The officer rallied quickly from his surprise. Women had snapped at him before, and yet still been won over. He smiled, and Jane found his demeanour deeply wounding because he so obviously felt that her resentment was temporary, and had continued confidence in his own charms. He raised his hat and was gone before she could come up with any suitable reproof.

Her mother seemed to be taking a long time, and Jane was so agitated that she thought it best to return her gaze to the window so that her expression did not betray her to the many passers-by.

Williams' heart leapt when he glimpsed the mass of red curls pinned back into a bun and topped with a little straw bonnet. He had not seen Jane since they returned, although even when most exhausted she had seldom left his thoughts. The girl was wearing a sea-green dress with a short laced jacket over it.

'Good morning, Miss MacAndrews.'

Jane's face showed annoyance as she turned in surprise, and then softened in recognition. 'Mr Williams,' she said, and even in her still-disturbed mood she lavished a smile upon him. 'This is a happy chance. I did not know that the regiment was in the town?'

'We are not yet,' explained Williams. 'I have been sent to help make arrangements for us to embark. That is my errand now, and I have to find Captain Wickham.' He was pleased to see the flicker of displeasure the name prompted, even though his suspicions of the man's intentions towards the girl had faded away in the dramas of the last weeks.

'Then perhaps I should not detain you.'

'Well, may I first . . . That is, I am truly glad to encounter you.' He had planned what he meant to say, but the words crumbled in the face of reality, and so he sought refuge in courtesy. 'Your mother is well, I trust?'

'Indeed. You may see her in a moment as she is engaged in purchasing a few minor things.'

'And is young Jacob in good health?'

'Good health and even stronger voice.' They both smiled, but in neither case was their attention truly on the conversation. Williams barely noticed the many strangers passing in the street, but felt that what he wanted to say ought to be said in a greater degree of privacy.

'Miss MacAndrews, may I draw you away for a walk along the battlements?'

Jane still seethed at the impudent assurance of Wickham. Did he see her as a fool, or as an innocent to be led easily astray? She barely heard the question.

'I beg your pardon.'

'I wondered whether you might like to walk.'

Jane frowned. 'Do you not have your duties, Mr Williams?' She tried to forget her annoyance and instead indulge her taste for mischief. 'Or is your wish to lure me away from my mother for some nefarious purpose?'

'Given the time we spent alone in recent days, you should be better placed to judge my intentions.' Miss MacAndrews smiled in approval, and then Williams worried that she might think he referred to their brief physical encounter and he panicked because he knew he longed to hold her again, but that was not what he had meant. Then the next words tumbled out without restraint. 'I wish to ask you to marry me.'

In spite of herself Miss MacAndrews gasped. His intentions and efforts to draw her away now seemed so obvious. Only her preoccupation could have prevented her from understanding his purpose.

'That is an honour, sir. I am flattered and do not quite know how to respond for the question is unexpected and so much has happened.'

She had not yet refused, and his hope soared. 'The reply need not be made in haste. One single word could make me the happiest fellow in the world, but I will wait for ever to hear it.'

Jane was not quite sure what he meant, and then remembered something. 'You are kind.' There was something endearing as well as infuriating about his odd mixture of passion, worship and calm reason. 'And yet it is but a few months since you told me that you were in no position to ask for my hand. I am surely entitled to know what has changed. I am not aware that you have come into a fortune.' Miss MacAndrews glared at an hussar officer who was lingering and obviously eavesdropping on their conversation. The sense that she was being watched offended her.

'That is sadly true. I have little to offer.' He also turned to stare at the officer, recognised the captain he had met at Sahagun and nodded amiably. The hussar sauntered off. 'I know I have so little to offer.' He leaned closer to her and dropped his voice. 'I simply love you, Jane.'

He was genuine. She could tell that. The tremor in his voice was not affected. An hour before and she would no doubt have responded, an open street or not. Instead, the gesture reminded her of Wickham and she sickened herself remembering her former excitement at his attentions and how close she had come to ruin.

'You have not answered my question, Mr Williams? I cannot see how matters have changed.'

Williams shrugged; he did not wish to be indelicate. Surely the truth was obvious? He stated it anyway. 'We have travelled since then. Alone, and for days on end. And we have . . .' He stopped himself. Did she not understand? 'It is a question of honour.'

'Honour?'

He failed to catch the angry inflexion. 'I would not have the slightest tarnish on your reputation.'

'Would you not?' He had not managed to say anything in the way that he had planned. Williams knew that he had angered the girl even if he did not truly understand why.

'Would you not?' repeated Miss MacAndrews. Her voice was quiet, but absolutely clear, and her speech was fast. 'And so you would deign to marry me, disgrace or not? As a favour, and a kindness. No one else would have me so I should be grateful for your condescension, even though you openly confess to be a man without wealth or obvious prospects.'

'But . . .'

'Disgrace, sir! What disgrace? I do not recall any moment of disgrace. And I might add that if such had occurred then you would have been responsible, and would not you who speak of honour be the cause of dishonour?' She thought of Wickham and his obvious lechery.

'I did not mean . . .'

'How can you expect any woman who is not truly degraded to appreciate an offer made so discourteously? Oh, you are generous, sir, so generous to speak now of marriage! The proud and kind gentleman and the wayward girl!'

She had to draw breath at some point, and Williams just managed to make a weak protest. He was confused and more than a little angry. 'My admiration of you is long standing. I first told you of it when we were still in England so that you can be under no illusion that I speak from pity or a sense of obligation. If I were not involved I would have spoken no differently. My life, my everything, will always be at your disposal to save you from the least harm, whether to person or reputation.'

'I do not recall asking for your protection,' said Jane, although she remembered how he had rescued her and knew that in truth she was both grateful and flattered. Everything was happening the wrong way.

'You have it anyway, for I have no choice in the matter.' He almost flung the words at her, and his face had grown red. 'I do not believe such a thing is dishonourable, but whether or not, it is beyond my control.' Many of the passers-by were watching. Williams no longer cared, but Miss MacAndrews was wishing they had not chanced upon each other at such a time and place.

Mrs MacAndrews rescued them before worse was said and greater offence taken.

'Ah, Jane, they found the material in the end, so we have enjoyed success.' She appeared to notice her companion for the first time. 'Oh, Mr Williams, I am most pleased to see you. You must tell Dobson that his grandson thrives, and that when it is convenient I wish to have a word with him to discuss the boy's future.' She permitted him the briefest of replies. 'I understand that you are helping to arrange the transportation. Do you have any news for us?'

'The cavalry and artillery are already embarking. The baggage will follow for each division, so you may be sent for this evening or tomorrow morning. The major sends his compliments and says that he hopes you will both be put on board the same ship as him, but that nothing is yet certain.'

'Then I am sure you have much to do, and we must not detain you from your duty.' Mrs MacAndrews stared fixedly at him. 'I trust that duty will not prevent you from obtaining a more suitable item of headgear.' Williams was still wearing his bedraggled forage cap, and wondered whether this was a reproof for not having removed it. He raised it now, bade them good day and hastened up the street. Williams felt more battered and bruised than after the fight at the bridge, and a good deal more confused. He was simply uncertain whether or not his hopes and thus his life were in ruins, and tried to tell himself that if he were not sure then there might still be some faint chance.

Esther MacAndrews looked at her daughter. She had still only wormed a little out of her about her escapades. Jane looked flustered, but she was nineteen and the mother could remember that when she had been young the important and desperate emotion of one day had faded by the next. There was no indication that anything too terrible had happened, either during her adventures or in the last few moments.

'It seems that Mr Williams has been taking care of you once again, my dear.' The mother spoke with as much innocence as she could muster, and consciously or not the accent of the Carolinas became stronger.

Jane looked briefly angry, but did not wish to be drawn.

'A chance encounter,' she said. 'We spoke only for a few moments as I waited for you.' It seemed better to move her mother on to a different subject. 'May I see the cotton roll?'

'It is wrapped, so better to wait until we are back at the hotel. I think you will be pleased, though.' Esther MacAndrews was not about to be so easily diverted. Jane's own sense of mischief was inherited from her mother, along with much of her character, if not her appearance. As Williams passed beyond earshot, Esther smiled warmly at her daughter. 'I have become very fond of that young man,' she drawled.

'I believe that Mr Williams also holds himself in very high esteem.' Jane was not inclined to be fair at that moment.

'Well, Jane, you know him far better than I,' responded her mother, with an emphasised lack of conviction.

Jane was unsure what was meant by the comment. Her mother was already expecting another man's child when she met and fell in love with her father. They too had their adventures, hunted by the militia as he escaped from captivity to reach the British lines. Was her mother suggesting that Jane's own recent behaviour was similar? Surely, given her own history, she would not be disposed to judge, but what conduct would she consider to be natural and so assume had occurred?

'There is a great deal I do not know about Mr Williams – a very great deal indeed,' Jane declared.

'There seems no doubt of his valour, and men value that considerably.' Esther MacAndrews was determined to continue her daughter's discomfort. Although she might not discover the details of what had happened since Christmas, she was confident of discerning Jane's mood more clearly.

'Ensign Williams has his virtues, I am sure,' Jane said primly. 'Yet they are accompanied by a considerable pride, and too little sympathy for others.'

'You know best, of course.' Esther now felt sure of

considerable attachment on both sides, whether or not either was willing to admit it. 'It is a pity he dresses like a ragamuffin, for in many respects he could be considered well favoured in his appearance.' Jane's face went rigid. 'Of course,' her mother continued, 'I am simply an old woman, and should leave such judgements to the young.'

Jane, long accustomed to such blatant insincerity, glared at her mother. 'This is scarcely the place to speak of such things.'

'What things, my dear? I have simply expressed a good opinion of one of your father's officers, and a gentleman who is a friend to us both. I do not see anything indiscreet in such a conversation.' Esther MacAndrews lied with practised fluency. 'Still, we must not linger. Little Jacob will most likely be awake by now. Come, carry this package for me.'

On the way back to the hotel, their talk was solely concerned with babies and their care. Jane was relieved after the morning's encounters, and apart from that delighted in the theme as much as her mother.

28

'Halt!' MacAndrews' order was more of a remark than an instruction for the 106th had already stopped in its tracks as soon as they heard the French guns. He flicked open his watch and saw that it was just past two o'clock. No wonder everyone from the general down had assumed that Marshal Soult was not planning any attack. Both armies had waited all through the morning, the French on a higher ridge and the British on a lower line of high ground some two miles south of Corunna. The Reserve Division was ordered to be at the harbour to begin embarkation at four. Sir John had chosen them to go first of all the infantry as an acknowledgement of their services as rearguard.

General Paget rode past. 'Turn them around. I dare say we'll be going forward soon!' He sounded positively cheerful. Mac-Andrews sensed that the 106th and all the other regiments shared his enthusiasm. They had been happy to head for the ships. In spite of the likely discomforts of transport ships, it would mean days or weeks of little work and light discipline, and rations would be more reliable than in the last few weeks. It was not to be for the moment, and he could see no sign of regrets. They turned about, frustrated only because no order had yet arrived for them to move forward.

They were on the right of the British line, but held back some distance from its centre. The French held a peak some way ahead of them, which he could just see over the closer crest. Paget had explained to them earlier that the general was deliberately making his right appear weak, so that Soult would see a path through to the harbour. He wanted the French to come that way, to tire themselves crossing a land cut by gullies and split into small walled fields. With some of their energy already gone, the enemy would suddenly be hit by two of his divisions, with the Reserve Division in the lead. It was just a question of waiting for the order. MacAndrews patted his horse on the neck and sat listening to the guns pounding.

The French guns were loud, and the answering noise of the British artillery seemed almost puny by comparison. Soult had forty guns, a dozen of them lined wheel to wheel in one battery shooting down at close range on to the village at the centre of the British line. Sir John had barely a quarter of this number, and three of those were back with the reserve. The rest of his guns were already on board ships, along with all the cavalry. There was not room for most of the horses and only the best were being taken. Hundreds more had been slaughtered in the streets or on the beaches.

Bobbie shied as Williams tried to take the mare past a row of dead cavalry chargers. The troopers had struggled to kill them efficiently with their pistols. Tearful men had flinched, and wounded rather than killed, so that some horses suffered horribly. They were then ordered to cut their throats as a surer and quicker means of killing, so the earth around the bodies stank from the dried blood, and his mare would go nowhere near them.

Giving up, he took her to the side and turned back into town, threading through the streets to go out by a different route. When they heard the opening salvoes of the enemy artillery, all of the officers detached from their battalions had immediately asked Wickham for leave to rejoin their respective corps. Most were on foot, and so were trudging as best they could, but Williams knew that Bobbie was close by and did not think that Pringle would object if he borrowed the mare. Wickham, whose own pair of horses had already been embarked as too valuable to be left behind, let him borrow a saddle. He declared that he would like to go himself, but must remain at his post, but Williams did not even bother to listen.

He passed along a stretch of quayside, and wondered on which of the ships the major's wife and daughter were. Miss Mac-Andrews' behaviour still baffled him, and he had thought over their conversation – and indeed all their conversations – many, many times without reaching any certain conclusion. He threaded through the streets, got lost, but managed to obtain directions from a sentry and eventually emerged on the main road.

In half an hour he saw the columns of the reserve waiting, their Colours flapping in the breeze. Before he reached the 106th, General Paget's chief of staff beckoned to him.

'It's Williams, isn't it? Where is Captain Wickham?' he called out.

'Still at the harbour.'

'Indeed. Well then, we are short handed and you have a horse, so you must serve in his place. Take this to General Moore.' He handed a folded note. 'Follow the road till you reach a little village. Then cut due south over the fields for Elvina. He should be there.'

'But, sir . . .' Williams tried to explain that the horse was not his.

'Damn it, sir, do as you are told!'

Williams rode off, passing close to the 106th. 'Your family are embarked, sir,' he called to Major MacAndrews, who acknowledged with a wave.

Pringle pointed, lifted his glasses off, and then put them on again as if to confirm what he was seeing. 'He's taking my damned horse again!' he shouted out, and the grenadiers laughed.

The sound of cannon fire grew heavier as Williams approached the centre of the battlefield. He passed wounded men, limping or supported by comrades. By now he could hear bursts of musket fire, both sporadic shots and heavy volleys, and then the wind carried chants of '*Vive l'empereur!*' and the beating of many drums, which fought against the skirl of bagpipes. He could still see little, as the ground rose in front of him and hid

301

the fighting. There was a volley and then a cheer that he knew to be British.

He came over the low rise and saw a line of Highlanders driving back the head of a French column. More redcoats were charging alongside them, and disappeared into a maze of low houses and walled gardens. Their regimental Colour was a red cross on black, so they must surely be the old 'dirty half hundred'. A battalion to his right was inclining its right wing so that the line now formed an L shape. Once in position it resumed steady platoon volleys to the front and side, the fire rippling up and down the companies.

There were a few horsemen clustered near the battalion. Moore stood out. His horse was unusual, for it was a light cream colour with a black face, but that only enhanced the impression he made. It was obvious that the rider was in charge, and as Williams rode towards him he felt a sense of awe at simply being in the man's presence. Sir John noticed him, nodded in recognition, without stopping as he dictated an order to one of his aides. Graham waved to him. Two more men waited with messages. The second was delivering his as Williams reined in beside them.

'Sir David's wound is grievous, but does not appear mortal,' said the staff officer. 'He may lose an arm.'

Sir John acknowledged the report. 'I pray that he does not. Ride now, and inform Sir John Hope that he succeeds to the command if I should fall, now that Sir David is unable.' The man rode off.

'Now, Mr Williams, I see that we have you at staff work after all.' Major Colborne took and scanned the message he had brought. 'Sir Edward informs us that the Reserve Division is in position and awaits your orders. Judging from the time he cannot have received your instructions.'

'You know the ground, John. Ride to Paget and take him along the stream to drive back the enemy right, but tell him not to go too far.'

'Sir.' Colborne immediately set off. Williams was about to follow, when the general stopped him.

'Stay, Mr Williams, I may well have need of an additional officer as the day goes on.'

The fighting in the village was hard to follow. They heard bursts of very heavy firing, and French and British cheers. The 50th had surged right through the houses, but the attack had lost momentum and some had become cut off when the French counter-attacked. The Highlanders of the 42nd were on the edge of the buildings, firing steadily. One company was on the slope, and Sir John now rode over to them to get a better view of the combat.

Round-shot from the French battery skidded over the grass, sometimes falling between the horses. One ball took the leg off a Highlander below the knee. The man screamed in his agony.

'Carry him back to the surgeons,' said Sir John with quiet authority to a sergeant standing in his place at the rear of the company. 'My good fellow, don't make such a noise – we must bear these things better.'

The soldier did not reply, but his cries slackened as two of his comrades supported him between their shoulders. Soon afterwards the company charged down to reinforce the fighting. The broken ground gave few chances for whole battalions to fight in formation. Companies went in on their own, and often found themselves split up into little clusters of men, fighting small, savage and often private battles.

It was soon clear that the momentum was shifting back to the French. The two British battalions were forced back from the village on to the slope behind.

Sir John sent orders for the two battalions of the First Foot Guards to come to their support. Williams took the order, and would long cherish the reaction of the brigade commander at the sight of his battered forage cap. His expression mingled profound distaste with a strong disbelief that any officer could so resemble a scarecrow. Yet reaction to the order was prompt, and as he cantered Bobbie back to the general, the Guards were already marching over the crest.

Some of the companies of Highlanders saw their relief coming, and so their officers took them backwards. Williams came up to Sir John just as he reached one of the retreating companies.

'Why, sir, are you withdrawing?' asked the general.

'We have used all our cartridges,' said a young, gap-toothed captain, 'and must go to fetch ammunition.'

'My brave Forty-second, join your comrades.' He pointed down the slope to where much of the battalion was still engaged. 'Ammunition is coming, and you still have your bayonets! Recollect Egypt!' The last time the regiment had fought in a battle had been eight years before.

The captain saluted, and Williams thought he saw him exchange a glance with one of his sergeants. 'Fix bayonets,' the sergeant called out in a voice tinged more by London than the Highlands. There was the familiar clicking sound as the sockets were screwed on to the muzzles of their firelocks. The company went back down the slope with quiet determination. To Williams they looked unstoppable. Sir John raised his hat in salute.

'Fine fellows,' said Graham. 'Good Scotsmen,' he added to one of the general's English ADCs.

Bobbie had been chewing the grass and now took the opportunity to rub green-tinged spittle all over the rump of the general's cream-coloured horse. Williams felt his head shift, and glanced down in horror to see the handsome charger so abused. He was still pointing back towards the two columns of approaching Guardsmen, but now his main hope was that the general had not noticed what his mare was doing.

Sir John Moore was jerked from the saddle and flung down on his back just by the feet of Colonel Graham's horse. Williams thought he just glimpsed a blur of movement as the eight-pound shot whipped past. The general sighed softly, but did not cry out and seemed unscathed. Then he shifted, trying to push himself up, and Williams saw the blood on the left side of his chest near the arm. An ADC sprang down from his own mount and took the general's right hand. Williams joined him. The blood was spreading quickly and they unwound Sir John's crimson sash and tried to staunch the flow. With Graham and another aide, they lifted him as gently as they could – there was only the slightest involuntary hiss of pain – and laid him with his back resting on a soft bank of earth.

'I must go and inform Sir John Hope,' said Graham in a voice of forced calm. Moore gave a gentle nod of approval and the colonel left them.

'How do the Black Watch fare?' The general's voice was weak, but had lost none of its confidence or precision. He was staring intently at the line of Highlanders as they charged once more. Williams assured him that the 42nd were advancing. Another shot hit the turf not far from them and skidded over their heads. The ADC gestured to Williams and with the help of a Highlander they took the general back behind the cover of a stone wall. A surgeon was near by, plying his trade in the shelter of a large boulder, and the man immediately came over.

Williams watched as he examined the wound and his heart sank. Sir John's left shoulder appeared smashed by the glancing strike of the ball. His arm hung by no more than a strip of skin. Much of his jacket had gone, exposing pieces of bone and bare muscle over his chest. The blood kept pulsing, even though it was hard to believe that it could continue flowing at such a rate.

The doctor's expression betrayed nothing of the hopelessness of the situation. He cut away a fragment of jacket and a couple of buttons forced into the ruin of the shoulder.

'I can do no more at present,' he said.

'Thank you. But my good man, you can do me no good – it is too high up.' Sir John's face was very pale, but his voice was steady.

'We should get him away,' whispered the aide.

'Sergeant,' Williams called to an NCO of the 42nd. 'Bring five men and a blanket.' The Highlanders came quickly. They were big men, and two were old soldiers who had fought under the general's command at Alexandria. Their touch was tender as they lifted and slid Sir John on to the blanket. The general gasped when his sword became tangled between his legs.

The aide went to unbuckle it.

'It is as well as it is.' The instruction was firm. 'I had rather it should go out of the field with me.'

'You will need it again, before too long,' said the staff officer. Williams tried to agree, but the words refused to come out.

The general leaned his head to stare at the wound. 'No, Hardinge, I feel that to be impossible. You need not go with me. Report to General Hope that I am wounded and carried to the rear and place yourself at his disposal.'

Williams appeared to be forgotten and so walked behind the Highlanders as they carried the general down the track. He had let go of Bobbie's reins and could not see the mare anywhere. A sense of helplessness oppressed him, and he went with the general in the vague hope that his presence might serve some useful purpose or give even the slightest comfort.

Bobbie ran for a long time, fleeing the noise and the stink of battle. She splashed through a little stream and ran on, weaving her way between the rocks and enclosures of the fields beyond. Hanley saw her first.

'Isn't that your disreputable mare?' he said to Pringle. The Grenadier and Light Companies were in advance of and to the left of the battalion, occupying a boulder-strewn ridge. Ahead of them a long skirmish line formed by the 95th extended to the right. The greenjackets were pressing forward steadily, and there were puffs of smoke and shots as they skirmished with the French. The fight was moving away, but the flank companies of the 106th were ordered to stay where they were and secure the low ridge. The rest of the battalion advanced in column behind the 95th.

Pringle followed Hanley's gaze and saw the mare walking slowly now. He whistled and called her name. Bobbie stopped, and began to crop at the long grass.

'Damned animal,' said Pringle. The French were now some

distance away, and certainly beyond the range of any accuracy. He jogged forward, calling to the horse softly. The mare turned its back, and then walked away from him.

'Be like that,' he said, and gave up, walking back up the slope to the grenadiers. He heard hoof beats closing rapidly and the mare was beside him, messily nuzzling his face, before he reached the company. 'There's a good girl. Mucky as ever. Now where have you been?'

'We saw Bills riding him about an hour ago,' said Hanley.

'Yes, I should not think anyone else would have such bare-faced cheek. Hope we haven't lost him again.' He looked carefully, but could see no traces of blood on the saddle.

'He's probably fallen off,' said Hanley, but there was doubt in his voice. MacAndrews had mentioned that both General Moore and General Baird had been hit. It made everything seem less certain.

'Oh, you bitch!' Pringle had been inspecting the rest of the horse when Bobbie chose to lash out and caught him on the thigh, knocking him over. 'Damn all bloody horses to hell!' He got up, rubbing his limb. 'I don't know why I bought you in the first place.'

'Must be for her charming temperament,' suggested Hanley. 'Or your looks, my darling.' He smoothed her long head and then pulled his hands away to avoid her snapping teeth.

'I sometimes wonder if she is still loyal to Napoleon at heart!'

They turned to look as the 95th reach the low crest ahead of them. The brigade continued to advance, but the grenadiers were ordered to wait and hold their position and so they stood and watched.

'We're winning, aren't we?' asked Hanley, and Billy Pringle was once again baffled by his friend's lack of confidence when it came to understanding the business of soldiering.

'Oh yes, we are winning the battle.' He thought of the ships waiting to carry them away. 'What it has all been for is another matter, because it rather looks as if the war is lost.' Pringle paused for a moment. 'I do hope Bills is unscathed.'

29

'Look familiar?' Pringle said sourly as they boarded the grimy little ship. It was the *Corbridge*, the same merchantman that had carried them to Portugal.

'That fellow does,' said Hanley, to whom one ship looked very much like another, but who had noticed the man in a shabby blue coat and round hat. The ship's master was a bald, inhospitable Northerner, who had only once invited the officers to dine in all the weeks of their voyage. Unable to forbid them all access to the deck, he had ensured his men made them feel unwelcome, constantly moving them aside to attend to urgent tasks. He was standing on the dockside, glaring at the ragged and dirty soldiers.

The recognition was mutual, as was the lack of goodwill. 'Told you I'd be back to collect you,' said the sailor bluntly. Britain's military adventures in the war with France had more often than not ended in disappointment and evacuation. Pringle, Hanley and Williams all found themselves reluctant to walk up the gangplank and board the ship. The optimism of the summer and its victories made the sense of defeat stronger. They had beaten the French at every meeting, but Spain had fallen to the enemy anyway, and no doubt Portugal would follow soon enough.

'Have we failed?' asked Hanley suddenly.

'Someone has,' said Williams, 'and no doubt there will be scoundrels in London who will blame a fallen hero, unable to defend himself.'

Pringle looked surprised. 'I do believe you are becoming political, young Bills.'

'The general was a great man,' he said with belligerent devotion.

Billy Pringle patted him on the shoulder. 'Yes, he was, and he will be universally mourned. I do not feel any fault was his.'

Williams had rejoined them only that morning, as the detachment was moving down to the quayside. He had waited with the general throughout his final hours, watching as his staff did their best to comfort him.

'Are the French beaten?' Time and again Sir John addressed the same question to every new arrival. He seemed desperate for reassurance, and it appeared to be his overwhelming concern. Williams had been moved when the general's French servant burst out crying on seeing his master, to be told simply in his own language, 'My friend, this is nothing.'

Closest to him was Colonel Anderson, who sat by his side, holding his hand, once the surgeons had abandoned a brief attempt to examine him more thoroughly. The pain they caused was too great, and nothing they could do would change the outcome.

'Anderson, you know I have always wished to die this way.' Williams only just caught the whispered words. 'Are the French beaten?' The question was to Major Colborne, who had just arrived.

'Yes, in every point of the field. You have won.'

'We have won. I hope the people of England will be satisfied.' His breath was coming with more difficulty, but the voice was still strong. 'I hope my country will do me justice.'

One of the few chaplains in the army prayed in the long spells of silence. At times, Sir John revived. He asked always after his aides, and his staff hid the truth that one lay dying and another was feared dead. He told Anderson that they must ensure that Colborne was made a lieutenant colonel, and then he tried to give a message to his mother, but lost the thread of his thoughts and trailed off into silence. When Graham and General Paget arrived he did not know them. The light in his eyes was failing. From the expressions of the others Williams guessed that his words were making less sense.

He did see Stanhope, and the last words were definite. 'Remember me to your sister.'

A gun boomed out from the flagship in the harbour. Anderson closed the general's eyes. 'Eight o'clock,' he said. One aide was sobbing, and most had tears in their eyes. Williams wished that he could cry. A sense of duty and courage made him feel that a man should rarely be moved to tears, but bear things with fortitude, and yet at that moment he felt it must be a great release.

He waited, eating listlessly when food was set before him, and he heard some of the staff talk of the jealousy of the ministry and its failure to support the campaign. When dawn approached they went up to the citadel. A few of the staff wondered who Williams was, but Graham and Colborne spoke for him. He was not sure why he stayed, and mourned so deeply a man he barely knew. They laid the general to rest inside one of the bastions of the fortress. A fresh grave was already there, for one of the brigade commanders of the Reserve Division had died almost as soon as they had reached the safety of Corunna.

There was no coffin even for the commander of the army. Sir John was still in his uniform, and then the body was rolled in a blanket like that of any soldier and lowered into the grave. His cloak was put across him. The service was short, for as the light grew the French artillery started to bombard the British outposts. A party of redcoats began to shovel earth over the cloak, and at first they worked with a tender care, until Graham told them to hurry. He knew his friend was not one to stand on ceremony or worry about himself when the good of the army required so much to be done.

Williams left them and wandered on his own through the streets, looking for his regiment. Battalion after battalion was moving down to the harbour, and he realised that he must look for them there, but he walked in a daze. Hanley saw him first and prodded Pringle, and then they had both halloed heartily. Pringle needed to be cheered up. There was no room for horses unless the mount was of high quality or belonged to someone of seniority. The orders were to kill all the others, but he had not been able to bring himself to perform the execution and forbade anyone else to do it. He had unsaddled the mare, patted her on the neck, dodged her teeth, and then let her loose on the beach.

Williams' expression made it clear that he was scarcely likely to lighten the mood. He told them briefly of the general's last hours and his burial.

'We were wondering whether we had lost you again.' Hanley explained how they had found the horse.

'I should report to the major,' said Williams.

'Not practical, old boy. He's already taken most of the battalion to another ship.' Pringle appreciated his friend's sense of duty, but suspected he had another concern. 'His family were already on board.'

'I know.' Williams thought of Jane and that plunged him into deeper gloom.

A harassed and weary-looking Captain Pierrepoint came through the press and ordered Pringle to take the Grenadier Company on board the *Corbridge*. 'No time to be lost,' he called, and then was gone back into the teeming press on the docks. Two other companies from the 106th would join the grenadiers. That was the same allocation as on the way out, when the *Corbridge* seemed crowded. Pringle guessed that it would be more roomy this time, in spite of the fifty of so stragglers from other units who were already below decks. The 106th was not much more than half the size it had been just sixth months earlier. They had lost dozens of men in the retreat, although a lot fewer than many of the regiments in the army. Compared to Portugal, there were few dead and wounded from the previous day's battle. Only one of the grenadiers had been hit in the fighting, and several others helped Eyles on board. He had been shot in the leg, but had every hope of recovery.

Little was said as the three officers followed their men.

The next company came after them. Williams chanced to look

back and returned Scammell's nod. Just for a moment he also spotted Hatch staring at him with a look of pure hatred. The man caught his glance and gave a smile with just a hint of mockery. They had exchanged no more than the briefest of greetings since his return, and he had to admit that the other ensign continued to baffle him.

The men were sent below, and after claiming a tiny room for themselves and the officers of another company, the three friends returned to the deck and watched as the ship moved out into the bay. They ignored the less than subtle hints from the captain that their place was to be stowed away with the other cargo. After months of campaigning, they were far less easily bullied.

Dobson marched along the deck, his gaze defying any sailor's inclination to stop him, and stamped to attention beside the officers.

'Beg pardon, sir,' he said to Pringle, 'but may I have a word?' His voice was at its most formal. Jacket stained and patched, his trousers torn, and with a thick beard far darker than his grey hair, the old soldier still stood with drill-book precision.

'Of course.'

'Well, sir, it's just that I would like to ask your permission to marry.'

'Good God,' said Pringle before he could stop himself.

'Mrs Rawson and I have grown close. Annie . . . I mean Mrs Rawson, would like to have it done soon.'

'Good God. I mean . . . I am sorry.' Pringle thought of the prim and religious sergeant's widow. 'Of course, of course, if you are sure.'

'Thank you, sir.'

'Congratulations, Dob.' Williams was even more shocked than Pringle, and yet he found himself beaming like a fool and pumping the old veteran's hand. His friends quickly followed his example.

'Would you ask the captain for me, sir?' asked Dobson. 'Annie would prefer a chaplain, but God knows when we'll see one of them.'

'Yes, yes, of course.' Pringle thought that this should ensure an interesting encounter with the ship's master.

'Thank you, sir. Well, I had better go and tell Mrs Rawson the good news.' He stiffened to attention, saluted, did a perfect about turn and marched away.

'Well, well . . .' said Pringle, for the only other things he could think of saying were profane in the extreme and he knew that Williams disliked such loose speech.

'It seems a little sudden,' ventured Hanley, although he guessed that life as a soldier's widow was unlikely to be easy.

'Often the way in the army.' Pringle smiled. 'Have you heard the old story? An officer met a pretty young woman just a few hours after a great battle. She was sobbing, and he told her how sorry he was that her husband had been killed. "Thank you," she says, "but it's not that. I have just this moment received a proposal from a sergeant, and it is not twenty minutes since I accepted a corporal." ' He roared with mirth.

'They do seem most unlike in character . . .' began Hanley, still finding the whole business odd.

'Oh my good God!' Pringle spoke over him, and his knuckles were white as he gripped the rail.

Hanley caught the movement first, and Williams followed his gaze and saw the shape moving through the waves. It was small and dark brown and he did not know what it was, until it was lifted on a swell. A horse was swimming towards them, its head held above the water. It was Bobbie. She was close enough for them to make out her empty eye socket. She was swimming fast, but as the wind caught the sails the *Corbridge* was moving still faster.

Pringle broke down, tears coming in floods, and for once it was not seasickness which forced him below deck to seek refuge in his cot.

The French guns opened fire ten minutes later. With the British withdrawal, the enemy's gunners had flogged their teams to drag the cannon up to high ground overlooking the harbour. Williams and Hanley watched as the first shots provoked a flurry of movement on board the ships nearer the shore. Within minutes, several were moving.

'Cut their cables,' muttered the captain. 'Daft buggers,' he added.

They were too far away to see the details. Williams had a sense of panicked movement on masts and rigging. White sails dropped from spars as ships set every stitch of canvas in their rush to escape. He could see two ships moving fast at such an angle that they must surely hit each other. Then one seemed to gain, and he was willing to credit their captains with unusual skill, until he watched the ships shudder and knew that they had bumped. Behind them another pair of ships were hopelessly locked together.

'Daft buggers,' repeated the master.

Hanley pointed to another ship, its masts at unnatural angles, and its deck canted up to one side. 'I think it's run aground,' he said.

''Course it's bloody run aground,' came the gruff comment from behind them.

Soon there were boats in the water, rowing hard, away from the foundered ships, carrying their crews and passengers. The French artillery were still firing, but perhaps because of the distance neither Hanley nor Williams saw any sign that their shot was actually hitting any of the ships.

'Biggest balls-up since Yorktown.' The expression had come into Williams' mind from nowhere, and Hanley was surprised to hear his pious friend employ even such a mild vulgarity. The master of the *Corbridge* gave a brief snort of laughter.

The *Corbridge* was running ahead of the wind now, and the captain took them near an old ship of the line with its guns removed to serve as a transport. An officer on deck screamed vitriolic abuse at the master for cutting across them so recklessly. The *Corbridge* continued blithely on its way, rushing between a pair of sluggish old merchantmen whose hulls were long overdue to be cleaned.

Hanley tapped Williams on the shoulder. He said nothing, and simply pointed. Two ladies stood at the rail of the ship to starboard. One was tall and dark haired and held a bundle in her arms. The other was smaller, her red curls flowing in the wind, and she was waving.

Miss MacAndrews shouted something, but the words were lost and she looked equally uncomprehending when he called back greetings. He wished that he had his telescope, so that he could watch her for longer as the ships grew apart, but he would not run below and fetch it for that would mean losing sight of her now.

Williams was happy. Hanley sensed it, and could not help smiling as well.

'Well, I suppose that we are going home,' he said, even though he did not really have one.

Williams did not appear to be listening, intent only on the diminishing figure of the girl as they rapidly left the other ship behind.

'I love you!' he bellowed as loudly as he could.

'I'm sure you do, lad,' said the master gruffly. 'Now you can both damned well get off my deck.'

HISTORICAL NOTE

Beat the Drums Slowly is a novel, but like its predecessor, *True Soldier Gentlemen*, it is fiction firmly grounded in fact. The 106th is a fictional regiment, and so are all the characters associated with it, but I have tried to make the details of regimental life accurate, and the speech and behaviour of the characters reflect the reality of the period. All of the senior officers in the army are real, and I have done my best to portray them as faithfully as possible, at times in their own words.

Lord Paget commanded the British cavalry with considerable skill, both in the dramatic moments of the charges at Sahagun and Benevente, and also in the even more demanding business of forming the rearguard and skirmishing with the French. He may well have been the ablest cavalry general the British produced in this period. Soon afterwards, however, he eloped with the wife of one of Wellesley's brothers, and this was the main reason why he did not serve again in the Peninsular War. By the time of Waterloo, Wellington and Paget – who had by now become the Earl of Uxbridge – had become more reconciled, and the latter received command of the cavalry in Belgium and led them with the same skill he had shown in Spain.

'Black Jack' Slade received much criticism and little praise for his part in leading Moore's cavalry. On one occasion he was ordered to lead a charge, but stopped twice to adjust his stirrups and in the end the attack was led with great success by the colonel of the regiment involved. Unlike Lord Paget, and in spite of his limited ability, Slade would hold farther commands during the Peninsular War. Seniority and personal connections counted for a great deal in the British Army of that era.

Sir Edward Paget led the Reserve Division with both skill and hot-tempered determination. His conduct commanded wide respect and the contrast between the behaviour of the regiments in his division and most of the remainder of the army was striking. He returned to Portugal later in 1809, but was badly wounded and lost an arm during Wellesley's victory at Oporto. When he eventually went back to command a division in Spain in 1812, he had the bad luck to be captured by a French cavalry patrol.

Thomas Graham is one of the most remarkable and appealing characters of the period, and the story of how he raised his own regiment and became a soldier at the advanced age of forty-three reads like a romance. His wife's fragile beauty was captured in a portrait by Gainsborough. She died of consumption, while they were touring the Mediterranean on a yacht in 1793, and the mistreatment of her corpse prompted him to join the forces besieging Toulouse as a volunteer. It was there he met the young Lieutenant Colonel Moore, beginning a deep friendship, ended only by Moore's death. Graham subsequently commanded the British forces in Cadiz, and won the Battle of Barossa in 1811. In the last years of the Peninsular War he was one of only a handful of men Wellington was willing to trust with independent commands.

Several of Sir John Moore's staff, including the Honourable James Stanhope, who was the nephew of Pitt the Younger, and Colborne and Napier, went on to have distinguished military careers. All were devoted to his memory, as indeed were many other army officers. Stanhope's sister, Lady Hester, was if anything an even more fervent admirer of the general. They did not become engaged, in spite of rumours to the contrary. In the years after his death Lady Hester travelled widely in the Middle East, defying most of the conventions restricting the activities of noblewomen. She died in Lebanon in 1839. A second brother, the Honourable Charles, was a major in the 50th Foot and was killed at Corunna.

Sir John Moore is still venerated by the British Army, especially by the regiments inheriting the traditions of the light infantry and rifle regiments – today principally The Rifles. In the popular consciousness, now that Charles Wolfe's poem 'The Burial of Sir John Moore' is no longer a staple of the schoolroom, he tends to be overshadowed by the Duke of Wellington. Probably Moore's greatest importance was as a trainer, most especially when he commanded a brigade of light infantry at Shorncliffe camp on the South Coast from 1803. A new system of drill was introduced, treating the individual soldier as more than an automaton, encouraging individual initiative, accuracy in shooting, and a reliance on personal pride and honour. This was a remarkably modern concept and in many basic principles is still reflected in the army today. Moore did not devise the system, but he was a serious and conscientious soldier, and did much to foster its success.

In 1808 many considered Moore to be the ablest British general – Wellesley certainly had a high opinion of him. Moore had served as a subordinate commander in Egypt, and in smaller operations in the Mediterranean. He assumed command in Portugal when Sir Hew Dalrymple, and his second-in-command Sir Harry Burrard, were recalled following the outrage at the Convention of Cintra. Wellesley, who although a lieutenant general had held the rank only for a matter of months and so was junior to Moore, had also signed this agreement and so also returned to London to answer charges. Cintra allowed the French army in Portugal to be evacuated to France in British ships, taking their weapons and loot with them. It did mean that the invaders were ejected from Portugal without farther bloodshed, but was generally seen as a poor outcome after the victory at Vimeiro. (I have taken one liberty by having Hanley quote Byron's condemnation of the treaty several years before the publication of *Childe Harold's Pilgrimage*.)

Moore had not arrived in time to be implicated in the

negotiations at Cintra. He was the most senior officer left in Portugal – as well as the most prestigious – and therefore automatically took charge. There is considerable doubt that the government wanted this. He was seen as a Whig and they were Tories, and he was also an extremely vocal critic of corruption and incompetence in the army and in government in general.

From the very start, the government's instructions to Moore were vague and confused. There was widespread enthusiasm for the Spanish patriots who had rebelled against the French invaders, and a complacent belief that the war was won. There was a sense that Moore would find something useful to do in support of the Spanish armies, but little idea of how he might achieve this. Naively, no one seems to have considered that Napoleon might not meekly accept the reverses in Spain. Instead the Emperor led over a quarter of a million of his best troops across the Pyrenees. The Allies were convinced for many months that the French had no more than eighty thousand men in all of Spain. The government of Spain and the administration of its army had been thoroughly dislocated by the removal of the royal family and the French occupation. It would have taken far more time than they had to organise an effective defence against the second, and far larger, French invasion. It would also have taken money and resources which simply did not exist. Napoleon and his marshals routed each of the Spanish field armies in quick succession. It was no mean achievement that many of these managed to salvage a nucleus of a new army from the survivors, but the desperate state of La Romana's Army of Galicia at the end of 1808 is not exaggerated. The soldiers were lacking basic equipment, were seldom fed and almost never paid, and diseases such as typhus were rampant.

Moore and his army of 35,000 could not hope to fight the French on their own, and had not been in a position to take part in the early struggles. He was on the brink of withdrawing to Portugal on at least one occasion. The decision to advance was a bold one, encouraged by the captured dispatch which revealed that Marshal Soult's corps was isolated and vulnerable. Moore failed to inflict serious loss on Soult, but he did draw Napoleon and the bulk of the French forces northwards. This prevented a rapid advance into the south of Spain and then into Portugal. Had this occurred so early in the war, it is possible that all serious resistance would have been permanently crushed. Instead the French effort shifted against Moore, and this gave time for the Spanish armies to reform and prepare defences in the rest of the peninsula.

The British had to retreat, and retreating in the face of the enemy has always been a difficult thing to do. Advancing farther into Spain meant that this would be an especially dangerous operation. It was also winter, a time of the year when armies rarely took the field, and the route led through extremely rugged terrain. The distances were smaller, and the weather less extreme, than in Napoleon's more famous retreat from Moscow, but that should not make us underestimate the genuine hardship endured by Moore's men.

Yet the speed with which discipline collapsed in many regiments remains surprising. Moore was clearly dismayed. Given his own approach to training and discipline, the readiness with which so many redcoats abandoned their sense of honour and duty was especially shocking. His orders to the army, and especially the officers, were clearly intended to shame them into greater efforts. Whenever there was the prospect of fighting, he and other observers were amazed by the rapid change in the redcoats' attitudes and behaviour. Orders to withdraw quickly plunged them back into despair and indiscipline.

Drunkenness was a common problem in the army of the period – and indeed in wider society. Throughout the Peninsular War, large numbers of redcoats would drink themselves insensible at any opportunity. Looting was also hard to prevent – and when provisions were short was often quietly ignored. In the retreat to Corunna both were made worse by a sense that the Spanish villagers were unwilling to fight for their own country, or welcome the allies who were risking their lives on their behalf. The British soldiers felt humiliated and angry at having to retreat, and readily vented this on the property – and occasionally the persons – of the Spanish in their path. It was unfair, but is surely understandable.

Wellington's army would suffer a major breakdown in discipline in many regiments during the retreat from Spain in 1812. Moore's army was less experienced, and certainly far less hardened to campaigning. The British Army was still in the process of learning how to wage war on the continent of Europe. It was especially inexperienced at the higher levels of command. Generals and their staffs were having to learn how to lead and control large formations. Mistakes were made. The story of the dragoon who got drunk and failed to deliver a dispatch is true. Sir David Baird was blamed for this, since Moore's ADC, who delivered the message to him, had offered to carry it himself if given a fresh mount. Instead Sir David followed the normal routine, and in this case the order was not delivered and several brigades underwent an unnecessary and especially arduous march at a time when the men were already fatigued. There were many failings in the supply and intelligence-gathering system. In time, such things would improve, and if mistakes were never eradicated altogether they became fewer. Later in the Peninsular War, Wellington's army did all of these things better, but his system was a gradual creation taking much time and effort.

Moore commanded the army at a much earlier stage in its development, and in a strategic situation of extreme peril. The redcoats suffered severely from weather, hunger, disease and inadequate clothing. Many men ended up barefoot, their often poor-quality boots completely worn out. They had already marched a long way before the retreat began, and too many of the supplies stockpiled for the army's use were destroyed rather than distributed. Once the retreat began, Moore drove his army on at a fast pace, determined to get ahead of the French pursuit. The marches were long by the standards of the day.

In spite of Moore's best efforts, all of the regiments were accompanied by many of the soldiers' wives and children. Some officers' wives also shared in the hardships of the campaign. Two battalion commanders – both of whom were killed – had their wives with them. It is unlikely, however, that any officers brought with them an adult, unmarried daughter. As in *True Soldier Gentlemen*, Jane MacAndrews' presence makes for a good story, but is not based on any real incident.

Soldiers' wives were a tough breed. They helped to look after their own men, and also were paid to clean and mend the regiment's clothing. Some were as prone to drunkenness as their menfolk, and the episodes of unconscious women lying in the snow, and in some cases freezing to death, are firmly based on reality. Others were said to be highly enthusiastic looters. Some were more respectable. The very proper Annie Rawson is based on a real sergeant's wife, who carried her dog in a basket throughout the retreat. Speedy remarriage was very common for the women of the regiments.

Readers may struggle to believe that Jenny could have given birth and then fled so soon afterwards, but this is also firmly based on fact. With so many women following the regiments, it was inevitable that some were in more or less advanced stages of pregnancy. A significant number of women gave birth during the campaign in conditions that can only have been appalling. Some did so in the open air, and without any medical assistance, and it is unsurprising that sometimes the mother or the child or both perished. Several memoirs mention such terrible sights. Another remembered finding a six- or seven-month-old boy trying to suckle from the breast of his dead mother. In this case there was a happier outcome. A staff officer took the child, wrapping him in his cloak, and announced, 'Unfortunate infant, you shall be my future care.'

One memoir tells of a Highlander whose wife went into labour near the end of the retreat. Comparatively fortunate in having the shelter of an outhouse and the attentions of the regimental surgeon, they dropped behind the column and the baby was born during the night. The surgeon left them, telling the soldier that he should surrender. The following morning, however, his wife refused to let him do this, and they both set off on foot to catch up with the army. The woman was barefoot, carrying her baby wrapped in an apron, and they had little or no food. Somehow they reached the British outposts.

The Corunna campaign was a grim business, and episodes from it clearly haunted many of the survivors for the rest of their lives. Yet many also took great pride in the conduct of their own regiments.

The British hussar regiments did well during the campaign, in spite of the unsatisfactory condition of their mounts and a woeful lack of horseshoes, and especially the nails required to fit them. At Sahagun, the 15th Hussars charged and broke two French regiments. At Benevente, the 10th Hussars drove the chasseurs of the Imperial Guard back across the River Esla. General Lefebre-Desnouettes was captured – probably by a German hussar, although the credit went to a private from the 10th Hussars. He spent much of his captivity in Cheltenham, where he was subsequently joined by his wife. Eventually he broke his parole – the promised word of an officer not to escape. Napoleon evidently approved and he was given a command in the attack on Russia in 1812.

I have attached the fictional 106th to Paget's Reserve Division, which formed the rearguard for the bulk of the retreat. The battalion's experiences are a combination of those of several of the genuine regiments in the reserve, and in particular the 28th and to a lesser extent the 20th. The action at Cacabellos on the 3rd January 1809 occurred much as described in the story. The day began with a punishment parade, and a number of men were flogged, although Paget gave a last-minute reprieve to a pair of redcoats due to be hanged. The lone soldier from the 95th who shot the French general was a wild individual named Tom Plunket, who on several occasions faced disciplinary action after bouts of drunkenness. The feat became legendary among the riflemen, although the only descriptions come from men who were not present at the action, and contradict each other in matters of detail. Although it is sometimes claimed that the incident was famous for the long range of his shot, it seems more likely that Plunket's coolness was most admired.

Many of the other incidents in the novel actually occurred, including General Paget's encounter with the paymaster and the subsequent abandonment of the army's treasury. I have slightly telescoped some of the details of Sir John Moore's wounding, for instance his words to the Highlander from the 42nd who had lost his leg, but apart from the presence of Williams, nothing has been invented, and his final hours and burial were as described. The same is true of the wider details of the Battle of Corunna.

Moore does seem genuinely to have considered fighting a defensive battle at Lugo. Both there and at other stages during the retreat he was concerned that the French might outflank him and threaten or even cut off his retreating army. The whole episode of Williams and his ragtag group of stragglers holding the bridge is an invention, exploiting this genuine strategic fear. A large force of stragglers from many different regiments did rally under the command of a Sergeant Newman of the 43rd Light Infantry and drove off the French cavalry as described in the story. This formed the basis for Williams' private army. Having described so many scenes of discipline collapsing, it was also important to show just how ready to fight most redcoats proved themselves at every opportunity. Polish lancers of the Legion of the Vistula and a Provisional Regiment of French Cuirassiers were serving in the Iberian Peninsula at this time, but neither played any direct role in the operations against Moore's army.

Some of Moore's officers were critical of the pace he set from the beginning of the advance, feeling that he exhausted the troops. It was also suggested that he should have spent more time with the leading divisions, rather than tending to supervise the actions of the rearguard. Most of this was unfair. It was natural to want to be with the rearguard since this was directly under attack by the enemy. A serious defeat in any of these encounters would have threatened the entire army.

The British Army endured the rigours of the retreat, fought a successful rearguard action on a bigger scale at Corunna, and was able to embark and escape to England. Soult's batteries opened fire while the ships were still in the bay, and there was considerable confusion and some losses, but the evacuation was an undoubted success. As at Dunkirk, one hundred and thirty-one years later, Britain was able to save its army from a campaign that had gone badly wrong. Also as at Dunkirk, the evacuation was a sign of failure, but it permitted the war to continue. In the months that followed there was a rather squalid – and depressingly modern – scramble to assign blame for the failure.

Moore had many critics, but his defenders were both zealous and extremely determined. Like all other generals, he doubtless made mistakes, but it is impossible to see how anyone could have produced a more successful outcome to the campaign. The threat posed by his army dislocated Napoleon's plans. The Emperor left for Paris after failing to trap Moore's army at the River Esla. It seems clear that he realised the campaign was unlikely to produce an outright and overwhelming success, of the sort that had concluded all of his campaigns up to this point. Therefore, he left Soult to manage the rest of the campaign. The marshal did the job competently, but for the remainder of 1809 the French armies in Spain proved unable to complete the subjugation of Spain and Portugal. The Peninsular War would continue, and the last judgement on Moore's importance is best left to Wellington, who said simply that 'We'd not have won without him'.

In April 1809, Sir Arthur Wellesley, as he still was, would return to take command of the British forces left behind by Moore to defend Portugal. He would not leave the Iberian Peninsula until he led his armies across the Pyrenees into France four years later. The 106th will accompany him for much of the way on that long and difficult journey.